Wilde's Army

Darkness Falls: Book Two

A Division of **Whampa, LLC**
P.O. Box 2540
Dulles, VA 20101
Tel/Fax: 800-998-2509
http://curiosityquills.com

© 2012 Krystal Wade
http://krystalwade.blogspot.com

Cover design by Harvey Bunda
http://soulspline.deviantart.com
and Ricky Gunawan
http://ricky-gunawan.daportfolio.com

ISBN: 978-1-62007-064-2 (ebook)
ISBN: 978-1-62007-065-9 (paperback)
ISBN: 978-1-62007-066-6 (hardcover)

TABLE OF CONTENTS

Chapter One..7

Chapter Two 15

Chapter Three..23

Chapter Four..30

Chapter Five...37

Chapter Six...50

Chapter Seven..68

Chapter Eight...82

Chapter Nine..94

Chapter Ten 99

Chapter Eleven 114

Chapter Twelve 127

Chapter Thirteen 143

Chapter Fourteen 155

Chapter Fifteen.. 169

Chapter Sixteen.. 182

Chapter Seventeen 203

Chapter Eighteen 218

Chapter Nineteen 239

Chapter Twenty.. 249

Chapter Twenty-One.. 263

Chapter Twenty-Two 279

Chapter Twenty-Three 291

Chapter Twenty-Four... 299

Chapter Twenty-Five.. 315

Chapter Twenty-Six 336

About the Author:.. 344

More from Curiosity Quills Press 345

Every book I write is for my family, but I have one family member in particular who goes above and beyond in the support department. Without this special person in my life, I'm not sure I would have found the strength to keep moving forward, to fight against people who tried to hold me back, and to finish Wilde's Army.

This book is for you, JoAnn Pepe.

CHAPTER ONE

Everything of importance in my new world has disappeared. The people I hold dear to my heart have been betrayed by two of our own who have been working for Darkness. The children, my sister, my mom, my friends, and *my Arland*—they were taken while I was asleep. But for whatever reason, someone protected me before I could be captured.

A few weeks ago, I didn't know Flanna, Lann, Tristan, or anyone else from Encardia aside from Arland—and him I knew only through dreams—but now that I do, I know I have to save them.

Saving things seems to be what my life is all about, at least according to the sun god, Griandor. He may have told me who I am and what I'm capable of, but knowledge doesn't do much to fill the hole in my chest.

I have to fight a fallen god, kill his army of daemons, and hide my identity from the Ground Dwellers. The only people of this world who'd like to see me fail.

And I've already failed everyone in so many ways, but I will find them, and I will do what I must to rid this world of Darkness.

"Hello, *Katriona*," a man calls, low and guttural, from behind me.

My body ignites in flames, fueled by fear and old magic. I draw my sword and turn from the empty space where my bedroom used to be, bracing for my first fight—of many fights to come—and I see Perth.

"Do you intend to kill me with that . . . *wife?*"

He regards me with the same ice-cold gaze he did the first time I met him in the training room. The blue flames reflecting in his pale, green eyes don't help much.

"I will kill you, if you take another step forward," I say with as much confidence as possible. I will not be forced into a marriage with Perth to repay the Ground Dwellers for building the bases. I will end this war between the gods, and I will free myself of this world's desires for my future . . . somehow.

"What if I take two?" he asks, moving forward *three* steps, leaving about enough distance for me to easily strike through him with my claymore.

"*Don't. Test. Me!*"

Perth takes one more step. A wicked smile stretches across his ivory face, and I push the tip of my sword into a spot above his heart.

"How foolish do you and Arland think I am?"

Arland. Anger fills me at the mere mention of his name.

"Why? Why did you betray all these people? Was it just to prove a point?" My voice comes out in a growl.

"*Me* betray these people? I did no such thing," Perth says, shaking his head.

Inching forward, I push the sword harder against his chest. "If you didn't betray everyone, why are you still here?"

"If you would stop trying to kill your future husband, I would be happy to tell you," he says, taking a step back when I pierce his skin with the tip of the claymore. Blood soaks through his white linen tunic and forms a red stain down to his belt.

I'm not playing games. Stepping toward him, I dig the blade back into his chest over the bleeding wound. "Why shouldn't I kill you? Right here, right now?"

Perth puts up his hands in surrender. "Because we are not so different, you and I."

"Go on. I'm listening," I say, *without* backing off.

"I had trouble sleeping and was walking in the forest. That is why I was not taken with everyone else. The children were screaming. I ran here to see what was going on, but there were too many daemons for me to try to do anything. When I entered the base to check if anyone was left, I found you."

8

I point to the closest table with my sword. "Sit."

Perth takes a chair at the table in the center of the room.

I seat myself opposite of him. "Why are we not so different?"

I have not sheathed my sword. I don't trust Perth as far as I can throw him . . . and since I'm short and don't weigh more than one-hundred and twenty pounds, I'm guessing I can't throw him very far.

Our eyes lock.

"We are both just pawns in a power play. I did not ask to be used against your family any more than you asked to be Bound to me," he says without any edge of humor to his tone.

I'm speechless. I think I *might* believe him. When people lie, they don't do it looking you straight in the face.

"How did you know who I am?"

"I visited a Seer on my own, three years ago. She told me my hatred of the Light Lovers would come crashing down the day I met *the* Light. I laughed at her. The thought of *not* hating the Light Lovers was absurd." The normal Perth has just returned. He leans back in his chair, fingers clasped behind his head, and a smart smile plays on his face.

I glare. If he's trying to help his case by telling me this . . . it's not working.

"Just hear me out, please." He rights himself in the chair. The smile vanishes.

I nod.

"For all my mocking, the Seer did not stop giving me the prophecy. She said I would recognize the Light immediately because she would not look at me as a monster, at least not the first time we met. The Seer also told me the Light was not my rightful future, and if I tried to obtain that future, I would live a life without love. She said the Light belongs to Arland Maher and him to the Light."

Closing my eyes, I think of Arland's smile, of his warmth. We were made for one another, to come together and fight a war, and yet we're apart. Separated by God only knows how much distance. I have to get to him.

"I love my father, Katriona," Perth says, drawing my eyes open. "I would not want to do anything to displease him, but when I met you—a Light Lover—and you did not look at me as a monster, my heart felt something it never had before."

"And what's that?"

"Hope. Hope that our two kinds could live in a world without turmoil."

"So, why did you try to kill me that day in the training room?" I hope his head still hurts where I hit him with my sword.

He laughs. "I was not attempting to take your life. I was angry. The Seer was right, and I knew I was going to have to fight against my father."

I want to take Perth for his word, but if he desires our two kinds to be united, why has he kept this from Arland? "Why haven't you said anything before now?"

"Do you believe Arland—or anyone—would have trusted me? He has told you about my kind. How did his mood change when he spoke of me?"

"Point taken."

The first time I asked about Perth, Arland ignored my question. He had to take me out to his favorite thinking spot by the river—as close to The Meadows as he could get . . . as close to his mother.

Resting the sword on the table, I release my grip on the hilt. I don't think Perth is making up this story. The sun god, Griandor, told me to trust in those around me, and since Perth is the only one left at base . . . I should start with him.

"Why are you telling *me*?" I ask.

"There are three reasons. You are the only other Draíochtan here, and you are going to need me if you want to survive. And Morgandy Domhnaill." The corners of his mouth twist up into a wry smile.

"Morgandy Domhnaill? My mom's fake name?"

"Yes. My Aunt Shylay used to tell me stories about Morgandy Domhnaill. She was a fabled, ancient goddess who lived by the sea. She treated the mortals with love and took care to ensure they always had food and a place to sleep. She was a goddess of kindness, and everyone trusted her."

"What does this have to do with my mom?"

"I believed her stories to be just that, but my Aunt told me if I ever met someone who called herself by the goddess' name, I should trust her and those she loves. When your mother spoke her name, I was taken aback. I never expected to hear the name 'Morgandy Domhnaill' again in all my life. I should have confessed then, but the way your mother regarded me—the way they all do—made me second guess what my Aunt instructed me to do."

Something tells me my mom knew Perth wasn't all rotten. I bet she even had a reason to treat him the way she did that night. My mom knows so much. I need to get back to her. There are so many things we need to discuss. No matter what impact she thinks it may have on my future, I want to know . . . everything.

"Why do our two kinds fight for power?" If I am supposed to unite everyone and form an army, I should be aware of exactly what divided us.

Perth raises his eyebrow. "Arland has not informed you of this? What *have* you two been up to?"

"You are not in a good position to ask questions you have no business knowing the answers to," I say, putting my hand back on the sword.

He watches my fingers thrum against the metal. "You enjoy killing things?"

I stand. "*Perth.*"

"Fine, fine." He waves. "Long ago, we were all considered equals, but Foghlad, the Leader of my kind at the time, wanted more."

Sitting back down, I release my death grip on my sword.

"Thank you." Perth tips his head in the direction of my clasped hands. "He used our magic against the Light Lovers, twisting the thoughts in their heads, turning them into spies, killers, whatever he needed them to do at the time."

"But how? Flanna mentioned your powers are used for dark things, but Arland said our powers cannot be used to fight."

"I wish I knew. Our magical powers are not supposed to be used to fight, but somehow he manipulated the magic to work against nature."

"And your people just supported him?" I ask, leaning forward.

Perth snorts. "Foghlad spoke eloquently to his followers, and over time—and I imagine with the help of magic—all of my kind believed in his mission to conquer the Meadows and take control of Encardia."

I narrow my eyes. "Why? What was he going to do with the control if he got it?"

"He was an evil man. Plain and simple. I am not positive what his final plans were, but Foghlad taught all of my people how to use our beautiful magic in dark ways. The battles have gone on for so long, not many of my kind understand how peaceful life could be if we would stop trying to conquer the world."

I lean back in my seat; the twisted roots of the chair poke into my shoulders. "Have you ever told anyone this?"

Perth shakes his head. "Unfortunately, if my father or anyone knew how I felt, I am sure they would kill me."

I feel as though uniting all of the Draíochta to fight might be more difficult than Griandor led me to believe—not that he gave me much information in the first place. "How long have the Ground Dwellers been fighting for power?"

"The first battle began one hundred and twenty-three years ago."

One hundred and twenty-three years? Uniting them after that much time might not be difficult—it might be impossible. "So, what do we do now?"

Perth smiles crookedly. "Since you are the one glowing with ancient magic, I was hoping you would come up with a plan."

He may find this funny, but I'm *not* smiling. I narrow my eyes.

"Sorry. The blue flames *are* somewhat distracting." He wipes his hand over his face, smoothing his expression.

I draw in deep breaths. My mind reaches out to all corners of my body, grabbing the flames and folding them in. I'm taking control. Not asking, just doing—like Griandor told me. The magic works its way into my chest, and the fire disappears above my heart.

The room is now pitch-black.

"Solas." I light a candle sitting in the center of the table with a spark from my hand.

"If I had any remaining doubts about your identity, your control over old magic just made them all wash away," Perth says, with childlike eyes.

"Did you see where the others were taken?"

"I followed them to a cave three miles north of here. I am not sure if they entered, but with only a knife for protection, it was too far for me to continue on alone."

"Are the animals—?"

"Daemons have no use for our animals; they are fine."

"Good, then let's ride out to the cave and check it out. If they aren't there, we'll come back. If they are, we'll fight."

"You want to ride straight into a trap?" Perth crosses his arms over his chest, looking at me like I'm an idiot. "The daemons will expect retaliation. We need to track them, gather information, and attack when the time is right."

"Well, we can't stay here. We have to get to them soon, or the daemons will kill them!" A lump forms in my throat. I have to save the others before it's too late; if a single life is lost, it will be too much for me to handle.

"You are correct. We cannot stay here." Perth tips his head toward the hall. "It appears someone hid your room, which tells me *someone* believes whoever called for the attack knows who you are. The daemons know you are here; they will wait for you. They might be mounting another attack as we speak. We should move to Willow Falls. There will be other soldiers who can help us. We can use the chatter box in the communications room to send word we are coming."

It's apparent Perth wants me to abandon the idea of finding the soldiers. He's never seen me fight; he has no idea what I'm capable of. Until my conversation with the sun god, *I* had no idea what I'm capable of.

"We don't need to bring any other soldiers into this. I can handle the daemons that took the others. We'll send word to Willow Falls about their capture, and we'll let the Leaders know as soon as we rescue everyone, we'll go there." I had no trouble fighting off hundreds of coscarthas and hounds in the forest, and that was before I knew much about myself.

"It will be a suicide mission."

It's also apparent Perth has no faith in me.

"Are you going to come with me, or am I going alone?"

"What kind of man would I be if I allowed a woman to go into a battle on her own?" He places his cold hand over the back of mine. "Especially one who belongs to me."

I jerk my hand free. "Thank you, but I don't belong to you."

"Try telling my father that." Clasping his fingers on *his* side of the table, Perth laughs. "And do not thank me. We are both going to die. So, do you know how to use the chatter box?"

"No."

"Neither do I. You should try to use the magic you have been blessed with," Perth says, heavy on the sarcasm.

Grabbing my sword, I point it toward the kitchen. "Lead the way."

CHAPTER TWO

Walking through the dark, empty base is unnerving. Even when I've been alone here, the place never had the lifeless feeling it holds now. With each heavy step, the sounds of the soles of my leather boots connecting with the dry earth pound in my ears. Every shaky breath I release hints at my unease. I have to be strong for those I love; otherwise, I'm not sure I could handle putting another foot forward.

Signs of a struggle are all throughout the dining room and kitchen. Tables are knocked over, chairs lie on their sides, and dishes are broken and scattered all around the floor. Light from the candle I carry illuminates trails of blood. My heart skids to a stop and so do my feet.

I gasp.

"What is it?" Perth asks.

"B-blood." I point to the line of blood on the floor, trembling as I walk along the stains with Perth behind me. The trail leads up the stairs.

"Someone was injured," he says, his voice void of emotion.

Swallowing hard, I raise the candle to see his face. "I understand that, but who?" The question leaves me breathless. Intuition numbs my limbs, telling me the stain is from Arland.

Perth steps over the line of crimson then takes hold of my elbow. "It does not matter. We must keep moving."

It may not matter to Perth, but it does to me. This war has already consumed two people I love: my father and my best friend Brad. At least he's been promised a second chance at life, if I succeed, but no one else shares that same opportunity. With suppressed apprehension, I keep moving.

We enter the communications room. The table is broken in half and the chatter box lies on the floor, buzzing with static. I pass the candle to Perth then rush to the corner, pick up the strange device, and tap it. I don't know why; a natural reaction maybe—like when a security camera flickers out and a guard taps the monitor.

The rectangular box is about a foot long. It's made of wood and has little holes cut out in a circular pattern. The box still reminds me of an old radio, but there are no wires attached, and I don't see a speaker inside.

"If we talk to each other telepathically, what's the point of this thing?" I look back to Perth.

He eyes the contraption in my hands. "From what I understand, the chatter box creates order to how messages are sent and received, but I do not know how to use it any more than you do."

When Arland took me on tour of the base, he told me connecting mentally through the chatter box requires a lot of concentration. Instead of questioning what the purpose of the thing is, I might as well get started. I sit on the floor, cross my legs over each other, then place the thing in front of me.

Perth walks up beside me. "What are you doing?"

"What does it look like? I'm concentrating."

I have no idea what I'm doing, but Perth doesn't need to know this. Closing my eyes, I think about the little wooden rectangle by my legs and about where I need a message to go. Weeping willow trees pop into my mind, as well as waterfalls. No one has ever described Willow Falls to me, but when I hear the name, those are the two things I relate the place to.

I imagine a telephone wire linking Watchers Hall to Willow Falls, imagine I'm in that wire, running along the fifty miles between the two bases. Tingles replace the connection I have to my arms and legs, then everything goes numb. I open my eyes and look down at myself . . . I'm floating outside my body.

"This is so amazing!"

Perth doesn't respond. He's watching the stationary me. He cannot see the floating me . . . or at least he doesn't look at the version of me hovering in the room.

The only thing to do now is figure out how to get my apparition from here to Willow Falls. I look at the box and study the small, round holes cut into the red wood. *The holes.* I swim through the air, reach out, then place my hand over the openings. The device sucks me in and sends me hurtling through a vast, dark space so fast my stomach rises to my throat.

"Willow Falls, Willow Falls, Willow Falls." I repeat where I want to go because I'm not sure how else to get there.

I'm surrounded by complete and utter darkness. Chills creep up my arms. I hold out my hands at my sides, but no longer feel like I'm moving. The air is stagnant . . . my head crashes into a wall, leaving me with an instant, throbbing headache.

I rub the knot above my eye and swim closer to a dim light filtering in on me through the inside of what appears to be another chatter box. My skin is polka-dotted with about twenty faint-white spots. I reach my hand to the holes but cannot pass through.

"Hello?" I have no idea if there's a chatter box protocol or not, but hello seems universal enough.

Someone passes by. Muffled voices come from inside the room, but I cannot make out anything being said.

I bang on the space next to the holes.

"Hello?" I draw the word out longer this time.

A mouth appears in front of me.

"State your name and location," a man's voice booms.

"Kate. Watchers Hall."

"Kate? Watchers Hall? I am sorry, but I do not know who you are," says the big mouth.

"It doesn't matter who I am; we've been attacked. I need to speak to whoever is in charge. Immediately."

17

"Drustan, notify High Leader Maher. He will want to speak to this woman. She says Arland's base has been attacked."

"Yes, sir. I will return with him shortly."

Hinges squeak as, I presume, Drustan exits the room.

Arland's father is here? I thought he was at Wickward. Butterflies swarm in my stomach, and I rub my palms together. I'm about to meet him without Arland's calming presence. What will his dad think of me? What if he doesn't like me? What if I can't make *my* father's friend proud?

"Oscailte," says the man, waving his palm over the chatter box.

I reach my hand to the opening again, but this time I pass through and am deposited in full apparition form into a room much like the one I just left.

"Who are you, and what happened?" The brown-haired man stands with his strong arms folded over his chest. The middle of his forehead presses together, and he narrows his blue eyes.

"My name is—"

"Leave us." A commanding voice reverberates from behind me.

I turn around. The man standing in the doorway, watching as the others rush out of the room, makes my heart ache. Arland is the spitting image of his father—minus the wrinkles around his eyes and the gray hair. Holding back the tears drains the strength out of me. Arland and I have only been apart for a short time, but there's no telling what condition he's in, or if we'll ever see each other again.

High Leader Maher closes the door after the last of the soldiers exit. "Katriona, it is nice to finally meet you. You must have questions, but there is not enough time. Who has been taken?"

He's right. I have *a lot* of questions, but most of them will have to be saved for another meeting. "Everyone besides me and Perth Dufaigh."

His face drains of color. "Is Perth aware of your identity?"

"Yes. He's just said he's known the entire time, but I don't think he is as bad as the other Ground Dwellers."

18

Leader Maher looks beyond me and rubs his chin between his thumb and index finger—another trait he shares with Arland. "Katriona, do not be fooled. Ground Dwellers are all bad. It is unfortunate, but you are going to have to stay with him. Use him if you must, but do not believe anything he says."

Of course Leader Maher thinks they're all bad. Perth said if any of his people knew how he felt, they would kill him. He's had to lie to everyone his entire life. I feel a sudden need to defend Perth. He could have left me here to rot by myself, but he didn't. That has to amount to something good in him.

"We are going to rescue the others. Perth wanted to come to Willow Falls for help, but I don't need it. He saw where the daemons took the others. We are going to check it out and possibly attack."

Leader Maher's eyes return to the present, and he gives me an approving stare. "I am happy to see how confident you are with your abilities. The last time I spoke with Arland, he informed me you were still unsure of yourself. Much has changed, no?"

I nod. Much *has* changed. I was visited by two gods, given information about myself and the war which has plagued this world for twenty years, had my best friend murdered in front of me, and my family and the love of my life were ripped away.

"You must not trust Perth, Katriona. I am sure he *did* want you to come here with him. His father is here. With the others captured—possibly dead—he would not have to worry about Arland standing in his way. He could have you for himself and take his position as Second Leader over his people—he needs a wife before that can happen. Given the family's reputation, I fear they may be up to something even bigger. Save the others, bring them here. When you arrive, keep your distance from Arland. You must protect him. I know it is intended to be the other way around, but if you want this to end well for the both of you—and I am positive you do—you must adhere to my advice. Do you understand?" His intensity is almost threatening. I'm sure if Leader Maher could touch me, he'd be shaking my shoulders right now.

"I-I do." I'm not certain who to trust anymore. Is Perth bad or not? Are Leader Maher's fears founded? Why couldn't Griandor have been more specific?

There's a tugging sensation at my apparition. My muscles burn as if I've been lifting weights too heavy for me. Staying in this room becomes more difficult by the second. I need to tell Leader Maher the rest, fast. "I need an army."

He squints. "We have an army."

"No, sir, *I* need an army," I say, pressing my palm over my heart; it's well over its maximum beat per minute range. I'm stepping on some major toes right now; any second, I'm sure I'll hyperventilate.

"I need men and women willing to fight and follow *my* orders."

"May I ask what for?" he asks with a hint of amusement.

I sigh. "To fight a war against a god."

He moves in closer to me. The ferocity in his green eyes is overwhelming.

My breath catches in my chest—I know how he became High Leader; no one could question the authority in his stature.

"What information do you have?"

"There is no time. We will speak more when I arrive with the others—assuming they're okay. Will you form an army for me?" My hands begin to dissolve and float toward the box.

"It will not be an easy task to convince people to fight. We have lost many lives already, but I will try. Many Leaders are gathered here to discuss our current situation. I will speak with them; however, I fear you will need to do most of the work yourself."

"Why?" I ask as all of my body dematerializes.

The chatter box sucks at the particles of my broken apparition.

"You will understand—"

I cannot hear the rest of his answer; I'm zipping through the black space just as before.

"Watchers Hall, Watchers Hall, Watchers Hall."

My head doesn't slam into a wooden wall like it did before. I fly straight through the holes and into my body. Feeling returns to my limbs. I wiggle my fingers and toes and open my eyes.

"Give up?" Perth asks.

I startle and look up at him. "Give up? I've been gone for at least ten minutes."

"Interesting. I did not see you move a single muscle. Did you deliver the message?"

"Yes. We are to rescue the others and bring them to Willow Falls," I say, leaving out details about who I had a discussion with.

Perth kneels beside me, offering his hand. "Will they be sending any soldiers to our aid?"

"No." Scowling, I take hold of him, and he pulls me to my feet.

"We don't need them. I've told you this." His lack of confidence is annoying.

"Were you aware of a Leader's meeting at Willow Falls?"

Perth's face falls flat. "No. Who did you speak with?"

"What does it matter? Perth, I will not marry you. If you lied to me before, if I discover you ever lie to me, I will drive my sword into your heart. Do you understand me?" Flames spread over my body. I'm sick of being in the dark, and I refuse to be a pawn in *anyone's* game or power struggle. I brush past him, heading straight for the hall.

He grabs my upper arm before I storm out of the room, pulling me around to face him. "Katriona, I swear to you what I said before was not a lie. Who did you speak with?"

I scowl at his hand on my arm.

He releases me.

"I spoke with Kimball Maher."

Perth arches his eyebrows. "They allowed you to speak directly to the High Leader?"

Playing into his obvious insecurity, I smile. "I wouldn't say allowed; he required it."

His eyebrows return to their normal location, then he stares at something on the floor. "And he spoke of me?"

Perth wants to do right, I can tell. I hear it in his voice, I see it in his eyes, and yet I torment him. He knows no one will ever trust him, but he needs trust in order to do the right thing.

"Yes. He says I shouldn't trust you, and I defended you. If you do anything to make me regret that—"

The floor no longer interests Perth; he looks at me with wide eyes and a genuine smile—the cold look turned warm. "You will kill me. I understand."

"We need to leave. We have wasted too much time already— something the others don't have. We'll take the horses."

"Okay."

I turn on my toe, and we leave the communications room.

CHAPTER THREE

Relief washes over me after Perth and I enter the stables and find all the animals unharmed. I didn't realize how worried I was. As soon as I hear the familiar clucks and occasional moos and nays, I sigh.

"How are the animals going to survive if we leave them?" I ask.

Perth casts a sideways glance in my direction. "Willow Falls may not send soldiers to *our* aid, but I guarantee you, they will send them here for the livestock. It may take a day or two for the boats to arrive, but arrive they will."

It sounds as though Perth has lost faith in his fellow Draíochtans. High Leader Maher didn't say he wouldn't send soldiers to our aid; I never asked for them.

"Collectors, right? I think that's what Arland called them."

"Yes."

Just in case it takes more than a few days for the Collectors to come for the animals, I grab a feedbag then fill the food troughs for the chickens, cows, and goats.

He enters the chicken coop after I finish feeding them.

I drop the empty burlap bag outside the goat pen and follow Perth inside. "What are you doing?"

"We are going to need food. There is no telling when we will have a meal again." He chases after one of the white hens, then catches it by her bumpy, orange feet.

She pecks at his fingers, but Perth manages to get his hands around her neck.

I turn my head and close my eyes, but still hear the distinct sound of bones breaking.

"It would be better if we could bring more, but the meat would rot before we could eat it all," he says, carrying the dead chicken in his hands.

I might not eat for days.

"Why not let it live?"

"Too noisy." He dangles the bird in front of him, indicating for me to leave the coop first.

We round the corner toward the horses. Their ears flatten against their heads. Mirain seems more nervous than the others, stomping and swishing her tail.

"What is it, girl?" I ask, approaching her with my hand held out, palm up.

"It is me. Animals have never liked me very much," Perth says, still standing in the storage area, backed against the hay bales.

I eye the dead chicken in his murderous hands. "I cannot imagine why not."

Leaving Perth, I gather Mirain and Bowen, then lead them from their stalls and into the storage bay near the stable doors.

Perth holds out the bird as I pass. "Here. Tie this onto Bowen for me?"

I crinkle my nose. "No, you can do that yourself."

He doesn't move.

Great. He's afraid. He can easily kill a chicken but is scared of a horse?

"Have you ever ridden?" I hope he has. Otherwise, there's not enough time to teach him, and he'll have to ride with me. The thought makes me cringe.

"We do not have a need for these creatures where I am from, but I have ridden. Neither the horse nor I will enjoy this much."

"You should ride Cadman's; he's gentle and won't fight you as much as Bowen will." I point toward the end of the stables.

"He's in the last stall." Never mind the fact I don't want him touching anything belonging to Arland.

Perth still doesn't move.

"No, Perth, really, I'll get him. Don't you worry at all." I march to the last stall, unlatch the gate, then lead the stallion out next to Mirain.

There's an uneasy tension in the space between the animal and Perth. They stare each other down. Neither breathes. Both stand still.

"Are you going to get on?"

The horse and Perth startle at the sound of my voice.

"Why are we bringing three?" he asks, his feet still planted to the ground.

"I'd like to take them all. If we rescue the others, we're going to need them, but I cannot imagine leading eight horses through the forest being the quietest adventure, can you?"

If Perth ever betrays me, I'm going to stick him in a barn with a hundred horses and let them scare him to death. This is ridiculous.

"You are bringing Bowen for Arland. You may admit it, it is okay." The creepy Perth is back. His eyes lose their decency, turning into cold slits, and he puts on a wicked smile.

I climb Mirain and grab Bowen's reins. There isn't anything to tie him to Mirain since I ride her bareback, so I'll have to lead him.

"Get on the horse, or I'll leave you here." I look over my shoulder where Perth stands, frozen.

There's no chance I'll find the others if Perth doesn't follow, but I cannot imagine he wants to stay here by himself. I turn from him and wave my hand in front of the door. "Oscailte!"

Holding my breath as the doors open, I prepare to fight anything that might run in to attack. But no daemons jump out at us. There's nothing in front of us other than the cold, eerie silence of the Darkness.

I click my cheek. "Let's go, girl."

Mirain trots outside the stables, then pauses. A few seconds later an extra set of hooves clop behind us, and I know Perth is following.

Mirain turns toward the nervous Ground Dweller.

"Where to?" I ask.

He looks up from his hands squeezing the horn of the saddle. "Go left, then left again, so we are heading north. We should travel in a wide arc and go beyond the cave. We will double back. The daemons will not expect us to come from the north . . . if that is where they are."

"Are you capable of leading us, or are you too scared of the horse you're sitting on?" I tease.

This seems to strike a nerve in Perth. He straightens his back, squares his shoulders, and kicks his feet into the horse's side. They trot right by me, into the forest of Darkness.

I dig my heels into Mirain and follow along on a trail not well traveled. Tree branches hang low, and I have to move them out of the way in order for us to pass. These three miles—or more if we go beyond the cave—are going to take forever.

Perth rides about ten feet ahead of me, but it's so dark I can only make out the white of his tunic. I'd love to have a torch or something right now, but we don't need to bring any attention to us.

Moving along at a snail's pace, I think of my sister, my mom, the children, and of Arland. Out of everyone, Brit is probably the most afraid. The children and Arland have lived this nightmare their entire lives. My mom prepared for this from before I was born, though she hasn't lived here since these rough times began.

No, I'm positive Brit is out of her mind with fear. Just a couple days ago, she was upset about us being in the dark, about missing college, about losing a boyfriend, and not knowing her prophecy. Now she's been captured by daemons and may not be alive much longer.

A tear races down my left cheek at the thought of my sister being dead. I wipe the tear away. My eye is still swollen. I almost forgot about it. Griandor took the pain from me but not the mark itself. The black eye is like a constant reminder of everything I've lost, of everything I stand to lose.

Reaching up, I move a branch out of my way and my vision fades to black. I cannot see Perth in front of me, or even Mirain. I struggle

26

to maintain control, but lose feeling in my hands and feet. Tingling sensations work their way throughout my body.

My eyesight returns gradually, but I'm not riding in the dark forest on Mirain. Torches hang on gray-rock walls and are burning brightly, revealing a cave full of daemons and soldiers. Rushing around and tying people up, the daemons are a kind I've never seen or encountered before. These beings are tall and have black, hairy legs and hooves for feet. Their torsos are human-like with broad muscular chests and big arms. They have heads of men and eyes the color of blood.

Lann comes into view as my vision clears. He's not tied up, and he's speaking directly to one of the daemons. Judging by the way Lann throws his hands around in conversation, it looks as if they're arguing. I cannot make out what they're saying. They move closer and stand in front of me.

My heart thuds hard in my ears; my fingers are numb. I'm cold. I'm wet.

"This is the girl's sister. She is the one I spoke about to you. If you want to kill the one who brings Light, you must use this one against her—and him"—Lann points to someone next to Brit—"This one is her lover."

Arland! Anger, rage, and hatred all surge through me. Why would Lann betray his people? He's a high-ranking soldier. What does he stand to gain from this?

The eyes I'm seeing this disturbing scene through fill with blinding tears. "Kate, if you can hear me, Lann is with the daemons. We're in a cave not far from the base . . . please, help us!" My sister's voice comes out in a whimper, in my head.

She turns her neck to the left and stares at Arland—the pain of this turn radiates through my neck. Arland's head hangs, his hands are tied above him, and he's been beaten. Cuts and fresh pink bruises cover the side of his face, and blood drips from his mouth.

"Do you know if Kate can hear you or not?" he asks, his voice ragged. He doesn't lift his head to look at her.

"I haven't told her I hear and sometimes see her thoughts; I'm just praying she hears mine, too," Brit whispers.

My sister and I *are* connected. I heard Brit in my head last night when the daemons attacked Brad—she told me to stay with Arland or he would die.

Brit must have wanted me to see Lann talking to the daemon.

I want to make Lann hurt. I want to kill every single daemon that has laid a finger on Arland and anyone else. I want to kill *Dughbal.*

The vision fades.

I open my eyes and a tree branch smacks me in the face, knocking me from Mirain.

"Ow!" I wheeze for air.

"Katriona, are you okay?"

I hear concern in Perth's distant voice, but I cannot see his face. Sparks of black and white light explode in my eyes.

He slides his arms under my back and legs, picks me up, then props me against a tree. "Can you hear me?"

I nod. My sight has not completely returned to me yet, but Perth is beginning to take on the form of a person rather than a blob.

Kneeling beside me, he laughs. "Who has the problem with the horses now?"

"L-Lann," I manage to get out through gasps for air.

"No, I am Perth. You must have hit your head." He runs his hands over my scalp, inspecting for injuries.

I shake my head and take a short breath without wheezing. "Lann betrayed us."

"How do you know this?" He removes his hands from my hair.

Telling Perth about my powers seems like a dangerous thing to do, considering what Leader Maher told me, but this one Perth needs to know about. I think.

"I have visions of things that can happen. And from what I experienced just now, I think I have the ability to connect to my sister's mind," I say, pinching the bridge of my nose. My head does hurt.

"And what do you see in these visions?"

Closing my eyes, I take a shallow breath. "Death, destruction, things that leave me confused."

"And what happened while you were in Brit's mind?"

"They are in a cave."

"Can you recall the details?"

I open my eyes. "Details?"

"How many daemons were there? What kind? How badly were people injured?"

I cannot answer all of these questions. Paying close attention wasn't on the top of my priorities list. "The daemons had hairy legs and hooves, but the rest of their bodies looked like men. That's all I know."

Perth shakes his head. "Tairbs. They are strong, but their numbers are weak. I saw coscarthas leading them from base, did you see any?"

"No."

"Do you have any control over the connection to your sister's body?"

"I don't know."

Perth purses his lips, stands then offers me his hand.

I take it, then he pulls me to my feet.

"We should continue moving. Lingering in the forest is dangerous. I know a place along the river where we can set up camp. It is north of the cave. The daemons should not be looking for us there. Are you okay to ride?"

"Yes."

Perth cups his hands; I step on them then climb onto Mirain's back. Once I'm settled on her, he climbs his own horse. With the push of a branch and a kick of his feet, he starts riding again with Bowen and me following behind.

CHAPTER FOUR

We arrive at the river after several grueling miles traveled in the densest forest I've ever seen, but now the trees are behind us. The ground is no longer covered in leaves and dirt; instead, rocks line our path. We lead the horses up a steep hill.

"This is it," Perth says after he reaches the end of the stone trail.

"You're kidding, right?" We're on a ledge above the river—out in the open where bats or coscarthas or any type of daemon could find us.

"Do you trust me?"

"Not entirely."

He sucks in a sharp breath. "Have I done anything deserving of your distrust?"

"Not yet." I clamp my hand over my mouth.

"If you would prefer, we can make camp down in the forest where the daemons would expect to find us, *or* we can set up here. Sometimes hiding in plain sight is the best plan." Perth slides off the horse.

I climb from Mirain. "I'm sorry if I've offended you. What should we do with the horses?"

Perth turns his head in the direction of the river. "We can tie them to some trees about twenty feet below us—by the water. We will cast a few spells to protect them from being seen."

This sounds like a problem. Arland never showed me how to cast complicated spells. I was so horrible with the simple door opening and closing and spark creating, we never moved beyond to more important magic. "I don't know how."

"Do not worry. I will take care of the magic, as long as you take care of the animals." Perth hands me the reins to his borrowed horse.

"Deal. You lead the way."

The trail to the river is winding, but thankfully not as steep as the one we climbed to get here. At the bottom, a twenty-foot mossy area spreads in front of us with a few trees sprinkled around.

The animals walk up to the water's edge, then take a drink.

I sit in the middle of the damp area, listening to the river rush by while Perth walks the perimeter and whispers spells to the wind.

Griandor and Leader Maher's words repeat themselves in my mind: "Trust in those around you; most importantly, trust in those you love. That trust will be your guide," and "Ground Dwellers are all bad." Everything seems like a cruel joke. I feel not only a pawn in Perth's father's game, but I also feel like a pawn for the gods.

If I'm so powerful, why not tell me exactly what I need to do to unite the Draíochta, so we can end the war; or better yet, deliver me to Dughbal so I can burn him with my fire? It's wrong to question higher powers, but I cannot help myself. With everything I've ever loved gone, I'm beyond worried about who I am. I'm angry.

"Katriona?" Perth says beside me.

I look up. "Yeah?"

He offers me his hand. "It is done. The animals will be secure. We should head back up."

"Why don't we just stay here? It seems safe enough. You just cast protections over us . . . ." It *seems* like a waste to go anywhere with such a nice, secluded spot by the river.

"While we would be guarded against anything getting in, we are not guarded if the animals get loose and run out. If that were to happen, our position could be compromised. If daemons discovered us here, we would be trapped . . . unless you wanted to use the river, but I do not believe either of us would enjoy swimming in *that*," he says, giving the river a fearful glance.

"What's in the river?" I follow his gaze to the water, barely visible through the blanket of Darkness.

"Serpents." He shudders.

I take his hand, and he helps me up.

"Can serpents get out of the water?" I ask, ready to high-tail it back up the ledge.

"I have only ever seen them in the water."

"So, the horses should be fine?" The thought of leaving three innocent animals here does not give me a warm and fuzzy feeling, but I'd rather be as far away from the serpents as possible.

"I told you." Perth laughs, probably amused by my sudden fear. "We are safe from anything getting in."

I turn on my toe then head up the trail—back into the open.

He follows behind me.

Perth still gives me the creeps. His eyes are always watching. Even his blonde hair seems spooky in contrast to the Darkness, but he has lived up to his word so far, and I'm supposed to trust those around me.

I stop in the center of our *hiding* spot. "What now?"

He takes a seat next to my feet. "We wait."

"There isn't any time. We need to get to the others now!"

Crossing his legs, Perth clasps his hands and places them in his lap. "Daemons rest as we do. We will leave at three in the morning. I will take the first shift if you want to sleep."

I cannot stand this. Daemons have my family and my heart. Sitting on this ledge out in the open for fifteen hours is *not* in the cards for my day. "*No.* We will not waste time. How many daemons did you see leaving with the others at base?"

"Too many to count." Perth draws circles in the dirt with his finger. "When you were in your sister's mind, what did you see?"

"Why?" Propping my hands on my hips, I stare down at him the way my mom always did when she was punishing me.

He doesn't meet my eyes. "I want to see if you were given clues about the trap you want to run into."

The first thing I heard when I was in Brit's thoughts was Lann telling the daemons to kill me, they had to use Arland and Brit against me. Giving up, I sit down.

"So my suspicions are correct?"

I'd like to smack the satisfaction out of his tone. "Yes, Perth, you're right. Lann told the daemons to use Arland and Brit against me."

He raises his eyebrows. "Nothing about your mother?"

"No. My mom wasn't mentioned." I don't remember seeing her in the cave either. There *are* forty-five soldiers, and tallying them and their locations didn't cross my mind, but now I'm worried about her more than I already was.

"I believe you should try to use your connection to your sister to learn more about the situation. It will be the safest way to gather information. We will move in when it is safe to do so."

Uhh, great, but I'm not sure how that connection works. "Is this going to be like the chatter box? Do I have to figure everything out on my own?"

Perth stops drawing in the dirt like a two-year-old and locks his cold gaze on me. "You seem to have quite a bit figured out already. Why do you doubt yourself so much?"

I ignore him and close my eyes.

"I will keep watch," he says.

"Keep quiet while you're at it, please." I know I'm being unfair, but I'm annoyed by how he's taking everything in stride—like this is no big deal.

Taking deep breaths, I clear Perth from my mind and think of Brit. All these years, she's sensed my emotions because we share a connection. Before I had left for college, she used to come to my room almost every night. The nightmares—which I now know to be visions—occurred more frequently than ever before. Mom and Gary didn't bother going to her room to wake her in the mornings because she was always next to me, sleeping with her arm draped over my back.

My legs tingle, but I don't fight against it like last time; I welcome the transfer of myself to Brit, then open my eyes.

Perth isn't in front of me.

I'm inside the cave.

Control over my hands and feet returns, but it doesn't feel anything like what I'm used to—they're not my own. There isn't enough time to think about how weird being removed from my body is. Brit is tied up to a cold cave wall, her mouth gagged. It feels as though there are a thousand cotton balls on my tongue. The wet rocks send chills up her back . . . my back.

She aches, she's tired, and she's starved for food.

The torches on the walls are still bright with flames. The air smells so strongly of rust and mold, I find it hard not to vomit. Brit's chest hurts as she holds her breath. She pushes the stench from her thoughts, but when she does draw in a deep, ragged gasp for air, it has to pass through her nose—starting the cycle again.

"Brit?"

"Kate? Kate! *Can you hear me?"* Even her thoughts sound frantic. She cringes; she needs to breathe. When she does, it takes everything in me not to let go of our connection.

"Is everyone . . . a-alive?"

"Yes. T-the d-d-d-daemons are torturing people for information about you."

I swallow hard. *"How many daemons are there?"*

"I-I don't know." She scans the room, but I only see soldiers. *"I think I saw twenty? Are you coming for us?"*

"I'm trying. Who is the second person who betrayed us?"

"I only know about Lann."

"There is someone else. Try to figure it out."

Tears well in Brit's eyes. *"Please, hurry, Kate. I'm scared."*

"Can you show me where everyone is?"

Brit turns her neck. Sharp pains radiate from my shoulder up the back of my head. I want to rub the spot, but my hands won't move. My wrists burn; rope is intertwined between them. She shows me Arland.

My breath hitches in my lungs.

He's worse than when I saw him earlier. The bruises have turned purple. Arland's shirt is gone, and his chest has multiple cuts. Blood stains the ground beneath his feet.

I shake in my very core. *"Oh God! Tell me they haven't poisoned him!"*

"No, b-but he's been hurt the worst."

"I can't stand this. Show me the others."

The children. Please God, let the children be okay.

Brit squints as her eyes reach out into the dark cave. Tristan and Saidear are next to Arland. She stares across from where she's tied, showing me Enid and all the children. Next to them are Mom, Gavin, Dunn, Flanna, Cadman, Ogilvie, and everyone else—they're alive, but their heads sag and shoulders droop. Except for Mom; she stares at Brit.

Hooves clap against the stone floor of the cave, echoing around us.

Brit stiffens, and her stomach turns. *"Someone is coming."*

"Stay calm." I'm not sure if I'm telling her or me.

Two tairbs come into view. "Aengus was wrong about the affection the girl possesses for these pathetic Draíochtans. If she wanted to protect them, she would have been here by now. Kill them all. We will find another way to get to her."

The taller of the two daemons pauses and looks over at Brit. "Start with that one first; make it slow and painful. Maybe the girl will hear the screams from where she hides."

He smiles wickedly and walks away.

The other tairb grins, turning his red eyes to my sister.

This cannot be happening. Griandor, please stop this. Help me. Help them. Please kill the daemons for me. Give me the power I need to stop him.

Tears threaten to spill over Brit's eyes. Thinking of her fingers, her toes, her heart, I search for a way to take control of her, for a way to take her place so she doesn't have to feel the pain of death. I have to find a way to make this end.

The vile creature walks up to my sister, licking his blackened lips. "I am going to enjoy this."

He rips open the front of her shirt.

Trembling, she screams through her gag. Her heart races and sends so much blood to her head, it resonates as it throbs through her temples.

The daemon draws a knife from a pouch on his back then cuts a small hole into his hand. "Do you know what my blood will do to you?"

She doesn't respond, but I do. I shake my head back and forth. Brit's head moves with mine.

"My blood contains a poison so strong, it will eat through your flesh in minutes and allow me to feed on the magic locked inside your worthless soul. One day, we will be powerful enough to overthrow the gods you so absurdly worship. You do not see the gods here now, do you?"

He raises his hand and shows her the blood dripping from it.

I cannot believe this hideous beast believes *we* are worthless. They feed on innocent lives for what? For the magic we possess? Is he so stupid he thinks they can actually overthrow gods? Does he believe Dughbal will come through on his promise of new life for them?

The rumbling feeling always preceding the flames builds in me, more powerful than I've ever felt it, but before it can take full control, the connection to Brit begins to fade.

My vision fills with black spots as the daemon collects his blood on the knife and lifts it to her face.

"Please help me, Kate!"

And in an instant, I'm back in my body.

CHAPTER FIVE

I'm screaming. I have no control. Opening my eyes, I jump to my feet. Flames erupt from my chest and spread to my arms and legs like fire on dry straw. I run to the winding path leading down to the horses, without sparing a second to tell Perth what's going on.

He calls to me.

I'm vaguely aware of shrieks coming from the forest, but I don't care. That monster was about to kill my sister, and I couldn't do anything to stop him. I'm not going to cry. I refuse to let anything happen to Brit.

The gravel on the path crunches and echoes inside my ears as my feet make contact with the ground.

A hand clasps my shoulder, pulling me to a stop.

"Where are you going?" Perth asks, breathless.

"I told you there wasn't any time, but you didn't listen. Now they've probably already killed Brit, and I couldn't keep the connection to her. I'm going to stop this. Let me go, or I will kill you, too." I knock his hand from my shoulder and run again.

Perth follows.

Mirain waits by the edge of his perimeter, facing toward the south.

I turn my head toward the sky. "Thank you, Griandor, for sending her to me."

Her body glows a brilliant-white, and she rears. When she returns to all fours, I jump on her back then look at Perth.

He stares at my horse; his eyes ask questions before he even speaks. "Did you just thank a *god* for your horse?"

"There's no time. I heard the daemons in the forest. Your hiding spot didn't work either." I kick my heels into Mirain's sides and take off . . . alone.

Lead me to them, Griandor.

Mirain moves so smooth and fast, I know the sun god is aiding us. Galloping at considerable speed, she jumps over huge fallen trees, turns just in front of boulders, and bounds though small streams leading to the river. She huffs white clouds of steam from her nose, but nothing slows her down.

Branches crack, and water splashes behind me; I glance over my shoulder. Bowen is following with Perth on the stallion.

Breaking through a line of trees, Mirain slows then stops about forty feet before we arrive at a large rock formation. Small cracks in the stones allow light to escape.

This is it.

I slide from her back then draw my sword. Body on fire and heart full of rage, I march toward the cave.

A hand clasps my shoulder again.

"Wait," Perth says with a hard edge to his tone.

"Why?" I try to knock his hand free of me, but he digs his fingers into my skin.

He glances toward the rocks. "We have about three seconds before we are spotted. Turn off your flames."

I think about everyone in that cave before I answer. "No."

"I have a plan. Now, turn off your flames." He growls.

"Your plans don't work." I want to hit Perth, use my magic against him.

Trust him, Griandor's voice booms in my head.

As if listening to its creator, the magic flickers and retracts from my extremities, folding itself into my heart. The anger inside me dissolves.

"Please, trust me," Perth says.

My shoulders sag, and I stare at the ground. I sigh. "What's your plan?"

"A distraction. I will ride a horse in front of the cave, get their attention, then ride off as fast as possible. When the daemons follow me, you can move in for the soldiers. Once they are free, I will understand if you do not try to rescue me—I doubt I will live long enough for that, but I would appreciate you trying."

I look from the ground and lock eyes with Perth. "Are you saying you're willing to sacrifice your life to save all the others?"

"Yes," he says with no hint of a lie in his tone at all.

I shouldn't have treated Perth as unfairly as I have. "I will come for you. Ride fast. Head north toward Willow Falls. Stay as close to the river as possible, so we can use it as a guide."

A small smile grows on his face. "I will. Cadman's stallion will not be able to ride as far and fast as your Mirain, but I will do my best to stay alive. Be safe and watch for their tricks."

Maybe all Perth ever needed was someone to trust him. Maybe that's all any of the Ground Dwellers have needed, except for possibly his dad. Perth mounts the stallion, creates a blue flame in his palm then transfers it to his sword. Old magic in the iron holds the fire.

"Oh, and Perth," I say before he rides away.

He looks over his shoulder.

"Thank you."

"No, thank you for trying to trust me. You have shown me more kindness than most. I hope for all of our sakes this is not a trap." Perth kicks his feet into the horse's sides and rides up the path leading to the mouth of the cave.

I wait until he reaches the top.

Perth lifts his sword, and the horse trots in.

Ten dreadful seconds pass; I don't dare take a breath.

Snorting precedes the glow of the blue flames and Perth. Tairbs and coscarthas chase the horse. Ten, twenty, thirty creatures rush out of the cave, grunting and screeching. I'm not sure how they keep up with the stallion's speed, but they do.

When no more exit and they're all out of sight, I move in.

Mirain and Bowen follow behind, then stop by a tree just before the path leading up to the cave.

Prickles of fear ripple along my arms and grow stronger the closer I draw to the entrance. I take a deep breath and release the magic from inside; there's no telling if all the daemons followed Perth out or not. Bringing my sword to my chest, I put my back against the rocks and use my ears to check for clues as to what I'm about to walk into.

Other than the sound of my nervous breaths and heart pounding in my chest, there are no noises.

It's now or never.

Stepping in front of the entrance, I see everything just as I had from Brit's mind—minus the daemons. Arland is at the back of the cave; we lock eyes.

I gasp.

Crimson soaks through his pants. Open wounds are carved on his chest. Dirt and blood make him barely recognizable. Brit is next to him. Both of them are alive, but I can't imagine they will be for much longer. Every advance my feet make seems to take too long. Concern for anything lurking disappears and my pace picks up.

I drop my sword by Arland's feet and work to untie the ropes around his hands.

He lifts his head.

"Thank God you're alive."

Stop. Griandor's voice booms in my head again.

It takes monumental effort to make my fingers obey his command.

Pick up your sword and untie your mother first, he instructs.

Arland's forehead creases, and he squints as I back away from him.

My heart aches. I want to help him, hug him, kiss him, but I set aside the look of confusion on his face then turn for my mom. Each step feels like I'm carrying ten pounds of lead in my boots.

Even in the dim light with a gag secured in Mom's mouth by rope, I see relief on her face. With my focus off Arland and Brit, I see a look of relief on everyone's face.

I rip through the bindings around Mom's feet, face, and then hands. She opens and closes her mouth a few times, rubbing her red wrists.

I glance over my shoulder at Arland. *Why can't I untie him? Why am I being punished even more?*

"How did you know?" Mom asks, removing the ropes from Gavin next to her.

"Know what, Mom?"

She points toward Arland and Brit. "That those two are shifters."

"Excuse me? Arland said shifters only imitate animals."

"Apparently they can do more than we thought." She finishes Gavin and moves on to Dunn.

"So you didn't know?"

Shaking my head, I follow her lead and untie Flanna. "If they're shifters, why don't they escape now that I know what they are?"

Mom stops and looks at me over her shoulder. "I am not sure."

We continue releasing people; each time someone is freed, they turn and help the one next to them until all but Arland and Brit are unrestrained.

"Why didn't you release him then?" Mom asks, offering her hand to Enid.

"Griandor sent me a message."

Everyone snaps their head in my direction—even the children.

I look down myself. I'm glowing, *and* I've just told a cave full of people I spoke to a god. My power is no longer a secret, but then, the only person who I needed to hide from has always known who I am.

The soldiers fall silent, as though I spoke a terrible joke in front of a bad audience.

Mom glances around, then rests her eyes on me. "We will have to discuss this more later. We need to find the real Arland and Brit, and those two are the only ones who could know where they are."

She points to the shifters. "This is going to get hard."

"*Get* hard? When has this been easy? I've lost everything and gotten it all back so many times, I don't even know how I'm standing right now. But we have to find them, and fast, because we have to rescue Perth, and there may not be much time for him." I turn on my toe then march right up to the imposters. Using my sword, I slice through the ropes holding the gags in the fake Brit's mouth, then Arland's.

"Kate, you must trust me. Look at my eyes and tell me I am not the man you love, tell me I am not the man you committed your life to last night." Arland's voice cracks.

He needs water. I want to caress his face, tell him everything is going to be okay. He looks so much like my Arland.

"They steal memories, too?" I ask.

"Apparently," Mom says.

But the pain filling me from his words is too great. Just last night, while next to our bed, Arland said he wanted me to be buried with his people. I can think of no greater future than to spend my entire life with him. Closing my eyes to escape the torment, I see two forms of pulsing energy. Black strands looped around a solid white core stretch out like bands of elastic and snap back over and over.

My flames burn out of control; I look at the shifters. "What did you do with them?"

"Kate, please, it is me," he begs, green eyes watering.

"They cannot be far. Shifters must stay close to those they emulate." The sureness in Mom's voice startles me.

I stare at her. "H-how do you know?" It's not that I don't trust my mom, I just don't understand how she can have any knowledge of shifters . . . no one knew what they were capable of, and she didn't live here.

She wipes tears from her eyes. "My sister and I were telepaths. Like you and Brit, we could connect to each other. Our annual hiking trip was a way for me to gather information from her about things that were going on. We could connect any time, but the closer I was to the portal, the stronger our link was."

"*Was*, Mom?"

"The night before our trip, when I got sick, it was because she was murdered."

Murdered? My chest constricts, forcing all the air from my lungs.

"We connected all the time." Mom sucks in a sharp breath.

"We were sharing information when she was killed. I felt her fear and her death as it happened. It was awful. *I* wanted to die." She presses a trembling hand to her pale cheeks.

"When I asked why you were sick, you said it was nothing! Why don't you tell me things?" I ask, shaking my head.

She covers her eyes, hiding pain she's never shown before, truths she hasn't been able to talk about. Yelling at Mom when she's just told me her sister died makes me feel horrible, but I hate secrets. I want the truth. However, after what just took place between Brit and me, I can only imagine how awful losing someone while connected to them mentally would be. "Was her name Cairine?"

Mom jumps at the name. "Yes, but how—?"

I wrap my arms around her. "Arland told me he and Cairine used to keep in contact, but he hadn't heard from her recently."

"I forgot how close the two of them were," she says into my shoulder.

"My sister was the last telepath in The Meadows. I'm sure without her, everyone there is worried."

Pulling out of our embrace, I glance at the two shifters. "I was in Brit's mind not long before I got here . . . what happened to the real Brit and Arland?"

Mom gasps. "They were taken away."

"Are they a-alive?" I ask, clenching my hand around the hilt of my sword.

"Yes, but we have to find them, Kate. They may not have time."

"So, what do we do with them?" I point at the shifters.

She turns toward them and scowls. "Kill them."

"You don't want to do that," Brit's shifter says, green eyes big and honest just like my sister's.

"Oh, I do," I say.

Brit's imposter smiles a broad, sinister smile. "If you kill us, you will never find the two you love."

I look at my mom, hope sinking to my feet.

"I don't know, Kate," she says.

Closing my eyes again, I lower my head. *Griandor, please help me.*

Along the ground, two black pulsing bands stretch from the daemons in front of us and out of the cave.

"Keep watch," I tell Mom, turning away from the imposters.

"Cadman, Flanna, come with me."

Cadman and Flanna stop talking to the other soldiers and follow. Keeping my eyes closed, I track the bands outside.

"Kate, I know *we* are not the ones you were looking for, but can you at least look at me?" Flanna asks in her sarcastic tone, but there's something more to it. Something uneasy.

"We don't have time, Flanna. I need you and Cadman to lead me around any obstacles. I'm following bands of—I don't even know what they are. I'm just following something stretching out of those two daemons, and I'm hoping it's going to lead to Arland and Brit." I step on a large stone and roll my ankle, nearly losing my balance.

Flanna takes hold of my arm with a clammy hand. "Sounds like a plan."

"I would feel safer if I had a sword," Cadman says.

I hold out my claymore for him.

"Thank you."

"You're welcome. If either of you sees anything, protect yourselves first; I can handle myself if something comes my way."

Flanna puts her left hand on my right shoulder. Judging by the echo of boots, Cadman walks behind me. The bands stretch down in front of us. Opening my eyes, I see we have to descend the rocks leading to the river.

We move at a slow pace, placing each foot carefully in front of the other. Jagged stones crash down the steep cliff side, cracking as they tumble to the bottom.

Flanna slides a couple of feet and lands on her butt. "Did we really need to come this way?"

"We're almost there . . . just a few more steps."

We jump onto solid ground, earth thudding under our feet.

A quick blink reveals the bands turn to the left and lead into another cave. The entry is small and dark.

My gut tells me this is a trap.

I point ahead of us. "The black things lead in there. I don't have a good feeling about this, but I don't know what else to do."

"I say we follow the only clues we have," Flanna says.

"I agree with Flanna, but you are correct, this does seems strange." Cadman doesn't look at me. He's on guard, searching in all directions for danger.

"You guys stay here. With only the one sword, if something is in there, you will be unable to protect yourselves. I've got magic on my side."

Flanna and Cadman exchange a worried look.

"Kate, are you sure it is a good idea to go by yourself?" she asks.

"I will be fine," I tell her. "Cadman, keep her safe."

He nods.

"Don't come looking for me, if I don't come back."

"And then what would we tell Arland when *we* find him?" Flanna laughs. "Just go, but be careful."

Keeping my eyes open, I drop to my hands and knees then crawl into the cave. I have no time to be afraid, no time to search for the black bands. I follow instincts and use my Light to guide me now.

"Arland? Brit?" I call.

My quivering voice echoes, betraying my nerves, my fears.

The tunnels are about three feet wide and four feet tall. I cannot imagine how daemons could have gotten Arland and Brit in here without a struggle, but I don't see any signs of one. No blood, no tracks . . . nothing.

The path makes a sudden, sharp slant downward. A hill so steep, it takes all my strength to keep from sliding forward. Turning around, I crab-walk down the slope; my muscles twitch and burn from holding myself up.

When the ground levels out again, the walls open into a large space and reveal three possible paths. I stand, close my eyes, and search for the bands—they lead to the right.

"Arland? Brit?" I call again.

The deeper I get, the creepier this situation becomes. A constant hissing noise grows louder and louder. Instead of getting colder the further underground I get, the cave fills with a damp, warm air.

I shudder. Goose bumps prick up my arms and raise the hairs on the back of my neck. The walls close in again; I return to my hands and knees. Time drones on. I don't even know if I'm following the right clues, but I will not give up on Arland and Brit, on love, or on family.

Another hiss echoes in front of me. I try to place why the sound is so familiar, and then it comes again—louder. Hissing is not a normal sound for a cave. It reminds me of . . . collecting eggs from the chicken coop, but why?

Again the sound echoes.

When I was seven, a black snake lashed out at me when I was gathering eggs from under a chicken. The snake was using the hen's warmth and eating her eggs; snakes are smart, vile creatures. But this sound is too loud to be any normal snake.

Serpents!

Perth said he's never seen them outside the water, but of course they come out, and what better place than in a low cave next to a river?

My hands and knees propel me forward at an alarming pace. I shouldn't rush into this when I know nothing about what I'm going to face, but the thought of the daemon being near my sister or my love is my driving force. Closing my eyes, I look at the ground to make sure I'm still on the right path.

I am.

"Arland? Brit?" I yell.

The hiss is deafening, making me pause in my tracks. I listen for any other noise that might give me information I need, but cannot hear anything else, so I continue crawling. The walls open up again. My fire fills the space ahead of me, revealing something I've never imagined.

Standing at least forty feet tall is the biggest snake I've ever seen. It looks like a cobra with brown and white scales the size of tables. Its hood is puffed out, and it hisses at Arland and Brit. They appear to be tied to the wall by their arms and legs, but there's no rope. Closing my eyes again, I see the pulsing black bands covering almost every inch of their bodies.

I have no sword. *What was I thinking leaving it with Cadman?* The fire rages inside me. Arland and Brit turn their heads in my direction. Their eyes widen when the serpent follows their gaze.

I need you, magic. Fill this cave and burn that daemon.

Sprites peel themselves from the ceiling, from the dirt floor, and from pools of water around my feet. At first, they maintain their natural shape—like rocks, dirt, and beads of liquid—but when they see the serpent, they turn into balls of blue flames then swirl around him. He spits, hisses, then snaps at them as they drive through his body.

Using the distraction caused by the sprites, I run along the path leading to the wall where Brit and Arland are bound. There are so many bands wrapped around their bodies, I'm afraid to touch them.

I need more. Help us. Cut these bindings and free Arland and Brit.

Flames break off me then burn through the daemon's bands; they writhe and slink away.

Arland slumps to the cave floor.

Brit falls to her hands and knees.

Neither speaks.

Blood covers their bodies. Their top layer of skin is dissolved.
They're dying.

My hands fill with painful nerves; my heart can't decide if it wants
to stop or beat at a million miles per hour. "Arland? Brit? Please . . .
say something."

Neither responds.

I cannot touch them, cannot move from where I stand.

The battle between the serpent and sprites continues behind me.
It needs to end. *I* need all the help with my love and my sister I can
get. Anger boils in the pit of my stomach. Turning from them, I
march toward the serpent. He lunges, but magic forms a blue wall in
front of me.

Kill him! I command.

Flames stretch from my body and engulf the hissing creature. My
strength grows weak, but I do not back down. He bares his fangs;
poison drips from them, landing near my feet. Taking two steps back
to avoid the deadly fluid, I push even more fire from my soul. Blue
flames swirl around then drive inside the serpent. He wails and sways
but remains standing.

The daemon lowers his head and hisses right in front of my face,
blowing my hair from my shoulders. His hot, rank breath moistens
my skin, fuels my anger. I'm certain death would come rapidly if any
of the yellow substance leaking from his fangs touches me. I take two
more steps away; I'm standing between two motionless bodies.
Arland and Brit.

Throwing my head back, I look up toward the heavens—even
though all I see is our stone tomb. *Griandor, please help me.*

I raise my hands over my head. "Fill me. Use me. Kill him."

From every direction, bright, yellow light rushes into the
cavernous space and into my upraised arms. A power flows in my
veins and nearly knocks me off my feet, but I push through it and
stand my ground. The serpent spits then lashes out toward me. I
jump forward and thrust my hands and magic in front of my body.
Light pours out of me and directly into his open mouth.

The creature collapses to the ground, but he continues to spit, hiss, and snap. Putting my hand on his neck, I focus all the Light into it. The magic severs his head from his body.

His black, beady eyes go blank.

I look up into the vast openness of the cave and at all the sprites flying around. The stone walls reflect the color of the sun in the sky from the Light on my body. I return to Arland and Brit.

"Now heal them!" I lay my hands on their shoulders, transferring power from my body into theirs.

In an instant, old magic covers their skin. I watch and wait as their wounds close, their skin regains color, and their arms and legs wiggle.

The sprites disappear, but Griandor's Light still shines through me.

Arland and Brit stand and appear to be in perfect condition.

My legs weaken, and my head spins. "Arland? Brit?"

Their forms twist and fade before my eyes.

Arland manages to get his arms around me just as I lose control and black out.

CHAPTER SIX

"Kate?" Arland's voice bounces inside my head like a broken record.

Splitting pain radiates from the base of my neck to my temples. What happened to me? My body aches like I've been hit by a tractor trailer, but I don't remember being touched by anything.

I moan.

"Brit, I think she is coming around." Relief floods his soft words.

"Kate? Oh God, Kate, are you okay?" Brit's voice is piercing and cuts through me like a knife.

My brain hurts so badly. I wish she would just be quiet, but hearing her speak calms the tension inside me—*she's alive.*

Fabric rips. "Take this. Get it wet with water from one of the pools," Arland says.

"I'll be right back." Brit might as well be speaking into a microphone. Her fast-paced footsteps echo around the cavernous room.

Arland puts one hand under my head, and the other caresses my cheek. "I know you are awake, and I am almost positive you are in a good deal of pain. What you did with the magic was incredible, Kate, but I understand now what your mother said about rest—you have not had enough of it."

My fingers come to life, and I take hold of his hand over my face. "My head hurts."

He chuckles under his breath. "You slipped out of my arms before I had a good grip on you. You hit your head pretty hard. Can you open your eyes, or does it hurt too much?"

I have to see Arland and Brit's faces for myself, make sure they're healed—make sure I'm not dreaming. My eyes flutter open, but everything around me spins, and I shut them again. "I think I'm going to puke."

"Just keep your eyes closed. I will carry you out," he whispers.

"You can't. The passages are too narrow." Too much talking. My stomach rises in my throat. I roll to my side . . . just in case.

"Here," Brit yells.

Water drops on my face, cold and shocking.

"Thank you, Brit. Kate is okay; she is worn from using the magic, and her head hurts," he whispers so quietly I strain to hear him.

Arland dabs the wet cloth across my cheek.

"Oh. I'm sorry, Kate. I'll be quieter." She mimics Arland's tone. "What are we going to do, Arland? We can't stay in here. W-what if another one of those s-s-snakes comes in?"

Ever since a snake bit Brit at our favorite swimming hole, she's hated the legless reptiles. Being in here is probably freaking her out more than I can even imagine.

Grabbing onto Arland's forearm, I sit up. The effort is great, but I don't make it far. I fall into his lap. Pushing aside the overwhelming nausea, I open my eyes again, focus on his face, and take slow, deep breaths to keep from throwing up. His clenched jaw and the crease in his forehead make me wonder if I'm the one who was trapped by shifters a few minutes ago.

"You are going to have to help me up."

He pushes my hair behind my ear, leaving tingling trails where his skin touches mine. "I believe you should rest." Arland's voice has the power to soothe every worry I've ever had, and right now is no different.

I fight an urge to go to sleep on him and grab onto his arms again. "There's no time, Arland. Brit's right; we cannot stay here. Other serpents can come in, there are two shifters in the cave we still have to take care of, and we have to rescue Perth."

Arland holds my arms and slowly lifts me upright, but I'm too weak to support myself. I lean my head into his chest. Black spots appear in my vision, and blood thrums in my ears.

"Rescue Perth?" he asks, rubbing my back.

I press my hand to my mouth as if that will hold back yesterday's lunch. "Yes. If it wasn't for him, I would never have found or been able to save you guys."

Arland holds me out then narrows his eyes. "Kate, please tell me he does not know who you are! Tell me you did not show him what you are capable of!"

The sudden jerk in my stomach does me in. Salty fluids fill my mouth, gurgles from the furthest reaches of my gut rumble—I lean over and throw up.

"I am sorry; I did not mean to make you ill," Arland says.

Brit hands me a wet cloth. "Here. I ripped some off my shirt in case you needed more."

Sitting up on my own, I take the bit of fabric and wipe my mouth. "Thanks."

"Kate?" Arland's eyebrows pull together so tight, I'm afraid to tell him anything.

Swallowing hard, I decide it's better to speak, to share everything. "Arland, P-Perth knows. He always has, but he's not bad. Perth doesn't agree with what his people do. He wants peace between our kinds, but he's scared to go against his father. Perth led me here; he even put his own life on the line so I could rescue everyone. The daemons followed him from the cave. He's heading north along the river toward Willow Falls. I promised to come for him."

I stand slowly, but have to hurry to turn my head from Arland. I throw up again. After I'm finished, he wraps his arm around me for support. Brit does the same on my right side.

"Can you walk?" he asks.

Even though I nod, Brit and Arland don't move from my sides. Together, we start toward the small hole I crawled through to get here.

"I do not trust Perth, Kate." Arland keeps his eyes focused ahead of him.

"He gives me the creeps, too," Brit chimes in.

"I know, Arland. Your father doesn't trust him either." I sigh. "When I spoke to him, he said all Ground Dwellers are bad, but I have advice from Griandor to trust those around me. And since Perth was the only one around me . . . . "

Arland stops then turns to face me, clenching his jaw and breathing heavily through his nose. I rest my hands on his shoulders for support. What is he more upset about: Perth or Griandor?

Arland arches his eyebrow. "You spoke with Griandor?"

The white-haired god it is. "Yes, and I had the unfortunate pleasure of meeting his brother Dughbal. I know what this war is about, and I know how to end it. The first step is getting to Willow Falls to form an army."

Arland shakes his head. "We have an army."

"That's the same thing your father said, but Arland, *I* need an army."

He smiles. "And what did my father say when you told him the army was for you?"

"He said he'd see what he can do." I laugh. "Griandor said it would be hard because your father, Dufaigh, and someone named Murchadha are afraid for any more lives to be lost, but I would have to find a way to unite both sides and have them fight for me."

Pulling me closer, Arland's fingers tense on my back. His intensity burns right into me. "Did he say how you would have to unite our two kinds?"

I don't like how nervous he's become. My heart rate picks up. "No, just that I need to do whatever it takes . . . ." As I'm speaking, it becomes clear what could unite our two kinds: a willing marriage to Perth. Arland realized it the instant he heard what Griandor wants me to do. If *I* had realized it sooner, I might have had something to say to the sun god.

"Arland, I won't. I can't. That's not what I want for my life. You know that. You know what I want." I hold his gaze—he needs to know how serious I am, how much he means to me and how much my life will remain in my control.

"I'm confused. What exactly is going on?" Brit asks.

"The only way to unite our people with the Ground Dwellers is for Kate to marry Perth," Arland says, without taking his eyes off me.

"No, Kate, you can't! That's not fair! Why would you fight in this war for anyone when in the end the life you get isn't what you want? Screw this! We'll find another way." Brit's angry voice torments the ache in my head.

I'm glad she's supportive, but I cannot look at her . . . only Arland.

I press my fingers to my temple, trying to hold back the throbbing. "I won't do it, Arland. Griandor's sister Gramhara didn't give me her power of love for nothing. There has to be another way, and I will search for one. Your father told me to keep my distance from you when we arrive at Willow Falls, so my guess is your prophecy said something will happen there. Something big."

"If you feel we can trust Perth, we are going to have to come up with a plan involving him. We need to get to the others and find him, but first . . . ."

Arland leans his head forward. I try to move away—I've just thrown up—but he pulls me closer, closes his eyes, and meets my lips.

Warmth floods me. Strength. This is why I will fight: for love, for a life with Arland—no matter how short. The touch of his fingers along my back, his smooth, soft lips on mine . . . wrapping my arms around his neck, I give into him.

"I'm going to go. You two obviously need alone time," Brit says with a hint of disgust, turning away, but going nowhere—she doesn't know the way out.

Arland steps away first. "I love you, Kate."

The room fills with golden light radiating from our bodies. The kiss has restored my energy. I wonder if this is what Griandor meant when he said Arland protects me in many ways. A few moments ago I couldn't even open my eyes, and now my heart swells with happiness.

"I love you, too."

From the corner of my eye, I see Brit staring at something on the cave wall as though she's looking at the most fascinating thing in the world.

I laugh and nudge her shoulder. "I'm sorry, Brit. We can go now."

She turns around with a half-smile. "Kate, you have no idea how happy I am to see you like this, but if you are supposed to keep your distance from Arland at Willow Falls, you are going to have to learn to hide your feelings better."

She waves her hand at us.

"The Light?"

"And your face. Your face lights up like a beacon when you see him."

Heat fills my cheeks.

Arland snickers.

She wags a finger. "You, too, Arland. Those eyes of yours plaster themselves to her as soon as she steps into a room. I've got years of experience hiding things from people. I'll do my best to help."

Now Arland's cheeks turn red.

"What do you mean?" The only thing I know Brit hid from me was an old bottle of rum in the woods, but the way she talks, I think she has a lot more secrets than she's let on.

"Not down here. I'll tell you anything you need to know, up there." Brit points above her head.

"You're right. We need to get out of here, but I want you to tell me everything *after* Perth is safe. Now, follow me." I lead them toward the exit.

The tunnels seem even smaller on the way back up to the surface. The impenetrable stone on all sides could crush us if there was an earthquake, entombing us forever. I crouch on my forearms, the walls brush my elbows, and Brit keeps bumping into the back of me. Finding our way out is easy, though; the now visible bands of the shifters guide us. I wonder if the magic killed them, if *I* killed them, or if freeing Brit and Arland only wounded the daemons.

We crawl into a vast open area, stand, then stretch our legs.

I point to a narrow passage. "It's going to get slippery, but we have to climb that."

Brit heads over and takes to the rocks. "Thank God Gary signed us up for those climbing classes," she says, looking over her shoulder.

"Somehow I don't think it was his idea."

Brit doesn't respond; she's already halfway up the incline. My mom must have carefully chosen every activity we ever participated in, knowing we'd wind up in Encardia, a land so far behind on modernization.

Arland gently pushes my back. "We better get up there, or she is going be out in the open without protection."

I take a few tentative steps up the rocks, and pick up the pace when I realize it's not a difficult climb. So much easier than coming down. "Cadman and Flanna are out there. She'll be fine."

A loud scream reverberates around us.

"Oh my God, Arland, that was Brit!"

"Go!"

Without devising any sort of plan, I climb as fast as possible in this small space. My head bumps into the ceiling, my shoulders into the walls. My knees ache from the hard stone, but I keep going.

The exit appears about ten feet before we reach it. I cannot see any movement outside. Even if an entire army sat out there waiting for us, I wouldn't know because of how dark it is.

I stop so fast Arland runs into my butt.

"Why have you stopped?" he asks.

"Should we just go out? What if it's a trap?"

"Kate!" Flanna's frantic whisper echoes, hiding the location of its origin.

I glance around. "Flanna? Where are you?"

"We are outside with Brit. Hurry up, but be quiet; her *scream* might have already drawn attention—and make sure you are not burning."

Arland listens to every word she speaks as though searching for hidden clues, then presses me to go forward. "I do not believe this is a trap."

Crawling through the opening, I find Flanna, Cadman and Brit all on their hands and knees as close to the rocks as they can get. "Why did you scream?" I ask, maintaining a quiet tone.

Brit rests her trembling hand on mine. "D-daemons." She stares up the cliff.

Arland exits after me, and the calm, cool demeanor of his Leader self oozes from him. He straightens his back then looks around in all directions before acknowledging Cadman and Flanna. "How many?"

Arland didn't even question *if.* He already knows.

"All of them, sir," Cadman says. "We watched them enter, but I do not believe they saw us."

All of them. That means there are at least thirty. What does that mean for—"*Perth* . . . . " The name escapes my mouth and hangs in the cool, dark air like the threat of death we continue to face.

"They have that little traitor," Flanna says, nose turned up.

"Traitor?" Brit asks, glancing at my fiery friend.

Flanna puts her hands on her hips, her red hair pale next to the anger coloring her cheeks. "He has to have something to do with this."

How can she make that assumption about Perth? I look between Arland and Flanna.

He doesn't take his eyes off the hill of rocks between us and an exit—or death. "Flanna is angry because she holds out hope for you and me, Kate . . . amongst other things. *And* she knows nothing of what you told me about Griandor and trust."

Flanna tears her gaze from my sister then turns to me. "Trust? Do not tell me you trust him? I am sure that little weasel had a hand in setting us up." She's angry, but her voice never goes above a whisper.

"I didn't trust him at first, but I do now—and I don't think he had anything to do with our set-up. There were two working against us. Lann was one. Do you guys have any idea who the other was . . . other than Perth?"

Flanna scowls then returns to face the cliff.

"Lann did not have anything to do with it, ma'am," Cadman says.

"I saw with my own eyes . . . well, through Brit's mind."

Brit shakes her head. "I was wrong, Kate. I'm so sorry. That wasn't Lann—he shifted into something else soon after you left my mind, and I forgot to say anything when you came back. Somehow they knew about our connection. They tricked me. Just like when the daemon threatened me with his blood. As soon as the connection faded, we could hear your screams from here. That's when they brought Arland and me down to that s-snake thing."

Information swims inside my head. Every time I feel like I know something, everything changes. "So Lann isn't a spy?"

Arland grits his teeth. "No, a shifter in the form of Lann was the spy. He is the one who allowed the daemons to enter the base while we were sleeping. When I came out to see what was going on, I saw his true form."

"But you said they only shifted into animals. How come we couldn't tell?"

"I do not know the answer." Arland shakes his head. "It certainly explains so many of our own turning against us."

"Does this mean the real Lann may be out there somewhere, and we still have no idea who the other spy was?"

"Are you sure there were two?" he asks.

"I'm not sure of anything, but a certain someone said he had two daemons working against us." I'm keeping details about my meeting with Griandor secret from as many people as possible. Knowledge is power, just like Arland's father always told him, and what I know, others will want to as well.

"Well, if there were two"—Flanna rolls her eyes— "I have a pretty good idea one of them was Perth."

She's getting under my skin. "Are the other soldiers still up there, or did they leave before the tairbs and coscarthas got here?" I ask, pointing up the cliff.

"Where would they have gone? You were taking care of Arland and Brit. None of the soldiers had weapons; there was nowhere *to* go." Flanna's tone borders on hostile.

I know she loves her people, but she acts as if I should have left Arland and Brit to die. No matter how hard I try, I cannot protect everyone.

Arland towers over his cousin. "Control yourself."

Her expression softens, and she covers her face with her hands. "I am sorry, Kate. We have never had anything like this occur. I love Lann and cannot imagine anything happening to him."

"You *love* Lann? I wouldn't have known," I say, trying to calm my frustration. Love certainly explains her current behavior, and maybe even some of her others.

Brit gives me a pointed look. "See what I mean about hiding things?"

Flanna drops her hands; her face blanches, making her blue eyes blaze in the Darkness. "Kate, I have been sharing a room with a daemon for . . . I do not even know how long."

I wrap my arms around her, and she sobs into my shoulder.

"We can discuss our love lives later. Right now we need to come up with a plan—one that does not involve us standing here waiting to get caught," Arland says.

Flanna backs away and scowls at him.

Cadman casts a weary glance in the direction of the cave. "Is there another way out?"

"There must be, but we have no reason to run and hide." Arland tips his head in my direction, and for a moment, I get an urge to turn and run the other direction. But this isn't just my life in danger; it's everyone in the world.

Cadman holds up the claymore. "Other than this sword, *we* have no weapons, sir."

"Kate, how do you feel?" Arland asks, rubbing my arms. "Do you think you can handle what is up there, or would you prefer to go back into this cave?"

So many dreams I've had of us dying in a cave, or rather just outside of one. I'd like to get as far away from the rocks . . . and, well, daemons in general as possible, but I don't want to hide. Both stowing away in this cave and fighting in the one above hold consequences I'm not sure I'm ready to face; however, with Arland beside me, I don't feel weak. "I say we fight."

A grin spreads across his face. "Are you sure? Once we start we cannot stop."

"We can't leave everyone up there in the hands of daemons. They'll kill them when they find four captives missing. Besides, we need to get to Willow Falls and work on that other thing." That *other* thing being my army.

Arland takes my hand in his. "Cadman, give me the sword. Would the three of you feel safer waiting here or coming with us?"

Cadman hands the sword over as if he's giving up an arm or a leg. "I would prefer to fight, sir. I just wonder what use I will be without a weapon."

"When Kate's fire burns, think of the things you love. Connect your mind to those things then command the magic to do your will. It will be the only weapon you need, but we must work fast. The magic drains her. She has not had enough rest, but if we all work together, it should make her job easier."

My mouth hangs open as I stare at Arland. "How do you know all of this, Arland?"

Glancing sideways, he smiles. "What do you think I was thinking about in every battle we have endured so far?"

Flanna groans. "Love lives later, right Arland?"

I hate how upset she is. I know it's not my relationship with Arland bothering her; Flanna did her best to push us together, but I can't worry about her right now. My sister is trembling.

"Brit, are *you* going to be okay with this?" I ask.

She wraps her arms around herself. "I-I d-don't know how to use the m-magic or a sword. The only thing I do know how to use is a b-bow, and I don't have one."

Freeing my hand from Arland, I embrace Brit and rub her back, trying to ease her nerves. "Stay behind me and Arland. Do you understand? Not in front, not to the side, but behind me—within inches."

Teeth chattering, face pale—she nods.

I lace my fingers with Arland's again then lock eyes with him. "Let's go."

He leads us along a path running about a quarter mile around the left side of the ledge. The daemons are quiet, and so are we. We creep up the hill, and the only things I hear are our footsteps.

"Wait until we reach the top to release the magic," Arland says.

An eerie silence blankets the cliff, making it difficult to keep the magic inside, but I do. I have no choice. With our backs to the rock formation, we slink along toward the mouth of the cave.

Hooves clop on the stone. Muffled voices rise in a panicked state. Groans echo into the night.

Arland leans next to my ear. "Now would be a good time to release the magic, Kate. When you do, step out where they can see you, and do not let go of me."

Closing my eyes, I send my mind searching through every part of my body for strength, for love, for all the things I think of when I need control. I see the horses, my sister, my mom, my friendship with Brad, but most of all I see Arland, and I *feel* Arland. Grasping onto those images, I will them over my heart and push out the Light. I take a step into the open with Arland by my side, Brit, Cadman, and Flanna all behind me.

Daemons startle and rush to the narrow corridor leading to the exit, then pause. Their mouths foam, excited by our sudden appearance at their prison. The tairb's eyes widen and glow red. The coscartha's shrieks—loud, agitated sounds—pierce my ears. There's even a hound or two in the group.

A howl rings into the Darkness.

The daemons advance.

We brace.

"Okay, everyone, remember what you need to do. When the old magic comes to life, command it into fire and burn the daemons. Do you understand?" Arland stares at me, but he speaks to all of us.

"I cannot wait." Flanna leans forward and growls.

We don't move from where we stand. Arland and I hold hands and Brit's are on my shoulders. Cadman and Flanna flank our sides.

Wake up!

I speak no other words to the magic. Stones, leaves, beads of water, bark from trees, blades of grass—all the representations of nature come alive in brilliant blues, greens, whites, and thousands of other colors to fight by our sides. The sprites swirl around, lift our hair, cover our skin and caress us with their soft wings.

Blue flames light all of us on fire.

Arland closes his eyes. Other than Brit and me, everyone's eyes are closed. Cadman, Flanna, and Arland whisper inaudible words.

He squeezes my hand, reassuring me, reminding me I am in control. "Now, Kate, send the magic to the daemons."

"Turn to fire. Burn them!" I command.

Transforming from soft, ethereal creatures into blue fireballs, thousands of sprites fly into the cave. Flames reach from my body and into the daemons as they continue their advance. With outstretched claws, bared teeth, and growls so loud they rumble in my chest, the daemons jump to the side to avoid the magic. Some are burned and killed instantly while others seem to ignore our attack.

Releasing a low, guttural sound, a giant black hound bounds toward us through the flames.

Flanna raises her hands above her head and smiles wickedly. "Mharúdó!"

One large, blue flame forms above her. She points her lifted arms toward the creature; the fire stretches out then lands on him. With a whimper like an injured pup, the hound burns until all that's left is a pile of ashes.

Flanna winks at me.

Ten more coscarthas approach. Before I have time to react, Cadman, Flanna, and Arland all control the magic, shouting commands. The power flows through us as it did when we were healing Brad. A heightened sense of connection to them, as though their existences are attached to me, tugs at my core. The power dwindles as it spreads into them, stealing strength from me, but empowering them.

My knees shake.

Arland squeezes my hand. "Just a little while longer, Kate."

Give her strength, Griandor. Arland's voice plays in my mind.

Looking at him, I notice his eyes are locked with a daemon a few feet in front of us, his mouth closed.

P-please, let us l-l-live. This time I hear Brit.

Lann. Lann. Lann. Flanna.

Sunshine. Cadman thinks the word as though he sees the sun, and it's the most beautiful sight his eyes have ever beheld.

No one speaks aloud, but I hear their voices. The magic must be providing a mental connection.

Blue sprites swirl between the monsters created for war and us.

Everyone except for Brit commands the beings to attack the daemons as they draw closer and encircle us. Fifteen tiarbs, hounds, and coscarthas stand on all sides. Some drool, some growl, and some are burned and bloody. They still appear hungry for a fight, yet they don't advance.

I look toward the endless black sky. "Finish this!"

Radiant sunlight breaks through the Darkness and beams down on us from the heavens. Magic flows through and out of my body, blasting into the daemons. It takes every weakened muscle to try to remain standing, but my knees buckle. Arland, Flanna, Cadman, and Brit grab hold of my arms to support me; their hands are hot but comforting.

"Stop! Unless you want me to kill him, which I would not mind doing." A sadistic voice penetrates my concentration.

The Light retreats upward.

Turning my head to the left, I see where the voice came from. A tairb stands about twenty feet away from us, holding onto Perth with one of its claws at his throat.

Crawling over the rock formation, climbing up the slope behind us, appearing from everywhere, hundreds of daemons surround our small group of fighters. I spin around, trying to find escape, trying to look for a weakness in the daemon's plan to trap us, but find none. The shrieks in the forest when I ran away from Perth, how simple it was for him to lead the daemons out of the cave . . . this has all been a trick.

A smile stretches across the tairb's face when I return my eyes to his. "So you see, you are trapped. If you wish the boy to live, you will surrender."

His blood red eyes flit between me, and Perth's neck.

"Do not surrender," Perth squeaks.

The tairb growls, and a coscartha kicks Perth's gut. He groans. Tears run from the corners of his eyes.

I will not surrender. I will not allow them to hurt Perth or anyone else. At my core, anger, rage and power all struggle for control. I clench Arland's hand in mine as the daemons take a few steps forward. My body trembles as magic tries to escape, as if trying to shake off my skin. Fire erupts on all of us, and without any guidance from me, the magic flows around Perth and into the tairb. The glow from its red eyes fades, and it drops to the ground in flames.

Perth runs toward us, flashing me an apologetic look. He takes a stance behind Arland and shouts commands to the magic with the others, sending fire toward the remaining daemons.

Shrieks, howls, and grunts fill the air as old magic consumes our enemies. The others control the power flowing from me so well, there is very little I have to do, but my legs are like jelly. My vision fades in and out, and before I have time to stop myself, I fall.

Arland quits fighting and pulls me upright. "Just a few more, Kate, then I promise you can rest."

When my sight returns, I smile, but when a hound leaps off the rocks, my happy expression disappears. "Arland, behind you!"

He looks over his shoulder, but before he has time to react, Perth jumps in front of us, arms outstretched, magic crackling from his fingers.

"Sruthándó!" Flames flow from him and engulf the beast.

The hound falls to the ground, howling an agonizing, low-pitched cry until its life is stolen.

The air smells of death.

The shrieks and howls have stopped. Water rushing in the river is the only thing I hear.

"Well, that was unexpected." Flanna breaks the silence, staring at Perth.

Cadman glances in all directions. "I believe he was the last of them, sir."

"You can let the magic go now, Kate." Arland hands my sword to Cadman, wraps his arms around me, then lifts me to my feet.

I rest my head on Arland's chest, soaking in his earthy scent. "It would be nice if they could stay. Let us enjoy the light for a while, you know?"

He tightens his hold on me. "You cannot stand up, Kate. You need to let them go, so you can rest."

"I know."

Thank you for helping us.

Sprites disappear into the earth, leaving everything dark, gloomy, and cold. Encardia is miserable again.

I pull my head away from Arland; everyone smiles at me.

Perth catches my gaze.

"What happened?" I ask.

He shrugs. "They caught up to me about ten miles from here. The horse could not outrun them."

"Well, thank you for trying *and* for risking your life."

Arland gives a disgruntled sigh, sounding more like a growl. "Kate, I am going to move you inside the cave. Do you feel sick like you did last time?"

His question brings my attention to the muscles screaming inside me to sit down. "Not sick, just tired."

He scoops me into his arms.

"What are you doing? We cannot stay here. We need to return to Watchers Hall or move to Willow Falls, but staying here is not an option," Perth yells, holding his hands out at his sides.

Arland's arms tense. "In case you are not aware, we only have two weapons between the nearly fifty soldiers and children: Kate and her sword. Since Kate is too exhausted to stand on her own, we are going to have to sleep here tonight."

The ice-cold look returns to Perth's eyes. "If you had done your job better, we would not be in this predicament. You have been so focused on your love affair, you missed that we had traitors in the base."

"May I hit him, sir?" Cadman asks.

Arland sets me down by Flanna and Brit, then turns around and storms over to Perth.

I cannot watch what's taking place.

Arland balls his fists. "No. I will hit him."

Flanna and Brit watch with smiles and wide-eyes.

Appalled, I gather as much strength to put in my voice as possible. "No!"

Arland stops and looks over his shoulder. The pain in his eyes is unbearable. Perth is a constant representation of everything that has been taken from Arland. Me siding with Perth must hurt like a betrayal.

"No one is going to hit Perth." I catch his eyes and scowl. "Perth, if you want people to trust you, stop being an asshole. If it weren't for mine and Arland's *love affair*, as you so called it, there would be no end to this war. If you want to put yourself to good use, why don't you take the time I need to rest to ride back to Watchers Hall to get weapons?"

He looks at me with indignation, but even from where I stand, I meet his angry look with one of my own. I'm trying to trust him, and I'm trying to get the others to as well, but he's not making this easy.

Perth shakes his head then takes a few steps back. "I will gather the weapons and more horses."

Arland unclenches his fists. "Cadman, will you willingly go with him?"

"If you wish me to, sir."

Arland nods then returns to scoop me back up. "We will free Gavin and Ogilvie then send them, as well. Cadman, go release them now."

"Yes, sir."

Cadman heads into the cave with Flanna and Brit following him.

"Hey, Arland," Perth calls.

Arland turns. "Yes, Perth?"

"Try not to let anything else happen to Kate while I am gone." Perth laughs, then disappears into the Darkness.

Arland's eyes meet mine, full of rage.

I place my hand on his cheek. "Let him go," I whisper.

CHAPTER SEVEN

"She's beautiful, isn't she?" Mom's voice drifts into my peaceful sleep.

I'm not dreaming—not while Arland is around protecting me from *all* nighttime visitors—and I know I'm with him because I cannot imagine anyone else's lap being so comfortable. My back and legs ache from lying on the cold stone surface, but the pain is easy to ignore now that I'm safe in the arms of my Coimeádaí, my love, my protector. I open my eyes, but everything is dark. The torches illuminating the cave earlier no longer burn. I make a slight shift to sit up, but Arland clamps his hand on my shoulder and holds me down. After I stop my attempt, he releases me then caresses my arm.

"Beautiful does not even begin to describe her," he whispers.

Flanna telling me Arland thought I was the most beautiful woman in the world, the way he touches me and looks at me as though he cannot get enough—these things make me wish for a million more moments like this. A million more stolen kisses on the hand and lips and sneaking away for warm baths together. But Arland didn't make me stay down to tell my mother I'm beautiful; I'm sure their conversation is about to switch to a more serious nature, and he doesn't want my mom to hold anything back.

"I have never seen her so happy, Arland. Not even the horses make her light up the way you do." I envision her looking down at me and smiling, eyes full of tears—like she did when I graduated high school.

The pace at which Arland's hand runs along my skin quickens. "Tell me, Leader Wilde—"

He goes rigid and stops tracing along my arm.

"Please, call me Saraid. I have lived a lie a long time, Arland, but hearing that name reminds me too much of my husband. Maybe more now, while I am so close to home."

The desperation with which Mom utters her words drills through me and settles in my chest. There is so much about her I don't know, and I cannot imagine what it must have been like to hide the painful memories without ever speaking of them.

"It must have been difficult on you all those years. How did you manage to keep your true self locked away? What information I have of Earth does not suggest those humans take kindly to us." Arland runs his finger along the side of my face, down my neck and arm, sending chills all over.

"So much changed during the time the portal was closed. I am sure you have noticed how Kate is much different from any women here." She pauses. "Her sister more so."

"Yes, Brit is quite . . . " Arland hangs on the word quite, as if looking for the right thing to say, "forward."

I smile. Forward, blunt, sarcastic . . . .

Mom sighs. "It is a good thing we were instructed to travel there. The people have grown to have fantastic imaginations and are learning to accept themselves and other diversified cultures. It was not as difficult to fit in as Brian—" She chokes at the mention of my dad's name.

Arland stops tracing the lines and circles with his finger and rests his hand on my shoulder. "I am sorry. He was a great man. My father respected him, and while I was only a boy, I respected him as well."

Arland means it. He's spoken of my dad before, and even now Arland's voice resonates with earnestness.

"Thank you, but I did not sit next to you to speak of my love, Arland. I sat here to speak of yours. I am aware you want answers, and I think it's time I furnish some."

At this whispered announcement he jolts, but immediately returns to tracing. "Is Kate going to be killed?"

This is not the question I wanted him to ask, but I understand why it's at the top of his list. Mom already told me she doesn't know whether he's going to die or not, but we never established anything about my life.

"I had a feeling you'd ask me that first. We all die at some point in our lives." Her response is almost exactly what she gave me when I asked about Arland.

"Saraid, please, I must know she will survive this war." Mom's half-truth answers are infuriating; Arland's agitation makes his voice an octave deeper.

"*She* will not die in this war, but I do not know about you—or anyone else for that matter. Let me tell you a few things. Kate will possess knowledge—a knowledge not even I have—regarding why Darkness is here. She might already know, but I'm not sure where she learns it. When the Seer envisioned Kate's future, an obscure scene played in her mind which she could not translate the details of—"

"Kate met Griandor." He sighs.

"She only told me after she rescued *us*. She said she knows why we fight and what she must do, but she has been too busy saving our lives for me to be able to obtain the information from her." The layers of sadness in his voice leave me feeling as bleak as his words.

"Arland, do you feel you have let her down in some way?" She sounds more like my mom now—ready to give advice.

He takes a deep breath, then releases. "I have let her down in every way."

What? How can he possibly think this? If I didn't want to hear where their conversation is going, I'd sit up and protest.

"Explain to me how that's so. What I see is my daughter in love, alive, knowing full well who she is, controlling her abilities, and making friends with enemies. How do you suppose you've failed her?"

I couldn't have said it better myself.

"Perth knows who she is, Brad is dead, and we are stranded in a cave . . . weaponless. Well, weaponless except for her."

How can he take fault for any of these things? Perth has always known who I am. Brad died—well he's not actually dead; Arland doesn't know this though—because I didn't pay attention to my visions. And we're in a cave because, well, because Dughbal needs to die. *Not* because Arland has failed me. My head spins, my pulse pounds in my ears. I'm going to get up and set the record straight—

"None of which were things you had control over. What are you truly afraid of, Arland Maher?"

He returns to caressing my arm and run his hands up to my shoulder. "That she will never live a normal life. I want Kate to be happy and to experience Encardia for what it truly is. I want to spend the rest of my life with her. And I am afraid if I continue to fail—or things continue to happen outside my control—that no matter what I want, or what she wants . . . none of it will ever be true."

I squeeze his calf. I want him to know I'm listening. Of course, he does know, but I hope the gesture makes him realize I don't like what he's saying. I don't want him to think there's no future. I want him to have hope; *I* want to have hope.

"If I told you, in the end, you will both be happy, would you believe me?" There's a slight edge in Mom's tone.

"No, Saraid, you have made it quite clear my father has been giving me half-truths my entire life. Why should I expect anything more from you?" He slides my hair from my face then runs his fingers through, playing with each knot until it's smooth.

Mom sighs again. "I deserve that. It is not easy learning of your children's future before they are born."

There's a long pause.

The sun moves through the sky in my mind while fifteen, twenty, maybe even thirty minutes pass. Water trickles into a puddle somewhere in the cave. Deep sighs and light snores come from the soldiers and children.

The silence is unbearable. He has to have more questions for her because *I* have more questions . . . .

"You know," Mom says, breaking the silence, "Kate has the power to do anything. If she wants to spend the rest of her life with you, she will. I do not doubt that for one moment. In case I am killed before that day comes, I want you to know you have mine and her father's blessing. Here, I have something for you. Give me your hand."

Arland removes his right hand from my hair.

"Ceangal Katriona agus Arland le grá."

The only thing I take from Mom's strange words is mine and Arland's names.

His body shakes. "What are you doing? You will be punished if you Bind us."

She was going to marry us?

"My father will not go back on the trade made between the Ground Dwellers and our old High Leader. You think just because our love is Bound they will not want someone as powerful as Kate connected to their side?" Arland asks.

"Will you ever love another?" Her voice is soft and firm all at once.

"No," he says with finality. "But—"

"Kate, will you ever love another?"

I'm frozen.

"Kate, I know you are awake. It's okay. I am glad you have heard everything, and I am glad you will be awake for the remainder of the conversation; there are many things you need to hear."

Pushing myself up, I turn around and face Arland and my mom. They're barely distinguishable; the glow of a small fire burning at the mouth of the cave is the only light I see. Soldiers and children lie on their sides, sprinkled around the floor like refugees in a shelter, identities hidden by the dim light.

She smiles. "Do you have an answer for my question?"

Arland and I meet eyes; I hold his gaze as I deliver my answer. "No, I will never love another."

He straightens and takes me by the arms, panic in his wide-eyed expression. "Kate, we cannot do this. Your mother will be punished, and if we cannot be together, we will be miserable."

"Arland, my mom is a grown woman and can make her own choices. And I would be miserable without you whether we were Bound or not."

I look at Mom. "Now explain what you were about to do, and what it all means."

"During *normal* circumstances, Draíochtans choose love freely. We do not have big ceremonies, but when a couple wishes to marry, they go to the woman's parents and ask permission. If permission is granted, a Binding spell is cast—"

"A spell leaving a touch of magic—that can be seen by all—on the hands of the couple until the marriage has taken place. The spell serves as a tool, to show the world the two are committed." Arland narrows his eyes at Mom, then turns back to me.

All his anger fades. "Kate, if this is done, and we are Bound but in the end cannot be together and you are with someone else, the mark will reappear and burn you forever. The burn will serve as a punishment of sorts. Do you see the problem with this?"

At some point over the last few weeks, Arland lost his confidence for our positive future. He's so concerned with who I will end up with, he has forgotten there is no one else for me. Not Brad, and in no way Perth. I cannot imagine another soul in Encardia bringing me as much happiness as Arland. I look between him and Mom. "You do not want to do this because you think the only way for me to unite us with the Ground Dwellers is for me to marry Perth?"

His gaze falls to something on the floor. "Yes."

"Arland, is there something else you aren't telling me? You promised you would never allow that marriage to happen, and I swore to you I wouldn't go through with it. Even with Griandor's advice that I must do anything, I will not do *that*. You said you wanted the things happening between us to be accepted; and here acceptance is being offered, and you refuse." Keeping my voice down proves to be impossible; I've never been angry with Arland.

Mom places her hand on my forearm. "Kate, I think Arland is—"

He brushes her hand from my arm. "I know you are tired, but do you feel like taking a walk with me?"

I don't like where this is going. "I can walk, but there are other things I want to talk about with my mom."

She smiles reassuringly and nods. "I will be here when you get back. You should talk to Arland."

Defeated, I sigh. "Okay, let's go."

He stands then takes my hand—and with it, my confidence.

My legs are a little wobbly, and my side is numb from being on the ground so long, but strength returns the more I move. We leave the cave and walk to the left, down the same path I followed to get here when I was afraid for Brit, where I left the horses.

The horses!

"Arland, I forgot all about the horses—"

I run toward the trees where I left Mirain, but Arland yanks my hand, pulling me back to him.

He laughs. "They are fine. After you fell asleep, Perth returned and told Cadman about them. They rode Bowen and Euraid to Watchers Hall."

Arland stops at the edge of the rock formation. "This is where the protections end. We should not go any further than this. Sit next to me?"

"Of course."

He takes a seat then rests his back along the stone. When I do the same, he puts his arm around my shoulders and pulls me close.

"So, what did you bring me out here for?" I ask, staring at the blisters on his palm, praying this conversation does not end with my heart crushed.

"Kate, there is nothing in this world, or any of the others, that could make me happier than spending the rest of my life with you, but there are many dangers associated with your mother casting her spell. If we walk into Willow Falls with a visible Binding on our hands, we will be obvious deviants from a High Leader's ruling—and one which will affect the Ground Dwellers to the core—and become targets for any of them to attack."

Moving from his protective arms, I stare into his intense green eyes. "We both want the same thing, Arland. Why should we deny ourselves of that? I know this might make me seem as *forward* as Brit, but if my mom Binds us and there are no ceremonies, how do we go about the marriage?"

A wide smile stretches across his face. "Once there is a Binding, we must consummate the relationship to be Bound. Only then would the magic fade from our hands."

I inhale a sharp breath. "All it takes is to do things we almost already did to be considered married here?"

He sits up and presses my face between his hands. "Well, yes, but if we had done those *things* we would not have officially been Bound without your mother's spell. I am sorry, Kate. I should never have allowed us to come so close without you knowing our customs. My betrayal of your trust is just one more reason why I am failing you."

Flashes of us in the straw, in our bed, and in the bathroom at Watchers Hall cross my mind, but I'm not angry with him for where we were going during those times. I'm upset Arland didn't tell me about Draíochtan customs—and by his continuous thinking he's failed me—but more than any of these things, I *want* the Binding. I want forever after with Arland. "I want the Binding with you, Arland."

Arland moves his hands from my face then laces his fingers with mine. "We cannot do it now. We would be unable to hide our relationship until we were Bound. If we plan to unite the Ground Dwellers, they must at least believe you intend to be with Perth—and I do not like the idea of you being burned for any amount of affection you may have to show him in the process."

Nerves course through me—Arland might be accepting this idea. I could be Katriona Maher. The vision I've had so many times of us with children in the meadow might be our future.

I shudder.

No, I will not wish for that exact vision . . . one where I wound up alone, Arland and our children dead next to me. My wish is for us to have those children, the rolling green meadows full of wildflowers and endless happiness, but not the death. "What if she Binds us at Willow Falls, and before anyone can see us, we sneak off to follow through with the marriage?"

A genuine, warm, melt-your-heart-kind-of-smile grows on his face. "You are sure I am who you wish to spend forever with?"

An uncharacteristic giggle erupts from my chest. "Do you even need to ask? I'm about to bully you into marrying me."

"You will never have to bully me into anything."

"Promise?" I bite my lower lip.

Arland's eyes gleam. "Promise."

He trails his fingertips up my arms, sending chills running down my back. His lips are parted. I imagine how soft they are, how warm. Closing my eyes, I lean into him and gently place my mouth on his.

We kiss, slow and sweet, but passion mixed with craving for more burns into me. My lips tingle, parts of me wake up that have been asleep forever. He grabs my waist and pulls me against him with such force, I gasp.

"Mmm. Sorry. I do not know what came over me."

"Don't be sorry for loving me, Arland." I repeat words he spoke to me once, kiss his nose, then sit next to him. Leaning my head on his arm, I look toward the heavens and see something I've never seen in Encardia before . . . stars.

"Arland, look up."

In a small patch above our heads, millions of white dots twinkle in the sky. The sight of them brings tears to my eyes.

He tightens his arm around my shoulder. "They are here because of you. Like the first time you awakened the magic when the sky opened up and revealed the sun to us. You have grown so strong, Kate. It appears you have brought permanent light to this spot."

I cannot take my eyes off the sky. "No. They are here because of *us*. The magic wouldn't have come to me if it hadn't been for you."

From the corner of my left eye, I see a look of wide-eyed wonder filling Arland's face. We rest against the rocks, staring at the wonderful gift from above, watching shooting stars dart through the small open patch of Darkness.

"Should we tell the others?" I ask, even though company is the last thing I want.

He shakes his head. "Not yet. Let them rest. This is your moment. Besides, I imagine when they wake up to the sun shining down on us, it will be much more impressive to them than the stars."

Tearing my gaze from the sky is painful, but seeing how much pride Arland wears makes it worthwhile. "I could stay out here all night with you, but we have to figure out what we're going to tell my mom and what we're going to do for the Binding."

He laughs. "Maybe after we figure those things out, we can return to this spot and sleep under the stars."

"Deal."

"To answer your question from before, if your mother Binds us at Willow Falls, we either have to wed before anyone notices, or escape—and being alone is not the safest option. You said my father told you to keep your distance from me when we arrive. Did he indicate any reason as to why?"

A lump forms in my throat. "He said if I wanted this to end well, I must protect you by keeping my distance."

Arland's eyes glass over. "There may be something in my prophecy about our marriage; something he has not told me—I fear there is a great deal he has not told me. We should speak to your mother and see what she knows. She seems to be in a sharing mood tonight."

"Are you saying you're willing to be Bound to me?" I'm beginning to wonder if either of us has any self-esteem. Arland said I wouldn't have to bully him into anything, but he never actually said he wanted marriage. Permanence.

His eyes return to the here and now, smiling at me. "I always have been, Kate, but we will be outcast if we are caught breaking away from what a High Leader has ruled. The only way we would ever be able to redeem ourselves is to win this war."

"I have every intention of winning this war," I say with a lot more confidence than I've had in a long time.

"I knew you would say that. We should return inside and discuss your conversation with Griandor and our Binding with your mother."

Arland stands then offers me his hand, and I take it. He wraps his arm around my shoulders, and we walk up the short incline to the mouth of the cave, but we stop before entering the dreary hideout.

"I love you, Katriona Wilde."

"I love you, too, Arland Maher." I return his formal tone.

Bending down, he places a gentle kiss on my lips. One that leaves me wanting so much more . . . especially after our talk of marriage. The thought of being Bound to him makes me giddy. He pulls away, and I touch my fingers to my mouth, trying to hold the tingling remnants of him there.

When we reach the back of the cave, I see Mom has kept her promise. She sits in the exact place we left her. Mom grins.

I drop my hand from my lips.

"Did you two work everything out?" she asks.

We take seats next to her. "Yes, and we have a lot to discuss, Mom. Do you swear to be honest with us?"

"I swear to be as honest as I can."

That little earnest statement seems to be the best I will ever get from my mother, and I guess it's going to have to do. "We want to be Bound, but not here. Arland doesn't think it's safe for us to escape, so how will we perform our Binding at Willow Falls without being caught?"

Her grin widens. "Well, I couldn't be happier. I have a few ideas for the spell. We will come up with a plan later," she says as if the ordeal is all worked out in her head.

"But, Mom, Leader Maher told me to keep my distance from Arland once we arrive. We suspect he knows something of our marriage. Do you know if something will happen?"

"No, I am not aware of anything that will occur at Willow Falls."

I want to believe her, I genuinely do. After so many years of her keeping things from me, I find it a little difficult, but I move on. I will press her for more, later. "If we keep our distance, the only people aware of our relationship will be those here."

"The soldiers all have a great deal of respect for Arland; requesting their silence should be relatively easy. But since Perth is aware of your relationship, we do have a concern—"

I wave my hand. "Perth is not a concern. We should include him in our plans. If he truly doesn't have any desire to marry me and believes in uniting our sides, then he will only agree with anything we come up with."

Arland and Mom both glower at me.

Before either has a chance to protest vocally, I go on. "I do think we should keep the Binding thing a secret . . . from everyone."

They continue their silent treatment.

"Will anyone ever trust me?" I throw my hands up.

"We trust *you*, Kate, but trusting someone we have grown to have a genuine hatred for is difficult," Arland says.

Everyone is so quick to judge, so quick to hate. There has to be a reason why Griandor told me to trust those around me when he did. He must have known Perth was the only one there. There's a way to make everyone trust him, but I'm missing the connection. All the interaction I've had with him doesn't amount to much. And I haven't seen him interact with anyone else . . . except for Mom.

I focus on her. Long brown hair falls in front of her eyes, making her appear younger than she is. Innocent. "Mom, why did you tell Perth your name was Morgandy Domhnaill?"

She looks around the dark cave then leans forward.

Arland and I do the same.

"A long time ago, Morgandy was a goddess loved by many. She was pure and kind and did not think so highly of herself to live in the heavens. She wanted to be near her people, so she could help them in times of suffering."

"She didn't want to live in the heavens because she didn't like the other gods?"

Mom shakes her head. "She preferred being near those who prayed to her."

"Was she a primary god?"

"Yes, how—?"

"Griandor told me . . . ."

She takes my hands in hers. "What was he like?"

"Mom, the name . . . ?" I say, pulling my hands away.

"Right. Well, one particularly dirty man came to her door and begged for food. It was her nature not only to offer him food, but her home. She allowed him to bathe, eat, drink, and sleep. When he was clean and well fed, he thanked the goddess and offered her payment by telling her a story. She listened to the story about his life with great interest, and when the time came for him to leave, she was saddened. It was unusual for Morgandy to have feelings so strong about a Draíochtan man, so she offered that he stay longer. He tried to refuse, but she all but forced him to remain with her. He continued telling her stories, and in return, she told some of her own. So, as the story goes, the two fell in love and had a child. The child was my great-grandmother, times three. Every new generation of women on my side of the family is told the story about Morgandy. Not many Draíochtans know of her, but those who do, know she is good. The Seer said I would need to use the name when I returned here."

I'm related to the gods? Maybe this is why they chose me, because some of their blood runs through my veins, because, in a sense, the powers belong to me? Does this mean I'll live forever? No. That's ridiculous. Sitting back, I think over her story before I speak, trying to piece together what it all means and how it applies to our situation.

"Perth's aunt told him if he ever heard anyone use Morgandy's name, he should trust the person. In fact, it wasn't until *he* used the name that I decided not to kill him."

Arland snickers.

I glance sideways at him, heart lifting from his moment of pure enjoyment. "His aunt must have had some sort of idea someone would offer him Morgandy's name in the future."

"I imagine a Seer instructed her to tell Perth that, but she might not have known why. It still does not make me want to trust him, but because trusting him is what you wish for, I will do it," Mom says.

"Thank you, Mom." I turn and face Arland. "Arland?"

"If trusting him makes you happy, I will do it, too." The muscles in his face tense, suggesting he's not lying; he's *only* doing this to make me happy.

"Okay, when the soldiers wake up, we tell them to keep mine and Arland's relationship a secret. When Perth returns, we should sit down with him and come up with a plan of action to show ourselves as united at Willow Falls. I'm still trying to figure out how we can trick everyone into thinking I'm willing to marry him. Maybe there's another way to go about uniting our kinds . . . ?"

"Would you mind sharing with us what the war is about?" Mom asks.

What I'm about to say is not going to make her happy, but my knowledge of this war is the one piece of power I hold over everyone, and I'm not about to let it go easily.

I take a deep breath. "You tell me what I need to know about my future, without holding *anything* back, and I'll tell you everything you need to know about this war."

Mom's mouth falls open—I've just offended her—but she closes it, then frowns.

I've got her cornered.

CHAPTER EIGHT

A pebble tumbles through the cave, breaking the silence. I look up and see my mom's silhouette walking toward us. Before she left, I wondered if she was going to find a way to punish me, to tell me I was acting petulant, spoiled or ridiculous. She's explained why she hasn't told me anything about my future, but it's not like I'm going to head for The Clearing then jump through the portal back to Earth . . . there's too much at stake.

She reclaims the seat she left an hour ago.

Arland releases me from his embrace, leaving a chill on my skin where his arms were, and we sit up. I enjoy the understanding between us. He must know if I ever want information from anyone, the knowledge Griandor gave me is what I will use to bargain. Of course, that will only go so far, but I will use it as long as I can.

Mom sighs and crosses her arms over her chest. "What do you want to know?"

"You can start by telling me what's going to happen to Arland at Willow Falls."

She waves her hand. "Oh, Kate, I already told you I do not know."

"And I'm telling you, I don't believe you. You've successfully lied to me and everyone I know my entire life." Agitation echoes off the cold cave walls.

"I have only ever done what I was told. It was the only way to protect you, do you not see?" Her voice reminds me of my childhood when she'd scold me for disobeying.

"No, Mom, I don't see. Why don't you try to explain it to me? You want Arland and me to be Bound, you tell me you know we're stronger together, you tell me you know everything about my future, but when I ask you for details, you say you don't know." Okay, so that came out more cross than expected, but I don't want half-truths. I don't want *you'll stray from the path of Light*. I want answers, honesty, and I want it now. This is my mom I'm asking for information, not some stranger, and I'm not asking for much. Just enough to help me survive, to give me hope.

Arland places his hands on my shoulders and puts his mouth beside my ear. "Kate, I know you are angry. You have every right to be, but you need to rein in the fire before everyone wakes up—everyone who is not already listening, that is," he whispers.

I'm burning. Bright blue light fills the cave. Flames stretch from me in all directions, illuminating tiny beads of water sliding down the moss-covered walls, and revealing the clenched eyes of a few soldiers.

Heat fills my cheeks. I cannot believe I allowed my emotions to get out of control. "Sorry."

Mom clasps her hands in her lap.

Arland watches me and rubs my shoulder.

Closing my eyes, I focus on the magic, the power, the anger that released the Light and fold it in over my heart until the fire is gone.

"So . . . ." I clear my throat. "Instead of just allowing things to happen, Mom, I think it would be wise to tell me what you know. I'm not going to walk away from what I have to do, no matter how hard my future may be."

She purses her lips into a thin line. "Fine. I only know about you, Kate, and not about everyone else. Something happens to Arland at Willow Falls, something that makes you angry with the Leaders. I do not know what it is, but it is enough to provoke anger in you that will define Encardia for generations to come. That is assuming you do not fail in the remainder of the war."

Revolutionize comes to mind as well as Griandor's other words, "You could still fail." They twist and warp around in my head until

I'm dizzy. What could I revolutionize? What is it I'm missing? If I am ready, willing, and fighting, why might I still fail?

Arland leans in close to Mom. "Why would you want to Bind us if you already have a good idea we are going to be punished for it?" His words come out like a growl.

Mom offered us what we want, but as always, it's just a part of the game. I'm beginning to think Arland is right . . . there will be no future for us. We are doomed before we even begin. He and our children always died in my visions . . . I've been warned. I reach for his hand, and, for a moment, sickness rises in me. If I don't figure all this out, hand holding, occasional kissing, and a short-lived marriage could be it.

Betrayed. That's how I feel. *Again.*

She rests her back against the wall. "Because, Arland, do you not want as much time with Kate as you can get? I would kill for one more day with Brian. For one more whispered *I love you* from him. I can give you something no one can ever take away. Some may try, but a Binding spell is permanent. We would be breaking laws, but would a proper marriage not be worth it?"

Arland squeezes my hand. "Every moment with Kate is worth it, but I do not want her to be exiled for our union."

Maybe she's not playing a game with us. Maybe she truly does miss my dad and wants us to be happy like the two of them were. All I know is I couldn't care less if I'm exiled, punished, or put to death for being with Arland. He is exactly what I want.

"Arland, Kate will be fine. That much I know. She will give some sort of speech—"

"Wh—?"

"Before you ask"—she shakes her head—"no, I do not know what you are going to say, Kate. You will give a speech that wakes everyone up and somehow unites our people."

I cross my arms over my chest. "How did you know I have to unite everyone?"

Mom mirrors my action. "I know a lot, but I still do not know what this war is about."

She went from being a concerned mom to know-it-all again. I'm still not sure if I can trust her. "You know a lot, like you knew about Brad? Why did you lie to me about him, Mom?"

Leaning forward, she takes my hands in hers, but I yank them away then slide closer to Arland. Whatever her justifications for hiding things and confusing me about my future with Arland are, I don't understand why she would let anything happen to Brad. He was a victim, made to look evil and used against me by Dughbal.

"Do you know how hard it has been to keep these secrets from you?" Her eyes fill with tears. "After I lost your father, you and Brit were the only things keeping me alive, but the Seer instructed us to keep everything from you until the time was right. Of course, she never said when the time might be right—"

"You didn't think you should try to prevent Brad from coming here? From being roped into a war that has nothing to do with him? To at least attempt to save an innocent life? All because I'd ask too many questions?"

"Kate, but you see, Brad was not innocent. He—"

Now I believe nothing. I will let her Bind me and Arland so we can have acceptance, but I may never trust her again. "Yes he was, Mom, and you know it. You erased Brad's memory when *Darkness* tried to manipulate him in the forest when he was ten. You knew Brad was a target, you knew he'd die, and I know you could have done something about it."

She looks at me with her biggest demure eyes.

Shaking, I struggle to maintain control, to prevent flames from bursting out of my core and attacking the woman who gave me life. "Don't, Mom. Griandor already told me the truth, and he said you were a fool to keep things from me. I want to feel bad for you for everything you've had to do for me over the years, but I lost my dad the same day you lost your husband . . . and I *never* got to know him. Then I lost the normal life I thought I lived. And while I may not be sorry for it, I'm mad. Mad you never prepared me for any of this, and that you continue to lie."

"What's going on?"

I start at the sound of Brit's voice then turn to face her.

My sister's eyelids are heavy and she yawns.

Looking around, I realize all the soldiers are awake and leaving the cave. *Great!* So much for controlling myself. "I was just telling Mom how I'm sick of the lies and want the truth."

Worry lines Brit's forehead; she looks between Mom and me. "Well, why are you yelling about it?"

"Mom knew Darkness wanted Brad, and she let it happen. He wasn't obsessive, Brit, it was the poison and Mom knew that, too. And I'm sure she's withholding a lot more." I give Mom a pointed look.

Arland shifts his weight.

"Mom?" Brit asks.

Mom nods.

"Why would you do that to Brad? Why would you let Kate believe he was evil when he wasn't?" Brit plops down next to me then wraps her arms around my shoulders.

Her support stifles my tremors, but as they calm, I realize she, too, is trembling.

"It had to happen. Everything has to happen. Just because we know the future doesn't mean we can change it." Mom's tone borders on defensive.

"You don't know that, Mom. Besides, at the advice of the Seer, you took me out of Encardia to save my life. You've already changed the future!"

"I-I—"

"Have no excuse not to tell Kate the truth," Arland says. Calm, cool, straight-forward. Always supportive.

"Okay." Mom sighs. "I am sorry. There was no class for Your-Daughter-is-Going-to-Save-the-World-Now-What? I *am* trying."

"We know it wasn't easy, and we know you *had* your reasons, but can we all agree to be honest?" I ask, leveling my emotions.

"Yes. I think it's time to be honest, but please try to control your temper?"

"I cannot promise you, Mom, but I will try not to get angry."

"From the time of your prophecy, I was aware of Brad's involvement in the war. But even if I tried to prevent him from being tainted, Darkness would have found another way to get to him, Kate. No matter what we did, he would have been used against you, and I am sorry for that."

She reaches for my hand again, but this time I don't yank it away. I hold onto her, allow her love to comfort me. We may have a lot of trust issues, but she is my mom and I still need her support.

"Brad isn't dead, Mom. Or he is. I'm not sure how it works, but Darkness is living inside him. Part of Brad is still there though. I've seen him; there's a battle going on in his eyes." I shudder, remembering the touch of Brad's cold skin on me.

"Griandor said he would restore his life after the war." So he has to be dead.

Brit rests her head on my shoulder. Tears soak through my shirt.

I lean my head on Brit's. "I know you're right. He would have been used against me somehow, even if he never went on our camping trip, but I hate myself for ever doubting him. Reverse our roles, and he would have been a better friend to me than I was to him. He *was* a better friend to me than I was to him. Before he was stabbed, he fought against the poison controlling him to apologize, and he didn't have anything to be sorry for." Words are painful to speak. My face and hands burn, and a lump forms in my throat, rendering me mute.

Arland moves in closer, sandwiching me with support between him and Brit.

"It's okay, Kate. You said Griandor will restore Brad's life. Everything will be okay." Brit sniffles.

She rubs her hand up and down my back, but it does little to make the guilt disappear.

I lift my head then stare into her eyes mirroring mine. "*If* I don't fail, Griandor will restore Brad's life. But if I do fail, everything will be lost. And Brad does not deserve to be involved in any of this. His only crime was loving me. It seems like loving me might be a crime for everyone." I turn to Arland.

He runs his hand along my leg. "You cannot blame yourself for what happened to Brad. And loving you is not a crime, but acting on that love seems to be."

"Arland!" Brit scowls at him.

Arland's right. Daemons attacked Brad after he shared his hidden love for me. Arland is in a position where it's impossible for him not to love me, yet that love is forbidden. We want to spend the rest of our lives together, and in committing to each other, it's possible we both get in trouble. Maybe love is not for me. Maybe that's why it took twenty years before I ever kissed anyone, before I ever thought about taking my clothes off for a man. So why *did* Gramhara give me her power of love? I'm at a loss.

He cups my face with his hands. "The more I think about mine and Brad's love for you and everything loving you means, the surer I become of my father's reasons for you to keep your distance from me at Willow Falls. He is aware of your mother's intentions to Bind us, Kate. He has to be." Arland faces my mom. "Is there anything you can tell us about Willow Falls? You said something angers Kate, but what? You must have more details."

She shakes her head. "All I know is how important it is for you to follow through with the Binding. I believe it is important to both of you, as well. Am I right?"

"You are aware of what the spell means to us, but why else is it important?" Arland asks, his voice flat.

"The closer you two are, the more you share, the stronger both of your magic will be. By the end of this war, many will conjure magic the way Kate does, but it starts with your marriage."

Brit bolts upright. "Wait, now you are marrying Arland and not Perth?"

A smile stretches across my face before I have time to stop it. "Yes, but you cannot tell anyone."

She looks between Arland and me as if she wants to bolt to the nearest bridal store . . . too bad for her they are all worlds away. "Oh my God, Kate, that's awesome news! Of course I'll never tell anyone, but how—?"

Mom arches an eyebrow. "We are going to need *Perth* to side with us, and we are going to have to make sure everyone around here remains quiet about Arland and Kate's relationship."

"It doesn't sound like you think Perth will help them, Mom," Brit says, excitement fading from her voice.

"I do not."

I place my hand over Mom's knee. "Well, I do. I will talk to him—"

Arland clears his throat.

We lock eyes, and for a moment, I get a glimpse of our future. Lazy days spent on picnic blankets with warm sunshine beaming down on us. Laced fingers. Tangled legs. Stolen kisses. Kids with curly locks, running around. Horses. I don't know if what I'm seeing is an actual vision, but I pray it is.

Blinking away everything I want with remorse greater than I've ever felt, I see Arland staring back at me. "Arland and I will talk to him."

He tears his gaze from mine and squeezes my leg. I wonder if he saw what I did, if Griandor and Gramhara shared the vision of our future with both of us. If they did, maybe Arland will have more hope for a positive outcome—I do.

"What else of Kate's future do you know?" he asks, looking at Mom.

"If Kate does not give her uniting speech, or it doesn't work, I am afraid I do not know what will happen. But if she does, you and an army will be sent to seek out the Leader of Darkness. The search will take months. It will be bloody, tiring, and you will be faced with more horrors than you can imagine."

Turning to face Mom, Brit narrows her eyes. "You didn't say *we*, Mom. Are you not going to fight?"

Her hands tremble. "No."

Brit appears as though she wants to wrap her arms around Mom, but something keeps my sister rooted in place.

I move my hand from Mom's knee to her shoulder, giving a nudge to get her attention. "Why are you crying?"

"I am going to stay at Willow Falls. As a Leader, I will not be permitted to fight." She hangs her head.

"There is no truth to that statement. Do you forget you are in the company of a Leader?" Arland glares at her, breathing heavy, agitated.

She lifts her head; an expression as frail as the tree in Watchers Hall's courtyard fills her face. Mom has never shown emotions or allowed them to control her. I feel like our roles are reversed and I should reach out, tell her everything will be okay, but I don't know if that's true or not.

"As a Leader punished for running away, I will not be permitted to leave Willow Falls—I may not be permitted to live. Brian and I disobeyed a High Leader's law when we passed through the portal."

My face burns as tears fight their way to my eyes. Mom and Arland lock eyes in some sort of silent duel, each trying to prove to the other who knows more, who is telling the truth. Mom may be many things, but I do not want her to die. This war has claimed so many lives already, why would any Leader take the life of someone who sacrificed everything to protect this world?

Arland rubs his chin, eyebrows turned down. "You may be punished, but my father would never kill you. You are friends. He respects you and Brian for everything you were willing to give up."

She covers her face with her hands. "We are friends—dear friends—but it will not be your father's choice—"

"He is High Leader. It will most certainly be his choice." Arland's voice cracks in a way I've never heard before. Is he unsure?

"Arland, there are things we have to do as Leaders we do not like. What is the punishment for breaking a High Leader's law?"

He reaches for my hand then squeezes. "Death. But that means they will also kill me and Kate if they discover our marriage."

I gasp.

Mom shakes her head. "No, they will not kill their only hope. If your marriage is discovered, and either of you is penalized, I will take full responsibility. My downfall will please Dufaigh. Your father knows the only way for Encardia to survive is for the two of you to be together. Kate's happiness means Encardia's Light. Does that sound familiar?"

"Yes, it was part of my prophecy," he says, rubbing his thumb over my knuckles.

"Your father knows *you* are Kate's happiness. That was why we made the marriage arrangement in the first place. It was our biggest mistake. We should have left well enough alone, but I am sure Dufaigh would have found another way to torment my family."

"But, Mom, if they kill you, *I* will not be happy. How can I go out and fight for people who seek to destroy my family? My life?"

"You are not fighting for them," she says, her voice warm and comforting. "You fight for yourself, for all the other worlds. You fight for survival of goodness. You need not worry about me; my life has never been the same since your father died. I do not mind the thought of death. In my heart, I know he and I will be reunited."

My mom never loved my step dad. Gary and I might not have been as close as we should have been, but I'm sorry for him. Whenever this is over and his life goes back to normal, I'll have to visit.

"I'm glad I mean so much to you! What about *us*, Mom? Kate and I need you. *We* love you." Brit glances at mine and Arland's laced fingers.

"At least Kate will have Arland when you are gone, but what will I have? You don't even know if I'll survive this war, but you're willing to let yourself be sacrificed with my future just hanging out there?" She stands, face red with anger, rocking on her toes. She looks like she could run far away and never come back, but something keeps her in place. She's waiting.

I'm waiting, too. Waiting for my mom to redeem herself. To be what Brit needs, the way Mom always has.

"You should consider yourself lucky, Brites Wilde. Your life is your own to do with as you see fit. Not many in Encardia are even aware of your existence. They do not seek to destroy you or marry you to someone against your will, and they certainly do not seek to have you fight in wars that make very little sense . . . ."

Brit's lower lip quivers. She stares at our mom for a moment, mouth opening and closing as though searching for the right words, then turns and runs away. Sobs echo their way back to us.

Frowning at my mom, I jump to my feet. "She might have been the only person left who still trusts in you, and you basically just told her she's nothing. I know you didn't mean it that way, but I doubt Brit will ever understand that. When she calms down, we can talk about the Binding. For now, Arland and I are going to try to fix what you broke."

I turn on my toe then storm off with Arland following behind me.

"Kate! Are you going to tell me what this war is about?" she yells after us.

"When the time is right. Of course, no one has ever given me any indication as to when that time may be," I say, over my shoulder and run to catch up with Brit.

Outside the cave, almost everyone stares up at the sky—some with wide eyes, others with mouths hanging open.

The children point and giggle.

The soldiers talk amongst themselves as they look at the stars.

Arland and I share a smile, then take a seat on either side of Brit. She pulls her knees to her chest, face red and swollen from crying.

Seeing my sister this way rips my heart in two. Her rock solid strength has always reminded me of Mom. It was Brit who calmed her older sister when the nightmares struck, who lent an ear when school was rough. Now I need to be *her* rock.

I need to be everyone's rock.

Brit leans into me.

Wrapping my arm around her, I let her cry. "Everything is going to be okay. I promise, Brit. I will always be here for you."

My words only make her sobs louder, so I don't say anything else. She cries for so long, I think it must be about more than just Mom. I suspect Brit is crying for some of the same reasons I did when I first arrived in Encardia.

Arland comes around Brit then sits behind me. I rest my head on his shoulder and stare up at the sky while there are still stars to enjoy. We'll probably be here all night, but this is not how I envisioned us sleeping under the stars.

CHAPTER NINE

"Sir!"

I startle awake and scream.

Arland brushes my arm with his palm. "It is only Cadman, Kate."

Looking over my right shoulder, I see Cadman and follow his ogling to the sky—which is now one of the strangest sights I've seen. In the ever-present black night, a small round patch of the most brilliant blue cuts through, reminding me of the waters surrounding Hawaii. Not a single white cloud dots the gift from above, and just like last night, everyone stares, captivated by the sight.

Groups of children and soldiers have gathered near the edge of the cliff overlooking the river; smiles and excited murmurs abound. Smells of the sun's warmth fill the air, like a promise offered by the first day of spring after a long, snowy winter. I inhale a deep, renewing breath. Surges of energy course through me. I'm happy . . . at peace. This is where I'm supposed to be. Fighting this war. Bringing Encardia Light.

"Enjoy it. This is a sight none of these people will soon forget." Arland slides his arm from my shoulders, kisses my cheek, then stands. "I will be right back. I need to speak with Cadman."

"Okay. I'll be here . . . staring." I smile and watch Arland walk down the path toward the river to join the others. When he's out of view, I return my gaze to the sky.

Repositioning myself against the rocks, I nudge Brit's shoulder. "Brit, wake up."

She groans.

"The sun is out. It reminds me of your favorite part of the forest back home." I run my fingers through her tangled waves, separating the knots from each other.

Brit rolls over in my lap and looks up at me with her big green eyes, puffy from a night full of crying. She squints, then rubs her eyes with the back of her hand. "Oh. You weren't kidding. The sun really is shining."

"No, I wasn't kidding. The stars were out last night, too, but you probably didn't notice."

Brit shakes her head. She sits up, then leans back into my open arms. "It's not fair, Kate."

"What's not fair?"

"You know *what*. I want to know what my purpose is in the war." With a disgusted sigh, Brit digs at the dirt under her nails.

"I talked to Arland about that. He said if we find a good Seer, we can get your prophecy. If you really want to know, we can try to find one. Maybe one will be at Willow Falls."

Brit pops up then faces me, biting back a smile. "Really? You've already thought about this for me?"

I nod.

Wrapping her arms around me, she squeezes the air from my lungs with a huge hug. "I love you, Kate. You're the best sister a girl could ask for."

"Uh, cheese?" I laugh.

"Yes, but I mean every single slice of it."

"I know you do."

"I am sorry to interrupt, but the children need food," Enid says, tapping my shoulder with her cold hand.

Brit and I both start. I turn around and wipe the tears that escaped during my hug with her, then put on a happy face for Enid. She rubs her hands together, glancing back at the soldiers, then looks up at the sky.

"Is everything okay, Enid?" I ask.

"Yes. It has been so long since I have seen the daylight." She turns her head to me. "Do you know where we can get food? I would have asked Arland, but I cannot find him."

A broken chicken neck falling limp in Perth's hands comes to mind. "Perth brought a chicken."

I glance over at the small crowd on the edge of the cliff and spot Saidear. "Saidear?"

He turns, wearing a huge grin. "Yes, ma'am?"

"Where are the horses?"

"They were tied to a tree over there," he says, pointing down the path I climbed to rescue everyone yesterday.

"Thank you."

Saidear gestures at the sky with his hand. "No. Thank *you*."

I laugh and return my attention to Enid. "I'll go grab it and be right back."

She raises her arms and leans to the side like a yoga instructor gearing up for class. "Do you mind if I come with you? I need to stretch my legs for a bit."

"Of course not. Do you want to come, too, Brit?"

My sister shakes her head. "I'm going to sit here and work on my tan."

There may be sunshine, but not enough for tanning. "Uhh—?"

She shoots me an evil look, narrowing her eyes. "Don't ruin it for me. I know it's not a lot of sun, but it feels great."

"At least you don't need sun block." I get to my feet. "I'll be back."

Enid stumbles over her boots as we quietly head down the path toward the horses. She's never been much for talking, so the silence between us doesn't bother me. Her constant fidgeting and clumsiness, however, does.

"Are you feeling alright? Your hands are shaking."

She raises her eyebrows as though she wasn't expecting me to speak. "B-being out here, so close to my home, so close to where . . . where—"

I pat her on the shoulder. "You don't have to say it. I understand, Enid. I am truly sorry."

I've only been awake for a short time, but today has been full of perpetual reminders as to why I'm here. Pain. Loss. Everyone experiences them at some point in their lives, but here, people live and deal with them every conscious moment.

We reach the bottom of the stone path and find the horses tied to a tree. Bowen, Euraid, and Luatha stand still with their heads down. But Mirain flattens her ears, and she snorts.

"Hey, girl. It's just me." After crossing the short distance between the edge of the path and tree, I lift my hand and allow her to nudge my palm with her warm, rough nose.

She lets out a deep sigh.

"Good girl. I have to get a chicken from Bowen's saddle then take it to the children. We'll visit later."

At his spoken name, Bowen lifts his head.

"That's right, Bowen. I'm talking about you."

I trail my hand down Mirain's neck, along her side then stop at her hindquarters and give a pat.

"Y-you do have a w-way with horses," Enid says.

I look over my shoulder.

Her face pales. She has dark circles under her eyes, and her hands tremble even worse than before. Enid looks like a diabetic on the verge of a coma.

"When was the last time you ate?"

"Y-yesterday. B-before b-b-bed."

"Do you often get weak from not eating?"

She tilts her head to the side. Her blue eyes and dirty-blond hair do little to add color to her pallor. "Y-yessss."

"Well, let me get the chicken, and we'll hurry back to cook it."

Enid crosses her arms over her chest as if she's holding back the trembles.

The chicken dangles by a rope over Bowen's saddle. I rush over, then work to untie the knot holding the bird. I hate knots. I don't have long fingernails, so getting the tightly wound twine to come apart is nearly impossible.

"H-here." A shiny silver blade appears over my shoulder.

"Use t-t-this," Enid says.

I grab the blade and cut the twine. "Thanks."

Now the brown chicken dangles from the rope I hold in my hands.

When I turn around, Enid is gone.

A loud scream resonates through the air, hitting my ears and matching the misery welling inside me.

The chicken falls from my hands.

My legs lock in place. Black bands of pulsing energy crackle as they climb my body, burning and slicing through my skin like knives. I cannot move, cannot open my mouth. I want to scream, want to cry out for someone—*anyone*—to help. Pain constricts my breathing as the bands blanket me with Darkness. The wild beating of my heart pounds in my ears. If only it was loud enough for someone else to hear. Control of my fingers, my toes, of any muscle that would give me flight, vanishes.

White light flows out of me and into the bands of the shifter. Growing from the feet up, the daemon takes my form with a wicked smile. I've never seen such a perfect replica of myself—not even a mirror could provide quality so astounding—but I look tired. Small, swollen circles rest under my green eyes. My hair is mussed around my face as if I just crawled out of bed.

The imposter waves, turns, then takes off with my body.

My vision fades.

Brit! Help me!

CHAPTER TEN

Fingers, toes, mouth . . . I cannot feel any of these things. No smells fill my nose. No light shines in my eyes. I don't know where I am; I'm not even sure if I'm alive.

Wake up, magic. Help me. Free me. Kill the Shifter.

I've repeated these commands a hundred times since the imposter turned and walked away. Although, I don't know if that's true—keeping count is not at the top of my agenda, and memories are fading in and out. I think something, then the thought disappears. No control. I have no control.

Brit, Arland . . . anybody?

Where am I? Why isn't anyone helping me? I want to scream, want to run for help, but I remain paralyzed. My thoughts are the only sounds I can make.

Brit!

Maybe I've gone insane. Maybe I'm drugged. Why else would I not be able to feel or see?

"Kate?"

A flash of the daemon stealing my body sweeps through my mind.

"Kate!"

Maybe this is just a dream. How could a shifter take me over? You can't be trapped inside yourself. I must be dead.

"Kate, snap out of it. I'm here. Arland is here, too."

Brit's voice keeps popping into my head. I'm imagining things . . . or answering myself. This is how a ghost must feel when trapped between worlds. No body to cling to. No purpose. Nowhere to go. I'm a ghost. That's what I am.

"Kate! Shut up! You sound nuts."

I don't know why I feel the need to give in to my lunacy, but I do. *"Brit? Is that you?"*

"Of course it's me! Who else do you talk to in your head?"

Maybe I'm not dead. Maybe I am actually hearing Brit's thoughts.

"Listen to me. You're not going crazy. You've been attacked by a shifter." The voice sounds just like Brit's; her tone even has a nervous edge to it.

How could I not believe what I'm hearing is real?

"Where am I?" If I am talking to Brit, maybe she'll have a reasonable explanation for me.

"By the horses. Do you wanna know what happened?" She sighs.

"Yes. I remember the shifter, but—"

"On their way back from base, Cadman and Perth found Lann and Enid—the real Lann and Enid. They were covered in those same nasty daemon tentacles Arland and I had on us. When he realized Enid wasn't Enid, he came up to find her, and when I told him you had just gone off with her to get a chicken, he freaked. Cadman was carrying Enid in his arms when it happened. It was . . . I don't want to tell you what it was. Just . . . well, anyway, Arland grabbed his bow and ran over to rescue you. It was amazing to watch him release arrow after arrow into the daemon. Arland loves you, Kate. He really loves you. The shifter thingy is dead, but the tentacles are still covering most of your body. We don't know how to get them off. Not even Mom knows. Are you listening to me? Kate?"

There's no way I'm imagining this. I know my sister's voice. I can almost feel her presence locked in this formidable place next to me. *"I can't see anything. It's dark, Brit. It's lonely. I thought I was dead."*

"You aren't dead. Can you not see through my eyes like you did last time?" Pity. If I had to describe her voice, it's full of pity.

"I don't pity you, Kate. I feel bad, but not pity. Can you see through my eyes or not?"

"No, I cannot see through your eyes."

"Think, Kate. Think hard. What were you doing last time?"

"*I don't know, Brit. I . . . I can't remember.*" I try to think, try to force my mind to remember how I got into her last time, but it's no use. It's as though no brain exists to tell me what to do.

"*Maybe if I stay quiet and let you concentrate, you'll find your way into me again, and then you will at least be able to see.*"

"*No! Don't leave me, and definitely don't be quiet. I can't handle being alone again.*"

"*Relax. I won't leave you. I won't be quiet either, but you need to think; think of how you got into my head before.*"

Her calm, soothing tone brings me back to Virginia, back to the early days of my nightmares. She'd always tell me to relax, always talk me to sleep, but this is different. I'm not having visions of my future; here I may not have a future. I'm trapped. My body a prison.

"*Magic won't even respond; I don't think I can get into your head.*"

"*Okay, okay, don't get so jumpy.*"

Jumpy? I'm not jumpy. Maybe I am. It's not like I can feel anything. I'm practically floating in space. Or nonexistent. Honestly, I can find no accurate words to describe this.

"*So you can't feel anything?*"

"*No. It's like there is no me beyond my thoughts. Isn't that what it felt like to you?*"

"*I don't remember. If I felt or thought anything while the shifter took me over, I don't know about it.*"

"*Huh. Well, maybe that's a good thing. Can you tell me what you see, Brit?*"

"*I'd rather you see yourself.*"

"*Me too, but* please, *just tell me. I need something to hang on to. The only thing I see is black and it's . . . .*"

"*Okay. We're near the horses. Arland and Mom are hovering over you. Mom is crying. She swears she didn't see this coming. I don't believe her. I want to, but I don't. Arland is a wreck. Keeps muttering something under his breath about failing you. Perth . . . well, Cadman punched Perth after he made a snide comment to Arland about not doing his job to protect you. Flanna is making food for the kids. They're in shock from what happened to the real Enid, but even*

Flanna is having a difficult time maintaining her emotions. Lann is in pretty bad shape. Arland sent Cadman and Ogilvie to dig a hole—"

"*Wait. A hole? What happened to the real Enid, what happened to Lann?"*

"*She . . . she died. Lann may not live another hour . . . ."*

How poor of shape am I in? "*How did Enid die? And why didn't you tell me before?"*

"*I'm sorry. I didn't want to scare you. The tentacles squeezed Enid to death, but I don't think that will happen to you. The daemon isn't even alive to hurt you. You're just stuck. We can save you. I know we can."* Brit rushes out a steady stream of thoughts—she has no confidence.

"*Slow down, Brit. Do Mom and Arland know you're talking to me?"*

"*Yes. Arland practically begged me to get into your head."*

Arland. I may not be able to feel anything, but I know what he must be feeling. "*Did you tell him I'm okay?"*

"*You aren't okay, Kate. You're stuck."*

As if I don't know this. "*Does he know you're talking to me?"*

"*No."*

"*Why not? Go tell him. Now."*

"*Alright, boss."* Geez, Kate's not even here and she's telling me what to do—and I'm listening.

"*Uhh, Brit, I can hear you."*

"*Good! Next time say please."*

I know she's teasing, but it does little to make this better. "*Brit, please, just go talk to Arland."*

"*I am. I'm by him now. What do you want me to say?"*

"*Just tell him you're talking to me."*

"*Okay. Give me a minute."*

Silence returns. I wish I could look around, see something, bide my time twisting my hair around my fingers, but I can't. There are only my thoughts and a paralyzing nothingness.

"*Okay. Instead of hovering over you, now Arland's hovering over me. His eyes are red—I swear it looks like he's going to burst into tears. Anyway, he wants to know if you can use magic."*

"*Tell him I've tried, and ask him if he's tried to cut the bands from me."*

"*They won't. They're afraid you will bleed even worse.*"

"*Even worse than what?*" I'm afraid I don't want to know the answer.

"*Than you already are.*"

"*Brit?*"

"*Yes, Kate?*"

"*Am I dying?*"

"*No. You aren't going to die. We are going to free you. You will be fine.*"

My sister's thoughts drift out of my consciousness, and my own thoughts turn selfish. I'm going to die and never see Arland again. Never experience the joy his lips bring to mine. Never be married. Never . . . .

"*Kate! Stop that. There has to be a way for you to get inside my head. Maybe you can use the magic through me? I just suggested burning the tentacles from you, but I almost got punched for it by a certain red-head.*"

"*Flanna is with you guys now? Does that mean . . . Lann?*"

"*He's gone, Kate. Flanna is beside herself, but I think she's pouring all her sadness into you. She left the children with Shay and Kegan and came down here with food, thinking that would help. Seeing her like this . . . and with Mom and Arland almost as bad over you . . . you need to come out of this. Do you understand?*"

If I wasn't trapped inside myself, I could have helped Lann. Flanna kept her feelings for him a secret for such a long time, and she's already lost so many things she loves; this isn't fair. This whole war isn't fair. "*Brit. I love you. You are my sister.*"

"*Why does it sound like you're saying goodbye?*"

"*I'm not. Be quiet. I'm thinking, trying to get in your head. I don't know if it'll work.*"

"*Okay, quiet. I can do that.*"

"*Brit. We look the same. We were born a year to the day apart. I love her. We're connected.*" I don't know if thinking these things will work, but I have to try. Without my powers, everyone is at risk. Already people are dying.

"*Arland is back, Kate. He thinks if we all stand around you holding hands, it will help. I think he sounds desperate, but I'll do anything for you.*"

"*Why do you not sound desperate, Brit?*" I'm beginning to wonder if this *is* all a dream. My sister is not usually this calm.

"*Because I think if you were going to die—or are dying or whatever—your voice wouldn't sound so strong. I'm banking on to that.*"

"*Well, what are you waiting for? Go stand around me in a circle.*" This is like what we did for Brad, so maybe it'll work.

"*Alright, we're in a circle. I'm about to grab hands with Arland and Mom. Ready?*"

"*As ready as a person without a body or a sense of feeling can be, I guess.*" And it's not like I have any other options.

"*They want you to speak through me. You give the magic commands, but I'll say them aloud.*"

"*Wake up. Free me of these bands. Heal my broken body.*"

Silence.

"*I said it. Should I say anything else?*"

"*That's usually all I say. Do you feel anything, or do you see any sprites?*"

She doesn't respond.

"*Brit?*"

Nothing. The all-consuming black space around me wins out over my connection with my sister. I've either died and am stuck in-between heaven and wherever I'm at, or something's happened to her.

Rubbing my left hand, I try to get the blood flowing through it.

Wait. My left hand is tingling. *I have a left hand!* Warmth floods it, rushing up my arm. *My arm!* I could cry. Feelings, they are incredible, and they are everywhere. Feet. My feet are squeezed into tight-fitting boots and are on the ground. My hands are locked with two others.

I'm not myself. I'm inside Brit.

"*Brit. Can you hear me?*" Worry. I *feel* worry for my sister.

"*Yes, I'm here. Don't be worried about me, Kate, I'm fine.*"

"*I can feel you. I can feel Arland and Mom holding your hands. I can* feel, *Brit!*"

Concentrate. I must concentrate. Both hands I'm holding are moist. One is strong and rough, the other thin and dainty, but both are tense. Focusing on where my eyes should be, I think of what I'll see when I'm in Brit's head. My body will be motionless on the ground. It won't be pretty. I'm bleeding—I cannot allow the blood to scare me.

Light filters in, evaporating the darkness surrounding me. Blurry, yet satisfying, my vision improves. I'm whole, in control; I'm in Brit's body, but I don't want to see myself. Turning my head—Brit's head—I look at Arland. He *has* been crying. Streaks where tears have run through the dirt, line his strong, emotionless face.

"Arland," I say, which is weird because I sound like Brit.

He doesn't move. Instead, he stares down at me—the me I refuse to look at right now.

"Arland, I love you. Please, look at me."

Arland snaps his head toward me. His eyes are big, wet, and full of sadness. "Kate?"

I shrug. "In Brit's flesh."

He closes most of the distance between us, but stops short of hugging me. "I never should have left you alone," Arland says, not meeting my eyes.

Breaking my hold on Mom's hand, I place my palm on his cheek. "Stop. Don't blame yourself for this. I'll be fine. Now"—I look down at my body then squeeze my eyes closed before I scream from the amount of blood pooled on the ground around me—"let's get these things off me. Okay?"

I look up at Arland; he nods then backs away.

Raising my arms above my head, I focus on the light in my soul, the things I love, and the things I want to kill, all at once. The fire starts out as a flicker but builds and stretches out from the pit of my stomach to the tips of my fingers. Flames burst from Brit's body then travel into Arland, Mom, Flanna, Cadman, and Perth. When everyone burns, I turn my head toward the sky. "Wake up, Magic! Burn this daemon from my body, and heal the wounds he caused. Heal Flanna's broken heart. Take the children's pain away. Restore our peace."

A small opening in the sky releases red sprites. They descend from above, spiraling around each other like a tornado of magic. The trees, rocks, and ground all glow red from the light of the small beings. A few sprites blanket Flanna while others rush toward the cave. Upon reaching my body, they slice through the bands without driving into the remnants of the daemon, as they do during battles. Instead, my rescue comes slow, methodically. Sprites take turns with each cut they inflict.

My legs are freed first; my exposed skin is raw and swollen. The clothes I wore must have disintegrated. Mom rushes to Cadman and Perth, sending them away with a wave of her hand. I'm about to be naked and ugly, and she knows it.

Trembling racks Brit's body. I'm doing everything in my power not to turn around and vomit. The only thing keeping me from doing just that is curiosity. Horrified, I watch the sprites move up my waist, uncovering more damaged skin. Bruises, cuts, blood . . . everywhere. My breath catches.

"Brit, are you still with me?"

"I'm here, Kate . . . this is awful. Do you feel any of it?"

"No, but I will be okay. The magic will heal me." It has to. No one could live after something like this. I wonder if Brit and Arland would have looked this bad if I'd killed the daemons in the cave before freeing them. As it was, Brit and Arland looked terrible.

The sprites cut off the last bands around my face. My body is freed, but from head to toe I'm as good as dead. Chunks of skin are missing. What's left is pale, red, or black. My hair is caked with blood and dirt. I look like a monster . . . *a zombie.*

Arland's face does nothing to hide his emotion. He's blank. His mouth open. His hand loosens in mine.

I tug at him. "Arland. I'm alive. I'm right here next to you. My body will be healed."

He doesn't move. Doesn't speak.

Taking a knee, I get as close to the red sprites as possible. "Can you heal me? I cannot live with these wounds open, and I need more blood. Please."

The beings stop and stare at me. One flies right up to my face, transforming from her red flame and showing me her tiny cherub-like cheeks.

"What's wrong?" I ask.

She shakes her head, blond curls bouncing from side-to-side. The sprite reaches out her pink, glowing finger and touches my nose.

I feel nothing. It's as though I'm back in the darkest reaches of myself, but this time I can see as the sprite flies down to my body then touches my real nose.

I can't breathe.

Pain sears through me.

I gasp for air, but the burning on my skin is too much.

Screams build from deep within then erupt from my mouth. They do nothing to mask the pain. Nothing to ease my seizing muscles.

I've been lit on fire, and everyone is standing around to watch as I melt. Never have I wanted to be dead, but now death seems the best option.

"Kate." The voice. I recognize the voice as Arland's. It's warm, soothing—it's full of love, but I cannot respond.

Spasms shoot down my spine. My back arches in protest, lifting from the ground and stealing what little breath I've managed to fill my lungs with. The spasm releases its hold. Hands prevent me from falling to the earth, cushioning my head and back, but only add to the sting of my wounds.

Tentacles are inside me. The daemon has not finished his battle. My body fights to regain control over itself. I squirm, cringe . . . I scream.

I want to give up.

Give in.

Just die.

Here.

Now.

I don't care anymore.

My voice cracks. I'm cold, yet sweaty. The trembles have all but stopped, and my skin no longer burns like it's been sliced open by a dull razor. Taking a deep breath, I hold onto it for a long time before I slowly let it out.

"Kate, can you hear me?" Arland's voice is soft and close to my ear.

I'm afraid to open my eyes. Afraid somehow the pain will return.

"I . . . I can hear you." My voice surprises me. It's hoarse and makes my throat ache.

He pushes hair from my forehead. "The magic has left. Are you still in pain?"

I do a mental check of my body. My head seems fine. My arms, legs, feet—everything wiggles the way it's supposed to. "How bad do I look?"

Flanna snorts. "Kate, you look like you have just been touched by the gods. Your skin is glowing . . . unlike some people."

I'm still afraid to open my eyes, so I rely on Arland, Brit, or Mom for an honest answer.

"Is my skin really glowing?" I ask whoever will respond.

Arland chuckles, sweet and reassuring. "Your skin looks as beautiful as the day I met you."

"Great. So you're telling me I'm covered in dirt?" It's nice to joke. Wonderful even. I'll never take my body for granted again. I want to live before I die.

"Yep, that's what he's telling you," Brit chimes in. "Are you going to open your eyes sometime today?"

"I'm working on it." The fear of opening my eyes is unreal. I know I should let it go, but I'm not ready. What if they're just being polite and I'm a beast marked for the rest of my life?

"Do not rush her, Brit. I'm not sure I have ever seen anything quite so spectacular in my life. Kate is probably in a bit of shock," Mom says.

"I don't think I'd call that spectacular, Mom. That was more like something out of a horror movie." Brit's hostility towards Mom tells me the two have not reconciled . . . not that I was expecting them to just yet.

"Bri—"

"What Kate does not need is to listen to anyone fighting. We need to move her inside, get her something to eat and drink. Do you two believe you can handle that?" Arland asks, raising his voice to a level I haven't heard before.

"Yes," they say in unison.

"Kate, you will feel my hands sliding under you. Remember, you do not have any more wounds. Tell me if you experience pain, and I will stop." Arland sounds as though he's speaking to a small child.

I nod.

"Saraid, Kate's appearance is going to cause a scene. Can you clear the path for us back to the cave?"

"Of course," Mom says. Rocks crunch under her feet at a rapid pace.

"Brit, find Perth and Cadman. See if either of them had any forethought to bring clothes or blankets back from base."

"Clothes. I can do clothes." Judging by the sounds of quick footsteps, Brit also runs up the path.

"Flanna—"

"Get food, right Arland?" Flanna sounds empty, deflated . . . sad.

She's just lost her love, and she's being sent on food duty. Things she hates to do, but only does because she's one of the only women around.

"Yes, and something to drink," Arland adds.

The weight of Flanna's slow steps settles in my chest.

Arland places his fingers on my forearm. "Does this hurt?"

"No." My arm hurting is of little consequence right now. "Is Flanna going to be alright? Are *you* going to be alright? Lann . . . he—"

"We will be fine. Lann is not the first friend we have lost. Flanna will need some time, but time is not something we have at the moment. We need to move you."

So much death. So much loss. Now that I'm alone with Arland, I open my eyes. His brows are creased, but his expression brightens when he catches my gaze.

"This is kind of embarrassing, you know?" I try to improve the mood.

"This is not the first time I have seen you without your clothes on, and I am sure it will not be the last." He unbuckles his belt.

"What are you doing?"

"I am giving you my tunic."

I shake my head. "I don't need it. Brit will have clothes for me soon."

"Are you sure?" he asks, looking me over as if he'd like to hide me away.

I bite my lip, fighting back the heat rushing to my cheeks.

He grimaces but re-fastens his belt. Arland slides his arms under my shoulder blades and legs, then lifts me from the ground.

"Brit told me you are upset about me being hurt again."

My heart flips in my chest. "You aren't going to change your mind about the Binding?"

Arland shakes his head, then carries me toward the cave. "I am frustrated I continue to fail you, but my failures do not change my desire to spend the rest of my life with you."

"Arland, you couldn't have known Enid was a daemon. *I* could have, though; just like I saw the daemons that had you and Brit. If anyone is to blame, it's me." Being carried naked *toward* other people is strange, but I focus all my anxiety about my lack of clothes into Arland. I cannot always have him take the blame for what happens to me or anyone else.

"No, Kate, Enid's odd behavior should have been an obvious clue to her true identity, but we will not dwell on this tonight. There are too many other things to be worried about." Arland blinks hard.

"Like what?"

"Like burying Enid and Lann, and getting everyone to Willow Falls," he says, meeting my eyes. Arland is sad, but I know he's desperately trying to hide it.

"Do you think I ever knew the real Lann?"

"I doubt it."

"What was he like?"

"Lann was a good man. Similar to what the daemon portrayed him as, but I should have known something was wrong there, too. Lann would have told me you were at Watchers Hall from the moment I returned from Wickward. There were many clues I missed."

"Arland." I turn his face toward mine with my palm; his eyes fight some inner struggle. "Stop that! You cannot possibly take care of everyone."

He pulls his face away. "There are also good things to worry about."

"Good things to *worry* about?"

"Yes, for instance, being Bound to you." Arland keeps his eyes focused on the path in front of us, but his mouth curves up a tiny bit.

"Why is marrying me something to worry about?"

"Our marriage is not something to worry about in itself, but we have yet to come up with a plan to convince the Ground Dwellers you are willing to be Bound to Perth. We also have to find a good reason why you should not be Bound to him. One that will somehow unite everyone. If you ask me, our marriage gives us quite a bit to worry about."

"Well, my mom is in the cave, and I'm already naked. Why don't we just have her Bind us here and get it over with already?"

He arches an eyebrow, making me regret my words.

I give my best shrug.

Arland stops halfway up the path and stares at me. "As intriguing as that sounds, would you not prefer to be clean and rested, and not have our marriage combined with all of this?"

He turns us around in circles. Other than the small patch of light shining down from above the cave, everything is dark. The air smells of mildew, sulfur, rot . . . death.

"You're right. You always are." I glance down myself. "I'm pretty hideous right now, too, huh?"

"You could never be hideous while naked in my arms, but filthy . . . . " His green eyes reflect the sparse sunlight; his teasing smile torments my longing for him.

I can't stand this anymore. "I think I can walk, Arland."

He shakes his head. "You do not have to walk."

"Really. I'm okay. I think I *need* to walk." It's astounding what desire can do to a person. People have died, I'm a disgusting mess and was moments from losing my life, and all I can think about is marriage and sex.

He sets me on my feet then looks me over. "You have no clothes, Kate."

There's no need to hide behind Arland; I gave him my dignity a long time ago. I meet his wandering eyes. "I didn't have any clothes in your arms either."

I close the space between us then tug at the end of his tunic. "Maybe you should give me your shirt? It's long enough; it might cover most of me."

Grinning, he unfastens his belt and allows it to fall to the ground. "I believe my tunic *will* cover most of you."

Arland lifts the fabric over his head, allowing me to soak in the beauty of each perfectly sculpted muscle along his abs and chest, then helps me slip into the white cotton. Once my arms are through, I wrap them around his neck. He presses his hands against my back, bringing our bodies so close I'm aware of each breath he takes.

"You see? It covers everything—"

Arland's lips are on my mouth before I can say another word. He threads his fingers through my hair, sending electricity coursing through my veins. My hands shake as they roam his body, teasing with the tips of my nails. Our lips move in a frantic need for more of each other. He trails his hands down my back, stopping just below the bottom of his shirt, and he presses me into him—

Arland startles and pulls away all too soon, leaving me hanging on for more.

Confused by his sudden departure from our kiss, I look up at him as his eyes lock onto something behind me.

CHAPTER ELEVEN

Glancing over my shoulder, I follow Arland's gaze. Perth stares, holding out clothes. A chill hits my legs with enough force to make me want to crouch and wrap the tunic around them. I turn then back into Arland's protective arms, but I desire the promise of warmth and my spared embarrassment in Perth's hands.

The cold indifference he displayed when I first met him returns, except this time, one of his eyes is black. "Sorry to interrupt. I did not realize you two were incapable of keeping your hands off one another."

Perth takes a step forward, dangling my necessities in front of him, just daring me to jump out and grab them.

Arland tightens his hold on me. "Why did Brit not come?"

"Katriona, your mother asked Brit to stay with the children. Flanna cannot manage to stop crying long enough to prepare your food, and the children do not like me. So here I am, offering you clothes. Are you going to take them?" Perth does not look at or address Arland.

He's just been slighted. I cannot imagine this ending well. Nothing ever seems to end well in this world.

I turn my head to whisper in his ear. "Relax. Perth is a jerk. We know that, but he does act like he's trying. He's brought me clothes . . . things I need. I don't think *you* need to hold onto me as though he's going to drag me away."

Arland doesn't take his eyes from Perth.

"I am beginning to doubt your mother even more. Why would she send him out when she knew you were without clothing?" Arland keeps his voice low, but even as a whisper his tone is as rigid as his body.

"Maybe Leader Wilde realized you would give up your own tunic for Katriona." Perth inches closer to us.

Arland relaxes his arms and releases me, but stays within inches as I reach out to take the clothes from Perth.

"Thank you." I grab them then hide behind Arland to dress.

He faces Perth, acting as a shield.

The Ground Dweller turns away from us then turns his face toward the sky. "Your mother said you would not want to rest, but Arland would insist you did. She said the three of us had things we need to discuss."

Arland mutters something inaudible.

I shake my head.

"Ignore him. I have a feeling my mom did say that," I whisper.

The soft leather pants dissolve the cold ache in my bones the instant I slide my legs through, and the boots make me realize I have toes again.

So much better.

"We do need to talk, Perth. But first, can you tell me why you thought to bring clothes from the base for me?"

He laughs, shrill and mocking. "You have a knack for getting yourself into trouble. Cadman and I agreed to bring extra sets for a couple of the men, women, and children, but we were aware you would need them more than anyone else."

Arland's eyes widen. "Since when are you aware of Kate's clothing needs?"

"You act as though you disagree, Arland."

Perth has a way of digging holes for himself, but Arland finds a way to allow the comment to float off, ignored.

I lift the borrowed tunic over my head then give it back to him and replace it with the one Perth brought. "I don't have a knack for getting into trouble, and you know it, Perth. Why do you always instigate?"

He stretches out his arms at his sides. "I am sorry. It is in my nature. Years of bad traditions. You do have to admit, Kate, that you have been smacked in the head by a tree while on a horse, fainted when you fought off the daemons holding me captive—I do appreciate you saving me—and now a shifter has dissolved your clothing. However you wish to look at it, trouble finds you."

Arland shifts his gaze from me to Perth, looking like he'd enjoy jumping off the cliff about now. There has to be a way to make Arland stop feeling so responsible for me, but he loves me—and he's my Coimeádaí. I'm sure there's nothing I can do to make his negative feelings go away.

I put on my best annoyed face and cross my arms over my chest. "You can turn around now."

Perth turns on his toe with the grace of an ice skater, his expression closer to that of the ice than the skater. "I am sure I missed a few examples of you and trouble, did I not?"

"I have heard enough of this banter back and forth, Perth. Last time I checked, you were still under my direction, am *I* correct?" Arland squares his shoulders, straightens his back, and his tone levels and resonates with power. "We must talk, but this is not how it will take place. You are either on our side, as Kate says you are, or you are not, but there will be no more teasing. *Anyone.* Do you understand?"

Watching Arland transform from the sensitive man who loves me to the Leader he was born to be is amazing.

Perth looks Arland's total opposite, holding up his hands apologetically. "I am on your side, but that is the problem, is it not? The fact that there are sides when we all should be fighting against the same evil. I know you do not like me—no one does. Just like my people do not like yours, but we need to overcome this."

Arland pivots to face me. He takes my hands in his then holds my gaze. "Are you sure you do not need rest?"

Perth laughs and gives me a pointed look.

Now *I* have to ignore him. "I'm positive, Arland. We need to work out our plan and get to Willow Falls. It's dangerous staying out in the open. We have the children to worry about and—"

"Okay, Kate, I know you wish to take care of everyone." Arland tips his head in the direction of the cave.

"Take a seat up there. To give us some privacy, I will move those lingering outside the cave inside." Arland holds out his hand in front of us and waits for Perth to go first.

We move along at an easy pace. Arland wraps his arm around my waist, but tension rolls off him in cascading waves. From his clenched jaw to his heavy breathing, nothing about him is happy. Working things out between the two of them—between all the Draíochta—will be no easy feat. This must be one of the tests Griandor told me about. I have two men willing to work together, but even they refuse to trust one another.

At the top of the cliff, Arland takes off toward a group of soldiers then moves them into the cave. Some look back at Perth and I while we take our seats, but Arland keeps them walking, and within a matter of seconds, they're all gone.

"Tell me something, Perth," I say.

He rests his head on the rocks and stares up at the now magenta patch in the mostly black sky. "Yes?"

"If you want so much for us to be united, why do you always provoke Arland? You know it doesn't help your cause. You must realize it only makes my position that much more difficult, as well. So why do you do it?" I watch his face and wait for some human reaction I can use to judge him.

The twisted corners of his mouth fall. He sighs. "I am sure Arland hates me for all the same reasons I hate him. For years, he has been aware his future—you—had been stolen from him by me. My father put me under Arland to be a thorn in his side, and I played into it. I knew one day you would show up and be mine to marry, and it would kill him . . . and his pride. I was confident in my convictions until I met with the Seer, and then when I met you." Perth holds my gaze.

"So now, Arland is to me what I was to him, and I hate *him* for it. I could imagine no better woman to be Bound to than one just like you. You are strong, Katriona, stronger than most women could ever dream of being."

My mouth hangs open, and I don't even dare make a move to close it. How the hell am I supposed to make everyone happy? Brad is in love with me, but I'm in love with Arland and him with me. Now Perth tells me I'm the best woman for him. Brad has a reprieve coming, but Perth . . . I have no promise of a healed heart by a god for him.

"You can close your mouth. Life is what it is, and it appears Arland is a part of the same game you and I have been thrown into. I am just sorry I ever played along." He puts his hands behind his head and stares up at the sky.

"Since . . . since you realize this now, does this mean you will be nicer?" Worrying about everyone's happiness is not something I can manage, but Arland's happiness is something I will be concerned with for the rest of my life. And I know Perth's presence does not fill Arland with warm and fuzzy feelings.

Perth meets my eyes, and for a moment, I see a man full of pain. "For you, Katriona, I will be nicer to the *Great* Arland Maher. He and I have a sordid past, but one full of misunderstandings I never knew of until recent times."

His soft-spoken words hold so much loss. What must it be like, raised to be a tormentor with knowledge you've stolen someone's future from them and rubbing it in their face on a daily basis, only to realize it's not the life you want, and it's not a life that belongs to you? Perth is without a purpose. Just like Brit. Or at least I think that's how they both see their lives.

Rocks crunch under the weight of slow, heavy steps. I look over Perth's head as Arland exits the mouth of the cave, hands clasped behind his back.

He takes a seat next to me, facing Perth. Arland doesn't look in my direction, doesn't touch any part of my body. He takes even breaths in and out, rests his hands on his knees. "You have been under my charge for a number of years now, Perth. None have been pleasant. What do you stand to gain from this partnership?"

"Katriona and I were just having a discussion . . . ." Perth snaps his mouth closed, as if he doesn't want to admit he's been wrong all these years.

I could punch him. "Go on, Perth. Tell him what we were talking about, or he'll never believe me."

Arland looks between Perth and me, clearly waiting for someone to explain.

He sits straight, looking Arland square in the eyes. Respect— something I've never seen Perth offer anyone. "I stand to gain a real life, Arland. Friends, honor, maybe even one day a family that loves me and loves others. I was not raised with that, and it is something I would cherish more than life itself. The Ground Dwellers are not on the right path, and I want to make sure they get there."

This is a decent start.

"Why have you waited so long to come forward?" Arland asks.

Perth huffs. "You and I are both aware if I had come to you, you would not have believed me. I, as everyone does, had to wait until the right time. When I found myself alone with Katriona, I knew the time was right."

Perth pauses, shifts his focus from Arland to me then smiles. "She tried to kill me. Did she tell you?"

Arland chuckles. "You are lucky she did not, Perth. Think about all she has lost. Her home, her comfort, her closest friend—add us to the list at the time she was alone with you, I am surprised you are not wounded."

I glance at the spot above Perth's heart; he's changed his shirt, but I know the cut I inflicted must still be sore.

He catches me staring then rubs his chest. "She did bleed me, but I will live."

Arland pats my leg. "I am proud of you."

He removes his hand and his smile fades, demeanor serious again. "Now, we need to come up with a plan. If we show up with Kate at Willow Falls, your father will want to see the two of you as a pair. Do you know any reason he would allow you to avoid being Bound to her?"

Perth shakes his head. "When we arrive and he sees Leader Wilde, he will most certainly call for her to cast a Binding spell over Katriona and me."

I suck in a sharp breath. Perth was so adamant about getting to Willow Falls before. High Leader Maher said Perth knew all the Leaders were there. I pray I'm not putting trust in the wrong person. Pray he's not walking me into a trap.

"Are you aware of Binding spells?" Perth asks.

"Mom explained it to me earlier." I'm afraid revealing anything else would be too much. Mine and Arland's marriage should be just that—mine and Arland's. Private.

Perth cocks his head to the side, squinting, then turns to Arland. "I will attempt to convince my father we should wait before the Binding spell is cast. We can make a show of it. Festivals, long gazes, held hands, stolen kisses."

"I am sure you would enjoy that," Arland says, keeping his tone level.

"You know as well as I do, Katriona will never have the kind of passion she shares for you with anyone else. A Seer paired you, another told me I would be lost without love forever if I tried to obtain her, and Katriona herself cannot keep her eyes off you—she does not look at *me* that way."

Arland and I were paired by the gods, not just a Seer, but I'll take what Perth said as a compliment . . . in an offhanded way.

"Are you okay with this, Kate?" Arland asks.

No. I don't want to kiss Perth, don't want to hold his hand—no offense to him—but if it's what we have to do . . . . "If you believe it'll work, I will do what I have to."

"Good. My father will love the show. He will be thrilled to think he is hurting both your families—and in the public eye at that."

Perth nods—an approval to himself, I'm sure. "A pretend courtship will be the perfect excuse to avoid the Binding spell, but I worry about the two of you and your ability to hide your feelings for each other."

Arland and I exchange a quick, humiliated glance, faces flooding with red.

"Brit said she could help us with that," I say.

"When we are finished discussing our plans, you should confer with her. Your visible feelings will be the hardest obstacle to overcome—that and your magic connection. You two shine when you use magic together—in fact, you two shine when you are together. Period. You will need to stay as far apart as possible."

I nod. "We are aware the magic is more powerful when we're together."

"A couple more things you will need to work on, Katriona," Perth says. "You need to sound like one of us. Go by your given name, slow your speech down. Stop using combined words no one here has ever heard. While most of us understand you, it would behoove you to fit in more."

"I don't see—"

Arland takes my hand in his. "He is correct, Kate—Katriona. It will help. They may not notice the way you look at me if there is nothing for them to see."

"They may not notice you staring back either, Arland." Perth laughs. "You should not, at any time, allow my father to see either of you looking at one another. The punishment would be—"

Arland glares at Perth, shutting him up in an instant. But I know what he was going to say; it's probably the same reason High Leader Maher warned me to keep my distance: Leader Dufaigh would have Arland killed.

Perth reverts back to his submissive, childlike state.

Arland softens his expression, then he faces me. "Kate is not a name of any other Encardian, and if you speak like us . . . ."

"Fine, but I only have ever allowed people who are mad at me or in love with me to call me Katriona." I stare into Arland's eyes; he's called me Katriona a few times, and when he did, shivers ran through me. I suspect he may be thinking of the last time he called me by my name; his gaze roams my body, transporting me to our room in the base. I wish we had privacy and a bed here . . . .

Perth presses his hands on the ground next to him, shifting his weight. His eyes flit between me and Arland.

Perth has called me Katriona since we partnered at Watchers Hall, and although I'm unsure of his feelings for me, I doubt he feels love . . . or I hope he doesn't. "Or people who do not know me well enough to call me otherwise."

Arland clears his throat. "So, you two will pretend to fall in love, Katriona will go by her given name and work to speak like us, but how will we work our way out of the lies to form an army?"

"*An army?*" Perth asks.

"Yes, Griandor said in order for me to form an army, I would have to unite our kind with the Ground Dwellers."

"*Griandor* told you this?"

"Yes."

"So a god gave you a horse and told you to form an army?" Perth's tone is filled with as much disbelief as his words.

"He gave me the horse long before he told me to form an army, but yes, Griandor visited me before you and I ran into each other at Watchers Hall."

Perth's expression falls flat. "And he told you, *you* have to unite our kinds?"

"Yes, Perth, he told me *I* had to unite our kinds," I repeat in the same empty pitch. "I know we have been at war for longer than a century, but if Griandor told me to do it, I'm sure it can be done."

"And if it cannot?" he asks.

"It must. We will find a way," I say.

Perth's constant lack of faith irritates me.

I squeeze Arland's hand. "Why else would we go to Willow Falls and put on a show if we did not need something from it?"

Perth runs his fingers through his blonde hair a few times, then drops his hand back to his lap and sighs. "If an army is what you need, consisting of both Ground Dwellers and Light Lovers, where does that leave the Sea Dwellers?"

I glance back and forth from Perth to Arland. "The *what?*"

"Sea Dwellers are a more peaceful people than both us and your kind, Perth. There will be no issue with them," Arland says.

His confidence in their allegiance is soothing; being at odds with another group of people is too much to think about, but someone needs to give me an Encardian history lesson. I hate finding things out by chance.

Images of red-headed mermaids, swimming beside a wooden ship full of drunken sailors, pop into my head. I'm almost positive that's not what Arland and Perth are talking about, but I'm going to ask anyway. "Are we talking mermaids and—?"

Arland laughs. "No, Katriona, mermaids do not live in this world. Sea Dwellers are Draíochtans like you and I, but they chose to live in homes over the seas."

"Like boats?"

"Some live on boats. Others live in dwellings constructed over the water along the coasts, but that is unimportant"—he waves his hand—"Since the war began, they have been living at Wickward with the majority of our remaining population."

Wherever they lived before the war, they are now Ground Dwellers like everyone else—yet another tragedy this world and its inhabitants have faced. I hope I get them through it because if not . . . .

Perth's eyebrows draw together. "If Griandor only mentioned you need to unite the Ground Dwellers and Light—?"

"Griandor did not say I had to unite the Ground Dwellers and Light Lovers specifically; he just said I would have to find a way to unite *everyone*. He did mention another Leader, Murchadha, but I did not realize there were others. The confusion is my fault. So, before I try to wrap my head around this, are there any *other* Draíochtans I need to know about?"

"No, there are only the three kinds of Draíochtans. We have three main leaders: my father, Perth's, and Murchadha. There are a few other remaining Leaders under the big three; however, none hold the same power or importance," Arland says.

"What do the other Leaders do?"

"Not much of anything now, but before Darkness, they governed small towns and provided a voice for their people."

"If so many died, who will choose the future High Leaders?"

Perth laughs.

Arland and I both stare at the Ground Dweller.

"Katriona, do you not see the irony? My father forbids Ground Dwellers from fighting against Darkness. The longer the war goes on, the more Light Lovers and Sea Dwellers die, the better chance my people have for deciding our kind as High Leader."

"Are you telling me your father hopes for all current Leaders to die?"

Perth holds my gaze. "And anyone already chosen for the future."

Arland . . . and me.

He nudges my shoulder, casting a scowl in Perth's direction. "I am sorry we have not discussed more of this world. I focused all our time on moving us to Wickward and failed to explain the basics. I still wish I understood why your mother hides information from you."

I stare beyond Arland and Perth—above them—beyond the endless stars in the open patch of sky, and up to the heavens. Mom is so focused on me doing the right thing and staying on the path of Light, I think she forgets I'm committed to this world, but I do wish she'd share more.

Peace washes over me, ironing out the subtle tension in my shoulders and chest. I take a deep breath of the stale air and watch billions of twinkling lights above our heads. Whether Griandor thinks my mom a fool, the peace must be the gods' way of telling me she's already shared enough.

"Like Mom said—the same reason Perth gave—she has been waiting for the right time. In her case, it seems there may never be a right time." My gaze returns to the cliff, returns to Arland where it belongs.

"Anyway, Arland, your father told me all the Leaders are at Willow Falls to discuss the current situation. If I am supposed to unite everyone, I'm—oops—*I am* sure Griandor meant the Sea Dwellers, as well. Do you think Leader Murchadha will also be at Willow Falls?"

"Yes, he certainly will be." Arland stares at me, melting my heart with the intensity in his emerald eyes.

"Are you prepared to lie to all the Leaders of this world?" he asks, voice raspy and seductive.

Nodding, I smile. Arland and I will be married if we play this game the right way, but Perth was correct; Arland and I cannot be near each other for long without showing our love for one another. At this inappropriately timed, random moment, I don't care.

"Have you two forgotten I am here? This could be a serious issue," Perth says, loaded with sarcasm, but sarcasm Arland and I deserve to hear.

I ignore Perth and stare at Arland. We won't get many opportunities at Willow Falls . . . have to make up for it now. "Well, Mom says I am supposed to give a speech. Since I do not know what the speech is or what exactly it will be about, I guess we will have to play the entire experience at Willow Falls by ear."

He smiles. "I believe that is the best we can come up with."

"Great. We will go to Willow Falls, Katriona and I will pretend to be in love, you two will work on this issue"—Perth points between Arland and me—"and now you guys no longer need me?"

"No," Arland and I answer at the same time, without looking away from each other.

Perth jumps to his feet. "I will send your sister out for you."

"Thank you," Arland says.

"Enjoy the time with Katriona while you still have it, Arland, because soon those lips will be somewhere else." And with that, Perth walks away.

Arland's muscles tense, fingers squeezing around my hand. His gaze follows Perth into the cave, but somehow Arland restrains himself, relaxes, and takes a deep breath. "I know he tries to irritate me; therefore, I will not allow him. He is correct, though; I do not look forward to the days at Willow Falls when your lips will meet with his instead of mine."

The thought makes me shudder. "But we will get through it, Arland, and in the end, we will be together. Remember that. Hold onto it because it will be the only thing keeping me going."

He turns back to me. "I am sure I do not deserve you."

"*What?* Why?"

"Our world is in ruins, our friends are dying, our future together rests in the hands of our acting abilities, and somehow you remain strong . . . hopeful. I do not have the same outlook. Your visions all ended with death."

I lean into him. "Without hope or a positive outlook, what do we have? Our friends have died, but we still live. The world is in ruins, but we have the power to fix it. *Our* future together lies in the hands of my mom, and she is willing to help . . . even if her intent is a little fuzzy."

Arland rests his back against the rocks then pulls my head to his chest. "You are right."

I sit up. "We should go back inside. We need to talk to Brit. And Lann and Enid . . . ."

Pulling me back down, he runs his fingertips along my arm. "There will be time for all of those things. We have a long way to travel; enjoy the peace while we still have it."

I don't fight against Arland. Relaxing, I place my head on his chest then close my eyes; there may not be any more moments like this for a long time.

CHAPTER TWELVE

"We shouldn't be doing this," I say, pulling away from Arland.

He tucks my tangled hair behind my ear. "Shouldn't?"

I sigh then bite my lip. "Should not. We should not be doing this."

"I kissed your forehead. If you would prefer, I could arrange for Perth—"

"Arland!" I punch his shoulder. "I *am* serious. We are awful. Flanna just lost Lann. Enid . . . well . . . ." I cannot say how Enid died. What happened to her could have also happened to me. "What are we going to do with them—*for them?*"

He drops his hands in his lap and smiles ever so slightly. "Since I met you, Kate, I have not been myself. I am like one of our youth stricken with lust. Forgive me."

I laugh. "Are you seriously asking me for forgiveness? Yesterday I threw myself at you. Today—"

"You did nothing wrong. Again, it was me." The hunger in his eyes dissipates. "I sent Cadman and Ogilvie out earlier to dig a grave. I will go talk to them and see if they have made progress. We will bury the bodies, and if you are up for it, we can leave for Willow Falls."

Hearing Lann and Enid referred to as '*the bodies*' makes my blood run cold. Tears fill my eyes. I look away from Arland, back up to the sky, hoping the light will somehow make me feel better.

Faint-gray hues paint the hole in the Darkness—our gift—overtaking the twinkling stars and black night. The setting hardly seems fit for a funeral. There will be no church, no mourners dressed in black, no limos, no songs—Lann and Enid deserve more. They dedicated their lives to end this war.

"*I* will be okay to leave for Willow Falls, Arland, but what about Flanna and the children? And what about the daemons? You said they sleep as we do. If we leave now, will we not be more vulnerable?"

"Flanna and the children will be okay. Loss is something we have grown accustomed to. They know as well as anyone we must keep moving." Arland's voice is strong, but he clenches his fists.

Draíochtans may be accustomed to loss, but being used to it doesn't appear to make it any easier. Every word Arland speaks, every gentle touch on my hand, every sad smile he offers hints at the pain he tries to hide.

Arland turns his head toward the river. "And we will be more vulnerable the longer we wait here."

"Arland, Flanna and the children still need time for mourning—"

"I know, but the daemons will trap us here if we continue to wait."

I cross my arms over my chest. "Why did we not leave earlier then?"

Arland cups my cheek, soothing my frustration. "You needed rest, and we needed to speak with Perth. Doing so gave Flanna and the children enough time to compose themselves—or at least some time."

"You said the magic would hide us from daemons even if they passed through the spell—or at least, that's what you said about the stables. Does our magic not work out here?"

A coy smile plays across his face. "That's?"

"Are you going to point out every mistake I make now?"

"Perth may be a lot of things, but he was correct to mention the way you speak. The people here may not care enough to notice, but there are many at Willow Falls who will. And you do not have much time to practice."

I roll my eyes. "I do not like being told what to do, or what I'm doing wrong."

"I'm?"

Arland is right, but I don't have to like it. "Please answer my question about the magic before I go kiss Perth like you offered."

Eyes widening, he chuckles and threads his fingers through my hair. Arland pulls me so close his breath warms my lips. "I will stop correcting you. Please, do not run off."

"My question, Arland."

"Daemons *would* pass through, however, if any of them made it out of here earlier without being killed, then they might tell others of our location. They could wait for us, surround us, and we would have to fight them here . . . again."

"So risking everyone by leaving during the day is safer than staying put and waiting until the daemons go to sleep?"

He nods.

"Okay."

I take a deep breath, pushing aside my own grief, so I can tend to the others. "I will go check in on Flanna and the children while you talk to Cadman and Ogilvie about the graves."

Arland kisses my forehead, stands, then offers me his hand. I grab it, and he helps me to my feet. For everything I've endured today, I feel stronger than I think I should. I don't know if my courage derives from adrenaline or sheer will, but whatever it is, I'm thankful for it.

"Solas," I whisper. A blue flame appears in my hand and provides enough light for me to maneuver through the cave without running into anyone. I search through groups of soldiers. Most of them talk amongst themselves, but Flanna is nowhere to be seen.

Mom is sitting along the side of the cave with the children. Anna catches sight of me then runs over and latches onto my leg.

I've been a huge failure to these people.

"She . . . she d-died, Kate. She—"

I kneel then wipe the tears from her swollen face. "Anna, I know you were very close with Enid—or who you thought to be Enid—but she is in a better place now."

She throws her arms around me, body trembling. "I want to be in the better place, too."

A lump forms in my throat. I swallow it. I have to be strong. "No, Anna, you do not want to be in the other place. We are going to fight this. We are going to win, and when we do, you will live a happy, full life. Do you understand?"

She inhales through her stuffed nose. "Can I stay with you?"

"Come on." I stand then take her by the hand. "I am on my way to find Flanna; she lost someone she loves, too. Can you be strong for her?"

Anna wipes tears from her face with the back of her sleeve. "Mmhmm."

"Good."

We walk hand-in-hand through the dark, searching for Flanna in every hideaway, every group of people.

"Where do you think she is?" Anna asks.

"She is probably alone somewhere."

Faint sniffles come from the furthest corner of the cave. We follow the sounds, then find Flanna on her side, cowering in a ball.

Anna tugs at my hand.

"What is it, Anna?"

She looks at Flanna, then back up to me. "Did Lann go to the better place, too?"

"Of course he did."

Anna drops my hand then takes a few steps toward Flanna. She sits up, face void of emotion, void of the vibrant life I've come to depend on. Flanna catches my gaze. Her bloodshot eyes are tormented. She already lost her mother, and I'm sure many others, and now someone she loves even more intimately.

Anna takes Flanna's hands, sits next to her, then whispers in her ear.

"Is that what Kate told you?" Flanna asks.

I'm rooted in place.

"Yes. She told me Enid is in a better place, and Lann is there, too." Anna turns and looks up at me. The innocence in her big, green eyes, the way she's trying to help—she is such an incredible child.

Flanna grimaces. "Well, Anna, Kate is correct. It is hard to lose people we love, but we should not waste time crying over them. Kate lost someone she loved, too, and here she is, trying to help us." With trembling hands, Flanna groans and stands up, then gives Anna a hug.

"Thank you for coming to talk to me."

"You are welcome."

Flanna puts her hands on her hips and stares at me blankly.

"Arland had Cadman and Ogilvie prepare . . . ." I clear my throat and tip my head in Anna's direction.

"So Arland wants to have a funeral?" Flanna asks.

"Yes, then we are going to leave. Arland thinks the longer we wait, the more danger we are in."

"I had a feeling we would not be here much longer. Are you okay? I mean after the incident with the shifter?" Flanna's face pales and she presses her hand to her forehead.

"I was lucky."

She looks behind me; her eyes widen.

My heart races. Every time someone sees something behind me, we end up in some sort of fight or argument or discussion I'd rather not have. Holding my breath, I turn around slowly and find Arland standing in somber silence.

"Arland," Flanna says.

"Flanna, I am—"

"Do not say it, Arland. I know you are. He was your friend, too."

The two of them have shared grief before. If it weren't for Arland, Flanna wouldn't be alive, but I don't know how to respond. Should I hug Flanna, or Arland?

Arland takes a couple steps then stands next me, but keeps his hands behind his back, shoulders squared. "Cadman and Ogilvie are ready for us outside. Katriona, will you please gather everyone and bring them down the path toward the river?"

"Yes, sir," I say, trying out my new role: someone not in love with Arland.

He turns away then heads through the exit.

Not responding to Flanna's open mouth, I grab her and Anna by the hand then lead them toward the other soldiers.

"Kate, why did my cousin call you Katriona? And why did you call him sir?" Flanna whispers.

"We will explain everything to all the soldiers after . . . ." I don't know why I have such a difficult time forming the words funeral or graves, but for some reason, my mouth refuses to speak them.

She glares at me.

"When we arrive at Willow Falls, Perth and I are going to pretend like we are in love. He is going to *court* me to avoid an immediate forced Binding spell. Arland and Perth agreed in order for Leader Dufaigh and everyone else to believe the lie, I would have to work to speak like everyone else—to fit in—so people do not look at me, or catch me looking at Arland."

Flanna stops short and grips my forearm. "Did you just say Arland and Perth agreed?"

"I did, but it was not easy to get them to talk."

"That is because Arland knows Perth better than you do. Arland knows he should not trust him—"

"Flanna, I understand you do not like Perth, but you must know I have to do this. Griandor—"

She glances down at Anna who has been listening to our conversation for too long. Anna doesn't need to be involved in any of my problems; her life is already difficult enough.

"You are going to need my help at Willow Falls. There will be people you have to meet, dances, conversations, customs you are not familiar with—I will not leave your side." Color returns to Flanna's cheeks, life to her eyes—I've given her something positive to focus her energy on.

"Kate?" Anna asks.

"Yes?"

"Why are you going to lie to everyone about who you love?"

I run my fingers through her hair. "Because I have to, Anna. I know you do not understand. Neither do I. But can you keep this a secret and make sure all the other children keep it a secret, too?"

"Yes, but I do not like it."

Flanna shakes her head.

We split up. She gathers people from the right side of the cave while Anna and I gather people from the left. We shuffle everyone down the path then toward the river, where Arland and Mom and a few others already wait.

Hints of sunshine peek down from above, illuminating black mounds of dirt covering Lann and Enid. Anna and Flanna pause when we reach the graves. I stand between them, my hands squeezed by their grief. To the left, I spot Marcus alone in the crowd of people, staring at his sister, tears glistening on his face.

I lean into Anna. "Remember, you need to be strong."

She doesn't take her gaze from the earth but nods.

"Go to your brother. Comfort him." I prod her back.

She takes a few steps toward Marcus, stops, looks at the graves, then rushes over to him.

Flanna squeezes my hand harder.

"Please, do not leave me," she says with enough desperation to rip me in two.

"I had not planned on it."

We nudge our way through the crowd toward Arland, my mom, and Brit. After we reach them, I take Mom's hand in my left and hold Flanna's on my right. Arland pats Flanna's shoulder then steps away from us, staring at the ground. When he returns his gaze on the crowd, on the mourners, on me, I'm shocked by the amount of pain he reveals. His eyes are red, his face falls flat—not emotionless, but flat from an inability to control emotions.

He focuses on me then opens his mouth. "Times are difficult enough without losing those we love."

Memories of my visions come crashing down on me like a ton of bricks. All the death, all the misery of losing him, someone I love, someone I cannot imagine living without now that I know him . . . I pray the day never comes, that none of the visions becomes reality.

He averts his gaze from me then looks at every person gathered, pausing only long enough to make eye contact, then moves on to the next. "Lann and Enid were good people. While none of us knew the real Enid, we know the shifter emulated who Enid truly was. She loved children, loved her fear céile, and had a passion for life. It is a shame we could not do more to help her, but the current state of our world does not allow for such miracles."

Arland steps through the crowd, takes Anna and Marcus by the hands, then leads them to one of the graves. The other children follow close behind, gathering in a loose circle.

"The children were particularly close with Enid and, therefore, will have first wishes for her passing." Arland kneels, scoops a handful of dirt, then drops bits of it in each child's hand as they walk by him.

"Speak your wish or favorite memory of Enid to that which will cover her forever, then spread it over her resting place."

All the children bring the dirt to their mouths, whisper words for Enid, then spread the wishes over the ground. Trailing back into the crowd, they take their places, but with a little less sadness on their faces. Frowns even out. Tears dry up. Peace has been made.

Flanna leans into me.

I release her hand then wrap my arm around her shoulders. "It is going to be okay, Flanna."

"I will never find love again, Kate—I mean Katriona. Part of my prophecy said I would love until the end. I did not realize the end would come so soon, and I did not realize I would never have had a chance to tell him," she whispers, staring straight ahead.

"Y-you never told him?"

"I told the shifter, but Lann never knew." Flanna's face turns bright red, matching her hair.

"He did not respond. I should have known something was wrong. Lann told me two years ago he was going to make me his one day. I laughed, but from that day forward, I began falling for him. I was mortified after I told him I loved him . . . he did not say anything."

"I am so sorry, Flanna." I don't know what else to say. In a strange way, I feel responsible. I have the ability to see these things, to protect everyone and to end all of this, but so far I haven't been able to save anyone.

She tears her gaze from Arland, from Lann's grave, from the end of her love, and holds mine with such intensity I'm imprisoned in her blue eyes. "Promise me you will never stop loving Arland. Promise me you will never take him for granted, never miss an opportunity to love him even if it costs you everything. Love is the only thing in the world that matters, Katriona. Do you understand?"

I manage to nod. Of course I'll love Arland. Of course I won't take him for granted.

"I mean it. Do not fall for Perth at Willow Falls. Do not become fool to their games, Katriona, because a game is what I fear this is for him. Arland loves you, and the two of you have to be together. We will all die if you are not."

Mom leans forward. "*Flanna,*" she scolds under her breath.

Flanna ignores my mom and grips my arm in her hand so hard, I know I will bruise. "Promise me, Katriona."

"I promise, Flanna." I don't dare tell her Perth is honest, don't dare tell her we could all die whether Arland and I are together or not. She's grieving. I doubt she wants to cry in front of all the soldiers; Flanna is a Leader. I'm positive my promise is the only way she knows how to cope with her hurt right now.

"Lann was a Leader." Arland's voice booms with pride, interrupting Flanna's quiet outburst.

She straightens her back and watches him without a hint of the pain that was on her face moments ago.

"She will not cry where others may see her. You should remember this; it will help you earn respect," Mom whispers.

I mimic Flanna's Leader stature. Squaring my shoulders and clearing my face of what I'm feeling, I stare ahead.

"A good Leader," Arland continues. "He guided many of you through tough times, through hard battles, and through devastations none of us should ever have had to face. He was a friend of mine. I vow never to let what happened to him happen to anyone again." Arland pauses and locks eyes with me. "I will remain focused and be more vigilant when behaviors seem out of the ordinary."

I catch a few of the soldiers looking in my direction, but I'm not surprised. Arland said himself he's acted like a lust driven youth since he met me. They must have noticed, but somehow *his* behavior doesn't bother me one bit.

"If any soldier has a wish or something they would like to say, please come forward now," Arland says.

Glancing around, I watch as, one by one, soldiers line up, grab a handful of dirt, whisper their wishes or kind words, spread them, then return to where they stood before. Not everyone pays respects, so it doesn't feel awkward to stand here while the ones who do move around. Perth, Flanna, Mom, Brit, and I all hold our ground—as well as a few other soldiers.

When the commotion settles down, Arland glances at my mom, then returns to his feet. He stands in front of the graves again. "I would like to ask all the Leaders in our presence to come forward and pay their respects to Lann."

Perth and Flanna step forward, but my feet are unwilling to move. The soldiers are aware I'm from The Meadows, but most of them are not aware of who I am—only that I'm powerful. If I step forward, if my mom or sister steps forward, everyone will know—or at least have a lot questions.

Mom looks between Arland, me, Brit, and everyone else. I'm not sure if Mom is ready for this either; she's been in hiding for years and has told me she fears for her life when the other Leaders discover her.

She takes a deep breath then releases. "We may as well get this over with in front of people who *do* like us. It will be good for these people to know. They need to trust you, Kate."

"Katriona, Mom. Kate will not exist at Willow Falls." No matter how much I hate the idea of coming out of hiding, she's right. If I'm ever going to form an army, I need someone to trust me.

"Katriona then." She turns and looks at my sister. "You, too, Brit. You have just as much a responsibility to this land as Katriona. I am sorry for what I said earlier."

"It's okay. I know you're scared. I am, too," Brit says.

She's always been closer to our mom; the quick reconciliation is not surprising, but it does sting. I've always felt my relationship with Mom to be somewhat lacking. Now, only more so. Even though I've resigned myself with her reasons, I still don't fully trust her. I just need her.

Without allowing any more time to dwell on trust or relationships, Mom grabs me and Brit by the hands then steps forward. Flanna walks next to us, and Perth joins as well. We take our places beside Lann's grave, ignoring the whispers from the soldiers behind us.

Arland kneels again. He scoops more earth then drops some into each of our hands. When we're all holding the dirt, he whispers his wish then scatters it over the grave.

I don't know what I'm going to wish for. I'm not sure if Lann was himself when we met, or if the shifter had already abducted him.

Perth follows suit, spreading his dirt.

My palms sweat.

Mom and Brit whisper to their closed fists then sprinkle their wishes over the graves.

What could they have wished for? Neither of them knew Lann. I've never been to a funeral, only seen them on television, and I've never heard of people making wishes for the dead.

"Katriona?" Arland says, startling me by his closeness.

Some dirt falls from my hands and lands on my boots. I look up and around.

Everyone watches me.

It's my turn.

I take a deep breath, close my eyes then whisper the first thing that comes to mind. "I am sorry, Lann. I wish for you to meet Flanna again someday."

I scatter the brown, dry earth over his grave then turn to rejoin the others in the crowd.

Arland grabs my wrist, stopping my retreat. "Wait. There are things we need to talk to everyone about."

"Here? Now? Are you sure this is appropriate?" I ask, stage fright rippling through me.

Arland's lips press into a thin line, but the corners of his mouth turn up just a little. I'm sure he'd laugh if we were alone. He laces his fingers with mine, easing the tension of being in front of the soldiers.

We're about to confess everything to them.

"We do not have time to wait, and everyone is already gathered here," he says.

I sigh.

Arland pulls me closer to him then turns me around to face the truth.

"Before we leave for Willow Falls, there are some things we need to discuss." Arland's words bring the eyes of everyone upon him—even mine.

"I have been Leader of Watchers Hall for ten years, but my family was aware of my status as Coimeádaí to Kate from before my birth."

None of this is news to the soldiers, at least not the ones Cadman shared the information with. Arland better go somewhere with this quick, or interests will wane.

"You may have noticed I called the Leaders up last to pay respects to Lann. You also may have noticed who was amongst them. Kate—Katriona—is the first born child of Leaders Brian and Saraid Wilde—"

The soldiers cut him off with an uproar of conversation, drowning out my thoughts.

"Please, calm down," Arland says.

Tristan steps forward, arms crossed over his chest, eyebrows drawn together. "My parents told me stories of the Wildes. Said they were killed trying to flee with their daughter so she would not have to be Bound to Perth."

Saidear emerges from the crowd. He places a hand on the young soldier's shoulder. "I knew Brian Wilde. He did not abandon his people because of an unfortunate arrangement."

"There is not much time to answer questions," Arland says, quieting the crowd. "Leader Brian Wilde was killed in the early days of the war, but if it were not for him, none of us would be alive right now. The Wildes did not desert due to the Binding exchange of their daughter with Perth. A Seer instructed them to use old magic to leave Encardia to protect Katriona—the only one with the power to defeat Darkness."

I feel a sudden urge to hide behind Arland—or a tree.

"You were all aware I have been protecting her, but what many of you are not aware of is why. She will bring Light to Encardia again. Just yesterday, she almost singlehandedly defeated the daemons holding us all captive. The light above us now is there because old magic is alive again, alive because of Katriona. I have seen this light before, but as she grows stronger, the sky remains visible longer."

Gavin steps forward. "Why have you not informed us sooner, Arland?"

"Timing," Arland says, voice flat.

Gavin steps back, accepting the answer without further question.

"Katriona was promised to the Dufaighs, but it is clear, Arland, the two of you have a connection—as all Coimeádaís have with their keep. What will you do about the Binding?" Shay asks, glaring at Perth.

He tips his head in my direction, flashes a cocky grin, then turns to face the crowd. "Which is why Arland and Katriona need to speak with you all now. I am on your side—or rather I am on the side of Light. I do not wish to marry Katriona as a punishment, besides, she and Arland were *made* for one another. I have no doubt about that. However, when we arrive at Willow Falls, Katriona and I will put on a show—"

"Griandor wants me to unite our people, and Arland and Perth believe the best way to start is to play by the rules," I blurt out before I can stop myself.

Public speaking is not my thing. Everyone quietly stares at me. My knees buckle, but Arland squeezes my hand, reminding me this is one of the easy tests.

"Did you say Griandor wants you to unite our people?" Ogilvie asks, crossing his well-defined arms over his chest.

"She did," Arland says. "The sun god has been in close connection with her since she arrived in Encardia a few weeks ago. In order for us to succeed, we need to ask everyone here to keep mine and Katriona's relationship a secret. If Leader Dufaigh discovers our connection, his desire for power will likely overrule the forced peace between our kinds, and all will be lost. Can we count on your silence?"

Silence is what Arland asked for, and silence is what we receive now. Even the children appear lost in thoughts. No one moves or looks away from me and Arland. My hand is so sweaty it may slip out of his. My heart flips in my chest. What if no one will do this? What if they do and get in trouble for it?

Everyone should save themselves and forget about mine and Arland's problems—

Cadman takes a knee, places his fist over his heart—like Arland did when he swore his life for mine. "You have my confidence,

Arland and Katriona. If we are discovered, punishment in the name of Light will be worth it."

Arland tightens his hold on my hand and casts a sideways glance at me. My face flushes, and chills run along my skin—I'm responsible for so many lives, so many debts I can never repay.

Perth kneels next. "My father would kill me if he were aware of this conversation. I know I am on the correct path and he is not— and I know you two are, as well. I will not only vow silence, I will fight in the army Katriona needs to follow her."

"I will also fight and swear my allegiance," Ogilvie says.

Over and over again, soldiers, family, and friends take a knee, cross their fist over their chest, then swear their lives to the path of Light. When the last and smallest of the children takes her knee, my body numbs. All these people—willing to sacrifice their lives, sacrifice their freedom—have just pledged everything to me and Arland. If things do not go well, their blood will be on my hands. I should thank everyone, but I can't find the right words. What's appropriate when people put everything on the line?

"Thank you," he says, squeezing my fingers between his. "Katriona and Perth will begin courtship as soon as we arrive at Willow Falls. Please, do your best not to mention myself or Katriona in the same conversation. Hide any knowledge we even know one another."

A tear slides down my cheek. We're diving head first into a dangerous, shallow end, and everyone is following right behind us. I sniffle, but the air smells . . . different. Rot and decay have been replaced. The scent reminds me of camping, of some of my last days in the forests in Virginia with Brad and Brit, before life spiraled in a whole new direction. I inhale a deep breath and look up.

Smoke.

Something is burning, something big.

"Arland," I say, pointing above our heads.

A shrill scream resonates from the middle of the crowd. Keely, the five-year old little girl who makes beds and collects linens, is standing by a coscartha in our protected area. Mom rushes to Keely's side, scoops her up, then covers her mouth.

"Shh, little one. The daemon does not know you are here." Mom looks at Arland with wide, panicked eyes then rushes to our side.

Plumes of smoke rise around us; bright orange flames shoot fifteen feet or so into the air from the trees. My skin warms from the sudden burst of fire.

"They know we are here like you said?" I ask Arland.

He nods. "They are trying to smoke us out."

Stop, drop, and roll does not sound like an appropriate plan for getting us out of this. "What are we going to do?"

Arland takes me by the hand and pulls me close. "We have to fight, Kate. We have to fight."

CHAPTER THIRTEEN

Determination to protect the children drives me. No matter how well trained some are, they're not ready for a fight, not ready for another introduction to daemons or the harsh reality of Encardia. I've positioned the smallest and youngest Draíochtans in the middle of all the soldiers; Arland and I remain at the back. Everyone moves as fast as possible toward the horses, sprinting toward the path which will take us north to Willow Falls.

I glance to my right. Sweat beads on Arland's temples and drips down his face.

"What are we going to do when we get out?" I ask, heat and smoke making my lungs strain harder for air.

"Do we send the others ahead of us and fight the daemons ourselves? Or do we all stay together?"

Covering her face with her hands, Keely nuzzles her head into his shoulder and whimpers.

"You and I will step out first and see what we encounter. If we are attacked, the others must remain here until it is safe. If we are not attacked, we will all have to move fast," Arland says, sureness filling his every word.

"But the smoke. How will they—?"

Kegan coughs, deep and hoarse, confirming my concern for how everyone will breathe.

Smoke blankets over our heads like a thick, gray cloud. I fight the urge to rub my burning eyes, cover my mouth, or show any sign of weakness. I'm a Leader; if Flanna won't cry over losing Lann in front of everyone, then I won't allow the smoke to faze me.

Keely sobs and shakes with each ragged gasp for breath.

Arland rubs the back of her head. "We will have no other choice but to fight fast, Kate."

"*Kate?*" How I have the courage to joke in a time like this is beyond me.

"Katriona," he corrects without any hint of amusement.

We reach the edge of the protected perimeter, and everyone in front of us comes to an abrupt stop.

Arland and I run into the backs of Tristan and Dunn, knocking them forward and into Saidear and Kegan.

"Sorry," I say, but other than Keely's high-pitched cries, no one responds.

Cadman raises his hand, holding us here even longer, then turns around. "Sir, I believe you should see this."

Arland leans away from Keely, looking at her with the compassion of a father for his sick child.

"Keely, I have to put you down now. Will you promise to be good for Dunn?" His question is soft, gentle, caring.

"I do not want to get down. The scary . . . ." She draws in a ragged breath through her stuffy nose.

Brit makes her way through the crowd, eyes wide with fear, skin pale. "Kate—"

Keely interrupts with an ear-piercing wail. Squeezing him tighter and locking her legs around him, she fights Arland as he tries to peel her from his chest.

Brit glances at Keely clinging to Arland for dear life, then opens her arms. "Here, I will take her."

I don't know what Brit was going to say, but I'm sure offering to take a child off Arland was not her intention.

Keely peeks at my sister, face red and glistening with tears, then lunges in her direction.

"Your name is Keely?" she asks.

"Mmhmm."

Brit flashes a half smile at me, then turns and walks away with Keely latched on tight.

Arland stares after them.

"That was unexpected." I shake my head. Brit has never been as fond of children as me.

He takes my hand in his and leads me between the soldiers and the rocks along the edge of the cave. Everyone's eyes are upon us. I feel their fear in the weight of the air, their despair. A knot forms in my gut, but I keep my head held high.

"Somehow I do not believe your sister came to help, Katriona. She wears her concern on her face. Brit may be good at hiding secrets, but I am not positive she hides her feelings as well as she believes she does," Arland whispers, helping me climb over a large gray boulder.

Glancing up at him, I check his facial expression; his eyes are slightly narrowed. "You look worried, Arland. Do you think she will not be able to help us?"

He scans the crowd as we walk side by side. "We do not have much of a choice but to try, do we?"

"I guess not."

We stop next to Cadman.

Watching someone so much older look to us for leadership is strange. Growing up, if I saw someone with gray in their hair or wrinkles around their eyes, I'd think they were wiser, full of knowledge I didn't have. In Encardia age means nothing.

"The horses are gone, sir," Cadman says.

Mirain! Dropping Arland's hand, I make a break for the spot I last saw her.

He grabs the back of my shirt, stretching it taut against my skin. "Stop."

Cadman clamps his hand on my right forearm. "Did you wish to run into a trap, ma'am?"

I squint toward the tree where the horses were tied, but the light is not bright enough to shine through the low-lying cloud of smoke. "You don't think . . . ?"

Arland tugs my tunic, pulling me away from the perimeter. "No, Katriona, I *don't* think the daemons did anything to Mirain or Bowen or any of the horses. They are smart enough to run away."

"But they were tied up." I strain my eyes again, trying to look for signs of blood or anything else that would tell me if the horses are hurt.

"There is no time to worry. Wherever the animals are, they are," he says.

"What do you propose we do, sir?" Cadman asks.

Both men turn to look at me; I get a sinking feeling I'm the only one who can get us out.

I run my hands along my arms. "How far is it to Willow Falls again?"

"Fifty miles," Cadman responds.

"Do you think the daemons know where we are going, or do they only know we are here because they were the ones to bring you here in the first place?"

Arland rubs his chin then takes a deep breath. "I cannot answer that, Katriona. Daemons have never cornered me this way. When one discovered Watchers Hall, we were aware and killed it before more could be brought back for an attack—or so we thought."

He tips his head in the direction of the graves. The trees burn, bright orange flames lashing up toward the dark sky. "There could be hundreds or even thousands out there waiting for us."

The night we brought Mom and Brit through the portal, we were attacked by hundreds of hounds and coscarthas in the forest. During that battle, my sister was almost eaten by a hound and Arland was nearly overrun by coscarthas and then by a hound. I have more control over my powers now, but the thought of battling *thousands* of daemons with little help worries me. There has to be another way. We need to hide, or go underground, or in the water, but not through an army of thousands of daemons . . . not with the children. "I am not sure we can fight that many daemons with the children, Arland."

The air grows warmer. My skin tingles as the chill works its way out of me. If we don't move soon, we will be surrounded by fire. Soldiers and children alike clear their throats, gasp for air, or cough. Unfriendly reminders of how dire my need to make a decision is.

"Sir, the flames are getting closer, and the smoke is almost too dense to see anything. What are *we* going to do?" Cadman asks, raising his voice to a level impending on insubordination.

Arland holds my gaze; his green eyes possess as much power over me as the burning forests around us. "Katriona, this is your army, these are your people—Griandor wanted *you* to lead us. What are we going to do?"

Hide—it's the only thing I can think of while the children are here, but Arland said we have to fight, and the smoke will kill us before the daemons do if we stay here. Leaving is our only option. My magic is our only protection—or is it? The last time I had to leave a hideout because of daemons, my room had disappeared. In fact, we're all invisible to the daemons now. "How does the hiding spell work?"

Arland shakes his head. "There is no way we could manage to keep up the spell while moving. It takes a lot of effort to cast it in the first place. That is why so many of us work together."

"There is no way everyone else can keep it up, but if you tell me what to do, maybe I can—or *we* can?"

Gray and black ash falls from the sky, landing on everyone's hair and shoulders like drifting snowflakes. I bring the crook of my arm to my mouth then breathe through my shirt.

Arland wipes the burnt remnants of nature from his nose. "It is too great a risk. The spell must be cast over every inch of land around us."

I prop my hands on my hips. "How many people did it take to hide me at Watchers Hall?"

He scowls. "One."

"Who?"

"Me, but—"

"But nothing, Arland. Tell me what to do. We can do this together, remember? We just have to think of those we love, remain connected. Everyone can help."

He takes my hands from my hips. "Repeat after me: cheilt an maireachtáil leis an dúlra." Arland pronounces each word slowly.

I listen closely, soaking in the spell. "Cheit a maireachlateis an d-d—"

He tenses. "No. Listen carefully. If you wish to hide us all the way to Willow Falls, you will have to repeat this over and over. We will help you, but we have only ever been able to hide ourselves while in a permanent location. This will not be easy."

Cadman paces between the edge of the perimeter and me. Fingers rubbing his forehead, he stops and looks up, then holds my gaze. "Katriona, I have fought with you and been witness to the strength you and Arland have when you fight together. I do not believe we need to hide. With your powers, we are capable of handling the daemons, and we need to go."

His confidence in my fighting skills is encouraging, but I cannot get over my instinct to hide—to preserve the children. Thinking of everything I stand to lose and of everything I stand to gain, I concentrate my thoughts over my heart then release the fire inside me. Power flows through my soul, fanning out to my extremities, and encases my body in blue flames.

Arland and Cadman stand close to me, hold their heads high and smile, but the others move away and give me a wide berth—as though my fire could harm them.

"Cheilt an maireachtáil leis an dúlra," I shout as loud as I can.

Magic stirs through the air, rippling through the smoke as golden light lifts into the sky. I inhale a deep breath. My lungs no longer burn, and my eyes no longer fill with tears.

"Will it hold, sir?" Ogilvie asks, reaching out to touch the protective layer as it swirls around everyone.

"It will hold as long as Katriona remains strong. She has already used more magic over the last two days than she should have, but if we assist her," Arland pauses then smiles at me, "we should be able to get far away from here."

I'm happy the magic is responding, but am well aware the dangers we will face if it fails. "Everyone needs to stay connected. We should hold hands and move single file. Arland, I am not sure if you and I should stay at the back or in the front or where—"

He rubs his thumbs over my fingers, soothing away my indecisiveness. "Katriona and I will lead the way. Everyone take the hand of the person next to you. Do not let go. Repeat the spell while we move; doing so should aid Katriona's efforts greatly."

Each soldier grabs hands with the person in front of them, increasing the power of the magic, and adding an unexpected weight to my shoulders no person should have to endure. Thoughts not belonging to me flood my mind, inundating my brain with chatter I cannot understand. Shaking my head, I block out the thoughts of the soldiers, their concerns and fears, and focus on what motivates me: love.

Flanna holds my right hand. Cadman takes Arland's left then leads us forward—I'm sure as a way of protection. Cadman's loyalty to Arland runs deep. Flames spread from the four of us to the others in a domino effect. This scene is so familiar, yet so unsettling—I pray it doesn't end as badly as the last time when Brad was killed.

"Is everyone ready?" I ask, looking over my shoulder at a line of powerful Draíochtans.

Not a single protest comes from behind me.

"Let's go, then."

We start forward, through the original barrier, outside the protection created by regular magic. Nothing jumps out or shows sign of an attack, and I don't waste time looking. Instead, I repeat the words Arland taught me. "Cheilt an maireachtáil leis an dúlra."

Over and over I whisper the unfamiliar language and watch as more sprites join in the balloon of golden beings encircling us.

Arland, Flanna, Cadman, and everyone else recite the spell, glancing in all directions. Apprehension flows through our connection. I sense the overall unease of the soldiers who've just learned of my powers, sense the disbelief they have of their bodies covered in flames. Something rifles through me from their responses, satisfaction maybe, making me feel a lot more confident everyone will make it to Willow Falls . . . to safety.

The forest remains still except for our movements, and we continue on without disturbance. To our right the river flows at a rapid pace. Water rushing over rocks creates a peaceful soundtrack for our long hike. Twigs snap under our feet. Tree canopies thicken over our heads. The fire is long behind us, the smoke faint.

No one speaks, but from the shared connection, I know the silence is out of fear. I should be focused on getting these people to safety, but all *I* can think of are daemons feeding on the horses. I'm not sure if Dughbal has any interest in them, but Mirain is no normal animal. She's a gift from Griandor; she must have powers Dughbal desires.

"What is bothering you, Katriona?" Arland asks, stepping over the trunk of a fallen pine.

I trip over a branch from the same tree and yelp, but keep hold of Arland's and Flanna's hand.

"Having trouble with your feet, *Katriona?*" she asks, spitting my name at me with a hurtful amount of sarcasm.

I look into her scowling blue eyes. Is Flanna mad at me about Lann? Does she think Mom should've helped him rather than me? Part of me thinks she should have helped him. I have an ability to conjure magic and heal myself. He didn't. Or maybe Flanna's upset because I'm going to pretend to be with Perth? No matter how innocent he is, she blames him for this debacle we're in. Whatever her problem, she doesn't seem to have patience for the lies.

Arland laughs. "Did I frighten you?"

I look away from Flanna's angry face and soak in Arland's voice, his laughter, his warm touch on my hand—things that calm and soothe me. I already know how much I'm going to miss him. "Yes. I was lost in thought and . . . ."

"You are worried for Mirain?"

"Amongst other things," I say. How did he know? "Why?"

"Your thoughts are loud."

My hands tense. "What?"

"Your thoughts seem to fill my head when the magic is in use and we are connected; it began during our last battle with the daemons. Most are scattered, or I am only picking up bits and pieces, but I can almost feel you in my brain."

"I could hear all of your thoughts during that battle, but I thought only I could—"

"Why did you not say anything?" he demands.

I shrug. "Because I don't want to hear everyone's thoughts."

Arland cocks his head to the side. "But it is such an amazing gift."

"Right now, I know almost everyone behind us has lost faith this is going to work. They are all afraid they will be picked off by a daemon first. Flanna can't believe we're talking at all. Cadman wishes we'd shut-up before Darkness finds us. My mom, I can't hear anything she's thinking. Perth, well he finds humor in my outburst toward you." Turning, I scowl over my shoulder. I cannot see Perth, but I'd love for him to get a good look at my face.

Arland leans down to my ear. "I am not upset with you; I am just at a loss how you could keep quiet about something like this. We share thoughts. Do you not find it amazing?"

His question startles me more than when he spoke. There are so many things I've found amazing here in Encardia but have never had time to consider—I'm surprised this comes as a shock to him. Magic, magic *I'm* creating, protects us. This alone amazes me, but on top of that, someone I've dreamed of for over six years is holding my hand, swears his life to protect me, and is willing to risk that life to marry me. My sense of purpose is stronger than I've ever experienced, and even in the darkest of times, I'm happy.

He squeezes my fingers. "Your thoughts are clear to me now, too. I forget how many new experiences you have had here, Katriona, but being connected to your thoughts while invoking the magic is something I never dreamed possible. The thought of losing this connection when magic is not in use and when we are no longer near one another at Willow Falls saddens me."

His sadness evaporates the free space in my mind, nearly crippling my ability to walk another step toward our destination.

Arland laughs again. "I rather enjoy this connection. Hearing how you feel straight from your thoughts is almost more endearing than hearing words from your mouth."

While I have nothing to hide from him, I'm not sure *I* like Arland being able to hear my thoughts.

"Why not?" The smile on his face tells me he's the *only* one enjoying this. "You do not have to share—"

"Is there not a spell or something the two of you should be reciting? Does everyone else have to do it for you while you talk about your *love lives?*" Flanna says soaked with her usual level of sarcasm, except this time, I sense the pain in her words . . . in her thoughts. Every fiber of her being cries out for Lann, to be held, to be loved.

"*Can you hear me?*" The question passes through my mind in a perfect match of Arland's deep, resonating voice.

"*I can,*" I think.

He squeezes my fingers between his. "*She will overcome her grief, Kate. She just needs time.*"

"*And you? Are you grieving?*" I focus on the spell and repeat the words aloud, adding more magic to our protective layer.

"*Do you believe I should let my friend's death affect me the way it has Flanna? We are Leaders for a reason; if we cannot be strong, we do not need to be in these positions.*"

"*But, Arland, we are only human—*"

"*No, we are not merely human. We are Draíochtans—and Flanna has Leader in her blood. She will overcome this.*"

His dismissal of her grief makes me want to scream. In almost every dream I had of him, he died. In all those dreams, I reacted. Most I threw myself over his dead body, others *my* body tore itself apart, and some I allowed daemons to kill me. If Flanna loved Lann the way she described, or anywhere near the way I do Arland, her grief must be overwhelming every part of her heart.

"*I am not dismissing her grief. If Leaders fall apart, what will keep the others from doing the same?*" Uncertainty rolls from Arland and into our connected hands, into my thoughts, *my* heart. "*And, Kate, if I am killed, I want you to be stronger than what you saw in your visions. You must go on living.*"

He's always told me he won't die. He's always been so certain when saying so. Does he not know? Is he not aware of his future? What if his father hasn't told him, or worse, what if he has and Arland has been lying to me, hoping the future could change?

"*I have not lied to you. Please, do not fear my death, but do not think it cannot happen. It would be foolish.*"

"Cheilt an maireachtáil leis an dúlra," I say, closing my mind to thoughts, to emotions, to memories of Arland dying. I concentrate every ounce of strength I have into the words, into the meaning of them. The negativity I feel will not cause me to fail these people—I will not fail Arland. He will survive . . . *we* will survive.

Blue flames shoot from my center, arcing and creating an additional barrier around the soldiers. Their gasps do little to distract me from my purpose, but their sudden excitement that I am the one who can end this war is exhilarating.

Arland turns his face away from me, returning his attention to the path before us—or lack thereof. "Cheilt an maireachtáil leis an dúlra."

"Cheilt an maireachtáil leis an dúlra," I say again.

The more often I repeat the line, the more often everyone else does. I do not falter; there is no weakness, no exhaustion—just drive. The trail remains narrow and full of obstacles. Boulders and fallen trees, mud and large pools of water—these things slow us down, but we push forward for hours.

The light from our bodies reveals death all over the forest. Decaying small gray rabbits lie on the ground. Dry and brittle plants crunch under our shoes.

The smell of rot puts the smoke to shame.

My gift, the open patch of sky, from Griandor is already missed by everyone. When the soldiers are not watching out for daemons or obstacles standing in our way, they look up, look for a present or a sign, but we have moved well past the stars and well past the bright blue piece of heaven. We have a long way to go before we'll see it again, of that I'm sure.

CHAPTER FOURTEEN

Seven hours we've trudged through the dense, dead forest. Our pace has slowed to a near halt. The children drag their feet. Everyone's backs are hunched. Grunts and moans come from many soldiers behind us, but their thoughts are so tired and focused on food and water—even my body is racked with cramps—I cannot possibly make out who the complaints originate from.

"*Do you need to stop?*" Arland sends the question to my head, but his words carry little doubt.

"*Even if I didn't, they need to.*" I tip my head back toward the others.

"*Would you like to tell them we are going to stop, or shall I?*"

"*You can.*"

Arland tugs on Cadman's arm, stopping him in his tracks. "Hold up for a moment while I speak with the others. We need to rest, but I need you to continue reciting the spell."

Cadman moves his lips, but no sound makes it to my ears.

"May I have your attention?" The authority in Arland's stature, in his straight back, alert eyes, and strong face, commands their attention well before his voice does—people always watch him.

"We are going to stop for the night. Many of you are hungry, tired, weak"—he glances at Flanna—"grieving. We need to move to slightly higher ground, away from the river. Are there any willing to volunteer to set traps and hunt for food while the rest of us move uphill?"

"I will, sir," Gavin says from the back of the line.

"Snares are a specialty of mine; I will also help." Ogilvie smiles. My blue flames reflect in his teeth, reminding me of someone standing under a black light.

Arland raises his eyebrow then shakes his head.

I forgot he can hear my thoughts; he's never heard of the lamps that make everything look bright blue, not black.

"Should we drop from the line, sir?" Ogilvie asks, looking at me.

Turning my attention to Arland, I see the question in his eyes before he speaks.

"Katriona?"

My energy wanes. While maintaining my grip on Flanna, I bring the back of my hand to my mouth just as a yawn escapes me. "I cannot protect them if they are not within the circle of sprites around us, and if they break the line, it needs to be reconnected." *I think.*

"Make sure the line is closed as soon as they step away," Arland says.

Ogilvie and Gavin nod, and I hold my breath as they break the line. Tristan reaches for the hand of the old Healer, Keagan. The burden of the connection on my shoulders does not lessen. The circle around us does not break.

We are safe.

"Are you sure?" Arland asks.

"Yes."

He looks ahead and nudges Cadman to move forward. "Follow closely. If anyone has difficulties making it up the hill, please do not break the line. Ask, and we will stop. Do you all understand?"

Without giving anyone time to say otherwise, we start up the hill, up the slippery slope of decayed leaves and dry forest floor. My thighs burn. My calves scream at me to stop. Holding hands makes keeping my balance difficult, and many times Arland and Flanna are my only support when I lose my footing.

"We are almost there," he says.

"Where?" I ask.

"To our new hiding spot. I have been here before. In fact, most of the area along the river I am familiar with. My father had me memorize the land in preparation for times like these—or in our case, this exact time." Arland doesn't look at me, but doubt fills his voice, and his internal monologue fades away.

Why would he shut me out? I'm not sure what I'm doing, but I focus my concentration on his thoughts, on what he's feeling, on making a connection to him as I've done with Brit when I had trouble accessing her mind. I want to understand his doubt, want to know exactly what he's thinking.

Power builds in my chest, burns with excitement, sending waves of fire rolling out from my core. I imagine entering his mind through our connected hands, up his arm, shoulder, through his neck and finally to his brain.

Arland snaps his head in my direction. *"No, Kate."*

Descending his body, drawing back into my core and fizzling out, the fire withdraws. But the lack of magic gives way to anger. *"You're allowed to get into my brain, to know what I'm thinking and feeling and seeing, but I am not allowed to do it to you? I share thoughts with Brit, have heard Flanna and Cadman and your thoughts before. Why am I not allowed now? What are you holding back from me, Arland? Please, your feelings have been so full of doubt, your eyes, your emotions, everything about you tells me you know something, or don't know something, and it's driving me crazy. Spit it out already, what's wrong with you?"*

"We will talk later. We are here."

Convenient.

I refuse to look at him. I focus on where we are and everyone around us. A dense growth of winged sumacs looms in front of us. The thin, green leaves are shriveled and limp, but still provide hearty coverage and will protect us from being seen or getting wet—not that I've ever witnessed rain here. With our hands still connected, Cadman leads us inside and around the sparsely located branches. Once everyone is under the canopy, I sense the soldiers relaxing, feel their need to collapse.

"You may let go. Sit down and rest," Arland says, holding firm onto my hand.

As the soldiers and children drop their connections and take seats on the ground, the golden sprites fly away, returning to the earth from which they came.

"Once Ogilvie and Gavin return, we will reset the spell around us, eat, then sleep for three hours."

Complaints and angry scowls geared toward Arland fill our hiding spot. He remains unyielding, standing still, breathing even, as though their outburst doesn't bother him at all.

My mom stands. She squares her shoulders and holds her head high. "Calm down."

The authority with which she speaks mirrors that of Arland's. While the magical connection is broken, his agitation from her interruption rolls into me, making me take a step back. He's led these people for ten years; her help is unwarranted and unwelcome. For a glimmer of a moment, he narrows his eyes, then settles himself, taking a deep breath.

"I am afraid we need to continue moving until we arrive at Willow Falls. There is no telling if we left a trail, or if the spell covered any of our scents. A few hours should be sufficient to rest your feet. If you wish to survive, this is what you must do. You are all aware of this; tonight is not the first time any of us have been on the move."

A hush overcomes the complainers, taking with it their scowls. Mom sits next to Brit and Keely, never looking away from Arland. I'm not sure why Mom has a sudden need to overrule him, but if I had to guess, it's all a part of her overall plan.

"Wait outside for Ogilvie and Gavin with me?" he whispers.

"Okay. Will we talk?"

He purses his lips and furrows his brow, but nods.

I feel the soldiers' eyes on us, on our connected hands, on the hope we bring. Maybe we're still connected somehow, or I'm making it up in my head, but I'm glad to get away.

Besides, Arland has some explaining to do.

He pushes an overhang of leaves from our way then allows me to pass through the exit first.

"It is very dark here, Arland," I say as a way of breaking the tension. It's dark everywhere.

He lets the weeping branches fall back into place, clenches his left hand into a fist, then opens to reveal a small blue flame. The act is so simple, so normal, I almost laugh, but instead, I mimic his action with my right hand.

We carry matching fires through the dark to a nearby pine then sit on a pile of rust-red, dry needles and rest our backs on the trunk. I lay my head on his shoulder, irritated by my concerns, but somehow eased by his comfort.

Holding his left hand in front of him, he turns it over a few times, as if inspecting the quality of his magic, then puts it up to my right hand and laces his fingers with mine. Flames rush up our arms. "A few days ago, you could only burn with fire during battles, now you have learned to create light in your hand, hide large groups of people, connect with your sister—Kate, you are unbelievably powerful."

His compliments are a distraction. "What are you hiding?"

A long sigh fills the empty, dark forest with so much noise; I fear any daemon could find us. "I am not hiding anything but my concerns of the unknown, Kate. Your mother said herself my father did not share my entire prophecy with me. Your dreams have all predicted my death; your memories of those deaths—when I saw them in your head—were like torture to me. Seeing you broken, watching you allow yourself to be killed or wish death upon yourself—I do not want you to do any of those things if death truly is my future."

My breath catches in my chest, tight and constricting. I sit up then turn to face him, look into the beautiful emeralds I've loved even before seeing them in real life. The doubt I didn't understand before is there now. He doubts he's going to live, doubts he's going to be there for me, doubts our marriage will ever take place . . . he doubts *everything*. "You will not die, Arland. You said so yourself. I need you to believe in that. I have heard *everyone dies* so much since I've been here, but without you, I have no magic and these people have no Light—that much of your prophecy we understand. So, you will not die, Arland. Do *you* understand me?"

His eyes meet mine then look me over in such an intimate way I feel the need to check if people are watching. "Your confidence has increased, too."

Arland is wrong; it's not confidence but my will to live, to love, and to survive which makes me say these things. I shake my head. "There was a time in my life where I was sure of everything, but those times are long gone. Now, the only things I am sure of are the only things keeping me going. Does that make sense?"

He smiles. "As I said, your confidence has increased."

I nudge his shoulder. "You are impossible."

"*Me?* You refuse to allow me to pay a compliment when one is deserved. You know you are supposed to talk like us, yet when you become angry, you talk like your normal, beautiful self. Need I go on?" A smile lights his eyes.

"I don't feel more confident, but I guess I am. At least I'm not begging the magic and the gods for help. And I don't feel the need to talk *properly* while alone with you," I say with the urge to stick out my tongue.

He tugs my arm, and I give in, nestling into him again. "We were not alone when you decided to be angry about hearing the others' thoughts. You said Perth was enjoying your outburst at me, but I think Perth enjoys a good argument no matter who is involved."

I startle, but Arland holds me to him, forcing me to stay calm. "I didn't realize I wasn't speaking like . . . like whatever it is I'm supposed to. Like an Encardian, like everyone else."

He runs his fingers through my hair and down my arm. Chills course over my skin. "I know, but there will be no second chances at Willow Falls."

A crack of a dry branch snaps behind us. We jump to our feet and draw our weapons, flames covering us.

160

"Hey"—Brit shouts, holding up one hand in surrender while the other grips a torch—"it's just me. No need to go stabbing, or shooting anything with an arrow."

I slide my sword through the loop on my belt. "Maybe you should announce yourself next time. And where'd you get that torch?"

"I literally just stepped out from under the tree, but I'll be sure to shout so everything we're hiding from can find us before we're hidden by magic. And you can relax; I'm not a shifter. Go on. Check me out. Do whatever it is you do." She swirls the torch around in the air, surely drawing more attention to us.

"Cadman showed me how to make it, then he lit it for me because I don't have a natural knack for magic like you."

Not being able to trust anyone kills me, especially not being able to trust my sister. I close my eyes.

Reveal her true form.

There are no pulsing black bands of shifter. No threat. Just the inside of my eyelids.

"I'm glad you don't trust me. You're learning. After what happened, you shouldn't trust anyone."

Opening my eyes, I see the serious look on her face and relax. "Is everything okay? Why did you come out?"

Brit all but closes the large gap between us. "Perth asked if I'd talked to you about keeping secrets yet. When I told him no, he said I should because we'll probably not have another opportunity before Willow Falls."

She bats her lashes over her wide, expectant eyes. "So, you two ready?"

Arland doesn't think she's as good at hiding things as she believes herself to be, but she is our only instructor. He opens his mouth—

"We're ready, but first, what secrets have you kept hidden?"

"If I tell you, they won't be secrets anymore. Let's just say you'll never guess and leave it at that?"

Is she playing a game of her own now? "Brit, I—"

"Kate, whatever her secret is, it is clear she is not willing to divulge." Arland points to the tree. "Shall we sit?"

Brit pushes past us then takes our seat. She rests her back on the sap covered trunk. I don't understand why, but she's making me wish she'd go away.

The light from my glowing body glistens on her face, changing her green eyes to a warm shade of aquamarine.

She points her finger at me. "See that look right there, Kate. I know my attitude drives you crazy. The slight lift of your eyebrow does you in. You can't let your emotions show."

Great. So now Mom and Brit are telling me to control my emotions while Griandor tells me to let them free. "If you are going to tell me—"

"Whatever you're thinking just stop. What I'm going to tell you is this: every time you see Arland, I want you to picture something you hate. Think of Perth."

"Brit, he's not—"

"Then think of his dad, or the bad guy, or Brad—"

I march toward her, hands propped on my hips. She's really driving a wedge into my side. "Brad wasn't a bad guy, Brit."

She rolls her eyes, but I see something else there too. Confusion? Excitement? I don't know what it is; she's impossible to read right now.

"Don't tell me you still believe in him? Poison or no poison, not only did he punch Mark Evans, he punched *you* and spit in your face, and he's d-dead." The way she stumbles over the word dead . . . maybe Arland is right, she can't hide anything any better than us. Whatever Brad—or the poison controlled Brad—did to me, she must have a lot more good memories of him like I do. They were friends, too.

"I don't think he's entirely dead, Brit. He's still in there, and if . . . no, when we win this war, Griandor promised to restore Brad's life, heal his heart, and return him home."

Tears fill my sister's eyes, and she wipes them away with her tunic sleeve. I've seen Brit upset before—the worst was when she arrived here—but not like this. She doesn't cry.

"What do you mean he's still in there? Kate, he *hit* you. How is it possible you still see good in him?" she asks, hands flying out, eyes full of accusation.

Will Flanna react this way, too? I hope not. I don't understand why Brit is fighting against Brad so hard. I take a deep breath and squeeze Arland's hand for support—he hasn't heard everything I'm about to say either. "You cannot say anything to *anyone*. Including Mom. Do you understand? This is all I have."

She nods.

"When everyone was taken, Griandor visited me, but before that, his brother visited me in Brad's body. I don't doubt Brad felt betrayed when he woke up and found me and Arland together"—and he had every right to—"but his anger wasn't actually *his*. Dughbal tried—"

"*Dughbal?*" Arland asks, guarding tone.

Casting a sideways glance, I see his arched eyebrow. He's waiting for an explanation. "Yes, Arland, Dughbal. Do you know of him?"

A blank stare. "No. I have never heard of him."

"I don't understand. You knew of Griandor and his sister Gramhara, but not their brother Dughbal?"

He rubs his chin. "No, but please, go on."

I look away from Arland, back to Brit. "Well, Griandor told me his brother helped wage a war so powerful it destroyed the gods' favorite world of Elysia."

"So it *was* destroyed." Arland sighs.

"Yes." I nod. "Dughbal fights for the same thing as Perth's father. Power. The gods shift control over the worlds, to maintain balance, but Dughbal was unwilling to give up control of Elysia, and his refusal started a war."

He leans forward, much more interested in this conversation than my sister. "With Elysia gone, why does Dughbal still fight?"

"Well, when that world was destroyed, the gods vowed never to fight each other again. Griandor said it was peaceful for a long time, but his brother got bored and caused a lot of issues. Their father punished Dughbal by sending him to live amongst men. Unfortunately, he was able to convince the daemons to follow him, and he wanted to fight here because Encardia was second best only to Elysia. And since no one used old magic anymore . . . ."

"But the gods do not fight—why does Dughbal not leave?" Arland asks.

"He's hoped to pull them into the battle for years, but instead of fighting him they use me. Griandor and Gramhara picked me for— well that doesn't matter—they picked me, and I have to kill Dughbal."

Arland tenses, squeezing my hand as if he's gripping the hand of an enemy. "Kate, you just told us Dughbal is a god. How does Griandor expect you to kill a god?"

I cringe, and he quickly relaxes his hold on me. "Their father took Dughbal's immortality from him, but he is unaware of this. However, the more Draíochtans killed by daemons, the more power Dughbal gains. We have to kill him . . . no, I have to kill him."

Brit nudges my shoulder, reminding me of her presence. "This history lesson is great and all, but I don't see what it has to do with Brad."

I've never said it before. I'm not even sure the realization was there until now. *I have to kill my best friend.* Taking Brit's hand in mine, I pray she doesn't freak out about what I'm going to tell her.

"Dughbal is Brad," I say, remembering the feeling of Dughbal's snake-like tongue flicking against my cheek. "I have to kill Brad."

The world around me fades away. I have a vague awareness of Arland's hand in mine, but I could be a million miles away from him. *Will I have the courage to drive my sword through Brad?* Sure, it may not be Brad, but I saw the struggle in his eyes when Dughbal visited me. I know Brad is in there, and I imagine driving a sword through his chest will not only hurt him, it will kill him.

Brit jerks my arm nearly out of its socket. "Kate? Kate, where'd you go?"

"Huh?"

"I'm more than a little confused. You say Brad isn't bad, then you say he's Dughbal and you have to kill him. Explain?"

Memories of the coscarthas circling Brad's body, jumping on him and ripping open his flesh with their long claws, surface and make me cringe. I wish I could go back in time and take it all away. "P-poison. The poison, no, before that. When Brad was lost in the forest . . . remember I told you Darkness—or Dughbal—tried to get to him, but Mom took care of it? Well, Griandor said Brad was strong, and because of that, Dughbal wasn't able to taint him. When we came to Encardia, I'm sure the coscarthas wanted to kill Brad, but maybe their poison doesn't work the same way on regular humans. While Brad was in his coma, Dughbal was able to taint him through the power of the poison. When Brad woke up, it was the tainted Brad who punched me, who spit in my face."

"W . . . what about Mark Evans?" Brit is reaching for the same reasons to remain upset with Brad that I did.

"Griandor said Mark Evans had bad intentions for me, and Brad knew it. Apparently Mark got what he deserved."

She squeezes my fingers. "So, you have to kill Brad, but this Griandor will bring him back to life?"

"Yes."

Brit sits up on her knees. Her strained smile sends tears racing down her pale cheeks. "And you love Arland?"

"Um, Brit?"

"I believe I know your secret now, Brit," Arland says with an even tone.

She looks at him, then me. My sister hides her face with her hands, and her body trembles, sobs silencing her words.

I look between them. I'm not sure I follow. "Brit?"

"Kate, can you not see? Brit loves Brad."

I laugh at Arland. "No she doesn't. She was dating Taylor Evans. Never once did she say she liked Brad."

I pry back her fingers, but she pulls away. "Brit?"

Without lifting her head, she cries even louder. "It's true, Kate."

Finding my way to my feet, I ball my fists at my sides. She pretended this would be a happy conversation, that she could help me. But all she's done is add more hurt. "Why wouldn't you tell me? And if you liked him so much, why didn't you start hating him when you found out he punched Mark? Why were you dating Mark's brother? I have so many 'whys' for you it's not even funny. *You* were my best friend, the only one who never hid anything from me. Now you aren't any better than Mom, or Brad for that matter."

The woods are too crowded. Our hiding spot is too full of watchful eyes that aren't supposed to see me cry. I want to scream. I want to run away. Arland and Brit look at me with different expressions of equal parts shock, hurt, confusion and other things I'm not even going to try to understand.

I will find the river and look for the others, and I will find it fast. No second glances will be spared in my sister's direction. Aside from Arland, and maybe even Gary, everyone has lied to me. I thought I could trust Brit, thought she shared everything with me. No wonder she gets along with Mom so well. They are exactly alike.

I'm halfway down the hill, sliding on the dead leaves matching the rest of this dead world. I slip, arms flailing at my sides, but regain control then return to marching away from Brit.

Arland runs behind me, begging me to stop, but I don't, and I won't.

"Kate, stop." He catches up to me and grabs onto my shoulders, putting an end to my escape. "You have to go back up. We have just left them defenseless."

Guilt as well as anger, frustration, and self-pity fill me now. Gone are the days where Kate used to worry about Kate. Now I'm responsible for an army, for children, for my love—and it's only going to get worse. "She lied to me. She was the only one who hadn't, and now . . . ." A lump forms in my throat.

"Are you upset with her because she lied, or are you upset with her because Brad is the object of her affection?"

"What's *that* supposed to mean?" I push his hand from my shoulder then climb back up the hill. I have to protect the soldiers and children.

Little good my abandoning does, he catches back up to me then takes my hand.

Arland pulls me into him and holds my gaze. "Kate, he is someone you loved. I cannot imagine spending all the years you did with him and you not having a deeper connection than you admit to. Search your feelings. Did you never, not once, feel there might be something more with him?"

I want to yell out *no, why are you jealous*, but I don't. Arland is right. Although I know my relationship with Brad is nowhere near as strong as mine with Arland, there was a time I thought there might be more. I was so comfortable in the tent with Brad, so taken aback by him when he stepped into the water outside the portal. I do love Brad. I love Arland more, but there is love for Brad. A love that could lead to something more if I ever explored it further. The spark wasn't there when we kissed—at least not for me—but we are two compatible people . . . if we tried, I'm sure our friendship could catch fire.

Leaning my head into Arland's chest, I sigh. "Once."

"'Once' being your way of admitting you felt something more for him?" Arland wraps his arms around me then rests his hands on the small of my back.

"Yes, Arland. Once I felt something more for him. Right before we came to Encardia. In the swimming hole, and then immediately after, in the tent. He held me in his arms when I was cold. I felt something . . . comfort or safe or at home . . . but it doesn't matter because as soon as he kissed me, I knew I didn't love him the same way."

He pulls away, keeps his left arm around my shoulder then starts forward, back up the hill. "So are you upset with Brit because you feel she is taking him away or because she never shared it with you?"

"Because she never shared it. It would be ridiculous for me to say because she is taking Brad away. I love you and want to be with you."

"I am not asking because I doubt your love for me, but I believe you may love us both, but for very different reasons."

"Trust me. The only thing I'm mad about is being lied to. Think about everyone who's lied to me. Go ahead: my mom, Brit, and even Brad."

He glances at me. "I know."

"To tell you the truth, I always thought Brad and Brit would make an excellent couple. Usually they'd talk each other's heads off when I fell asleep, or they'd share drinking stories, or . . . but none of it matters because he loved me and Brit—"

"Has had to endure this lie, knowing how much he loved you, how much you did not reciprocate his love, and how much she wanted to be with him."

"I guess I came across like a jerk, huh?" I stare into his knowing eyes.

"Considering all the lies you have been told, no, but your sister has her reasons for withholding this secret. What good would it have done her to tell you? You would have mentioned it to Brad, and what would he have done?"

I suck in a sharp breath. "He told me he wanted to marry me. Before Shay put him in the coma, Brad said he knew from the moment he met me he wanted to be with me forever. It's not fair for either of them."

"When we win this war, Griandor will heal his heart and then maybe there will be a chance for Brad and Brit," Arland says. "Would you like to speak to your sister alone?"

Looking up, I see Brit sitting by the tree, arms crossed over her chest. She leans her head back, eyes closed. "No. She's an expert at hiding things, and we need her advice."

CHAPTER FIFTEEN

My sister's advice for hiding things is ridiculous, but considering how well it's worked for her, I have no other choice but to take it. From now on, anytime I look at Arland, I'm supposed to think of Perth or Dughbal or anything that generally displeases me.

Knowing her secret explains all the sour faces she's given Brad over the years. It also explains why he used to ask me if he smelled bad when we were preteens. I used to think he was self-conscious about puberty, but now I understand he was noticing Brit. I don't want to be mad at her about who she loves, but there's a significant part of me still crushed by her inability to trust *me*.

"So I'm gonna go back *inside* and talk to Mom now." Brit doesn't move away; she looks down and kicks a patch of pine needles over with her boot.

"Is everything okay?" I ask.

She raises her head, but she doesn't meet my eyes. "No. I'm sorry I never told you. I just thought one day you'd wake up and see how wonderful he is and want to be with him. And I guess . . . I guess I was just scared I'd get my heart broken, or I'd ruin your life or—"

I wrap my arms around her before she can apologize for anything else.

She squeezes back, nearly expelling all the air in my chest.

"Brit, if I'd known you cared for him so much, I wouldn't have stood in the way," I say after refilling my lungs with the dank, rotten air. "I do realize how wonderful he is. I love him dearly. Life wouldn't have been so much fun if Brad wasn't around, but you both deserve to be happy. I can't provide that happiness for either of you."

Brit hides her face on my shoulder. "You're wrong, Kate. You can provide happiness for Brad. You are the very thing that makes his world spin."

I step back, staring at her swollen face, her broken expression. "If I made his world spin, I'd be with him, and that's not going to happen. You may have been right when you said he was obsessed with me. Not stalker obsession, but unwilling to see the truth that there is no future between us. I hope once he does see that, he'll be open to your feelings."

She looks at Arland then to me. "I hope so, too, because I want what you two have."

I hold her anguish filled gaze. "One day you will have it because Griandor will bring Brad back, then he can be all yours."

Brit bites her quivering lower lip, then turns and heads toward the canopy of sumac.

Something festers in me as she walks away—something dangerously close to panic. My hands shake, and I wipe them on my pants. "Just remember, don't say anything."

She stops but doesn't turn around.

"I won't." Her words are soft-spoken, an unusual tone for my witty sister.

Brit told me she wouldn't say anything about Dughbal, and now I'm telling my sister I don't trust her. And I don't. I'm sure my request hurt, maybe even broke, her ego. Forgiveness is something I've already given her, but I cannot forget she kept a secret from me for so many years while I told her so much about myself. She knew my deepest secrets, my love for someone I dreamed of, my every fear, and yet she couldn't tell me hers.

Arland takes my hand, lacing his warm fingers with mine, leans down then places a gentle kiss on top of my head. "You no longer trust her?"

His eyes, they radiate with knowledge and questions all at the same time. "Yes . . . no . . . I don't know. Of course I love her and she's my sister, but Arland, she lied to me. I understand why she did it, and maybe I would have done it, but she knew everything about me."

He shakes his head. "She omitted more so than lied."

I step away from him. "Are you defending her?"

"In a way, yes."

I ignore the smile and the you-are-acting-childish look on his face so I can scold him. "How could you possibly defend lying or omitting or whatever you want to call it?"

"What good would it have done for her to tell you? You would have tried to pair the two of them together—to their dismay. Brad would have felt awkward because he was there for you, and Brit would have lost the ability to remain casual with him. Even if you had not made an attempt to pair them, you would have known her feelings and, therefore, *you* would have felt awkward when Brad made attempts—"

I clench my hands at my sides. "It wasn't like that. He only ever made an attempt once."

"Katriona," he says, pleading in his voice, "I took his memories from him; not all of them were tainted. You may not be aware of the other attempts, but he loved you for a very long time. There must have been hints or clues or affections shared between the two of you he never shared with any other."

Arland insinuates I'm naïve. Instead of the normal calming affect he has on me, I'm furious. "We were just friends. Or, I was just his friend. We never did anything until we came here."

Arland steps toward me, eyes locked with mine, making me want to run away or smack him for pushing my emotions, but I fight the urge. I love him and don't want to argue, don't want to raise my voice, don't want Brad of all people to come between me and Arland.

He takes my hands then closes the space between us. "So Brad never held your hand?" Arland asks, dragging his thumb across my palm.

"Never allowed you to rest your head on him? Never touched your hair? Never hugged you or held a door open for you?"

"No." Knowledge that I'm lying hits me with the weight of a wrecking ball slamming into a house. I've been lying to myself since I found out Brad loved me . . . no, before that. I knew on our trip, from the moment I rested my head over his heart and heard the rapid thuds of *his* lies. But the friendship we shared was so genuine, so pure, so perfect—or so I thought. Instead of being my best friend, he made me look like a fool, and I let him. Everyone knew . . . even Gary.

Tears blind me, but there's nothing I need to see. I'm right where I need to be, in Arland's arms, head resting on *his* chest—not Brad's or Perth's or somewhere it doesn't belong. I close my blurry eyes and listen to Arland breathe. Allow him to soothe me. He's like a healthy dose of medicine, taking away all my frustrations with just a touch.

He rubs my back then pushes hair from my face, tucking the tangled locks behind my ear. "Why do you cry?"

"I was so blind. I mean, when we first got here, I questioned myself. Asked myself why I was blind, but I just chalked it up to his affections not being obvious. B-but they were. We took almost every class together. He held my hand at concerts, played with my hair when I was stressed, hugged me every time I saw him. I'm so heartless, Arland. I let Brad treat me like a queen and never . . . . What if . . . what if it really was Brad who punched me? He had every right due to the kiss and him professing his feelings for me and me moving on, but what if *he* really hit me for everything I've put him through over the years?"

"Stop. I did not ask you to think about this because I wanted to see you upset. I was trying to help put you in your sister's shoes, and yet I have failed. Miserably I might add." Arland chuckles, shaking his head, then takes me by the shoulders.

"Listen to me, Brad did not hit you. Griandor told you that himself. And if a person is not honest with you, how can they expect you to reciprocate their affections? Think, Katriona, when I wanted you to know how I felt, what did I do?"

"You told me—and you kissed me." *And it was unbelievable, and you nearly died for it.*

"Yes, I told you, and you were given the opportunity to share your feelings. However, Brad waited until he thought death was upon the two of you. It was unfair and put you in a position to make a decision you clearly were not prepared to make."

When Arland puts it that way, my actions don't seem nearly as awful. "But—"

"There is nothing you should feel guilty about. Promise me not to stew over him again?"

"Okay." I bite my lip, but I'm not convincing anyone.

Crossing his arms over his chest, Arland narrows his eyes. "Katriona, promise you will let him go. We will save his life, then you will be able to make any choice you desire for your future. And while I am asking you to promise things . . . forgive your sister. She needs you, and you need her. Remember how lonely you were without her?"

"I have already made my choice for my future."

Arland smiles. "Then you have nothing to worry about where Brad is concerned."

"And I have forgiven my sister, but forgetting . . . . "

"She lived in the exact same position I am about to find myself in at Willow Falls. However, she has had to live the lie many years while I will only have to suffer for a short time."

"That's why you support her? Because you will have to go through what she has?"

"Her situation was much more difficult than what mine will be." Arland's smile fades.

"I am at least aware of your feelings and know when you make strange faces at me, it will really be because you love me. Brit did not have her feelings reciprocated, and she watched him adore you when she knew you did not feel the same while *she did*. Put yourself in her shoes, Katriona."

"I'll try. I promise to try. I just"—I glance in the direction of the hideout—"I've never been very good at giving people second chances."

Touching my jaw with his fingertips as though I'm a delicate flower, he turns my head toward him. "Then you need to work on that. You seem to be doing a fine job trusting Perth. Did you not say he tried to kill you when you first met?"

"He never lied to me though."

Arland grazes the back of his fingers across my cheek, looking into my soul with his knowing eyes. "He was never honest with you either. He knew who you were from the moment you met, yet you are telling all of us to trust him."

"You're right."

"I know." Arland pulls me against him and laughs. "Now, we need rest and food. I am surprised Ogilvie and Gavin have not returned. They are both expert hunters."

He steps back, glancing around.

Arland once told me our eyes adjust to the lack of sunshine, and to some extent mine have, but here, nothing can be seen except for the nearby scraggly, dried up trees. The light provided by the gods' gift to us must have made our vision weak again.

"I'm sure they're just having trouble finding food to catch. Did you notice all the dead animals on the way here?"

"I did." Arland takes another look around.

"I am concerned without food, trips away from bases will become too difficult for anyone to endure. This war must end soon. We should go back under the tree. We can wait for Ogilvie and Gavin there." Pulling me toward the sumac at the pace of a sprinter, he doesn't wait for me to respond.

Fearing the worst, I glance over my shoulder but see nothing. "Are you okay?" This question is beginning to give me déjà vu. I've asked so many others if they're okay. At some point, I know someone will tell me no. I wonder who that will be.

"I am fine. Concerned for everyone's safety, but *I* am fine." Arland's voice carries a hard edge, and I gather he's more than slightly concerned for everyone.

We've been out here for at least an hour without signs of Ogilvie or Gavin. The forest has been quiet with no noticeable noises—other than when my sister snapped the twig under her foot—so we cannot be sure whether the others *are* okay or not. Plus, we have hungry and tired soldiers and children with us, and the horses are missing.

My concerns have come full circle.

Thoughts of sitting under the sumac send a tingling of guilt through my chest. How can we sit and rest while others may be in danger? How can we talk of food while the animals are missing?

I stop in my tracks, and Arland nearly makes me topple forward, pulling me with his strength and speed.

He turns around, eyebrows pinching together, then rights my unstable self. "Why have you stopped?"

"We can't go in there."

He flashes a concerned glance in the direction of the shrubs. "Why not?"

"It's been at least an hour. Why aren't they back? And where are the horses? The others should rest, but you and I need to find Ogilvie and Gavin and the horses."

"I do not like this," he says, shaking his head. "We cannot leave the soldiers here alone, not without setting protections. But look at them"—Arland points toward the hideout—"they are all asleep. Three hours are not enough rest for the distance we have walked today, and certainly not without food."

Some soldiers lie sprawled out on the ground, snores erupt from their massive chests. Children rest their heads on Mom, Flanna, Brit, and Shay. While the four women prop themselves up with branches and trunks, their faces are tight, revealing discomfort.

"We can set the protection around them, then we'll come back after we find the others."

Arland looks me over as if he's my doctor and I'm his dying patient. "You are tired, as well. Your mind dwelled on images of food and beds on the trip here. We can set the protections around them together, but I will go alone to find Ogilvie, Gavin, and the animals."

"No. I won't let you go alone."

"Be reasonable. I can handle myself and know this forest well. I would feel a lot more comfortable if you would allow yourself to rest."

"And I would feel a lot more comfortable if you allow me to come with you—"

"Sir?" The faint call makes Arland flinch and sets him on alert.

Narrowing his eyes, he looks around. "Did you hear that?"

"Yes," I whisper, listening for another sign of the others.

"Sir?" The voice is louder, but the origination remains indiscernible.

Arland stares at something behind me then puts his finger over his lips.

Pins and needles poke at my skin, making my movements stiff and slow. Turning my head, I look over my shoulder and receive another shock.

"*Mirain.*"

Taking a couple steps forward, she whinnies, then Bowen and Euraid appear behind her. All the animals have cuts covering their bodies, are caked in mud, and have vines tangled around their legs.

Holding out my hand, I move forward. "How do you think they found us?"

Arland grabs me by the shoulder and pulls me away. "Check for signs of daemons."

"You think she's a shifter?"

He puts his arm in front of me then pushes me back. "I do not know, just check them."

Closing my eyes, I see nothing. "They aren't shifters."

"Thank the gods." He drops his arm then lets me pass.

"Sir?" The voice calls louder, coming from behind the horses.

"Stay here." Arland rushes down the hill and disappears into the shadows, leaving me alone to care for the animals and protect the soldiers.

"How'd you find us?" I ask, leading the horses to the pine where Arland and I sat before.

Mirain snorts.

I'm sure of two things: she can understand me, and I cannot understand her. Tying Bowen and Euraid to the tree, I glance over my gift from Griandor and her lack of reins. "You going to be a good girl and stay here?"

She bobs her head then moves closer to the tree.

"Thank you. I'm going to go wait for Arland." I rub their foreheads, then leave the animals to rest.

"*Kate.*" The familiar and unwelcome voice causes me to pause in front of the sumac, feet afraid to move forward, instinct telling me not to run, stomach turning in knots.

"So you recognize me still, huh?" Brad's tone is so cold, so not Brad.

Swallowing hard, I close my eyes. *He is just an apparition. He cannot hurt me.*

"Oh I can hurt you. I know where you are, where you all are. Your precious lover is out there chasing daemons he believes to be his soldiers, but his soldiers are clueless there is anything wrong. Those fools are still trying to catch dinner. The animals are dying, Katriona Wilde. The soldiers will not catch anything for days—if that. Who knew Griandor's creatures needed light to live?" A maniacal laugh resounds in my ears.

My lower lip quivers much like Brit's did when we spoke of Brad earlier, but our reasons are much different. I refuse to open my eyes to see my friend, to see the boy my sister loves, to see the struggle I know will be in *his* eyes.

"Oh, Katriona, I assure you he is in here. He fights so very hard to save you. The boy loves you. He is even aware of your love for the

Draíochtan, but cares not of this betrayal. All he desires is a simple touch of your repulsive skin, a mere greeting with your lips."

Shaking, I clench my eyes tighter, try to think of anything but what's happening around me. The trembles move into my chest, down my thighs, into my knees. I am weak.

"Yes, dear, you are very weak." An ice-cold finger trails my cheek, pulling warm tears out behind the touch I know so well.

"You should feel how he calls for you. I am almost intoxicated by what this makes him scream on the inside. Delightful really."

Brad. I cannot believe this is happening to him. He doesn't deserve the pain, doesn't deserve to be forced to fight against someone he loves with everything in him. Dughbal is so cruel, so heartless, so senseless. Why does he punish an innocent person? Boredom? Ignorance?

With balled fists and courage derived from somewhere deep inside, I face the god who seeks to destroy all. His wicked smile, stretched halfway up my best friend's face, melts all my resolve. I see Brad, the tension in his blue eyes. Dughbal may have Brad's body, but the fight has not been won. He blinks over and over, paces toward the trees, then back to me.

"Brad?" My voice comes out like a whimper. I don't know why I call to him. I'm not sure what good it'll do, but I have to know he's there.

His pacing comes to an abrupt standstill, hands straight by his sides.

"Kate?" He slowly shifts his gaze from the ground to me. Brad has little control.

"Fight him, Brad. Fight him with everything in you. Don't let him win. Don't let him take you away. You are my best friend, and I love you and want you back here. With me, with Brit, with *family*. Fight him for your dad. Just fight."

He runs to me, places both his frozen hands on my face, squeezes my cheeks. His eyes are filled with fear and intensity—Brad is in there, but not like I've ever seen him before. "Kate, what's happening to me? Where am I? Wh—No. No, you will not speak to her, human."

"*Kate*," Arland shouts from behind us.

Dughbal looks over my shoulder, and with a *snap*, he disappears.

Falling to my knees, I clutch my stomach. My hope, my heart, my resolve for the Brad situation gone.

Arland grabs my arm then lifts me to my feet. "He is gone now. Did he hurt you?"

Yes, he took away my sound mind. "No, but Brad is still in there; I talked to him. He doesn't know what's going on. He's scared and confused and—"

"Sir, if Darkness was here, should we not move?"

Arland holds up his hand.

A glance behind him reveals Ogilvie and Gavin standing with their weapons drawn, casting fearful looks into the surrounding trees. The men are alive and breathing. Closing my eyes, I see they are also both their true selves. "You found them?"

"Yes, by the water. They did not catch any food."

"I know. Dug-Darkness told me." I look pointedly at the two men behind Arland.

"Katriona and I need a moment," he says.

"Yes, sir," Gavin and Ogilvie reply together.

Arland tightens his hand on my arm, eyes focusing hard on me, and he leads me between the horses. "What happened?"

"Dughbal knows I'm an opponent, and he'll do anything to stop me and steal my magic. With you I'm safe; without you I'm open to attack." I rub my hands together, remembering my conversation with the sun god.

Arland grips my shoulders with a wild, uncontrolled panic in his eyes. "*What?*"

"When I asked Griandor how he and Dughbal came to me the other night—or why they hadn't before—he said there are many other things you protect me from. I'm guessing he meant they can't reach me when you're around. Which explains why I was able to hear

Griandor's voice in my head when I nearly freed you . . . I mean the shifter you in the cave, and why I haven't heard from him since."

"If I keep you safe, why do you believe he was able to reach you tonight?"

"I don't know, but what I do know is that you didn't hear Ogilvie or Gavin calling for you, it was daemons. They probably led you far enough away from me so that he could . . .visit."

"That does not explain why he was still here when I returned. This is bad. Very bad." He clenches his teeth and breaths heavily through his nose. "What do you think will happen if Dughbal pops up in the middle of Willow Falls, Kate?"

Chills creep up my arms. If Dughbal can get to me with Arland a few hundred yards away, what will happen when we have to keep an even greater distance between us?

"I have no idea how I am supposed to protect you when I am not supposed to be around you." He lets go of my shoulders then turns to walk away.

"We need to speak with Perth again."

I run and grab him by the hand, stopping his hasty march toward the sumac. "What could Perth possibly have to help us with our Dughbal problem? The more people I tell, the less power I have."

"While Perth is the last person I want you to tell your secrets to, he may be able to offer me a place on your security."

"My security?"

"Yes, I am willing to stake my life Dufaigh will want round the clock protection for you. You are, after all, going to save this world from Darkness and marry his son. Leaving you with an unlocked door would be foolish." He grins.

"Oh. Well, yes I am going to marry his son and save this world from Darkness. We should talk to Perth; my future husband will definitely wish you to be on my security since you *are* my Coimeádaí and all."

We burst out laughing. Exhaustion, hunger, frustration and everything else has given way to insanity. Nothing we've said is funny. It's downright disturbing, but what else can we do if not laugh at these things? We'd be miserable without humor.

Arland leans over, gripping his stomach, face red, veins throbbing in his temple.

My breath returns to me, and I inhale deeply, then cough out the last of my laughs. "I don't understand any of this, but I think Gavin is right, we should leave."

"She is intelligent, sir. " Gavin runs his fingers through his short brown locks and stares at Ogilvie.

Arland glares at the eavesdropping soldier, then turns on a softer, more concerned look for me. "Katriona, you have not had any rest since your ordeal with the shifter. We will cast the spell around us, speak with Perth, then you can sleep."

"They know we are here and so does *he*. We cannot stay."

Ogilvie rushes forward then places his hand on Arland's shoulder. "Sir? To the right. We are not alone."

Flames burst from Arland's bodies and mine. We turn our heads just in time to see a small group of coscarthas slinking back into the forest, their black, stringy hair swaying as they go.

Arland draws his sword. "We have to move."

CHAPTER SIXTEEN

Arland points at my sword, a silent command for me to draw my weapon, then turns toward the soldiers. "Gavin, wake the others. They are under the cover of the bushes to my right."

"Yes, sir." Gavin pushes through the leaves, shouting all the while at everyone to wake up.

"Could he be any more conspicuous?" Ogilvie asks, staring after his friend.

"Never mind him." Arland shakes his head. "Katriona and I will untie the horses."

"Shall I scout the path to the river?"

"Yes. Do you remember where we passed the coscarthas?"

"*More* coscarthas?" I ask.

They glance at me but ignore my question. Arland hadn't mentioned *passing* coscarthas. We've been resting for a little over an hour. No one has eaten, too many of us have not slept, and already we're on the run again.

"Yes, sir." Ogilvie removes his sword from its sheath, staring at the shiny metal blade with a wild-eyed look.

"We will have to pass them to get back down to the river. If you come upon too many for us to get by, we will need to find another way down; however, if there are only a few, kill them."

"With pleasure." Ogilvie smiles at his weapon like a madman, tips his head in my direction, then trots down the trail.

Arland grabs my hand then leads me to my horse. "I want you to ride Mirain."

"But how will we all stay connected if I'm on her?"

"I am not sure, but how else will we hide her—or the other two for that matter? They will be lost again if we allow them to ride off by themselves."

"So we potentially risk lives either way? We don't ride the horses, they get killed by daemons? If we do ride the horses, we get killed by daemons?"

Mirain nudges my cheek with her warm muzzle.

"What is it, girl? Should I leave you or ride you?"

"Unless her answer comes in the form of a yes or no, I believe you are going to need to trust *me*." I hear his frustration and recognize the meaning of Arland's words. My lesson to everyone has been trust; of all people, I should trust him.

"I'm sorry."

He cups my cheek in his palm. "I have not been strong enough for you since Lann died. Your doubts in my plan are reasonable, but please—"

"Stop, you have been more than strong enough for me, and I do trust you. It's me I don't trust."

Leaning forward, Arland sighs, clasps his hands and offers them to me as a stool.

Staying here and arguing about who's strong and trustworthy and who isn't is not an option, so I climb onto Mirain's bare back, then he mounts Bowen.

She turns, facing the soldiers and children who have left the hideout and gathered around us.

The children rub their eyes, and adults share looks of fatigue.

A nagging sense of responsibility forces me to speak. "We have to move again. There is no food to be caught in the forest—at least not enough to feed all of us—and Darkness and his daemons have found us."

Without direction from me or Arland, the soldiers position the youngest children in a line then take places at the front and back.

"Who will protect us if the two of you ride your horses?" Perth asks, instigating as usual.

Flanna stands in the middle of the crowd; her grief still showing in the bags under her eyes, the lack of smile and the way her shoulders hunch over. My eyes meet hers, begging her to take the lead. She looks from me to Perth, to everyone else, then nods.

Warmth fills me. I smile and pray this helps her recover who she is, her peace, her happiness.

"I will." Flanna steps around Cadman to take his place at the front of the line, tosses her hair over her shoulder, and glares at Perth.

"You should remain at the back, Perth. You are a skilled swordsman; I expect if anything goes wrong, you are capable of handling yourself."

"Sir, I have taken care of three coscarthas," Ogilvie shouts, stepping out of the cover of the trees and underbrush with brown, dried leaves stuck to his tunic. Blood soaks through his pants leg. He knocks the leaves off, slides his sword through the loop on his belt, then looks to Arland.

"Our path is clear to the river."

"Thank you, Ogilvie." He appraises his soldier's leg. "Were you injured by a daemon?"

Ogilvie looks down at his injury. "No, sir. I stumbled over a branch and cut myself with my sword. It was foolish, but I am not in pain."

"You should be more careful next time," Arland says. "Hold the center, between the children."

Ogilvie limps toward my two favorite children then takes each of them by a hand. Anna's face is pale and her eyelids are heavy. She closes her eyes, but Marcus leans forward and inspects the gaping wound on the soldier's leg.

Arland turns his attention away from Ogilvie then rides Bowen along the line; everyone looks up at their Leader as he passes. "Cadman, ride Euraid next to Katriona."

Cadman mounts his horse then rides her next to me, his face pale and sullen.

184

"Everyone stay connected as we did before. Flanna, I want you to walk as close to Mirain and Katriona as possible. Touch them if you can. I will remain at the back of the line. Perth, you should keep your hand on Bowen." Arland stops next to Perth, but looks up at me. "You ready?"

I nod but it's not like I have much of a choice. As much as I hate to think it, I cannot wait to get to Willow Falls. Food and sleep are at the top of my list.

"Do you remember the path we took to come up here?" Arland asks, his deep, fearless voice making me regret my wish for a quick arrival to Willow Falls. I could go without sleep for months just to spend time with him, to have him talk to me, look at me, smile at me. The drive in his eyes, the intense focus on protecting our people, his overall strength in frightening times—these are some of his most endearing qualities. Ones I'll miss when we have to pretend not to like one another, when we have to lie.

"Yes." My stomach grumbles. Go without sleep, maybe, but not food. I need to eat. We all do.

Please keep us safe.

"Good. Keep your eyes open and on the lookout, follow the path, and do not stop reciting the spell."

Focusing my strength and love into my magic, I unfold the power from inside, embrace it as it flows through and out of me. My body warms, my hunger and exhaustion fade. "Cheilt an maireachtáil leis an dúlra."

Sprites swarm the air around us. They come from all directions, from all plants, from every piece of nature. Green, blue, brown, white—all the beautiful lights of life. Their wings flap so fast near me, vibrations tickle my skin. Humming fill my ears.

Flanna places her hand on my calf, inundating my brain with everyone's connected thoughts. Nudging my heels into Mirain, we take off at a slow pace toward the river. Senses are keen, alerts high, exhaustions forgotten. Sleep is the last thing on anyone's mind.

Low hanging branches snap and fall to the ground with a thud when I move them from my way. Soldiers slip and slide on the hill covered with dried leaves and vines, but no one loses connection. The spell reverberates up and down the line, spoken by small, loud and strong, confident and proud voices alike.

"Cheilt an maireachtáil leis an dúlra," I repeat.

"I have not seen any daemons, Kate. The lack of them concerns me. If Dughbal knows where we are, do you not think he would have more of them out here?" Arland asks through thoughts.

Turning, I get a clear glimpse of him as though he's in the sunlight and we're treading water in my favorite swimming hole on Earth. His face reveals none of what he's thinking. The concern Arland has for these people, the fear we're walking into yet another trap, and worry something will happen to me display themselves as intent focus on the path ahead of us.

"I have no idea what he'd do, but we didn't see any on the way here either. They knew where we were then, too, remember?" I face forward, looking for danger and reciting the spell once more.

"I do. This is different. He was here, Kate. He touched you. He could have killed you—"

"No, he couldn't have killed me. Not yet anyway. Griandor said if Dughbal gets stronger, it would be possible for him to kill me, but tonight and the other night, he was just an apparition."

"An apparition should not be able to touch you, Kate. He had his hands on your face." Arland's frustration rolls through our connection, shaking my insides.

I thread my fingers through Mirain's white mane and squeeze. *"That was Brad . . . at first, but Griandor assured me if Dughbal was not an apparition, he would have killed me."*

I move another branch from my way. Sounds of the rushing river make me radiate with relief. *We made it.* The ground levels out. Everyone's thoughts relax, but we still have a long distance to travel. A left turn leads us north and on our way to Willow Falls.

The only conversation is the continued casting of the spell, but thoughts are excited and bubbly. Anna envisions a bath, Shay a bed, Dunn chicken stew. Ogilvie thinks about—

"Let go of me, Flanna. Now," I say under my breath.

"But—"

"Just do it, *now*," I repeat, this time with a greater sense of urgency.

Flanna drops her hand from my calf, and my connection to everyone's thoughts fades.

I turn Mirain, draw my sword, then trot to the middle of the line. "Everyone stop."

Arland abandons Perth then rides next to me. "Why have you stopped?"

Ignoring Arland, I eye Ogilvie with disgust and point my weapon at his heart. "Let go of their hands and step away, *shifter*."

The line parts and breaks away from him as if he has an infectious disease, but he holds on to Marcus's wrist, tight. The boy struggles to get away, kicking and screaming. A smile grows on the shifter's face, laughter rumbling in his chest. "I am no shifter, Katriona."

"Let him go then." I tip my head toward Marcus.

"Marcus does not mind standing with me, do you boy?" Ogilvie clasps his hand tighter around Marcus's wrist, turning the child's little fingers purple.

He contains a scream in his closed mouth, face puffing. Tears roll down his cheeks. It's obvious he's in pain.

Closing my eyes, I confirm the pulsing black bands snapping around the bright white core of light.

"Is he a shifter?" Arland asks, drawing his sword.

I scowl at the daemon. "He is."

Arland climbs from Bowen then holds the metal blade against the shifter's neck. "Let him go."

"Why should I? You are all about to die. Starting with him seems like a fine idea." The shifter sheds Ogilvie's skin; it falls to the ground and lands in a heap, leaving the true form of the shifter floating in front of us.

"The others have freed me from this pathetic being," it says, sending my attention to what's left of Ogilvie. "They are aware you know what I am, and they are coming for you."

Staring at the lump of clothes, crimson, hair, and a strangely twisted face that used to be Ogilvie, I freeze. Too shocked to react. Too afraid to save Marcus, the soldiers, or anyone for that matter, I swallow back the scream building in my chest, fight back the tears welling in my eyes.

"Kate, that was not Ogilvie. That is not a person at all." Arland directs his thoughts into my mind, but while I'm aware what's on the ground isn't Ogilvie, the resemblance is too similar.

The shifter lurches forward, bands cracking with energy. Mirain rears, kicking her hooves at him on her way down. Shaking my shock, I jump from her back then rush toward Marcus, but he's stuck to the bands of the shifter's body.

Dark, red blood drips from Marcus's arm, and wild screams escape his mouth. Matching high-pitched cries come from a tiny voice buried in the crowd. Without looking, I know it's Anna crying for her brother. I cannot face her; the shame I feel for this, the guilt—I should have known to check Ogilvie when he returned from scouting the path.

Protect him.

The shifter darts back up the hill, dragging Marcus behind.

I rush forward, but Arland grabs my forearm, preventing me from running after the daemon.

Marcus's feet drag through the dirt and leaves; he screams and claws at the shifter but is not strong enough to escape.

"This is not your fault, Katriona. Now, send the magic after him," Arland says, pitch flat . . . empty.

With every fiber of my being, with every ounce of love I can muster, I close my eyes, clench my fists, keep my feet rooted firmly to the ground then force the magic out of me. Instead of shaking from fear, fury rocks my body. Around my feet, sprites crack open the earth; explosions of flames burst from the ground.

The winged creatures fly in front of my face. Pebbles, leaves, water, sticks . . . life itself thrives in the forest, electrifies the air, makes *me* powerful.

"Kill the shifter," I command the magic with a deep, resonating voice. The strength it possesses takes me by surprise, but the sprites respond without hesitation and fly away from the river, forming a straight line, swirling in, out and around the trees. I hold my breath. Hold my hope. My sanity hangs on them finding the boy.

"K-Kate," Anna cries, breaking into my concentration.

Shay and Keagan hold Marcus's sister back, but I kneel then open my arms for her. She sprints to me and almost knocks me over with the force of her hug.

"You have to s-save him." She buries her face in her hands and loses herself to sobs.

"We will, Anna. We will."

Arland pats my shoulder. "Katriona, you need to stand up. *Now.*"

Pain pricks from my heart and spreads to my fingers as fast as fire does. Holding Anna to me in a giant bear hug, I stand, but am not prepared for what I see. Hundreds of daemons encircle us. Hounds, coscarthas, shifters and tairbs. All of them inch closer; all of them carry a different terrifying death threat.

Soldiers pull weapons from their holsters, notch arrows, or create fire in their palms. Preparing for a battle they are all too tired to fight, they form a barrier in front of the youngest children.

Flanna lights her arrow with a flame from her hand then looks to me. "What should we do?"

Griandor, help us. Help me. Give me the strength to fight for these people. Give me the strength to get through this.

Arland takes my right hand in his. "*You already have the strength, Katriona Wilde. Command your army. They wait for your instructions.*"

His thoughts fuel my anger, the rage I have for Dughbal's indifference toward life. Flames spread from Arland and me to Anna.

She leans back, and her gaze bores deeply into my eyes; there is no emotion on her face, no fear, no pain, no sadness, just a blank expression.

"Kill them, Kate." The power of the old magic flows through her, fills her with strength, with anger, and with the will to fight.

Anna glances at the daemons that advance too close to our people, too close to battle. Flanna waits for an answer . . . everyone waits for an answer. I open my mouth, feed the fire into my words, feed the hatred into the sprites swirling around the forest. "Kill them. Release your arrows into them, strike them with your swords, cut them open with your knives. Whatever it takes, burn these daemons. Send them back where they came from."

Arrows zip through the air from my left and right, streams of blue light trailing behind. Some daemons fall and burn under the power of the fire, but others move forward at an alarming pace.

I set my sights on the tairbs first—the fastest—focusing my hostility on them. "Steal back what they have taken. Return the magic to this land. Feed the power to the soldiers."

Sprites create a circle around us, spinning faster and faster until all I see is a flowing band of white light. The daemons stop and stare at the ring of magic, and after exchanging glances with one another and giving what appears to be a moment of consideration, continue forward.

"Now," I shout.

More arrows fly from the soldiers' bows, bouncing off the bristly fur of the hounds, but piercing through the gray, mangled skin of the coscarthas. The tairb's eyes flash red and angry; their hooves propel them forward. Within an inch of the ring of sprites, all the evil beings stop again.

"Kill them," I repeat.

Sprites break from the protective ring and dart into the tairbs, knocking them back then consuming their bodies with flames. Cracks and screams fill the night. Smoke rises from the forest floor.

A familiar and bone chilling hiss rustles the air behind us, blowing leaves by our feet.

Serpents.

"Anna, you have to get down. I will protect you, but you must go stand with the others. Arland and I have to fight, and we need both our hands. Do you understand?"

Her body shakes, and her wails break my resolve. She grips me tighter. The weight of her ten-year-old body pulls hard on my muscles.

"Please, do not make me go. I will help you fight. Please?"

Arland releases my hand, peels Anna's fingers from my back, then transfers her to her feet. Kneeling, he takes her by the shoulders; his hard face softens and he meets her eyes with a look of utter sweetness and sincerity. "Anna, I know you are afraid, but we have to fight. You must go."

Perth runs over to us, dodging a misfired arrow with a quick roll on the ground along the way. "I will take her to the others."

With an empty quiver and sword covered in blood, he comes to rescue a child?

She watches his hand as he reaches for her, then screams and grasps for me. Tears streak through her cherub-like cheeks. "Please, save him."

Her painful plea for her brother cuts me in two. "I will."

"Go. Now. I will cover you," Arland says, returning to his feet.

Perth yanks Anna's hand and rushes her to the others. She disappears inside their protective circle.

"She will be okay, Kate, but you should not have told her we would save Marcus. I fear it may already be too—"

Hissss. The serpent's breath kicks up the wind, carrying with it the pungent smell of death.

Daemons move in closer. Mirain and Bowen are the only calm amongst all this madness. They stand side-by-side in the path. Nothing attacks them; nothing even pays them any attention.

Arland takes my hand and follows my gaze. "The magic protects them. Look." He points at Mirain. "Her coat is glowing whiter than ever; the light surrounds Bowen and Euraid. They are safe. Maybe that is how they made it here without being attacked."

"So they would have been safe . . . ."

"I was wrong again, and I am sorry."

A quick check of his facial expression reveals a split second of pain in his eyes. "Don't blame yourself. You couldn't have known Ogi—"

Arland pushes me to the ground, draws his sword, then stabs it into a coscartha. The leathered-looking beast lands next to me with a thud, his hollow eyes widen, his hot breath rank and sickening. Black seeps from his mouth full of rows and rows of pointy teeth.

Pain radiates through my jaw; a tickling of metallic liquid flows onto my tongue. Wiping my face with my sleeve, I smear my shirt with bright red blood.

"There was no time to warn you." Arland offers me his hand. "Are you okay?"

Fighting the urge to vomit, I take his hand and stand. I wipe more blood from my chin from its unhappy meeting with a rock, then nod. "I am fine."

Hiss.

My hair blows back. My face moistens. I cannot see the serpent, but he is close.

I remember the snake in the caves and how difficult it was to kill him, how much magic it took to cut through his body. *Illuminate that which seeks to destroy us*, I pray, focusing everything I have over my heart.

Sprites rise from the ground and the water, descend from the sky and the tops of trees. Power and magic flow all around and through me, surrounding the group of soldiers, my mom and Brit—more than I've ever conjured before, more than I can handle by myself. I should feel weak by now, should feel the energy drain from my soul, but I don't. Someone is helping me. Someone besides Arland, Flanna, and Cadman. There must be.

Light brightens the black forest like the sun at noon, revealing two serpents standing at least forty feet tall with long fangs dripping with poison and at least another hundred daemons standing in the shadows to our left. They were probably waiting until we thought we'd won, waiting to move in and kill us when our guard was down, but their game has been exposed. I meet eyes with each one, hoping my stare is defiant and fearless, then draw my sword and call to the magic again.

The daemons from the shadows rush forward, tearing through the trees and underbrush, rumbling the ground with their stampede. Turning to our left, we have just enough time to raise our swords.

"We need to split up," Arland says.

"Stay close." I step into the sea of approaching monsters. Alone.

Arland and I stab and slash our way through daemon after daemon. Coscarthas attack first, shrieking and clawing. Three surround me, staring; I release a guttural scream as I use every muscle in my body to strike through the heart of one. Spinning around, I slice the neck of another, then the decaying face of another until they are all dead and burning.

A hound lunges from behind a tree, teeth bared, black fur raised on its haunches. He lands in front of me and takes three steps forward. White foam drips from his mouth. I meet his yellow eyes and see the reflection of the towering serpents behind me. They lower their bodies and circle the soldiers.

We are outnumbered.

Growling, the hound paces in front of me. Four more spring from the bushes to join him. I turn around, watch for any indication of an attack as they walk a perimeter, encompassing me. Their muscles twitch, their teeth shine from the light of magic. Sounds of swords stabbing into hard skin and bones, of arrows zipping through the air, of magic humming as it protects the soldiers—of war—fill my ears.

The smallest of the hounds jumps at me, grazing my arm with its claws as he flies past.

Blood trickles toward my hand. Stinging rushes to my shoulder.

The black beast returns to his feet. The others sniff the air. As if intoxicated by the smell of my blood, they inch closer, growls rumbling louder, and lunge at me at the same time.

I'm frozen. Powerless. Going to die.

"Bhrú," Arland shouts, sending a wave of blue flames from his chest into two of the hounds, but the other two land on me, knocking my sword from my hands.

My defense lies in a pile of leaves too far away for me to grab. All I have is my magic, but the pain searing in my arms and chest makes it impossible to move. Impossible to breathe.

"Kate, you have to get up," Arland yells from the middle of a fight with a tairb, coscartha, and hound.

There is no time to think; the mutts have already bitten me. I don't know if I'll die because of the wounds. But it doesn't matter what their bites will do to me, I cannot sit here and wait for more.

"Get off me." Pushing through the protest in my arms, I thrust each of my palms into the hound's chests.

The daemons burst into flames and whimper as death consumes them.

Jumping to my feet, I grab my sword. Pain and anger swell within me. I fight through the emotions and the horrible throbbing in my arms to evaluate our situation, but my breaths come quick. My vision is unfocused. My heart beats rapidly.

"Kate." Arland's voice is urgent but distant.

I bend over, stare at the ground. Blood drains from my arms, creating pools of red around my feet. My skin is cold, but sweaty—numb, yet full of stabbing sensations. The sword falls from my hand, splashing in the blood.

Sprites swarm around me, rush over my skin, seal the wounds created by the hounds, but the energy of the gods is not enough.

I'm dying.

I try to lift my head to look at Arland—to be loved by his eyes one more time—but I'm paralyzed.

Blood curdling screams of panic and anguish rise behind me. Magic is failing us. I am failing us.

I have no control.

A hand, warm, small and familiar rests on my back. Running along my spine, the touch of my mother sends chills over my skin.

"Katriona Wilde, you will not die. You must fight this. Fight the venom inside you. Use the magic. Call to the gods. This is who you are born to be. This will not be your last fight."

"I can't." Talking is too painful. Must. Stop.

"You can. Now call to the magic. Use what the gods have given you. Be the strong woman I know you to be."

My stomach knots and squeezes. Tears stream down my face. "I . . . I'm dying, Mo . . . Mom."

"Call to the magic, Kate. Let it flow through you. That is all I need."

My heart speeds to the point of one constant beat. I fall to my knees. "Arland . . . ." *My love.* With one last thump, my heart stops.

In its purest form, filling every inch of space as far as I can see is white.

Soft.

Edgeless.

White.

Darkness does not exist on this cloud. I imagine it would be impossible for Dughbal to live here, to breathe here even.

My skin is flawless and radiates with a perfect light pink hue. I inspect the bites. They're gone. I take a deep breath. The pain is also gone.

Standing, I find I'm no longer paralyzed. No longer in the middle of a war. No longer anywhere. This is different from when the shifter took control of me. I had no feeling. No body to connect to. No life. Wherever I am, I'm alive, able to move, to breathe and to walk.

Taking a step forward with my right foot, everything above and to the sides of me fades to black. My name rings shrill in my ears.

"Katriona," another shout from a voice so familiar, so warm it makes my insides burn to be near it.

"Where are you?" I call out.

"Her heart is not beating. *Keagan*, come here. We need you now."

The voices are frantic, high-pitched and demanding, but there is no one here.

I am alone.

"Hello?" I call.

Nothing.

Trees ignited with blue flames pop up on all sides of me. Smells of burned hair, dry and sharp, fill my nostrils. I cover my nose with my hand, try to filter the scent with my skin.

An invisible force strikes my chest, knocking me off balance and expelling the air from my lungs. Gasping, I turn to my side and cough up pockets of smoke. The strange force continues crashing into me. I'm pinned on my back.

Now everything is dark.

Tears run from the sides of my closed eyes. My arm stings. Glancing at it, I see the bite marks reappear. Blood covers my arm, and my pink hue has turned pasty white. I look up; three figures hover over me. They appear far away, but the blurs of peach, red, brown and green grow clearer with each blink of my eyes.

"I believe she has returned," Keagan says.

"Kate, can you hear me?" Arland whispers next to my ear.

"Arland?" My mouth is dry, filled with a bitter taste.

"She is alive." His voice shakes, but I hear his relief hanging in the word *alive*.

"Keep the line strong. Do not let the daemons get any closer. Have the serpents been killed yet?" Arland shouts, further away from my ear.

"Sir, we cannot continue to fight them off with what little weapons we have." Cadman's urgency drills into me. "We are out of arrows. The magic which protected us has faded. Without Ogilvie or—"

"Look out," Arland yells.

Humid air gushes past us. The ground shakes.

War. I'm at war with Darkness. I must lead these people, must fight. Transferring my weight to my elbows, I prop up my back and focus on what I have to do, what I love, and thank the gods I'm still alive.

"What are you doing?" Mom puts her hand between my shoulder blades and lifts my right arm. My weight is too much for one elbow to bear, and she lowers me to the ground.

"You are filled with poison. You were able to call magic before your h-heart stopped, but you were gone, Kate. Let us take care of this. One of the serpents has fallen. It will all be over soon."

She pushes hair from my face, allowing me to see the concern in her eyes. Her look takes me back to when I was a child and I'd broken my arm; Mom said it was her fault I fell off the horse, and she'd cried more than I did when the doctor set the bone.

"Mom, I cannot let them fight without magic. I'm alive. I feel fine." I reach out my hand. "Will you help me up?"

She sighs then pulls me to my feet.

When I glance around and see the predicament we're in, my heart almost stops for a second time.

Everyone has moved to form a circle around me. We're surrounded by daemons. The forest blazes; orange flames lick the trees and burn the plant debris on the ground. Smoke hovers above our heads. Children and adults lie motionless, sprinkled along the landscape like uncovered graves on a hillside.

I look away. Guilt for their lives is on me. I could have protected them, could have saved them. Yet I allowed myself to be killed. Allowed myself to be surrounded. By what? Daemons. *Dogs?*

The gods did not gift me with their powers for me to waste them in such foolish fights. The gods gave me their powers to kill their brother. And I plan to do just that. I'm going to start with every creature here.

Shaking, I ignore the protest of my muscles, ignore the eyes of my mother, ignore the carnage surrounding me and focus on what matters: life. Anna drags my sword. With a weapon too large for her, she attempts to fight a small coscartha. She will not have to fight anymore.

I break through the soldiers and children fighting to protect me, march to Anna, then grab my sword from her small hands. I stand in front of her then stab through the heart of the daemon.

Sprites spring to life, returning from where they hid, and create a protective barrier around every remaining soldier and child's body. Looking up, I watch as they swarm around my head and stare at their cherub smiles as they fly by.

"Kill the serpent, find the boy, power the Draíochtans, and leave the rest of the daemons to us."

With a crack, the sprites return to their earthly forms then fly away from me, back toward the serpent. He lunges forward, snapping his jaws in an attempt to kill Arland and Cadman. They jump to the side, avoiding a bite sure to kill. The beast lowers his neck then slithers closer to Arland.

Spinning in a halo over the beast's head, the magic separates and drives into him, pinning him to the ground.

Arland turns and looks at me. The corner of his mouth twists up, and flames ignite his body.

"Kill him, Arland. Do it now," I shout.

He and Cadman stand on either side of the serpent, raise their swords like axes, then come straight down over its neck. Its head rolls toward the river, then lies motionless while its shiny black body flails around on the ground.

Rising from the dead daemon, the sprites band together then dart into the trees.

Please find Marcus . . . alive.

If Arland wasn't a Leader, if he didn't need to show his strength or prove his ability to control his emotions, I'm sure he'd run to me right now. He kills every creature standing in his way, crossing the distance between us. Coscarthas fall with quick, effortless stabs of his sword. Daggers of fire shoot from his chest, killing hounds mid-air. He knocks tairbs off their hooves; Cadman follows behind and slits their throats. Shifters receive arrows to their pulsing cores from Arland's best man.

Arland is terrifying yet magnificent. His muscles tense. Veins bulge with blood, fueled by what can only be adrenaline. Dirt covers his exposed skin. Beads of sweat run down his cheeks. His sword bears proof of his kills, but his face bares his desire to be near me. Not once has he looked away. Not once have his eyes stopped smiling.

Magic aids his march across the forest.

Nerves weaken me.

Lowering his sword, he leaves no space between us, takes my face in his hand, holds me like he shouldn't while others are around. "You died."

I experience a sudden need to look away from his emerald eyes. The war around us has not stopped. Soldiers fight with everything in them; children do their best not to be killed. "Not exactly. I'm here, aren't I?"

He turns my face, forces me to meet his eyes. "That is not the point. You died, Kate. I have failed you. Repeatedly." Leaning down, he places his lips on mine, but there is reservation in this meeting. Uncertainty. Restraint he's never shown before.

"I love you," I say.

"As I love you." Arland backs away then raises his sword in a defensive position. "Are you able to fight?"

I nod.

"Good. The soldiers killed most of them while you were *gone*, but as you can tell"—he points at the bodies—"most of us have also been killed."

Cringing, I take count of how many are still here and alive. Me, Arland, Brit, Flanna, Mom, Cadman, Tristan, Perth, Anna, Keagan, Keely, Saidear, Dunn, Gavin, Kent, Muriel and Shay: seventeen of us remain. I'm going to be sick.

"We should hold hands and fight the daemons in a line. Share the magic like before . . . like on the cliff. We didn't need weapons then, and we don't need them now." I reach out for Anna then clasp my hand around hers.

"Anna, don't let go of me. Do you understand?" *I will not allow another child to die.*

The instant every man, woman, and child links together, fire explodes from us. Thoughts of survival, of salvation, and of winning fill everyone's heads and hearts. Daemons approach us on all sides, but I don't waste time looking at them. I don't recite spells as many of the others do; I meet the eyes of the creatures longing to kill us and command fire into them.

Magic hits the ground around our feet, knocking leaves, dirt and branches up in a cloud, but instead of rising into the atmosphere like smoke from an atom bomb, the debris launches itself away from us then smacks into the daemons. Wails rise from wounded monsters lying on the forest floor. Following behind the debris, flames consume any life left in our fallen enemies and grow from the feet up on the daemons left standing.

Our power amplifies. Our enemies dwindle. Serpents lie dead to our left, daemons lie dead . . . everywhere. The forest floor is barren, revealing only black dirt.

This battle is almost over.

Arland spares a glance at me then leans next my ear. "They are gone, Kate. You can release the magic."

I shake my head. "No, Marcus isn't here yet."

He tightens his hand around mine. "Do you—?"

"Yes, I do. He will be okay."

Anna looks up at me; she heard what I said. I still hear her thoughts. She's begging the gods for me to be right about her brother. Every part of her cries out for him to be alive.

The power has not stopped swirling around us or burning daemon bodies on the ground. The Light has not given up. I sense the sprites' searching, sense their desperate need to find the boy and bring him to safety, and I sense their excitement when they do.

I look over my left shoulder. White light glows in the forest and grows nearer to us. "He's coming."

Anna fills with joy, sadness, anger, emotions I can't quite name. We watch magic carry the boy in a protective white bubble, like the yolk of an egg. He's asleep or . . . .

Oh no. Please, Griandor, please let him be alive.

The beings lay Marcus on the ground in front of Anna. Magic spreads out under him like a sheet then seeps back into the earth. Everyone gathers round him, still holding hands, still holding their breath, still hoping.

Anna falls to her knees beside him, throws her arms over him, and cries. "Marcus, please be alive. Please be alive. Please be alive."

His face is pasty white. His arms are covered in blood. His clothes are tattered rags. The hair on his head looks black in comparison to the paleness of his face.

"*Heal him . . . .*"

His mouth twitches. He turns his head toward Anna. "Anna?"

She pulls away from him. "Marcus!"

Opening his eyes takes time. Time we don't have. He looks up at me, and his brows furrow, creating wrinkles he's way too young to wear. "You saved me?"

I don't know how to respond. My mouth refuses to move. My feet won't even move.

Arland kneels beside Anna and Marcus then runs a hand across the boy's forehead. "She did, Marcus. Katriona has saved us all"—Arland flashes a smile in my direction, then returns his attention to Marcus—"but we need to continue our journey. You have been through a terrible ordeal; we all have been. However, if we do not leave now, more daemons will likely show up to finish us off. Can you walk?"

"I . . . . Yes."

Anna pulls her brother to his feet.

He moans but covers his mouth and stares at the ground.

Arland watches them, I'm sure admiring the same courage I am, then puts his arm around Marcus. "Do not be ashamed to show pain."

"But you have never shown pain. You broke your nose in a battle with a tairb and showed nothing. I want to be like that. Like you." Marcus tips his head in my direction. "I want to be like both of you."

"You already are," I say, taking up his other side. "Now, you and Anna should wait here while we bury—"

"We must leave at once, Katriona." Arland does not stop moving forward. "We have thirty miles to travel yet. We are weak, wounded, tired and hungry. There is no time to bury the fallen. We must make peace along our journey."

Anna and Marcus watch us with what can only be expectant eyes. Wide and wet, red and swollen. For their sakes, I wish we could have a funeral, but at the same time, staying here could risk their lives again.

All eighteen remaining adults and children take hands then trudge forward through the scorched underbrush; the horses follow behind. Thirty miles is a long way, but we have to make it, and no matter what happens when we get there, I don't believe I'll ever forget what happened here.

CHAPTER SEVENTEEN

My feet ache as if I've been walking around a mall all day in a pair of high heels. I did that once. Some part-time job placed me outside a sporting goods store, asking people if they'd like to participate in a survey. Two days were all it took for me to realize retail was not for me. And right now, I realize these leather boots aren't for me either. What I wouldn't give for a pair of real hiking shoes. If there were a store here, I'd consider robbing it so I could outfit everyone with a pair.

I should be thankful though; the path is quiet. We have not encountered any other daemons, and everyone in our small group has held up without complaint.

Save for Perth.

About an hour ago, he broke hands with Brit then wandered close to the river, yelled over his shoulder something about a rabbit, then ran back empty handed. Arland and I exchanged glances and shook our heads.

Perth is starving. *Everyone* is starving.

I'd give anything to be back in Virginia, anything to eat a big juicy hamburger from a greasy fast food joint. My mouth waters at the mere thought of beef and cheese and ketchup and—

"Katriona?" Arland whispers, squashing my daydream of artery clogging sustenance.

"Hmm?"

He grimaces. "We have arrived."

I look around for something to explain to me where *here* is. "I don't see anything."

"Don't?"

I sigh. "Do not. I do not see anything."

He lets go of Keagan's hand then points ahead of us, into the wall of black. "Straight ahead, between the trees. If you look hard enough, you will see the glow of a burning torch."

My eyes have not yet adjusted the way everyone else's have, but I know with time they will. However, I don't see a flame or anything past the darkness in front of me. Squinting, I lean forward—like that will help—and shake my head.

"Sir, we have arrived," Cadman says, breaking the line to stand next to Arland.

"I am aware. Katriona cannot see the light." Arland chuckles, squeezing my hand.

I *am* the light, and I have the urge to knock him in the shoulder, but don't.

Cadman doesn't share in Arland's humor; instead, the red-headed soldier raises an eyebrow then crosses his arms over his chest. "Why do you believe her eyes have not fully adjusted when she has adapted to everything else with such ease?"

Arland gives me a cursory glance, his green eyes averting mine before they get locked into one of those looks we are no longer allowed to share. "I imagine it has something to do with the amount of light surrounding her. She is rarely in complete darkness in order to adjust."

"That sounds plausible. The less she uses magic at Willow Falls, the stronger her eyes will become . . . I pray." Cadman looks over his shoulder.

"Shall I travel ahead to scout for any possible dangers, sir?"

"No, that will not be necessary. We are safer when connected. However, please send Perth this way then take his position so Brit is kept safe at the other end of the line."

"Yes, sir." Cadman jogs toward Perth.

I already know where all this is going, and I don't like it.

Perth arrives next to me and takes my hand without asking. "I assume you wish to speak of a plan for our arrival?"

Arland regards Perth with a blank expression. "I wish to be on Katriona's security. Can you arrange that?"

Perth laughs. "I am sure it can be arranged, but you do know my father will be suspicious. You were her intended. He may interpret your willingness to help as a trick. And, because *I* am curious, why do you want to risk it?"

"I cannot sleep without him," I say.

Perth practically yanks my arm from its socket, jerking me to face him, and keeps walking, but backward. "Do you expect Arland will be sleeping with you, Katriona? Are you a fool? My father will kill him and have your family further disgraced. If anyone will be in your room in the evenings, it will be me, and I am not sure that will bother me at all."

A deep, guttural growl erupts from Arland's throat.

I squeeze his hand, hoping to calm his frustration with Perth. "No, not in my room with me, but as close to me as possible. He protects me from more than just daemons, Perth. He protects me from horrible visions. Visions that do not make sense for me to have. Visions ending in death, his death, my death, everyone's—"

"How close I need to be to her is yet to be known," Arland says, lowering his voice. "Darkness is able to confront her when I am not near."

Perth peeks around me. "May we stop for a moment? Speak about this in private?"

"Cadman," Arland calls over his shoulder.

"Yes, sir?"

"Keep everyone connected. Stay only a few feet from us, but make sure no one eavesdrops. Do you understand?"

The two men exchange an unspoken agreement with their eyes, then Cadman turns with his arms outstretched to corral the others. They only move a few feet away, but Cadman engages them in conversation loud enough for me to recognize he's offering a distraction.

"What do you mean Darkness can confront her?" Perth asks, leaning forward.

Arland clenches his jaw. "Kate has had dreams of Encardia her entire life, but when I sleep next to her, the dreams stop—"

A wide grin grows on Perth's face. "I am sure they do."

I ball my fists at my sides. How dare he insinuate Arland and I have done anything we haven't. Especially since I have been so desperate for *that*, and Arland has exhibited self-control to an almost annoying extent to avoid *that*.

Reaching back, I muster every ounce of non-magical strength I've got then launch my bony fist through the air, right into Arland's palm.

"What did you do that for?" Frustration stiffens me, rooting my legs where I stand.

"What would you have expected him to think, Katriona? I told you this would happen. We need only explain why it is so important." Returning my fist to my side, Arland speaks low then keeps his hands to himself. Good thing too, cause I might smack them away. Hitting Perth would've felt great.

"Hmm," Perth says, rubbing his chin in such an Arland kind of way. "So why is it so important for you two to be together?"

"I can answer that," Mom says, stepping away from everyone else.

"Mom, we can handle this."

"You said Griandor called me a fool for not sharing things with you, well gods forgive me, but he was a fool for not sharing things, as well. What did he tell you about Arland? Did he tell you without Arland and you together there is no Encardia?" She holds her hands out at her sides like an opera singer reaching the crescendo of a powerful song.

"Did he tell you if Arland is not with you, you will remain in constant danger from Darkness? Did he tell you not only does Arland protect you, but you him? Did he tell you—"

"Wait." Grabbing Mom's shoulders, I shake her from her mental breakdown long enough for her to look me in the eyes, to truly see me. "What?"

She shudders. "What, what?"

"Most of what you said, Griandor did tell me, except for the part about me protecting Arland. Griandor said Arland protects *me* from much, but not the other way around. So, not only do I have to worry about the visions and Dugh-Darkness appearing inside Willow Falls whenever Arland is not around, you are now telling me I also have to keep Arland safe? From what?"

Out of the corner of my eye, I see Perth shoot Arland a raised eyebrow look. "What does she mean *Darkness will appear inside Willow Falls?*"

I let them talk it out and focus solely on my mom. "What are you not telling me? Do you know if he will die? What do I have to keep Arland safe from?"

"His father."

"His . . . *father?*" I ask slowly, shaking my head. High Leader Maher isn't evil. Why would *anyone* need to be protected from him?

Arland drops all pretense of friendly conversation with Perth and pushes past him to stand between me and Mom. He towers over her. "What did you just say?"

"Kate-Katriona must keep you safe from your father."

Arland's stands stiff, unmoving. Inching forward, I place my hand on his back, along his waist—

Liar. Misguided liar. His most prominent thoughts inundate mine. I hadn't expected this; the touch was to calm him, but instead it connects us like before, when magic was awake. And something else exists inside him. Fear. Fear she's not lying, and fear she's right. Fear he knows nothing of himself, he's going to die, and he's going to fail me all wrapped into one big chest crushing burden.

Releasing my fire, I step in front of Arland then take his hands in mine. "*You will not fail me, but we are at the point we need to listen to her again. She has been cryptic. She has lied, she has kept things from us longer than necessary, but she holds information we need. I want nothing more than to hear why I need to be worried about your father."*

Arland takes a step back. Given the overwhelming amount of hatred he's directing toward my mom, I think it's the best he can offer.

Keeping his hand in mine, I turn around. "Mom?"

Perth watches, staring with interest surely feeding the ice-cold man's personality more than the new man who he's becoming, the man who cares . . . or at least pretends to.

"I have told you I know nothing about Arland's life, but I do, and you need to be aware of the information I have. Now is the time to share."

I've heard this before, and her rambling makes me think she's trying to apologize, but I'd rather she just explain it all.

"Arland, your father is scared you will be unable to keep your distance from Katriona and will send you away. On a mission. Not to hurt you, but to keep you safe. Unfortunately if he does, I am afraid one of the visions Katriona has had about you will come true."

"*No* . . . ." The word floats from my mouth and into our conversation. The world around me turns gray, worse than the cold blackness. Images of Arland drowning, of him being sliced open by coscarthas' razor sharp claws, of him being torn limb-from-limb . . . .

"Katriona," he says so close to my ear his breath warms me.

I don't know when he did it, but his arms are wrapped around my back, securing me to his chest. Resting my head on him, I breathe in his woodsy scent; it's tinted with a strong sulfuric smell. I pull away and realize the smell of sulfur is from the brown, dried blood covering his shirt.

"I am not going to die." His words are strong, yet soft. Arland speaks as though he has no doubt and wishes me to believe what he says, too.

I stare at our shoes—also covered in blood. "You cannot say that for sure. Your thoughts are layered with fear of death, fear of letting me down."

He holds me at arm's length, lifts my chin with his finger, forcing me to look at him. "We all fear death. And if my sole purpose in life is to protect you, do you not believe my greatest fear would be failure? You are all this world has for survival, and so far you have been injured in more . . . no, worse ways than most. If I allow myself to believe for one moment I have done a good job, you will be in more danger than you have ever been. Thoughts are a dangerous thing to be able to share; they cross through our subconscious and most we let go of, never to think about again. The ones we hold on to are the ones we speak. We should be more careful when sharing them."

I glare at him. When I wanted nothing more than to have a moment of peace in my head, he provoked me.

"I am sorry." Arland slides his hands down my arms, resting only when our fingers are laced.

"For?"

He smiles, warm and enchanting. "For invading your thoughts earlier."

"I am sorry, too."

"For?" he asks, mimicking my pitchy tone.

"For being so angry with you when you did."

Mom steps closer to us. Her smile beams in the golden light shining from me and Arland. Our magic must be growing stronger; it comes now when we don't even realize it. "You share thoughts already?"

Arland steps back, but keeps me nuzzled in between his torso and arm. "The more magic we use, the stronger our connection."

"This is good."

She's giving me something. I don't know what, but I just know she's giving me something I need to hear. "Why?"

"Do I honestly have to repeat myself?"

"Because the two of us together are the key," Arland and I say in unison, sharing the same annoyed tone.

"I still have not had my questions answered," Perth says, eyebrows drawing over his eyes.

Arland rubs my arm. "I do not know why, but since Darkness has taken Brad's body—"

"*Brad?* The man who hit you?" Perth rejoins us and stands next to my mom.

"Brad did *not* hit me, and how did you find out?"

"If he did not hit you, there was nothing for me to find out." Perth flashes his cocky grin. "So is it true?"

Frustration boils in my chest. "Br—"

"Brad is not from this world. He accidentally traveled here with Katriona, was injured by coscarthas, and was in a coma," Arland answers for me.

"One of the children overheard a conversation in the kitchen, and I overheard her telling another; that is how I know he hit you." Perth stares at me. His almost white eyes, stark in comparison to the Darkness, look greener than normal. They hold a less milky appearance, a light shade of parched summer grass.

"And I remember seeing the two of them brought in. I thought Katriona was dead, too. Her exposed skin was covered in blood and dirt. But none of that tells me why he hit her or why he has anything to do with Darkness being able to reach her."

"When we healed Brad, he was already too infected to be released from the hold Darkness had on him," Arland says.

"In a way, the poison continued to work. Brad was tainted, but we were unaware. We believed it to be jealousy when he hit her, but it was the confusion working itself into his brain. When we attempted to return him home, we were attacked. He seemed willing to die. Then, as if he was fighting the poison inside, he . . . " he pauses and glances down at me.

"I can handle it." Hearing how hard Brad fought against the poison can be no worse than seeing the battle.

"Apologized to Katriona. I knew something was wrong with his apology, but it was not until her conversation with Griandor that I fully understood. Darkness is Brad; Brad is Darkness. Somehow the connection Katriona and Brad share allows Darkness to appear as an apparition before her."

"Why are we worried about an apparition?" Perth asks.

"Because," I say, "the more magic Darkness steals from Draíochtans and Encardia, the stronger he becomes. His apparition will go from harmless to deadly. And he is already strong enough to touch me."

Perth cocks his head to the side, looking Arland up and down. "Arland protects you from this?"

"Yes."

"And if he is assigned to her security, High Leader Maher cannot send him away," Mom adds.

"How close do you need to be?"

Securing his hand on my hip, Arland pulls me against him tighter. "We do not know for sure. To protect her from her dreams it seems as if I need to be touching her, but to protect her from Darkness it only seems I need to be within one hundred feet of her, or have her in my sight. After what happened earlier tonight, I do not wish to have her out of my sight."

Perth paces back and forth, wearing down the already dead grasses.

Mom inches closer to us, leaning her head in as if she doesn't want anyone to hear what she's about to say. "What happened earlier tonight?"

"How did you miss it?" I whisper. "Brad was up the hill. He fought against Darkness, talked to me even, but it was Darkness touching me when Arland came back."

"I wonder if the harder Brad fights, the easier it is for him to *appear* before you," Mom says. "We have many things to consider."

Perth stops his grass trampling and looks up at us, with no ounce of confidence anywhere to be found on his face. "My father will be suspicious, but I could find a way to twist it, so he believes your standing outside her door as a guard is a punishment. However, I do not know how to keep her in your direct line of sight."

Brit steps out of the huddle of people. "I do."

Is anyone *not* listening?

Arland sighs an aggravated sigh, lets go of me, then crosses his arms over his chest.

Brit bounces on her toes. "At least, I think I do."

"Well, go on, Brit. What is it?" Mom asks, waving her hand in the air.

"My connection to Kate . . . I mean Katriona."

Mom shakes her head, Perth returns to pacing, and Arland releases another sigh.

"No one believes me?" Brit frowns.

"Why am I even here?" She throws her hands up, turns then storms off toward the others who probably don't need to be standing away from us since they all know what we're talking about anyway.

I should stop her, but I don't know how her connection to me is supposed to help either. If I'm supposed to be in Arland's direct line of sight, how could Brit being in my head do anything to help that?

"That's the point, *Katriona*. You're supposed to be in *my* head," she yells from next to Flanna who eyes me as if I'm a monster. "Like when the shifter took over your body. You were in *my* head and conjured old magic powerful enough to heal yourself. You touched Arland and talked to him. If you are in *my* head, he can see you."

Everyone stops what they're doing.

How could I cast her or her ideas to the side? She's my sister, and no matter what, she's always been there for me. "I am sorry, Brit. So sorry."

"It's okay." Brit shrugs. "I know you don't trust me anymore, but I believe in you, and I believe in Arland and what we're supposed to do here. And if this is the *one* thing I'm supposed to do in all of this, I'll help you as much as I can."

Trust. What is it? She's lied for so long, but about something so dear to her. Not me. Allowing her to feel alone when the one she loves has already suffered is just not right. "I mean it, Brit. You are so smart and wonderful, and I am sorry. You have never done anything for me not to trust you."

Her chin trembles then she puts her face in her hands and cries.

Everyone watches us, shifting gazes from Brit to me.

What did I do now?

I feel strangely self-conscious and confident as I leave Arland, Mom, and Perth and make my way through the soldiers and children to stand in front of my sister. "Why are you crying?"

Looking up, she wipes her tear-drenched face with her tunic sleeve. "I would have preferred if you stayed mad at me, Kate. At least it gave me something to prove. I have nothing to offer if my plan doesn't work. I already know Brad will never love me the way he loves you. What's the point? I don't know why I'm here. I don't know who would want to love me. I'm just done. With everything."

"You are here because this is where you are from. Brad is not from here. Maybe he is not the right man for you. Maybe there is someone you have not met who will love you more, who will be better for you."

She sniffles, looking me over with a raised eyebrow. "So you agree, you don't think Brad will ever love me the way he does you?"

I push a wavy lock of dark brown hair from her cheek. "Brit, I cannot answer that. I do not understand why he loves me as much as he does in the first place."

"Are you kidding?" Brit laughs. "You two were inseparable for eleven years. For the longest time, I was sure you'd end up waking up and marrying him someday. I couldn't believe how fast you fell for Arland, but I couldn't have been happier."

Glancing around at all the watchful eyes, I meet the only ones that truly matter, then return to face my sister. "Can we have this conversation later? When there are not so many people around to hear things they have no interest in?"

"You do it well, you know?" Her tone is flat, leveled, sad.

"Do what?"

"Fit in here. You already sound like them. You use magic better than any of them." Brit turns in circles, pointing at the remaining soldiers and children. "You fight like them. This is your world, Kate, but I'm not sure if it's mine. Not without purpose."

I grab her by the shoulders, jolting her from a dangerous act of self-loathing. "You have purpose. You have saved my life many times now. You have come up with the best idea for keeping me and Arland safe at Willow Falls. Please, do not give up. *I* need you."

All the confidence she's exuded over the years, the sarcasm, the humor, the love for me, the fun spirit she is—these things are all gone. Instead of the girl I grew up with, she's grown into something more, something strong but wild, something serious but cautious. She's a contradiction of herself, and for once in our lives, I have no idea how she's going to react.

Flanna moves forward, breaking the awkward silence between me and my sister with a tap to our shoulders. "Brit, your idea is brilliant. You two need to speak to one another in private, and we need to get to Willow Falls. Talk in your heads on the way there, okay?"

Nodding, Brit turns away from me.

"Kate?" Flanna asks.

"I understand." Turning around, I see the open mouths of Mom, Perth, and Arland, but don't know how to interpret their looks. I keep my head down, stare at my feet, then walk next to Arland.

"So you and my sister get to spend all your time together now, and any time you cannot see me, I will be in her head. Do you think this will work?" I ask, on the verge of tears.

My stomach is an empty pit stretching deep and limitless. I wrap my arm around it, try to smooth the unfamiliar ache, but nothing changes. I feel as though I've lost something, as though no one likes me right now, as though I don't like myself.

"The only thing left is a story. And I am sure when we arrive at Willow Falls, the four of us plus Brit and Flanna will all be whisked into some room to talk to our fathers about things none of us"—

Perth points at Brit, Arland, Flanna, Mom, and stops when he gets to me—"really wish to talk about. Are you okay, Katriona?"

I lift my head; we hold each other's gaze.

"Huh?"

Perth steps closer to me and Arland. "You are pale."

"He is correct. Are you feeling ill?" Arland presses his palm to my forehead. "Is it possible she is experiencing aftereffects of the poison?"

Mom meets my eyes, and I catch a glimmer of recognition behind them, then she looks back to Arland. "Yes, I do believe that could be happening. Once we get inside and speak with the Leaders, we will make sure she gets rest and medicine."

Arland looks me over once more. "We should go then."

"Katriona"—Perth holds out his hand—"are you ready?"

Knots form inside the pit, twisting and turning, and fill every ounce of previously available space. Ready? Will I ever be ready for these lies, for the potential to lose everything I've ever cared about? "C . . . can I have a moment with Arland?"

"It is too dangerous, Arland. I see the torches from here. We are well within scouting distance, and you two have already stood too close to one another," Perth says.

Mom whispers the hiding spell, walking in a circle around me and Arland.

Flanna, Brit, Shay, Keagan, Cadman—everyone spreads out around us, reciting the spell, providing us with privacy.

The more I hear the words directed at the magic, the looser the knots become.

Perth walks away from us then joins the circle.

Everyone turns their backs on me and my love.

"It appears we have been given the moment. Why the sudden sullenness?"

Throwing my arms around him, I press my head into his chest, allow his sculpted form to be my pillow, my tranquility, my Arland. "I do not know—don't know. I hate the lies. I want to be me. Want my sister and me to be friends again. Want the damn sun to shine. Want Brad back. I just want things to be easy and right. None of this makes any sense. Going to Willow Falls just seems like a waste of time."

He rubs my hair with his hand and lets out a silent laugh—the kind a parent does for a child when the child is afraid of something the parent is not. "Kate, Griandor said you must unite us, so you must. It will not be a waste of time. Your mother protects you. She may not tell us everything, but she is telling us what we need to know. You and Brit will be fine; trust is something hard to regain, and no matter how upset she is with you for not trusting her, I guarantee she is more upset with herself. And I promise you, through the lies and through the trickery, you will still be you. You are an incredibly strong woman, and when this is all over, the gods will give you your heart's content."

My face burns as I hold back the tears. My chest constricts. I attempt to speak, but a solid lump forms in my throat.

"I love you. No matter who you kiss inside those doors, I will always love you, will always protect you." He presses his lips to the top of my head.

"I love you, too," I say into his tunic, running my fingers down his arms until they find his hands.

"Are you ready?"

"Mmhmm."

"Remember, you hate me, you think I smell horrible, and you love Perth."

I nod, the lump now solid in my throat.

He nudges my shoulders, pushing me forward. "Go, take his hand. I will stay next to Brit on the other end of the line."

Turning around, I stare at him one last time, smile at him, soak in his beauty, his warmth, his love. Blood and dirt are caked in his hair and on his clothes; his tunic is shredded . . . he's a total wreck, but he's still mine, and I pray he always remains that way.

My steps are shaky, small, and it takes me a lot longer than it should to reach Perth. He breaks hands with Cadman and reaches out for me. I take the hand of my punishment, and his cold chills me straight to the bone.

"I will lead the way. Follow beside, yet behind, me, and do not touch or look at anyone. If any of my father's men are out here, we do not need them to form any opinions." Perth leads us toward the torches I cannot see, and I do exactly how he instructs. As much as I'd love to look at Arland, I will not risk his life, will not risk everyone's lives.

Instead of worrying about failure, I focus my thoughts and energy on what needs to be done.

Willow Falls, I must unite everyone.

CHAPTER EIGHTEEN

"I cannot believe we did not pass any Watchers on the way here." Flanna props her hands on her hips, fingers splayed.

"Does that not seem the least bit strange to anyone?" My fiery, red-headed friend has barely spoken or reacted since Lann's death, but now she's a little more normal, tapping her foot next to the wooden door in the ground.

When we stopped in the woods, we were closer to Willow Falls than I'd realized. It took us fifteen minutes to trek the remaining distance to the perimeter, and the trip carried the spookiest quiet I've ever experienced. Every breath of every soldier could be heard. A couple animals creeping around the underbrush scampered away as we neared, scattering leaves on the forest floor.

"It does seem strange, but unless we go in that door, we will never know why. So I suggest you go in now, Flanna. Or would you like me to go in first?" Arland asks, bending down to grab the rusty metal handle.

She stops tapping her foot and glares at Arland. "I am not scared of what is inside; I am afraid of *who* is *not* outside."

He opens the wooden door in the earth; the squeaky hinges sound like nails raking down a chalkboard.

Flanna jumps in without a second glance at any of the others; her pounding footsteps echo off the wooden planks. "Vanora. How fantastic to see a *friendly* face."

Her voice is muffled, but she speaks loud enough for us to hear, and I'm sure she does it on purpose. "It is safe to come down."

"After you." Perth holds out his arm.

"No. I will not go in until everyone else is safe inside."

He purses his lips into a fine, pale-pink line. "Understood, but please be sure not to disagree with me in front of my father, okay?"

I'm not positive I'm going to like taking direction from Perth to appease his father, but nod while motioning for the children. "Anna, you and Marcus go in first with my mom. She will make sure you are taken care of."

Anna holds her brother's hand in hers, then she and Marcus dash from the middle of the line. Looking up at me with her big brown eyes, she squeezes my waist before they enter the stairway into the earth. Mom pats my shoulder then disappears, followed by Brit, Shay, Keagan, and all the others until Arland is the last man out besides Perth.

I scowl at Arland.

He looks at Perth and me, then rests the door open on the ground. Arland steps in, taking the air from my lungs as he goes.

Perth stares into the abyss of our future. "Arland is right about one thing."

"What is that?" I ask, clutching at my chest.

"You are an incredibly strong woman. Your soul is pure, Katriona." He presses his cold hand on the small of my back. "Now, after you."

I'm not ready to step into this stairwell, not ready for all the possibilities Willow Falls holds. I look over my shoulder, searching for an excuse to stay outside longer, and spot Mirain and the other horses standing side by side behind us. "Who will take care of them?"

"I will send someone up as soon as possible."

"Visit you soon, Mirain," I whisper.

"My father frowns upon people in his family entering stables. He considers it beneath us. You may not see her again until we leave this place."

I run to Mirain, rub between her eyes, the best goodbye I can manage, then return to Perth. Following the others, I descend the dark stairs into my temporary prison. Each thud of the wood below my feet echoes in my ears and rattles my supposed *pure soul*. The door's hinges squeal in protest when Perth pulls it closed. He slides the heavy metal bar over the braces then turns three squeaky locks.

Perth trots down the stairs then returns his hand to my back. The touch would be natural for Arland, but I jump from the chill in Perth's hand, from the alien feel.

He leans into me and tucks loose hair behind my ear. "Remember, we love one another. You cannot jump every time I touch you. What will you do when we have to kiss? You know they will expect it."

"I know *you* will expect it, but why would everyone else expect a public display?" I whisper.

"Cold feet?" Perth asks, grabbing a fistful of my tunic.

Stopping in the middle of the stairwell, I pull his hand from me and squint through the darkness to see his stony expression. "No, this is what must be done; however, I do not understand the need for everyone to see it."

"Not everyone needs to see it, mainly my family . . . my father. We are near the bottom. Take my hand." He grabs my fist. "Starting early with our unity is a good idea."

Relaxing my tensed muscles, I lace my fingers with his. There is no strength or warmth, just cold and bones. "We would not want to make a bad first impression."

At the last step, Perth leans over then kisses my cheek. "We are safe, my love."

I catch sight of Arland standing with the soldiers, next to my sister, and shudder. He's holding her hand. We haven't even gotten into the thick of it and I'm ready to run away. Her hand shouldn't be in his. My hand shouldn't be in Perth's. What are we doing this for? Maybe Anna was right; we shouldn't lie. We should just be upfront about everything. Tell them all to go to hell if they don't like it.

Perth wraps his arm around my shoulders, drawing me closer, drawing me out of my dark panic.

"Why, Perth Dufaigh. It has been years since I have seen you," says a tall red-headed woman standing next to Flanna.

"And I see you have well forgotten about me." This beauty towers over Perth by at least a foot, with eyes bluer than the bonnets of Texas, skin matching Flanna's perfect cream, and gaze locked directly on me.

"I could never forget you, Vanora." A crooked smile grows on his face. "Katriona, this is my dearest friend Vanora. Vanora, this is Katriona—"

"Wilde? Katriona Wilde your future wife?"

"Yes."

Perth smiles, and I notice something cross Vanora's eyes. Disappointment maybe? Anger? Sadness? I'm not sure, but it only lasts a second, then she shakes her head and offers me her hand.

"Nice to meet you, Katriona." Her grip is firm, and her stare bores into me.

"Nice to meet you, too."

The corners of Vanora's mouth twist up.

I make every effort not to show how much her handshake hurts.

"Yes, well, your father will be pleased, Perth," she says.

He releases my shoulders then takes my hand again. "Speaking of my father, do you know where we may find him—and High Leader Maher?"

She tips her head toward mine and Perth's left. "They were in the great room, eating dinner about fifteen minutes ago. They may still be there, but I am not positive."

"Thank you, Vanora. It *is* good to see you."

"Good to see you, too." She glances at Arland. "Where are the others, *Leader* Maher?" Vanora spits Arland's status at him.

I gasp, but she doesn't spare another look at me.

"They did not make it." He walks away from her, ahead of the rest of us, and toward the great room, I'm sure. Arland has no reason to explain anything to Vanora, and from the sounds of it, she's not friendly.

"Nice meeting you," I say glancing over my shoulder as we leave, hoping to come across as the polite fiancée.

Vanora stares after us. Doesn't speak, doesn't move, just stares.

"She will warm to you. Everyone will warm to you, once my father instructs them to," Perth whispers, a wide grin reaching up to his eyes.

I laugh. A genuine, happy laugh—the kind that, when allowed, can bring on tears. People are going to be forced to like me because of what I am, not who, and that's supposed to make me feel better. The funniest part: Perth realizes how stupid this is; yet he still says it.

Arland hesitates before opening the door in front of us. He must want to turn around and see what made me happy, but after a split second pause, he pushes open the door. Everyone follows him into a huge, well-lit room.

A cathedral ceiling with massive wooden beams draped with dark, green ivy is the first thing that catches my eyes, then the sheer size. This one room appears to be larger than all of Watchers Hall. Hundreds of round-wooden tables with chairs parked around them are sprinkled throughout.

Potatoes and chicken and eggs and . . . oh there are so many wonderful, mouth-watering smells in here. My stomach growls loud and furiously for how long I've kept it empty.

Perth pats *his* stomach. "Hungry?"

I draw in a deep breath, savoring the yeasty scent of bread, the sweetness of carrots and the deliciousness of . . . everything. "Do you even have to ask?"

"We can eat as soon as we find my father."

"Perth," a man booms from the left side of the great room. He sits at a long table—not round, but rectangular—dressed with a red velvet cloth adorned with golden ropes. The gaudiness of the cloth can be compared to nothing I've seen in Encardia.

"My son has returned, with a woman in tow nonetheless. Tell me my boy, who is this beautiful jewel standing next to you?"

Leader Dufaigh. The cloth makes perfect sense now; it fits his twisted, rotten self.

I blush and smile at Perth, like a good actress. He tugs my hand, leading me through the room, past the mostly empty tables and right up to his father.

No one follows us.

"Father, this is Katriona Wilde."

Leader Dufaigh's fork falls from his hand and hits his plate with a loud clank. He pushes out his wooden chair—appearing more as a throne with intricate flowers carved into the edges, lined with red velvet—and stands, revealing an enormous round belly. He leans forward. "*The* Katriona Wilde? Does this mean her mother and father are here as well?"

Biting my tongue, I hold back the urge to blurt out *my father is dead you sick jerk* and manage another smile.

Perth keeps his head and eyes down. "Yes, father. This is *the* Katriona Wilde. Her mother is here, but her father is not."

Leader Dufaigh glances at our hands then scans the crowd. "I should like to speak to your parents. Do you know your father's whereabouts?"

I do not show the same submissiveness as Perth; I meet Leader Dufaigh's cruel gaze. "My father died."

"Oh, that is too bad. Too bad indeed," he says, shaking his head, jostling his double-chin. "Your hands are joined. Does this mean . . . ?"

"Yes, Father. Katriona and I have . . . ." Pulling me closer, Perth smiles wide. "We have fallen in love, sir."

Leader Dufaigh runs his fingers through his greasy, shoulder length blond hair. "I do not believe it. *I do not believe it.*"

"Oh God," I whisper, glancing over my shoulder. I cannot look at Dufaigh. I think I'm going to be sick.

Everyone's lives depend on our ability to pretend, but I'd never thought the Leaders wouldn't believe the beginning of the lie. I try to find my mom or Brit in the crowd, but the only person I see is Arland, and he's scowling. Those green eyes are supposed to adore me, look me up and down and make me blush while they do, not look at me as though I'm nothing but scum. He plays his role well—too well. My face burns. Fighting back tears with everything I have, I take a deep breath then let it out.

He doesn't mean it; his anger is all a part of the lie.

Perth squeezes my fingers.

Cringing, I turn away from Arland and look toward Dufaigh, allowing those tears to fall. I can do this. "I love your son, sir. And it would be nice if someone would trust in us."

Perth wipes my face with his thumb, leaving frigid trails on my cheek. "You are upsetting her. We have had a difficult trip, and we are all in need of food."

Dufaigh looks beyond us, resting his hand on his belly. "There is no time for food now. We need to speak in private. I have many questions for you and also for Leaders Wilde and Maher." He turns to his left then heads toward the end of the room.

A plate of unfinished food sits on the table. Potatoes, carrots, chicken . . . my stomach rumbles.

"Well, come now. Gather the others so we may discuss your Binding—amongst other things," Dufaigh says, pausing in front of round, wooden doors.

Perth starts after Dufaigh, towing me behind. "But we need food, Father."

He chuckles. "You have spent too much time with these Light Lovers, Son. Come with me now. Leader Maher, Leader Wilde, would you mind joining us?"

Mom, Arland, and Brit step out of the group of soldiers and approach us, but Flanna slinks back, keeping her arms around Keely. I don't think Flanna will be able to keep her promise to help me fit in here. She's still too wounded, and I don't blame her.

"The rest of you may stay here and eat, then bathe. You lot smell awful and need to prepare yourselves for a celebration. My son is getting married tonight." Dufaigh's belly bounces with his laughter. He glances at me again then pushes through the door.

"To . . . tonight?" I ask, taking a step back, ready to flee, ready to throw myself into a fire before being forced into a life without choice.

"I expected this. Do not worry. When we speak to him, I will convince him otherwise." Perth holds open the door then follows me through.

"Sorry," he whispers then lets the door swing closed in Arland's face.

"Why did you do that?" I demand.

Perth puts his mouth next to my ear. "You heard him yourself; my father already thinks I am weak from spending too much time with Light Lovers. I cannot be nice to Arland."

I sigh. "Fine. It makes perfect sense."

We travel down the dark corridor lit only by small, yellow candles in glass sconces on the walls, and follow Leader Dufaigh around corners, down stairs, and through doors. There are so many different passages I'm positive I could never find my way here again without a map.

Dufaigh stops in the middle of a spiral staircase leading further into the earth, turns to his right and pounds his fist against the gray, stone wall. An echo rolls around us; that was not stone he hit. The wall ripples. The gray rocks disappear, revealing a skinny wooden door I'm sure Dufaigh could never fit through.

"Follow me," he says, turning to the side and squeezing his way in.

Perth and I enter at the same time with Mom, Arland, and Brit behind us.

The door slams closed, raising the hairs on the back of my neck.

"Where are we?" I whisper.

"I do not know," Perth says.

"We are in the hall leading to the communications room, Perth. You would know these things if you paid attention during tours." Arland doesn't smile or walk any closer to us; instead, he keeps his eyes straight ahead and shows no emotion on his face.

Smirking, Perth glances over his shoulder. "Why would I pay attention during those early tours? I have no intentions of ever commanding the military. That will be your job, no?"

Arland laughs. "It will be my job. In fact, it will be mine and your wife's job to lead Encardia. How do you feel about your wife being a High Leader while you are a mere Leader to your dwindling people?"

"My wife will make a better High Leader than both you and I combined. So as long as I can call her mine, that is enough to satisfy my needs."

"Nonsense, my boy. No woman should ever be more powerful than her husband. She will relinquish her title of High Leader to you once you are married, and Arland will no longer be necessary. Only one man can lead at a time, and since you are one month older, Katriona's title will be passed to you." Dufaigh stops his forward progress, turns and puts his hands on Perth's shoulders.

"You, my son, will become High Leader of Encardia."

"On whose authority?" Mom demands.

Dufaigh peeks around Perth's shoulder, the Leader's face appearing as pleasant as someone removing toxic waste. "High Leader Maher's. And you would not wish to go against a High Leader's law again, now would you?"

"My father would do no such thing." Arland towers over Dufaigh, hands spread out at his sides. "He is not even aware of Katriona's presence. Why would he make such an arrangement?"

More lies. High Leader Maher knew we were on our way to Wickward; something has changed. Something not even Arland knows, and that frightens me more than anything.

Dufaigh drops his hands from Perth's shoulders then steps in front of Arland, staring at my love in a way dangerously close to making my fire burn out of control. "Ah, Arland. You believe us all to be fools. Why is it your father is unaware of Katriona's presence? Did you not inform him of her arrival because you were hoping she would fall in love with you instead of my son? You are quite lucky you are the son of a High Leader; otherwise you would pay severely for your lack of communication."

Dufaigh moves on to my mother. "And you, Leader Wilde. Unless you wish to be punished for your abandonment crimes, I would suggest you not give the child any wild ideas for not relinquishing her title. Her title saves your life."

He turns once more. "And who, may I ask, is this?"

Mom grips tight to Brit's hand. "This is my daughter."

"Your daughter? I was not aware you had another daughter." Dufaigh looks Brit over as if she's a piece of livestock at auction. "Does she come with the same powers as Katriona?"

Mom shakes her head. "No. She is nothing special compared to her sister."

Brit sucks in a sharp breath.

Perth's father paces in front of the three of them. "Tough living in the shadow of someone more powerful than you, is it not, child?"

She doesn't respond.

Mom wraps her arm around Brit's shoulders. I know the words were intended to protect my sister, but I don't doubt they hurt.

Dufaigh stops his sinister march and stands before Brit. "It is okay, child, you do not have to speak it in her presence. Her shadow must be a tall one to live in." He caresses her cheek.

Propping her hands on her hips, Brit huffs air through her nose. "You're wrong. My sister doesn't treat people that way—and there's no sun, so there aren't any shadows for me to stand in. Unless we're talking about the ones surrounding you."

"*Brites*," Mom says, frowning. "You cannot speak to him that way. He is a Leader."

Brit scowls at Dufaigh. "Well, apparently so am I."

Perth and his father exchange glances.

"She reminds me of you, Saraid. Tell her to keep quiet or I will find a way to ensure her fate is the same as yours."

Dufaigh pivots on his heel, marches another few feet, then passes through a doorway on the left.

"Please, Brit, control your tongue," Perth whispers. "This is not where you and Katriona grew up. You may have been able to get away with speaking to people that way there, but my father is not the forgiving type. I do admire you standing your ground, and he will have a great deal of respect for you as well, but he will also have his eye on you. Try to speak as we do, try to act submissive, or I fear what may happen if you do not."

"Thanks for the advice, but I'm not submitting to anyone, and I'm certainly not going to have him belittle me. Let me have the same fate as my mother. If more people would stand up to him, maybe he wouldn't be so feared." Brit brushes past us then follows the same path as Leader Dufaigh.

"Mom?" I ask, wondering what the hell happened to my sister.

Mom smiles but rubs her hands together. "She has had enough, Katriona. We need to find a Seer, or she will never be happy."

"Ar—" Dufaigh steps back into the hallway, and I revise my words. "Perth and I discussed that earlier. We will see if we can find one. I believe it will help calm her. She should not speak that way to anyone, let alone a respected Leader."

"Come along now." He points toward the doorway with his stubby fingers.

"Coming, Father." Perth places his hand between my shoulder blades and pushes me forward.

We step through the dark doorway opening into a room so familiar, I want to hide my face for fear the knowledge will somehow reveal itself.

I've been here before.

The communications room looks the same as the last time I was here, minus Arland's father. I try to look around with nonchalance; the brown-haired man must be here, and if he is, he will likely recognize me.

I spot him standing in the far right corner of the room, deep in conversation with Drustan—the other man who was here when I visited via the chatter box. They stop talking and look up at all of us.

Scanning through the faces, they each stop at me then return to their conversation.

Thank you, Griandor.

"Why did you bring us in here?" Arland asks, coming from behind Perth and me to stand before Dufaigh.

"There is a disturbance at Wickward. Your father is here monitoring it, and I brought you all back here to meet with him." Dufaigh waves his hand as though the disturbance means nothing to him at all.

"What kind of disturbance at Wickward?" Arland pronounces the word disturbance slowly, probably trying to hide the caution in his tone.

Leader Dufaigh smiles and claps his hand on Arland's shoulder. "It is unclear the extent of the damage, but the base has been infiltrated. Another failed Leader, Arland. Does this sound familiar?"

He brushes Dufaigh's hand aside. "Is this the reason there are no guards outside these walls tonight?"

"We brought them in to prepare for their journey to Wickward." The sinister, yet annoying, Ground Dweller points to a large piece of aged paper with names scrawled on it. "The ones on the list leave at three."

Brit approaches the table, running her finger down the long list of names and gasps. "Wait, so you're telling me another base is being attacked and you were out stuffing your fat face instead of trying to help?"

Dufaigh growls, low and throaty, and turns his attention on my sister.

Brit is playing a dangerous game. One that will surely have her locked up and ruining our plan before we ever get to eat. I try to make a connection to her, think of her and her alone.

"Brit?"

She keeps her eyes focused on Dufaigh standing before her with a blood-red face. *"What? This guy is pissing me off."*

"He's dangerous, Brit. Just shut up and let him talk without interrupting again. Please."

"I am a Leader, child. No matter what your bloodline, if you wish to live, you will keep quiet." Dufaigh turns to Arland.

"She clearly has a fascination with you to speak up that way. Learn to control her, Arland Maher, or you will be out of two wives."

Her scowl fades, and we lock eyes. *"What does he mean I have a fascination with Arland?"*

"As long as he doesn't think I do, we should be fine. Play into it. Arland is smart enough to figure it out."

Brit clasps her hands behind her back and looks at her boot, twisting it on the stone floor. "I am so sorry for talking that way in front of you, Arland. It was just hard to hear him speak to *you* that way."

Arland puts his arm around Brit's shoulders, pulling her into him—an act making me squirm on the inside. "You must learn to show respect. Even to those who do not always deserve it." He looks away from Brit and smiles broadly at Dufaigh.

Backing away, he huffs out a long breath. "I will very much enjoy watching you fall from grace, you—"

"That is enough," Arland's father commands, stepping into the room through a doorway in the far right corner. "You will not speak to my son that way. Is it not enough we are at war with Darkness, we need to war each other as well?"

Mom places her hand over her heart and bows her head, a sign of respect; though after what Leader Dufaigh just told us, High Leader Maher doesn't deserve it. "Kimball . . . ."

He crosses the room then stands right in front of my mother, towering over her by at least six inches. "Drustan, Annan, leave us."

Keeping his attention on the men, he waits for them to leave then looks at Mom again. "It is good to see you, Saraid. Where is Brian?" Leader Maher glances around the room, but he knows exactly where my dad is.

Mom buries her face in her hands. "He died a long time ago, Kimball."

Leader Maher pulls her into a hug. "He was a good man. I am sorry to hear of this."

The amount of acting going on here is incredible.

He holds her at arm's length, then tips his head in the direction of where he entered. "The meeting room in the back will be more appropriate for our conversation. After you."

Leader Dufaigh takes off first, followed by Mom, Brit, Perth and me.

"Wait here, son," Leader Maher says.

Peeking back, I notice he has his hand wrapped tightly around Arland's elbow.

"Keep moving," Perth whispers.

Arland and his father watch as Perth and I cross through the doorway. I can only imagine the questions that will be asked. Only imagine the lies unfolding before we have a chance to tell a large enough web of them. Of course Arland's father already knows the truth, but we need for him to stay on board, and we need Arland to stay here.

Alive.

Perth leans in close to my ear. "Do not worry; Arland will be fine."

"It is not only him I am worried about," I say as low as possible. "It is everything."

We lock eyes, and I'm positive he understands I'm worried about the lie. Positive he knows Arland's father will have to go along with it—at least the part about Perth and me.

"Me, too."

"They are such a lovely couple," Dufaigh says, interrupting my quiet conversation with Perth.

We've entered into a small room. One long table is situated in the center with a dozen or so chairs surrounding it. Clear glass jars filled with white wax and warm candlelight line the table. Hand-drawn canvass maps cover the walls, denoting bases and enemy hideouts in different colors.

Dufaigh sits in a chair at the head of the table—a seat I'm sure is not intended for him. Light flickers on his face, creating shadows under his milky-blue eyes and chubby cheeks.

I stop in the middle of the room, not sure where to sit and not sure I want to get any closer to him.

"Take a seat next to me, Perth. Katriona, do not fear, child. You may sit next to him." Dufaigh points to the seat closest to him.

"I was concerned you would have brainwashed your daughter against my son. Having her willing to marry Perth and not the least bit interested in Arland Maher seems almost too good to be true. Are you ready to perform the Binding spell now?"

"No, Father." Perth holds out a chair for me.

I sit down then take his hand again once he's next to me. Perth may be cold and lacking all of Arland's marvelous qualities, but having someone to hold onto does tremendous good for my nerves.

Dufaigh narrows his eyes. "What do you mean, son?"

"I wish to court her properly, sir. Our time together has been full of bloody battles. We could use some light-hearted fun before we commit to one another forever." Perth picks up my hand then places his frigid lips on my knuckles.

"Is that not what you wish for, too, my love?"

"I . . . I—"

His father rests his clenched fists on the table as if he wants Perth to see his anger. "This will not do. We need a wedding. Our people have endured great losses and need something to bring cheer. Your marriage—"

Perth lowers his head, reverting to a state of submission. "Father, I do not wish to displease you, but this is what we desire. A week or two is all we need, then once we are Bound, Katriona and I will go out and fight off this terrible Darkness."

"More nonsense. I will not allow you to risk your life out there." Dufaigh waves his hand toward the dirt ceiling.

"But how will we end the war?" Perth asks.

"Son, you will direct what little army we have left to fight out the war."

"But Katriona has the power to save us all."

Dufaigh wears a look resembling the man I once thought Perth to be: cold and hard. With eyes fixed on Perth, the heartless Leader stands and digs his fingers into his son's right hand. "You will not speak another word. If Katriona wishes to fight after you are Bound and she has relinquished her position to you, then so be it."

Perth reveals no outward signs of pain; he mirrors his father's angry gaze. "You would have me send my wife out to fight while I remain behind . . . in hiding?"

"She is a Light Lover, Son. It should not matter to you." Dufaigh looks at me then flinches.

"I am not quite sure how it is you have fallen for her. She bears the same distrustful eyes as the rest of them."

"Her life and my honor do matter to me." Perth squeezes my fingers so tight my bones ache. He fears his father; standing up to him must be terrifying.

"Do you want your time to court her, or shall I have Leader Wilde perform the spell now?"

"I will do no such thing without both of their consents," Mom says, slamming her fist on the table. "You have crossed the line, Dufaigh. Your son wishes to give the people the very thing you ask for, and you challenge him? And worse yet, you say he should send his wife to fight alone? How dare you! Have you lost all *your* fight?"

Dufaigh looks from Perth to the other side of the table, fingers still dug into his son's hand. No words are spoken, but there's fire behind the eyes of my would-be-father-in-law.

Mom shakes her head. "No, I see you have not lost all fight. Only you fight for all the wrong things. Nothing has changed with you over the last twenty years."

Arland and his father walk in. Everyone looks up or turns around.

Side-by-side the two men could be clones of one another, minus the gray streaks in High Leader's hair and the crow's feet around his eyes.

"I apologize for my tardiness. I needed a moment to speak with my son—alone," he says, stopping at the head of the table. "Would you mind moving from my seat, Dufaigh?"

Without a word, Dufaigh releases his grip on Perth then moves to the other end of the table. Leader Maher claims his seat while Arland sits next to Brit then takes her hand in his.

I try not to stare, try not to allow the faked affections bother me, but they do. She hid her love for my best friend from me for years, now she gets to pretend to be in love with my true love—gets to kiss, hold hands and have acceptance. This was my half-baked telepathic idea, but I hate it already.

"I hear congratulations are in order. It seems Brites and Arland have fallen in love as well as Katriona and Perth. This works out well." Leader Maher offers a smile reaching up to his striking green eyes, making his crow's feet grow to his hairline.

"However I am sorry, Brites. I must send Arland to Wickward to rescue the other Draíochtans. I am sure you understand?"

"I am so sorry," Arland whispers next to her ear.

I cannot take this.

"*You have to, Kate. I promise I will not do anything, and I promise not to enjoy this.*" Brit meets my eyes and smiles. "*Although his hands, his smell, his—*"

"*Stop!*"

She looks away from me, back toward Arland's father. "I understand, sir. He will be missed, but he is very good at what he does."

"I have a request to make." Perth watches the lying pair with his nose turned up in disgust.

I do my best to match his look. With the googly faces Brit's making, it's not a difficult task.

"What is that request, Son?" Dufaigh asks.

"I wish for Arland to be on Katriona's security."

Leader Maher laughs a low, almost bemused laugh. "*Security?*"

Perth doesn't look away from his father. "I know you do not trust Arland, and in many ways neither do I, but you cannot deny his ability to fight off daemons and unruly Draíochtans. Katriona will need security, Father. Think of all the men here who would wish to have her as their own. She will need a guard with her at all times."

"And you think my son will be the best security for her?" Leader Maher asks with a hint of disbelief. "I believe that to be a waste of his time and will put many lives at stake."

"I think it a perfect idea, Kimball." Dufaigh chuckles and rubs his chin. "The Great Arland Maher resorts to protecting his former intended. But can *he* be trusted? Look at all his recent failures, Son."

"He has failed no one," Arland's father says, overpowering everyone's chatter. "He must run this mission to Wickward. Would you prefer to have our people die just to protect one girl?"

Dufaigh bolts out of his seat then leans across the table, face red and wild. "One girl? *One girl?* Do you have any idea how powerful this *one girl* is?"

Leader Maher's wooden chair creaks as he stands, shoulders squared, face emotionless. "I do, but I also understand you want to strip that power away from her and make her nothing but a piece in *your* game for power."

He paces the length of the table, so much like Arland back at Watchers Hall. "We do not have time for these games, Dufaigh. We need to gather our people and form a more powerful army. I do not wish to fight any more than you do, but fight we must. We are dying. There are three bases of people left to our entire race. What will you or your son stand to gain when there are no people for either of you to rule?"

"Need I remind you the price for these bases you speak of? If it were not for my kind, no one would be alive now. My son's marriage to this *one girl* is finally the payment we have been awaiting." Dufaigh returns to his chair then leans back.

"If he wishes to have Arland on her security so there are no issues with that marriage, then that is what he will get. Unless you wish me to evacuate the remaining bases of all Sea Dwellers and Light Lovers alike? Or I could repeal our peace agreement and we can go to war now?"

Mom scowls, looking back and forth between the men as they tell lies, as they try to move their figurative chess pieces. She makes a slight shift in her chair as if she's about to get up and speak her mind, but Leader Maher shakes his head.

"Leave it, Saraid. If Perth wishes for Arland to watch over Katriona, and Dufaigh threatens to throw us out otherwise, then that is what we must do. Part of the arrangement made between our kinds many years ago." He rolls his eyes.

Arland stands so fast his chair falls backward on the floor with a loud *clack*. "You are giving in to his demands? Who will lead the soldiers to Wickward? Who will ensure they have a safe return?"

Something about the way his face turns bright red and his eyes narrow, mimicking the anger in his raised voice, tells me Arland is not pretending. He's upset about being stuck here. He loves his people. To know they need him, need us—it must be eating him alive. But Mom said he'd be killed if he went on his father's mission, and Arland knows how much he protects me . . . .

Everyone ignores him, even me.

"I would like him to be within sight of her at all times—except at night when I would like him posted outside her door. Is that agreeable?" Perth asks, breaking the tension.

Dufaigh raises an eyebrow. "What do you expect of the other men here, Perth?"

"Look at her, Father." Perth brings my hand to his lips and kisses it.

"I have. I do not see what attracts you to her, but if this is what makes you feel safe, then this is what we will do. I will assign one of my guards to be Arland's partner. Someone will need to relieve him for breaks and sleep."

Arland stands next to his father, arms crossed over his chest. "Are you seriously going to sit back and allow this?"

"My hands are tied." High Leader Maher shrugs. "This is the way things are."

"Who will go to Wickward?"

"We will gather our most trusted men. You may pick a leader, and they will leave in the morning."

He places his hands on Arland's shoulders. "I do not like you being stuck here any more than you do, but we do not always have a choice."

"Well, I believe my work here is done," Dufaigh says, pushing his hands on the table to help himself up. "Get cleaned up—all of you. I will send a dresser to your quarters, Katriona. She will prepare you for your outing as Perth's future wife. We will meet in the great room at seven."

Leader Maher grabs Dufaigh's arm before he walks away. "I need to speak with Arland for a moment, Dufaigh. Do you mind?"

"As long as he can see Katriona, I do not mind where he goes. Son, do you have an issue with this?"

Perth has to say yes. If he doesn't, his father will be suspicious. *I would be suspicious.*

"She needs to eat and prepare for the celebration. There is no time for Arland to speak with his father now. Can you not speak to one another while she bathes?"

The muscles in Arland's jaw jut. "Fine."

"Where will we find our quarters?" Mom asks.

"Ahh, I nearly forgot about you. You will need to remain here while your dear friend Kimball decides your fate." Dufaigh turns and heads from the room, snapping his fingers. "Let us leave them to it now, children. Follow me."

Brit scrambles from her chair then wraps her arms around Mom's trembling body. "I'm not leaving you, Mom."

"You must. This is my problem, dear. I have been expecting this for a very long time." Mom pats Brit's hand but looks at me. "Go.

Follow him. Do this. He will at least allow me to live long enough to see you married."

My breath catches in my chest. She isn't talking about me marrying Perth. She can't be. Dufaigh may believe that if he hears, her words may even bring him pleasure, but I don't think she has any hope she'll make it through our time at Willow Falls. She must have some knowledge that her last act as my mom will be to Bind me and Arland.

Perth tugs my hand, but I cannot move from my seat. My eyes lock with Saraid Wilde's—the only living parent I have left, and one who has given up everything for me.

"We must go. We cannot keep my father waiting."

Heat rushes into my face, around my eyes. Sweat beads on my forehead.

"If he has to come back, he will know something is wrong. Please, come. I promise you will see your mother again."

Everyone's gaze is on me, but the only one that matters is the one across from me, the one scared and alone, the one I have not trusted enough. "I'm sorry . . . ." I whisper.

"Go." She waves.

Shaking, I stand then allow Perth to lead me from the room, and Arland and Brit follow behind us.

Before the shadows hide Mom from me, before I somehow forget what she looks like, I glance over my shoulder and see her crying in High Leader Maher's arms.

I hope she knows how much I love her.

CHAPTER NINETEEN

The bath here is similar to the one at Watchers Hall—the only exception is there are multiple stone enclosures in the same room. Privacy is a thing of the past.

Hope is too.

Brit and I walk hand-in-hand into the dark washroom with our dingy-white towels slung over our shoulders. Neither of us has spoken since we left communications. The man who wishes to steal everything I am also wishes to steal everything that made me this way and everything keeping me this way.

My sister and I drop hands and separate; Brit goes to the enclosure on the left while I go to one on the right. Placing our towels on small wooden tables in front of the enclosures, we draw the linen curtain between us then slip out of our clothes.

Dust rises in a cloud around me. Remnants of war and death—including mine—all fly up to greet me. I sneeze.

"Bless you," Brit says.

It's the first thing she's said to me since we found out our Mom might die, and for whatever reason, it makes me laugh.

"What could possibly be funny?" Brit asks, voice flat.

"This—all of this. It's stupid and pointless. Dufaigh is an idiot. I have the power to destroy him, but Griandor wants us all united, and here I am, about to play dress-up and pretend I'm in love with someone I'm not, and you say 'Bless you'. It's so normal and appropriate, and right now our lives are anything but." Still laughing, I step into the water.

"I think you've lost your mind. You died, Kate. Arland saved you . . . again. You've seen blood and battles and—"

Faces of people from Watchers Hall flash before my eyes. Glenna, Enid, Lann, even the people I hadn't become friends with. Old and young alike, people have lost their lives because I have not ended this war. I swallow hard. "I know. I was there, remember? But I don't know how Arland saved me the second time. What happened?"

Air bubbles linger on my skin and occasionally tickle my back and arms as they rise to the surface. How simple it is for the air to return to where it belongs. I wish there were a way for me to make it to the surface, breathe fresh mountain breezes, soak in a healthy world, but I'm trapped. Stuck in a lie. Forced to play chess with a bunch of selfish men and women.

"I kept thinking you were going to turn into a werewolf or something after the hounds scratched you."

"Brit?" I can't help but giggle.

"I know it sounds stupid, but I always loved scary movies. Anyway, your body turned bright-red, blood poured from your arm, and you just froze. Seconds went by where you didn't move a single muscle, then you just kind of fell over."

The poison the hounds carry must have the ability to cause paralysis. I wanted to move, wanted to see Arland or go to him, but was like a statue.

"Arland must have killed a hundred daemons at once. So much magic poured out of him. Blues and golds filled the sky, and they were all coming from him. That's how I knew you weren't dead—at least, that's what I told myself. You need each other for this magic to work. So you couldn't be dead, right?"

Picturing what he must have looked like, a tinge of regret hits my heart. I wish I could have seen him. Seen how powerful he was. For me. For us. For Encardia. "I think so."

"Anything that tried to get near him just died. When the stupid things realized it, they backed off and attacked everyone else. He couldn't save you and protect us, but you were more important.

Mom and Keagan flipped you onto your back and told Arland what to do. He slammed his fist into your chest, then it was just like CPR."

Because of me all those soldiers and children are gone, because I died and was more important for Arland to save than them.

I grab a bar of soap from the ledge then scrub it all over my body, trying to get any remaining venom off my skin, any blood of my friends. Everywhere I look there's more, more loss, more proof of the senseless war going on around me. The water turns cloudy and brown, but it all flows away with the spring, flows outside with the rest of this dead world. As though the horrible things in the forest never occurred, the enclosure is clean, pure. "There was this white cloud or something. The most flawless white I've ever seen— seriously, cotton balls, sterile rooms, I'm sure nothing on the planet could compare. I stood up and took a step forward, and when I did, something smacked me in the chest and wherever I was turned black. Voices became clear, memories flooded back to me. Brit, I'm pretty sure I was in Heaven."

"Which would explain why after a few minutes of CPR, the magic faded, and the rest of us had to find a way to protect all of you. That's when most of the soldiers were killed."

My chest constricts. I rub my hand across it, pressing the tender flesh with the tips of my fingers. My skin is swollen, and I'm sure it's bruised, but even if every rib was broken, the pain would never be greater than the guilt I feel for all those lives lost because of me.

Brit says nothing for the longest time. The water swirls around me, and the room fills with the scent of sweet lilacs, but after what Brit just told me, the smell does little to calm my nerves.

Water splashes, the sound jolting my already tense muscles.

"Sorry. I had to wash my hair. The next time you die, don't go into the light. You really should have watched more movies with me, Kate."

Her sarcasm has played a horrible trick on me. Tears trickle down my face, splashing into the water. "Do you think they'll really kill—?"

"I won't think of it; I can't. But promise me if it comes to that, Kate, you don't allow it. You are powerful enough to destroy him. Those were your words. Promise me you will if you have to."

Such an awkward conversation to have while bathing and unable to see each other, but I don't have to dig inside her head to know how serious she is. "I promise."

"Thank you."

We fall silent, and I close my eyes and rest my head against the ledge but cannot relax. Hounds and coscarthas attack children in my mind, children I know—or knew. The serpent's humid breath full of the pungent smell of death has replaced the lilacs. Arland's comforting warmth is what I crave. These lies already hurt more than I ever expected. We don't need to break a Binding Spell to punish us; I'm already burning.

"He doesn't think he's good enough for you."

I bolt upright at the sound of Brit's voice. "How did you—?"

"I've always sensed when you were thinking about him—even before we knew he existed. And I can tell he thinks that by the way he looks at you: always sad."

"Right. Well I know he thinks that. It's crazy, though, Brit. The gods practically created us to be together," I say, relaxing again.

"I'm sorry I taunted you in the communications room. If it makes you feel any better, his hand was sweaty and tense. The only time I think he was comfortable was when he was arguing with Dufaigh."

My stomach turns in on itself. "I cannot sit in here anymore." Dunking my head, I rinse the last of the grime from my face and hair, then climb out of the stone enclosure and grab the towel.

"I'll be out in a minute," she says.

Wrapping the towel around me, I leave my old clothes in a heap on the floor. I walk out of the washroom and bump right into Arland. He grasps me at my elbows to keep me from falling backward. His warmth floods my body; his eyes mesmerize me.

"I . . . I—"

The hall is empty and lit only by faint candlelight. There are no windows, no paintings, no carvings like the ones at Watchers Hall. It's just as dark and gloomy in this hall as the Darkness is outside.

Arland looks both ways then closes his eyes as if trusting his hearing is better than his sight.

"All clear," he says, looking my toweled body up and down. "No visits from Dughbal while you were in there?"

"No." We have precious moments with each other, and he chooses to speak of this?

"I love you," I whisper. "I hate these lies. I hate this place. Your father caves to Dufaigh, why?"

"These are not conversations we should have while you are . . . you. Tonight, during the celebration, through Brit we will talk." He leans in then places his lips on my cheek. His kiss tingles my skin. "And I love you, too. You are so strong, so beautiful. I wish I could hold you in my arms right now."

Arland squeezes my elbow. "We will make it through this."

I stare into his eyes, into his soul, soaking in my other half. "I know we will. You always say that, at least."

Arland turns and looks over his shoulder, drops my arms then backs away. "Someone is coming," he whispers. "We should get you back to your room before anyone sees you like this. Did Perth not provide his lover with more adequate clothing? I am shocked. Usually that family is so . . . put together."

An unfamiliar man appears behind Arland. "Arland Maher?"

He turns. "Leader Murchadha, it is very good to see you."

Leader Murchadha is tall—much taller than Arland—with tan skin, lean arms and legs, and a white beard down to the center of his chest. They embrace each other, slapping backs in happy greetings.

"Who is this lovely young lady behind you?" Murchadha tips his head in my direction.

"This is Katriona Wilde, sir. I would give you a proper introduction, but as you can see, she is not decent." Arland looks over his shoulder then winks.

For a second, I forget I'm *supposed* to hate him.

Murchadha glances at me. "*The* Katriona Wilde?"

"Yes, sir."

He clasps his hands behind his back. "Does Dufaigh know she is here?"

"Yes, sir."

"Why are you with the girl? Has he changed his mind? Have you two fallen in love the way the prophecy stated you would?"

I stop breathing. No one is supposed to know about that. Leader Murchadha knows more than most. He must be well trusted, but *I* must do something to end this conversation before Arland or I say or do something we shouldn't. "In love? What prophecy said I would fall in love with *him*? He is my guard, and he is failing miserably at keeping me protected. Arland, can you take me to my room now?"

Arland points down the hall. "Walk that way. I will be right behind you."

"What kind of bodyguard does that? Good thing I am as powerful as I am, otherwise I would be dead." I storm past the men and trudge off in the direction Murchadha came from. If Arland tells the Leader anything, that's his choice, but no matter how much I hate it, I have to play this role so no one else dies.

Once I'm in the shadows, I stop. I have no idea where I'm going. Arland must not have actually wanted me to leave. And what I said to him . . . .

I was so mean.

He already feels he's not good enough, and I basically told him he was a lousy protector.

Keeping my back pressed against the wall, I whisper the concealment spell and hope to the gods it works.

"She seems nothing like her father or mother." Murchadha glances over his shoulder.

I hold my breath and stay as close to the wall as possible. Murchadha turns around to face Arland again, and I exhale.

"Her anger did not seem genuine, though, Arland. I am aware you do not trust many, but you do know you can trust me?"

A faint smile cracks on Arland's face. "I have always known I can count on you, but she has no interest in me."

Murchadha sighs. "I pray for all our sakes you are wrong. The way that girl looked at you, I can hardly believe she loves anyone else."

I'm failing already.

"You must have misinterpreted her behavior. Moments before you arrived, she was yelling at me for looking at her. I have to admit, she is like her parents—although blind to the games played by the Dufaighs—she is strong, stubborn, and confident. It is unfortunate Perth was able to sweep her off her feet before me, but I did not lose everything. Her lovely sister came as a consolation prize."

Murchadha places his hand on Arland's shoulders. "I have known you since you were a child, Arland; in many ways you have been the son I lost when this war began. Will you forgive me if I say I do not believe a word you speak? If you feel there is something important enough for you to hold back the truth, I will not press you any further."

"Sir—"

"I understand it must be quite important. You have always been the most honest man. I saw the way you looked at her, as well, and I have never heard you speak of a woman as some sort of prize to be won. Be careful. The others may not know you as well as I do, but if you are going convince people, you are going to need to try harder than that."

The hinges of the old wooden door to the bathroom squeak like they haven't been opened in a hundred years. Brit pokes her head out.

Murchadha nods, drops his hand from Arland's shoulder, then walks away.

"Who was that?" she asks.

"Someone I did a terrible job of convincing."

"Convincing of what?"

Arland offers his arm to Brit; she's wrapped in her towel, and I imagine I look just as silly as her—if anyone could see me.

"We have to find Katriona before anyone else does. Apparently our eyes have a terrible way of giving us away."

"Tell me you weren't caught looking at each other."

He doesn't speak.

Stepping out of the protective bubble of my spell, I allow them to see me.

Arland glances up first, big creases lining his forehead. "You heard?"

I attempt to smile, but nerves probably make it look more like a grimace. "I concealed myself."

"We need to get you back to your room, and to Perth," he says. "Stay in front of us while we walk, put your best worst expression on your face, and pretend to be mad."

Turning around, I march down the hall in my ridiculously skimpy towel and do my best to scowl. We pass doors and passages leading in other directions. No one crosses our path, and there are no sounds to be heard; however, smells of chicken, potatoes, fruits, and so many other wonderful scents fill my nose and set my mouth to watering.

"Something smells really good," Brit says.

"That is the feast for your sister and Perth, my love."

I do my best not to fall over my feet.

"Arland!" A man calls from behind us. "Hold up."

"Sorry, Brice"—Arland says without stopping—"I must get these two ladies to their rooms. You may follow us if you wish, but I would advise keeping your eyes pointed at the floor."

I don't even give the man the time of day. Failure seems to be the only thing I'm good at lately, and adding one more suspicious person to the list is not what any of us needs.

"At the floor? Why am I not allowed to look at them?"

"If you look at that one, the Dufaighs will kill you, and if you look at this one . . . ."

Whoever Brice is, he sounds young—at least no older than any of us. "Understood. So who is she . . . the one belonging to the Dufaighs?"

"Katriona Wilde."

"Oh. You were not having a laugh; they truly would kill me for looking at her. Well, I have been summoned to the great room for some sort of spell casting. Now I know why. We should talk more later, Arland."

"Nice to meet you, Miss . . . ?"

"Brites Wilde. I'm Katriona's sister."

"What does your father say of you holding on to her arm the way you do, Arland?"

"He says I should be Bound to her, Brice. So I advise you avert your eyes from her indec—"

"But . . . ?"

Arland growls. "You have things to take care of in the great room. Go."

Curiosity piqued beyond control, I spare a glance over my shoulder. Brice *is* young—no older than Arland—his light brown hair is the only thing I make out before he disappears back into the shadows.

Arland points to his left. "This is it, Katriona."

This door is different from most I've seen anywhere in Encardia; it's wooden, but has black steel reinforced bars across the front of it.

"Lot of crime in this neighborhood?" Brit asks.

He tips his head toward the door. "It is a safe room for valuable people. Go on in. Rhoswen should be waiting for you."

"Who?" I wrap my hands around one of the prison cell bars for support. My legs are weak. My will to meet anyone else or go into the great room for a party—actually my will for any of this is just gone.

"Dufaigh's dresser."

I stare at my sister's arm hooked through Arland's. "Where will you guys be?"

He points to a door right next to mine. It doesn't have bars on it. "Brit will be there, and I will be outside. Always here for you. Knock if you need anything."

Expecting to find it locked, I slowly turn the handle on the door, but it opens right up. The room is well lit by a thousand candles. Crystal chandeliers hang from the ceiling. Glass jars line the floor, and polished silver candelabras rest atop a large oak table between the four poster bed and vanity—everything reeks of extravagance. These must have been Dufaigh's quarters.

A short young woman with long blonde hair stands tapping her toe, hands on her hips. A green velvet dress and a pewter brush rest on the table in the middle of the room.

"Rhoswen?" I ask, securing my towel around my chest.

"Yes. What took you so long? We have to get you ready for a celebration and look at you . . . ." Her lip rises to her nose like I smell bad. "This is going to take quite some time."

"Right, well I will leave you to it. Again, Miss Wilde, if you need anything, just knock and I will be here." Arland backs out of the doorway.

The metal hinges creak behind me, breaking my resolve. "Wait!"

He flashes a cross look, but pushes open the door enough to poke his head through. "Yes?"

"Do not get too cozy with my sister," I whisper so low Rhoswen cannot possibly hear me.

Arland looks past my shoulder then places his fist over his heart. "I promise to love you—and only you—through life and into death, Katriona. Remember that."

"You, too." I cannot imagine what me kissing Perth in front of everyone will do to Arland, but I know what him touching my sister has already done to me, and I don't like any of this.

CHAPTER TWENTY

Rhoswen leads me to a mirror in the back of the room. With a hand on each of my arms, she smiles at my reflection. The girl looking back at me is not Katriona Wilde; whoever this girl is, the most obvious thing about her is how battered she is. A light mustard color creates a circle under her left eye. Cuts and scratches cover her face and neck—wounds she didn't even know existed—and she appears ten pounds underweight.

Reaching my hand to my hair, I touch the small intricate braids Rhoswen created. They run from the front of my head to the back, twisting around each other until they finally become one. The end of the braid rests between my shoulder blades—a style I'd never choose.

She smacks my hand away and glares at the girl in the mirror. "You should not touch them. Your hair was not cooperative and will likely fall."

"I am sorry," I whisper, but I don't care if my hair falls from the braids.

Inspecting the rest of my alien form, I think about my mom and if she used to dress this way before she and my father escaped. Would Mom approve of me wearing a green velvet gown? Would the clothes remind her of herself? Of happier times? I don't think it's possible. Judging by the garments everyone else wears in Encardia, this kind of clothing could never be deemed appropriate.

I cannot believe in the midst of all this madness Dufaigh has the audacity to dress me this way. He's turned me into a weapon of false hope against everyone, and I hate it. Katriona's here to save the world, but she can't have what she desires, so you're not going to get what you desire either. Not that he'd ever tell any of them that.

"I do not know what you see in that boy," Rhoswen says, still looking at my reflection.

A tear sits in the corner of my eye, and I wipe it away before she sees. "What?"

"Katriona, I may be a Ground Dweller, but the boy is just like his father. We are all sick of their evil ways. You had life in your eyes until Leader Maher walked away, and you cry at your own reflection . . . I doubt you are Dufaigh family material."

"He is a good man," I say.

"Who?"

"Perth."

Rhoswen grabs my arm. "Turn and look at my eyes."

Without turning all the way around, I look over my shoulder. Her eyes have even less color than Perth's, her skin is a sickening shade of white, and her hair is bleach blonde. She's as colorless as snow.

"You have the power to end this war, do you not?"

If I respond with an honest answer and this is all a trick to see where my allegiances lie, then we will all be killed for sure. But if Rhoswen means what she says, and I lie, then I lose a possible ally. I wish there were a way to see through people the way I do the shifters.

I close my eyes, but see nothing to help me decide if she's trustworthy.

"I do have the power to end this war."

She cups my cheek with her cold hand. "Then leave this place and fight."

Pulling away from her, I shake my head. "I cannot."

She sighs. "Is it for love? For the boy?"

"Love is involved, Rhoswen. I—"

A loud knock at the door interrupts our conversation.

"It is probably better you tell me nothing, but there is something different about you. Not just your magic. There is something special about *you*. When you saw all these worthless possessions of the

Dufaigh's and turned up your nose, I knew you were good. Do not let us down." Dropping her hands to her sides, she crosses the room then opens the door.

I'm standing right where she left me, staring into the mirror with my mouth hanging wide-open.

Perth enters the room. He's dressed in a tan velvet tunic, dark brown leather pants, and a matching belt is cinched at his waist. He stops walking when we meet eyes in the mirror.

"Leave us," he says with no warmth in his tone.

"Yes, sir." Rhoswen glances at me then disappears behind the heavy door.

Closing the distance between us, Perth places his hands under my elbows, taking care of me as he might a delicate flower. His chest presses against my back.

"Why are you so close to me?" I ask.

"We are about to step out for a celebration in our honor, and you ask why I am so close to you? You should get used to it." He takes a firmer hold on my elbow then spins me around to face him. "They will expect us to show affections for one another. Will you be able to handle that?"

"I honestly don't know the answer to that question."

"Don't?" Arland's voice startles me. He stares at Perth with hostility I've never before seen displayed.

Brit walks in behind Arland, adorned in a new tunic and pants— nothing fancy for her. I'm the only one wearing a dress. She closes the door then trails behind him over to where Perth still holds me up against his body.

Shaking free of him, I run to Arland then wrap my arms around his neck. "Do not. Are you going to correct me every time I make a mistake?" I ask for the millionth time.

"If it will save your life . . . yes." He holds me back. "It is too dangerous for us to hug even here, Katriona."

"Sorry." I back up then stand by Perth.

"His father will expect a show, so give him one. Kiss if you must, hold hands, sneak off, but do not go overboard. He will suspect something if you are too enthusiastic."

"So I have permission to kiss the Great Arland Maher's woman. How wonderful is this?"

I punch Perth in the gut.

"Definitely do not do anything like that in front of my father," he says, wheezing. Perth grabs my hand then laces his fingers with mine.

I stare at our hands.

"So what were you and Rhoswen discussing?"

"She said you and your father are evil and everyone is sick of your family's ways. She thinks I should leave and fight, and that she can sense I am good."

Perth's face drains; his color reminds me of the cloud I visited when I died. "We must tell my father."

"He will kill her. Why would—?"

He grabs my forearms and shakes me. "She was trying to trap you. What did you say to her? Did you tell her anything?"

"Get your hands off her, Perth." Arland sticks his arm between us, knocking Perth back a bit, then stands with his arms crossed over his chest and glares.

I watch the two, sure the testosterone will make one of them explode any moment. "What could I say? She asked if I had the power to end this war; I told her yes. She asked why I do not just go out and fight; I told her I cannot. Then she asked if love was involved, and I told her yes."

"And that is all?" Perth asks.

"Yes. Your knock interrupted us from talking about anything else."

"Do us all a favor. The next time anyone asks you anything, throw a fit. Whether they are on our side or not—and there are not very many Ground Dwellers who are—we cannot risk exposure. Be mean, threaten them, punch them if you have to, Katriona, but do not let it pass by lightly."

Throw a fit? Perth's father is deplorable; he'll kill anyone who stands against him, or he'll at least see them and their family diminished to nothing. I swallow hard. "Do you know which Ground Dwellers are on our side?"

"Yes, and Rhoswen is not one of them." Perth mimics Arland's stance. "You should be the one to tell my father."

"*Me?* Why?" I ask, throwing my hands up.

"You have something to prove to him; I do not." The corner of Perth's mouth twists up. "Put on your best demure face. Make him think you do not understand how anyone could say we are evil, and mention how she offended you to the core."

Brit rolls her eyes. "You've got to be kidding me? Kate would never speak that way."

"No, Brit, Perth is right." Arland stares at me, melting my insides with a combination of love and fear. "Kate has something to prove, and Dufaigh has spies. I do not doubt Dufaigh sent Rhoswen to test your sister."

"But she's a terrible liar."

"Why don't you lie for me then?"

He smiles. "Don't?"

"*Arland!*" I say, stomping my foot.

"I am sorry. I am only trying to protect you."

"I know, but I meant what I said. Brit is a wonderful liar, and I am not. You and I have things we need to talk about. Does it not make sense for her and me to switch places?" Never mind getting me out of kissing Perth and her Arland.

Now everyone in the room aside from me has their arms crossed over their chests.

"I am not going to kiss Perth for you. I'm not that good of a liar."

Perth makes a small squeaking noise.

She puts up her hands. "Sorry, Perth, no offense."

"Oh, none taken. I am just the man no women desire. Feels wonderful."

She raises an eyebrow then looks at me with the same impatient scowl as before. "Do you seriously not trust me with Arland?"

"I do. I am just . . . ."

"Afraid to lie? Afraid to kiss Perth and hurt Arland? Afraid for me to kiss Arland and it hurt you? I can read your thoughts without even being in your head. I'm your sister, remember? You are smart and confident when you use your magic, why not when it comes to other things? You need to do whatever it is we've come here for, and you need to do it fast." Brit turns on Arland; she's taking control. She's either not afraid anymore, or she's beyond her tolerance level.

"Out in the hall you told your dad to send Cadman and Saidear to Wickward, but Kate needs an army. When will they be back?"

"It is another fifty miles to Wickward. Assuming they have no issues with daemons and are able to regain control of the base, it could be a week."

She steps toward Perth, arms still crossed over her chest. "Okay, Perth, your dad said you could have two weeks to court Kate?"

His eyes widen. "Not specifically, but I believe we can get away with two weeks."

"Kate, you have to unite everyone?" Brit asks, turning to me.

I love watching her take control. She's just like our mom. "Yes. Where are you going with all this?"

"Well, the thing is, you've been given time to find a way to unite everyone. Perth's dad won't force him to do anything for at least two weeks, two of the best soldiers for your army will be back in a week, and all of that gives you time to do the uniting. I cannot do this for you; it was your task, your place in this world. We don't know what mine is, but I don't think it was to fill in as temporary Kate when life gets too tough. If you need to talk to Arland tonight, I won't get in the way, but I will not kiss him for you," she says, pointing at Perth. "And I won't lie to his dad for you either. So don't ask."

"You are right." I sigh. "This is my problem, and it was wrong for me to ask you to do anything. I will throw the fit to Dufaigh, kiss Perth—"

"You make that sound awful." Perth stares at his feet.

I ignore his pouty lips. "And then if I can borrow you for a while, I will talk to Arland."

"Okay," Brit says.

"Meetings with all of us will only draw attention—we should go." Arland holds out his hand.

Brit heads toward the door first, followed by Perth, but Arland stops me on my way by.

"I will not enjoy this any more than you, but please, do not worry about my feelings. I know where your heart lies." He kisses my cheek then nudges me to pass.

Walking away from him is like walking away from my foundation; every step cracks another piece.

Perth offers me his hand. "Ready?"

"I guess."

Brit opens the door, and the four of us make our way through the dark halls. The floor and walls are made of stone, but time has not done this place well. Dirt reveals itself through fissures, like nature is trying to reclaim what doesn't belong. The further along we travel through the ancient base, following along twisting paths and up staircases, the stronger the smell of food becomes.

Our pace quickens. Another set of stairs is a minor inconvenience on our quest for sustenance. Suddenly the worry about the lies and my mom and everything else fade away, and all I think of is chicken and bread and vegetables. The warm smell of wheat and flour transport me back home to the farm. Mom would bake bread on the weekends and serve it to me and Gary after long hard days of work.

Boots clack on the steps as we run up. Breathing heavy, we round another corner then come face-to-face with two huge, round wooden doors armed with guards easily recognizable as Ground Dwellers. The more I meet, the more I realize their lack of color and size is what gives them away. These guards don't carry spears or swords; instead, they are outfitted with leather battle armor on their arms and chests. Their eyes reflect no emotion. Their faces are hard and empty.

"Why does the great room need guards?" I ask Perth, tugging at his hand like an innocent child.

He kisses my forehead. "For your protection, of course."

"Are these big oafs planning to move from our way?" I bat my eyelashes.

The one on the left laughs under his breath and steps aside. "Katriona Wilde I presume?"

"Yes. And you are?"

"Not as important as you." With a nod and a smile aimed at me, the small man takes hold of the door's iron handle and tugs. He groans and pulls with considerable effort, and after what should have taken a strong man a few seconds, the door opens allowing light and smells and music to pour out into the hall.

"After you," he says, holding out his hand for us to pass.

Linking arms and thanking the guards, Brit and Arland go through first. I open my mouth to say thank you as well, but Perth pinches me.

"Ow. Why did you do that?"

He winks at the chivalrous Ground Dweller then looks down at my arm. "I did not do a thing."

I pinch him back.

"Ow. Why did *you* do that?"

Patting his hand, I say, "Stop playing games, Perth. I am hungry, and we have serious business to speak with your father about."

He chuckles. "This is why I love you. You are always about business."

The music stops. There could be no worse time for this. Hundreds of people fill the room, scattered about like small cliques at a high school dance, and every single one of them have their eyes on us and will surely hear what I'm about to say, but I have to say it. As much as I don't mean it, I have to say it.

Keeping my eyes on Perth, I squeeze his hand—mostly to keep from falling over, but onlookers won't know that. "And I love you because you have a way of making me smile in serious times like these."

No one speaks. The music doesn't restart, and I'm afraid to look at anyone. I gather up my courage and peek ahead at the Leader's table—it's about twenty feet away. Arland and Brit have already arrived and watch Perth and I as we approach; neither appear the least bit fazed by the exchanged I love yous. However, those sitting at the Leader table share mixed looks of wide eyes and wide smiles.

Two empty chairs sit behind the middle of the table while two more empty chairs sit behind its right side. I don't have to guess to know who the ones in the middle belong to, and it makes me sick. High Leader Maher belongs at the center of the table, and if not him, it should be Arland and me. Perth has no business there.

"Glad you could finally make it. We were beginning to worry your guard had failed you as he has failed so many others," Dufaigh says, standing. He looks down the other side of the table at High Leader Maher, Leader Murchadha, and the beautiful woman next to him, then my mother.

"Show some respect. My son is here with his future wife. Soon he will rule Encardia. Stand."

"There is not much for him to rule," someone calls from behind us.

I look over my shoulder, but cannot tell who made the comment.

Dufaigh shakes his head. "It is a shame you cannot control your people, Kimball. If any of my own spoke that way, I would have them killed."

Leader Maher glances into the crowd. The strong man from the communications room when I visited through the chatter box is not here. Something in him is gone. Fight. Tenacity. Passion. I don't know how to describe it, but the way he looks for whoever spoke out makes me think he'd like to tell the person to shut up and stop bothering him. Maybe he's ready to die or sick of the fight.

After twenty years of this, I'd be done too.

"Never mind who dishonored their Leader, right Kimball?" Dufaigh returns his attention to us and places his hand on top of his fat belly. "Please, Son, Katriona, come take your seats. Arland, Brites, you may have a seat at the end. Enjoy it while you can, for soon you will have no place at this table."

Arland squares his shoulders. "I would rather sit with the people. Keep your seats. Brites?" He offers his arm, and she links hers through, then they walk away.

I wish I was her right now.

"Suit yourself then." Dufaigh glares after Arland. "Make sure you are always within sight of Katriona."

If Dufaigh only knew how important that was to his own survival, would he still be playing these power games?

Perth takes my hand and leads me to the other side of the table. He pulls out my chair, and I take a seat next to High Leader Maher. He offers me a smile, but little else as far as pleasantries go.

Dufaigh snaps his fingers. "Camlin!"

A Ground Dweller comes from a door behind the Leader table then waits by Dufaigh like a dog waiting for commands. "Yes, sir?"

"Bring these two their meals. The girl should have extra portions"—Leader Dufaigh glances at me—"she could stand to gain a few pounds. And tell Abenzio to play more music. This is a celebration and everyone is standing around staring."

He faces the crowd. "Eat. Drink. Have a good time. My son is here with the long lost Katriona."

Heat rises into my cheeks. I should take his concern for my weight as a compliment, but coming from him, I know it's not—plus I've seen myself in a mirror, I'm not a pretty sight.

Perth leans next to my ear. "I believe you look beautiful. No matter what, and no matter who you truly love."

"Tha—"

Flutes tweet out a sweet melody, interrupting the chattering crowd and my thanks to Perth for his unwelcome compliment. Camlin returns and places a plate with a heaping portion of food in front of me.

Waiting for everyone else to get their meals is torture.

Once all the food has been delivered, including the servings to the crowd, I scarf down my chicken, carrots, and potatoes like I've never eaten. I'm vaguely aware of Dufaigh's eyes on me, but I don't care—he'll probably enjoy watching me eat like the heathen *he* is.

In a matter of minutes, I empty my plate. Camlin sets another one in front of me.

"No thank you," I say, wiping my face with my napkin.

"Go on, child. Eat. It is clear Arland not only failed to keep you safe, but he failed to feed you, as well. I promise you will never go hungry again." Leaning in front of Perth, Dufaigh pushes the dish closer to me.

One look at the Leader's oversized belly tells me he isn't lying.

"Thank you for the offer, but I have already eaten more than enough." While I have his attention, I should probably find a way to tell him about Rhoswen. I hope Perth was right about her; otherwise I fear for her life. Thinking about what I should say, I bite my lower lip.

Perth leans next my ear again. "Let go of your lip and talk to him. Do not wait much longer, or I am afraid he will think poorly of you."

Our faces are close, too close. Perth's breaths dance across my cheek, sending my neck hairs straight on end. He squeezes my sweat-drenched hand. I feel the eyes of his father on us—of everyone on us—and know this must be the perfect time for a kiss. Focusing my thoughts on what I love, on what this means, on why I'm doing this, I send magic out from my heart to—

"Perth, do not force the girl to display affections for you in public so soon. It is obvious the two of you care for one another, but you have just announced your courtship. Do not be so forward," a woman says, standing behind Perth.

He lifts my chin and smiles. "Public affection is not something she is fond of, Maura, but I am working on her."

I swear his eyes appear greener than before.

"Yes, well she is a smart woman for wanting to keep her affections private." The Ground Dweller squeezes between our chairs then offers me her hand. "My name is Maura."

Ignoring the chill in her skin, I stay firm in my grip. "Katriona."

"I have heard a lot about you, Katriona. I am Perth's aunt. If you have any questions about the family and our history, please, come to me. My brother will be too busy to answer most questions, and as a High Leader in training, Perth will be fairly busy as well. But of course, there will be scheduled visits and nightly dinners, so you will have time to ask him questions."

"Scheduled visits?"

"Oh yes, Katriona. You will need alone time, but not too much. We would not want you two to do anything before your Binding." A blonde lock falls in front of her eyes, and she swipes it away as someone might a gnat.

Part of me wants to laugh and the other part wants to vomit. I bite the inside of my cheeks to keep from smiling.

"Maura, if the children decide to do something before the Binding, it does not much matter," Dufaigh says, waving.

She turns on her heel and faces him, hands propped on her hips. "What is the purpose of the courtship then? Why not just allow them to consummate the relationship so you can strip her and the Maher child of their titles?"

"Maura, you make it sound like I am evil. Is this not what you want for our people?"

"It is, Brother." She pats my shoulder then works her overly plump self back through the chairs. "We will discuss things later."

"Thank you."

Maura stares at me as if she's never heard those words spoken to her, shakes her head, then returns to her seat next to her brother.

Should I not have said thank you? Should I not be nice? The more I talk, the more I feel like I'm digging holes. I need to speak to Dufaigh about Rhoswen *now*. "Leader Dufaigh?"

"Yes, Child?" he asks, gnawing off a piece of chicken from its bone.

"May I speak with you in private?"

He tears at another piece of chicken then shoves it into his mouth using his fingers. "Whatever you need to say, you may say here."

"No, sir, what I have to say needs to be spoken in private."

Dufaigh slams his fist on the table, ending every conversation in the room. "Perth, what is the meaning of this?"

Perth stares at his plate. "You need to hear what she has to say, Father."

"Guards." Dufaigh claps his hands over his head.

The two guards from outside the hall rush up to him. "Yes, sir?" they say in unison.

"Are you two capable of controlling her if she gets out of line?" he asks, pointing his disgusting, greasy finger at me.

They look at me with their milky-blue eyes and smile. "That one poses no threat to us, sir."

"Good. Come with us, but do your best not to listen." Dufaigh stands, grabs the chicken leg from his plate then heads toward the exit on the side of the room. He looks over his shoulder. "Are you coming?"

Perth and I stand then trail behind the Leader and his guards. We pass through the small door leading to the area where I met Vanora. The door squeaks closed on its hinges.

Everyone turns and looks at me.

"I . . . I need to . . . to—"

Licking his fingers, Dufaigh laughs. "You said you needed to speak to me, at this rate we will never have a conversation." He smacks his lips, turning my stomach in the process. "Get on with it."

"Rhoswen approached me before the celebration."

He stops eating, then hands his chicken to one of the guards. "Leave us."

"Yes, sir." The men don't even flinch at the disgusting behavior of their Leader; they just turn and walk away.

"Go on."

"Well, she said everyone is sick of you and Perth and your evil ways, and that I should leave and end the war."

He growls, narrowing his eyes, and walks closer to me. "And what did you say to her?"

"I told her I have the power to end the war, but I stay for love." When said that way, it almost sounds like I'm on board with this idea, and she won't be able to deny I said either of those things.

"Is that all?"

"Yes, sir."

"You are powerful, Katriona. The next time someone disgraces your family, I expect you to deliver an immediate punishment. I will handle Rhoswen." He brushes past me and back into the great room.

Perth stares after his father.

"That is it? Will he test me again? Is he going to—?"

"His reaction was strange. I do not know what to make of it. Give me time to think, but he *will* test you again, count on that." Perth takes my hand.

I squeeze his fingers; his support is priceless.

"Do you dance?" he asks.

I smile, remembering all the dancing lessons Gary tried to give me. "My sister is a better dancer than me, but my feet do not get in the way like they did when I was a child."

Perth pulls me close to him then wraps his arm around my shoulders. "Will you give me one dance before you trade places with your sister?"

Something about the tenderness in his voice, about the gentle way he wraps his arms around me, makes me sorry for him. "Yes."

CHAPTER TWENTY-ONE

Dancing with Perth in a room full of people—all with different expectations of me—is not as bad as I imagined it would be. The music is light and most of the candles have been snuffed out, creating a romantic ambiance, and almost everyone is smiling and having a good time.

It's fun switching partners, pressing hands together and dancing around each other. The room echoes like there are a million drums all playing the same beat. With each step I take, my hair falls loose around my face. I hike up my dress with one hand and laugh and kick my feet, then spin around to the next person.

We were only supposed to have one dance, but this is the most fun I've had in what feels like forever. Growing up I'd always dance around the family room with my mom—some of these same steps—and we'd laugh so hard we'd wear our stomachs out long before our feet.

I catch Mom smiling at me from the end of the table—from her position of disgrace—and thank the gods she's been allowed to live. Of course, Dufaigh probably intends to kill her as soon as I'm Bound to his son.

Lucky for her that will never happen.

Weaving my way around people, I continue to dance, continue to allow my hair to fall, continue to have fun . . . until I meet hands with Arland. His light touch, his radiating warmth—everything about him calls me to be near. The smile falls from my face. My laughter gets caught in my chest; I should be having fun with him, not Perth. I should not be having fun at all. What are we doing? The world is dying and we're dancing the night away.

Someone presses their little hands against my back, nearly pushing me over. "Oh, I am sorry," a young girl says.

I straighten myself. "It is okay."

So not to make my sudden mood change any more obvious, I dance my way back to Perth, take his hand then tug him toward our table.

"Tired?" he asks, breathless.

"Very." I take my seat. "And thirsty."

"Camlin"—Perth calls, mimicking his father's cold tone—"bring Katriona something to drink."

"Yes, sir." Camlin frowns at me then stalks off.

I wait for him to pass through a door leading into what I presume is the kitchen, then glare at Perth.

"Have I done something?" he asks, batting his blonde eyelashes.

"Is it impossible for you to show kindness to your own people?"

"It is possible . . . if I want to have my head chopped off."

Looking around, I check for his father or anyone who shouldn't hear our secrets. "He is heartless, Perth. You are ten times the man your father will ever be."

Perth's head snaps in my direction. A genuine smile grows on his face, and for once, he looks warm. His hand tightens around mine, and the chill fades away. "Those are the kindest words anyone has ever spoken to me."

I lean closer to him. "They are the truth."

We lock eyes, and my heart pounds wildly in my chest—this is another one of those perfect moments, but this is almost too perfect. I fear a kiss would mean too much to Perth now.

"Thank you," he says.

I laugh, high-pitched. "Ahh, so you do know the meaning of those words."

"I lie well," he says, cold returning to his features.

Camlin sets a golden goblet filled with a burgundy liquid in front of me. "Your drink."

"What is this?" I sniff the sweet, fruity fragrance wafting toward me.

"It is wine. Very hard to come by these days. Enjoy." Camlin tips his head then returns to his place along the wall with his hands linked in front of him.

"Wine?" I bring the goblet to my lips then smell one more time.

Perth slides his finger along the rim, pushing it away from my mouth. "Take one very small sip, then turn your nose up at it."

I do as he instructs, then set the goblet down. "Why?"

"It is poison."

"*Poison?*" I bring my napkin to my lips then wipe my tongue on it. *Good thing the room is dark.*

"Not that kind of poison." He smiles, watching me frantically lick the fabric. "It is something my father gives people when he wants information from them. He does not trust you, though I am not sure why. Are you positive Rhoswen did not say anything else to you?"

"I told you everything."

Perth caresses his finger down my cheek, tormenting my insides. "We are not putting on a good enough show."

"*Kate, can you hear me?*" Brit asks, invading my thoughts.

Finding her in the crowd, I nod.

"*Good. Do you still need to talk to Arland?*"

"*Yes.*"

"*He says you should talk now. After dancing comes some stupid speech by that asshole, then it's everyone to their rooms—according to Arland at least. So anyway, I think you're doing great. Well, you were until you got near Arland while you were dancing . . . are you stupid?*"

"No," I blurt then press my hand to my mouth before I say anything else.

"No, what?" Perth asks.

"Nothing. Sorry."

"Oh. I understand." He scans the crowd then stops when he sees my sister. "You are speaking with her?"

"Yes."

"I will remain quiet. Will she be visiting soon?"

"Yes."

"*Apparently you* are *stupid. You're supposed to be the smart sister. Anyway, you ready to switch?*"

Without answering, I focus on her, on connecting to the thoughts streaming through her head, on being inside her veins and controlling her muscles. My head tingles, my arms and feet do as well. The room darkens then everything fades to black.

I'm floating on air, drifting through the room toward my sister. People dance around me, through me. When I pass, they reach for something they cannot touch, smile up at me as though they can see me, then dance with more energy as if my presence is a drug.

My spirit floats into Brit's body. I wiggle my fingers and toes then look back at the table where Perth sits—he's laughing and talking to me, or Brit as me.

"You feel strong right now, do you not?" Arland takes my hand and laces his fingers with mine.

"How—?"

"Because every time you get near me, I feel it, too. This place—being surrounded by evil people, being forbidden to be near one another—it makes us stronger." He tugs me closer to him. "I would kiss you, but it would be unfair to use Brit that way."

I rest my head on his chest and breathe in the scents I've grown to love as much as the man who wears them. The dry leaves, dew, pine—earth—all these smells settle my nerves and calm my soul.

"I miss Flanna. She would find a way to make this all fun. Where is she?"

He caresses his hand up and down my back. "She and Shay are together. I believe Flanna is grieving for Lann now. Without having anyone to lead, there is no reason for her to be strong. Honestly, I believe that is where most of the soldiers from Watchers Hall are . . . grieving."

Pulling away, I look around the room. Arland is right; our soldiers aren't here. "I need to be with them, with her."

"She would like that very much. However, there is no other person in Encardia who holds more contempt for Dufaigh than Flanna. If you were to be nice to her in any way, he would become suspicious."

"Why do they hate one another so much?" I ask, resting my head on his chest again.

"Her mother should never have been attacked by daemons. Dufaigh made a poor decision that held our families in The Meadows too long. She blames him for her death."

"I think he is to blame for a lot of things," I say, realizing I haven't seen the man since we spoke. "Where did he go?"

"He grabbed Rhoswen and his door guards then left shortly after you and Perth came back in. Although, I think you were enjoying yourself a bit too much to notice."

I stare into his emerald eyes. "Sorry. I—"

He smiles and traces my cheek with his finger, forcing me to close *my* eyes. "Please, do not feel guilty. I rather loved watching you dance and laugh. I cannot wait for the day we have a celebration like this."

"Will we get one?"

"When we end this war, my love, we will have a celebration bigger than this one. The guest of honor will be the sun." Squeezing me, he kisses the top of my head.

Cadman bursts through the double doors then rushes up to Arland, creating an entrance so loud everyone turns their heads to see. "Sir, I need to speak with Katriona."

Arland drops his hold on me. "Lower your voice. She is right here, using her connection with Brit to speak with me. What do you need of her?"

Cadman draws in deep breaths, chest heaving as if no amount of air could help him recover. "I believe I have discovered why Wickward was infiltrated."

"And that reason is . . . ?"

"Shifters, sir. The very same problem we had at Watchers Hall. Katriona was able to see through their disguise, and I need to know how."

I glance around the room, hoping no one can hear us. "Cadman, I have no idea how that works."

His red brows furrow, enhancing his wrinkles, reminding me how old he is. "You do not understand how it works, but what do you do?"

"Close my eyes and pray their forms are revealed to me."

Arland laughs. "Have you prayed a lot recently?"

"More than you will ever know," I say, smiling.

Cadman gets down on one knee then takes my hand, looking at me with utter desperation. This is the kind of fight I expected to see in High Leader Maher, in more of the people here, but everyone is complacent to rot to death.

"It is your magic . . . no, it is the old magic which belongs to every Draíochtan that makes you able to see through them. You must teach me how to use it. We leave in six hours. Will that be adequate time?"

"Stand up," Arland says, narrowing his eyes and looking toward the head table. "*Now.*"

"Yes, sir." Cadman stands. "I apologize for causing a scene, but I must know, I must save these people and bring them here—we need them for your army." He tugs my hand, eyes wide and palms sweating.

"Close your eyes, Cadman, and focus on everything you love—not just the sunlight as you wished for on the top of that cave so long ago, but for *everything.* Concentrate love over your heart, let it grow inside you and turn to anger, anger toward Darkness and his daemons, toward whatever it is you seek to destroy. When that anger grows so big you cannot contain it in your heart any longer, allow it to spread through your chest, down your arms and legs, then command it to do what you want."

"And that will help me see the shifters?" he asks like an eager student.

"No, that will be how you control old magic. To see the shifters, you must use the old magic, close your eyes and ask the gods to reveal the shifter's true form to you. Do you understand?"

"Yes. I will practice this now. If it works, I will teach the others. Thank you." He turns my hand over then places his lips in the center of my palm. "I will be in contact, sir. Watch over her."

Arland claps Cadman's shoulder. "No. Thank *you*. Be safe. I will see you soon, my friend."

Arland watches his best warrior walk through the double doors, then returns his gaze to me. "The music is dying down, the people are returning to their seats. A kiss will be expected. Promise not to enjoy it?"

"Enjoying it is impossible. I will think of you and only you." I place my fist over my heart in the same way he did for me. "I love you."

"And I love you."

"*I'm coming back*," I think.

"*I know. And you're not stupid; I'm sorry for saying it. I don't know why I keep saying so many mean things.*"

"*I know you're sorry. It's okay.*"

My connection to Brit, and Arland's warmth, disappears. I'm floating through the great room again. I return to my body, and the strength of Arland is replaced by Perth's small, cold fingers laced with mine. Finding my love in the crowd, I see Brit showing him some of the same affections I just did. I don't know if she's trying to keep consistent with how we love him or what, but it doesn't make me feel good to watch. In fact, her head on his chest makes my heart hurt, my body ache. How will I survive two weeks of this? How will I survive another day of this?

Perth tucks a loose strand of hair behind my ear. "Stop staring at him, Katriona. People will notice."

"Sorry." First I'm apologizing to Arland for having too much fun, now I'm apologizing to Perth for looking at Arland.

I'm done.

"Can we go back to our rooms now? I am exhausted," I say, leaning my head on Perth's shoulder.

He rests his head on mine. "My father has a speech planned, and my uncle wishes to meet you."

I sigh. "Is it going to be like this every night?"

"Speeches, meeting people, and dancing—probably. You are the key to my father's success, remember?"

"Arland said he went off with Rhoswen and the guards after we talked to him . . . are you sure she is not on our side?"

"I do not doubt my father will punish her publicly just to make you cave and speak against him. Do not fall for his tricks." Perth lifts his head then draws my face toward his with his finger. "Shall we go meet my uncle?"

"I guess." I take his hand then follow him out into the crowd.

We approach his Aunt Maura standing with a man who looks more like Perth than Perth's father.

The thin man frowns when he notices us. "Perth, I was wondering when you would introduce me to your prize. Nice of you to finally bring her over."

Perth puts his arm around my waist, drawing me near at the hip. "I apologize, Uncle Lorne, it has been a whirlwind of an evening. Katriona, this is my Uncle. Uncle Lorne, Katriona."

I offer my hand but the same courtesy is not returned.

Uncle Lorne's eyes have no visible iris, and his skin is closer in color to the gray coscarthas than that of a normal person's. "Pleasure to meet you."

"Oh, the pleasure is all mine."

Jerk.

He tips his head toward Arland and Brit. "What do you think of your sister and her affections for that boy who did a terrible job protecting you?"

Noticing their linked hands, I scowl. "I cannot control who my sister loves."

Lorne laughs. "Good answer. I like her, Perth. And to think your father thought he would need to force his hand to get her to marry you. Apparently you have inherited some of his charms, no?"

Disgusting.

Perth smiles at me. "It appears I have—and a good thing, too; Katriona will make fine children someday."

I have to force myself not to blurt out who those children's father will really be.

"Speaking of my father and his charms, would you happen to know where he is? I expected a speech of some kind, and Katriona is exhausted—I told her we would rest after he releases us."

Lorne straightens and uses his eyes to exchange some unspoken agreement with Maura. "Your father will not be available for the remainder of the evening. Go on to bed."

"Oh, okay. Well, I will return Katriona to her room then meet up with my father." Perth tugs my hand.

Lorne grabs Perth's arm, yanking us back toward him and Maura. "On second thought, you should meet with him now. Say goodnight to Katriona then have Arland return her to her room. I will have Deverill and Cyric accompany them as well, so you or your father will not have any concerns."

Perth turns to me. This is it, the moment where I have to make my Broadway debut, the moment where I find out how willing I am to do this.

"Are you going to be okay without me?" He strokes my cheek with the back of his bony fingers.

I nod. "I wish we had more time to spend together, but I understand you must speak with your father."

He cups my cheek, sending chills across my face, sending a shock to my heart and knees. "I love you."

"I love you, too." I wrap my arms around him and imagine the brave man I'm watching him become, the man who wants honor and a family and to do the right thing. Then I imagine Arland and pretend I'm going to kiss him, because I can think of nothing else to make me want to do this. Strong Kate is gone, replaced by weak Katriona who only cares about her heart.

Perth closes his eyes and leans into me. Our lips meet. He parts mine slowly rather than sweetly, like he's never kissed anyone before. His mouth doesn't open, but the longer we're connected, the closer he pulls me into him, the harder he presses against me and then—

Everything is black. My stomach twists and rises into my throat. I'm going to be sick. Smoke from burning bodies fills the sky, making the air foul with the scent of charred hair and skin. Cries ring in my ears. Death is littered on the ground for miles. I look down at my feet and see Brit, gurgling, blood draining from the corner of her mouth and open wounds over her chest and arms.

"B-B-Brit." I fall to my knees then press my hands against her cuts, apply pressure to stop the bleeding, but I'm too late.

She's dying.

"Who did this? Who killed her?" I scream but receive no response.

Body trembling, her eyes roll back in her head.

"No . . . ." I ball my fists and look up.

Daemons approach by the thousands, led by Brad who's naked and covered in crimson. The Brad I knew struggles against Dughbal, stopping every few steps, slowly placing a foot forward, then making a considerable effort before moving another.

"K-kill him, Kate," Brit says, eyes returning to the here and now. "You have to kill him. C-come b-back for m-m-me."

Arland rests his hand on my shoulder—his warmth and smell give him away before I turn around. "You must leave her, Kate. Dughbal is your kill, and he is waiting for you."

We're surrounded.

"Foolish boy, do you honestly believe this pathetic Draíochtan woman can kill me?" The sadistic voice coming out of the guy with blonde hair, blue eyes, and a football player build, screams out insanity.

A tear falls from my chin then lands on Brit's cheek. Closing my eyes, I think only of her and the life stolen from her, I think of all the times we spent sleeping, laughing, and crying together. I imagine the life she would have had if it weren't for this god standing in front of me in my best friend's body. She could've had Brad, she could've had love, she could've had everything she ever wanted.

Flames grow from my core and spread like wild fire. Arland ignites as well as Perth on my left and Cadman, Flanna, Saidear, Tristan, and so many others who still live and fight with us.

"Your ancient magic will not be enough to save you. Fight and you will die a horrible death, Katriona." Dughbal licks his lips, the lips I've tasted, the lips that loved me once. "Give up and I will make it painless. Where you are going there will be peace."

"There will be peace until you steal our powers and ruin the Heavens, too. I will not give up, I will fight you and I will kill you."

"Very well. I rather enjoy a fight. Choose your death: swords, magic, or daemons?" Dughbal smiles, arms out at his sides, the tall, mangled coscarthas inching closer.

I toss my sword to the ground, glowing bright enough to illuminate miles of surrounding forest. "Magic."

"Wonderful choice," he says, raising his arms above his head. "Mharúgrá."

Black fog stretches from Dughbal and engulfs Arland's body, making him invisible against the night. He cries out, muffled but gut-wrenching.

"Not Arland, *no, no, no* . . . ." I run to him and close my eyes. "Save him. Save him, and kill Dughbal. End this *now.*"

Light fills the sky, bursts from the ground, descends from the trees and spirals around Arland and the billowing fog. The closer the magic gets, the dimmer the sprites become.

Drive the sword through his chest like you do his daemons. Griandor's words replay themselves in my mind. I glance at my sword lying on the ground near my feet, pick it up and abandon my love to kill Dughbal—it's the only way.

"You no longer wish to use magic?" He laughs and reaches out his hand, sword flying into his grip.

Marching toward him, I draw my claymore back and think of Arland's love and my sister's smile, then focus all my pain and anger into my heart. This will not continue. I will not lose anyone else.

Dughbal holds his arms out to the side and tips his head back. "Go ahead, child, strike me with your sword. I am a god. You cannot kill me."

It cannot be this easy.

I run to him then ram the blade straight through his chest. Thick black fluid oozes from his wound. He looks down himself, stumbling back a bit.

Dughbal's weapon falls to the ground with a thud.

With two hands, he pulls my sword from his chest then drops it. The metal clanks off his blade. The wicked god drops to his knees. "I do not understand."

I pick up my claymore, lift it over my head then drive it into his chest again. "You are a god, Dughbal, but your father took away your immortality a long time ago. You can be killed, and you just let me." I twist the hilt, ensuring his death is painful.

Over and over I remove the sword, plunge it into him and watch as more of his evil seeps from him and into the earth. The red dirt stains black around him.

"He is dead, Katriona," Perth says, clamping his hand on my shoulder and tugging me back. "We need to go."

"*Arland* . . . ." I turn, but Arland is nowhere to be found. "W-Where . . . ?"

Perth shakes his head. "He is gone."

"*No.* He's not gone. He can't be gone." My vision clouds, my knees tremble. "No. *No.* Not my love. Not—"

Perth's cold hands cup each of my cheeks now. His mouth is wide open, and I'm almost positive I'm kissing him in a way I never imagined I would. My eyes are closed, but everything appears blue— I'm glowing.

Pulling away, I offer him less of myself and drop my hands from his waist where I had my nails dug into his skin.

"That was . . . ." Perth whispers.

I spare a quick glance at Arland—his mouth hangs open, his eyes don't meet mine. He leans beside Brit's ear.

She nods and they turn and walk away.

No.

No.

Not Arland.

I lost him in my vision and in reality.

The wooden doors slam closed behind them. A piece of stone falls from the wall and crumbles on the floor.

No one watches Arland or Brit though; everyone stares at my body covered in blue flames. No one can possibly understand why my magic displayed itself. Arland cannot even understand *why* it happened.

But he must think I enjoyed kissing Perth.

And now I'm not protected from Dughbal. My heart sinks to my stomach. If Arland ever forgives me, I could lose him anyway. I hate this. I need to make the list of my visions, the list Brit suggested. I need to prepare for all Arland's possible deaths. I need to find a way to save him, and I need to end this war.

Lorne glances around the room. "Where has Arland gone off to? It is a good thing your father has other soldiers to help protect Katriona, Perth."

"I am sorry," Perth says, tearing his gaze from me to look at his uncle.

"Arland. He is gone. Deverell will have to escort her to her room. I will keep them posted outside her door tonight in the off chance Arland does not return." Lorne shakes his head. "Your father will have him executed for this."

"No, Uncle Lorne, my father will be very happy Arland ran off. Let him fall from grace publicly." Perth reaches for my hand again. "I will escort Katriona back to her room then meet my father."

Lorne laughs. "After that display, I do not understand why you do not go through with the Binding right now. You could have a very interesting evening."

I squeeze Perth's fingers between mine as hard as I can manage. He cannot believe I enjoyed that, or his uncle's comment.

Maura jabs the perverted Ground Dweller's ribs. He smirks, rubbing his side. "It was a mere suggestion, Maura."

She and I meet eyes; hers are the faintest shade of brown, like coffee with way too much creamer. "I believe Katriona needs rest, and Perth needs to meet his father. There will be no Binding tonight."

"And you know my father will get more enjoyment the longer we string this out and hurt the Light Lovers. If you see my father before I do, tell him I will meet with him shortly."

Perth rushes me out of the great room—everyone must assume we're going for more of what they watched, but in private. Once in the hall, he slows his pace then lets go of my hand. "What happened?"

I gasp, afraid to admit what happened, afraid to admit death may be Arland's fate. "I had a vision."

"That much I could decipher, but you went cold on me . . . you barely moved and I thought you had decided not to go through with the lie. Then you whispered 'No' in my mouth and kissed so . . . passionately. I have never experienced anything so wonderful in my life, Katriona. Please, kiss me again."

He pulls me into him, wrapping his arms around my waist, stealing my air, my hope, me . . . .

"I know you do not love me, and I know you never will, but please, one more time, kiss me like that."

Tears stream down my face, and I cannot stop them. Wriggling free from Perth's embrace, I run away. He follows, but I don't stop until I reach my room. I push through the door, slam and lock it closed behind me, then throw myself onto the bed.

Pounding comes—first in my head from crying too much, then at the door. I ignore whoever it is.

Dreams haunt me all night long. Sitting up in bed, I realize I fell asleep with my clothes on. I reach out for the sun to see what time it is—four in the morning, according to the position of the stars and moon.

My head still throbs, and my throat is dry. Someone laid out a baby-blue silk nightgown for me, so I slip from my ridiculous velvet dress and into the more appropriate one. I tiptoe to the door then unlock the top bolt, praying Arland is out there.

The hinges protest, echoing down the hall. Only the guards Deverell and Cyric stand outside my room.

"Can one of you get me a glass of water?"

I don't know which is which, but the same Ground Dweller who held open the door for me and Perth to enter the great room, is the same one who nods then walks up the stairs.

"Will you be needing anything else?" the other, short, blonde man asks.

"What is your name?"

"Cyric." He grins, looking me up and down with his beady, white eyes.

I hide myself behind the door. "Well, Cyric, can you bring my sister to me—and where is the other guard? I was told he had to remain in sight of me at all times."

"No one has seen Arland Maher or your sister since the celebration in the great room, but if I see either of them, I will be sure to send her your way."

My insides shake, but I remain calm on the outside. I know I can't keep this up though. "And Arland?" I purse my lips.

Cyric clears his throat, wearing an expression saying he doesn't care. "He will return, but whether he is put in charge of you again is up to your future husband."

"Thank you." The water no longer important, I close the door, go back to bed, then crawl under the covers.

Staring at the ceiling, I replay the events of the evening through my mind, but the disappointment on Arland's face haunts me more than anything else. His eyes, full of sadness, couldn't even meet mine. His expression, blank, empty, didn't reveal any of the warmth I've grown used to. If he ever wants to see me again, I'll have a lot of explaining to do—a lot of making up.

Someone knocks on the door.

I bury my head under the pillow and hum the song Flanna sang for me when I was afraid at Watchers Hall, her peaceful melody of words about Griandor and the sun, and try to sleep.

Another knock echoes through my head, adding to the pounding ache.

"Go away." I throw my lumpy down-filled pillow across the room then flip onto my belly. Unless Arland is outside my door, I'm not answering it. Considering how dangerous that would be and after what happened tonight, there's no way he's knocking.

Once the person outside my door gets the hint, I curl into a ball and sob myself to sleep.

CHAPTER TWENTY-TWO

Thump, thump, thump.

People banged on my door all night long. No one around here seems to learn. I'm sure if whoever it was had pressing matters, they would have barged in, but no one did.

Thump, thump, thump.

"Fine. I am coming. Just stop pounding my door." I throw the blankets from my legs then step onto the cold, stone floor with my bare feet. Wrapping my arms around myself, I pad over to the prison exit then turn the handle.

"Good morning, Katriona." Rhoswen holds up a tray of food with her left hand and carries multiple garments in colors of wine, blue, and gold with her right. Her face is swollen, black surrounds her eyes, and her lips are cut open.

"I brought you breakfast and clothes. Are you going to tell on me for something else today?"

I suck in a sharp breath, bringing my hand to my mouth, not sure what to say about her appearance. "I . . . ." I think about what Dufaigh told me, about how if anyone disgraced my family I should punish them immediately. As much as I hate to do it, taking in her wounds, I know I must. This has to be another test.

"I am not sorry. You insulted someone I love and therefore insulted Encardia . . . ."

She scowls. "May I come in?"

"Yes." I put my arm out and move aside.

Rhoswen hobbles toward the table in the center of the room then places the tray down. "You really should light a candle or two. Not good for the girl who brings light to be surrounded with so much darkness."

She snaps her fingers and all the candles in the glass jars on the floor spark to life.

"How . . . ?" I ask, spinning around to take in the sight.

"You have no idea how to play with Ground Dweller magic, do you? Only that ridiculous child's magic of the Light Lovers." She shakes her head, tossing the velvet garments over the tall mirror at the back of the room.

"And to think we thought you were different. You do not know anything at all. You are perfect for the Dufaighs. You may actually be worse, considering you have the power to end it all . . . you said so yourself."

I hate having to play this game—she's so convincing as someone fighting against Dufaigh—but I have no choice. How do I know who to trust and who not to? Griandor said to trust those around me, but does that apply to the dresser as well? Does it only apply to people I knew before I came here? The gods should have given me more. Why did they send me here to screw everything up? I could've just fought Dughbal; I didn't need to involve all these people.

Perth said Rhoswen was not on our side, and I know I can trust him, but everyone else told me not to. I want to scream, but resort to balling my fists and marching toward the wounded woman in my room. "Now wait just a—"

"Look," she says, bruised arms crossed over her chest. "Your words do not convince me, your anger seems directed elsewhere, and your love for Perth is as real as Dufaigh being a kind man. Do not lie to me—and do not for one minute assume I believe your lies. You are playing some game none of us understand, but we are smart enough to know we have never understood everything."

I move closer to her, try to send magic to her, to help heal her wounds. I don't know why, but I want to believe her. Why would she allow them to beat her so horribly if she were on the Ground Dweller's side? "We? There are more?"

Rhoswen narrows her light green eyes—

Her eyes. Yesterday they were nothing but white, and today, they have color to them. Just like Perth's have made slight changes. Could it be the Ground Dwellers who are on the right path have eye color? What if they can all be saved? Maybe that's how I unite our kinds? I bring the Ground Dwellers to the path of Light by interacting with them? Maybe I should tell her everything, help her understand what we're doing here. Maybe she'll tell others, and they'll help. "You—"

Stop. Griandor's voice booms in my head, nearly bringing me to my knees. *She is not ready and neither are the other Ground Dwellers. Your work here is not an easy task. Take caution. Take time.*

Rhoswen taps her foot, lifting a golden eyebrow. "You were saying . . . ?"

I shake my head. "Nothing. Would you be willing to teach me Ground Dweller magic? I would hate only to know the powers of the Light Lovers. Do the Sea Dwellers have magic, as well?"

"Amú ama, tá sí," she mutters.

"What?"

Rhoswen points to the chair, revealing a long cut running from her wrist up to the middle of her chalky-white forearm. She notices me staring and pulls her tunic sleeve down to cover the wound. "I said you are a waste of time. Even if I teach you the magic of all Draíochtans, it will not matter. The only way Darkness will ever be defeated is for all the worlds to be opened and for *all* people to fight together."

Please tell me she's not right, Griandor. Please tell me you only meant I had to unite everyone in this *world. There's no way we can travel into all the others with what little army we have left. I don't even know where the other portals are, or what madness we might face in those worlds. I only know of Earth, and I know no one there would believe this. Griandor?*

I collapse onto the cushy, suede-covered chair and close my eyes. "That does not matter to me. I will not be involved in the fight, remember?"

"You will die like the rest of us then," she says, dragging a brush through my hair without regard for the amount of tangles—or my scalp. "And I guess I will die *today* when you tell Leader Dufaigh what we spoke of?"

Gritting my teeth, I clench my fists around the armrests on the wooden chair. "I suppose so—and maybe you deserve it." *God, forgive me.* I've broken Arland's heart, made Perth long to kiss me, lost my best friend, have no idea where my sister is, don't know if my mother will live another day, and I've just sentenced this woman to her death.

"I will refrain from braiding your hair today. It appears you do not like Light Lover traditions even though that is your heritage. It is a shame you are not more like your parents—"

"*Enough!* Just show me what to wear then leave." I'm too conflicted to have her here. I want to help her, but can't. I want to protect her, but can't. I want to find Arland and escape this place, but can't.

Rhoswen gasps and drops the brush on the table. "Wear the burgundy dress; it will go best with your eyes." She pauses, looking at me hard and long. "I pray for all our sakes you change."

The doomed dresser pats my shoulder with her bruised right hand then walks out of the room.

Please let her live to see the truth.

I stand then walk over to the mirror, head hung low, body heavy, mind running over so many disturbing thoughts always landing on Arland's death. Where is he? Where is Brit?

"*Brit?*"

Silence.

"*Brit, can you hear me? Please, where are you? Where is Arland? I need to tell you what happened. Please?*"

Who am I? The girl I used to be would have run after Rhoswen and told her the truth. I would have done everything in my power to help. God, I hope all of this is important. I hope ruining that girl's life—and everyone else's for that matter—is worth it. I lift the blue-silk nightgown over my head then startle at the yellow bruising in the middle of my chest. I haven't looked at myself naked since . . . I don't remember when. This mark, this was my death, this was from Arland saving me. Who will save me from Dughbal now that Arland is gone? All his people are in danger—I'm in danger—so where is he?

Thump, thump, thump.

"Be right there." I grab the velvet dress, slip it over my head, then run for the door, envisioning his green eyes, his wide smile . . . .

"Good morning, love," Perth says before the door fully opens.

I sigh, grimacing at his way too cheerful expression. "Good morning."

He arches an eyebrow. "May I come in?"

The two guards in the hall snicker.

"Would you like me to end your lives now?" Perth scolds without taking his eyes off me. Grabbing my hand, he pushes me back into the room.

The men hush each other but return to laughing as soon as the door closes.

Perth rubs his thumb under my swollen eye. "You have been crying. I am sorry about the kiss. I do not understand what came over me . . . you . . . it—"

"It's not your fault." I knock his arms from mine, then make my way to the bed. "Have you seen him?" I ask, sitting and balling the comforter in my hands.

He shakes his head. "No one has seen either of them. It is quite possible they are in the room next to you, where Brit's quarters are, but their whereabouts are insignificant. My father does not wish to punish Arland because I made it known I am happy wherever he is, as long as he is not with you in the same respect I am."

I glare at him. "Your father is a pig."

"I know."

"So what does he have planned for us today? More dancing? More shoving food in our mouths? Meetings to laugh about Arland's lack of leadership skills?"

The corner of Perth's mouth twists up. "Probably all of the above."

"I miss Flanna. She'd be yelling at me right now. She'd be yelling at you, too. She hates when people wallow."

He stares at me, eyes drifting from mine to the scoop neck on my wine colored dress, then down to my hands folded in my lap. "Talking to Flanna would be a grave mistake."

"Arland already told me. Is something bothering you? You haven't moved from the doorway."

"I never realized how hard this was going to be for me, Katriona. I believed I would thoroughly enjoy kissing you, holding your hand, telling you I love you—and I do, that is my problem. I wish to have all these things, and you are like a tease to my heart. My first kiss was shared with a woman imagining someone else. And when I wanted nothing more but to experience that joy again, I knew I would never have it."

He sighs. "I should never have pressed you for more. I saw how much pain you were in, I saw how you looked at him after—I am afraid many saw."

"I—"

"Do not try to make me feel better." Perth stares at me, his eyes a more pastel shade of green. "You suffer much more than me. Complaining would not be in my best interest."

Crossing the room, he stands before me, knees grazing my knees, cold filtering through the velvet like I wear nothing at all. "There is more."

"M-more?" My heart races.

"My father felt your mother's punishment was not strong enough. He has called a meeting with High Leader Maher and Leader Murchadha, as well as a few of the others, to try to come up with something more fitting."

I try to stand, but Perth places his hands on my shoulders and forces me down. "Let. Me. Go."

"And what would you do?"

"I have the power to end this, Perth." I peel his fingers from my shoulders then jump onto my feet. "And I'm going to do just that."

"*Katriona!*" He chases after me, expression wild. "Take my hand. At least allow me to walk you to communications."

"Fine."

We lace fingers, and I lead him from the room, ignoring the snide comments about who's in charge by the ridiculously short duo outside my door. Perth and I wind our way through the dilapidated structure, nodding at the occasional passerby, smiling when necessary, whispering nothings into each other's ears.

Such a stupid game. They want to punish my mother for protecting this world. I'm so ready to tell these people to grow up, to tell them to move aside, to tell them to get over their petty quests for power and look around. There is nothing left here for them to fight over.

"We are here." Perth pounds his fists against the magical stone wall. It morphs into the wooden door before our eyes. "Promise to keep your cool?"

"Sure."

Walking through together, we step into the room where the two soldiers monitor the chatter box. Static buzzes through the little area.

"Perth," Drustan says, scooting out his chair. "We were not expecting you. Is there something I can help with?"

"Where are the Leaders?"

Drustan stands, eyeing me with his head cocked to the side. "In the back."

I drop Perth's hand then run for my mom. "*Mom!*"

"What is this?" Dufaigh's sinister voice greets me as I barge into the room.

Mom, Dufaigh, High Leader Maher, Murchadha, Lorne, and Maura all sit around the table where this lie first began to weave its way into the world yesterday. Mom's hands are bound.

"Mom?"

She glares at me. "What are you doing here?"

Dufaigh steeples his fingers. "Yes, child, what are you doing here?"

Perth runs up behind me. Taking my hand in his, he tugs me toward them. "She is worried for her sister."

"Ahh. Well, no one has heard from her or Arland Maher"—Dufaigh flashes a cocky grin toward High Leader Maher—"since yesterday. Now, we are in the middle of pressing matters. Please, leave us."

"We are sorry, Father."

Perth's *father* waves his greasy hand at us, returning his attention to my mom. "Just be gone."

Mom and I meet eyes, then she nods.

"Okay. I am sorry for interrupting," I say, backing out of the room.

Perth holds my hand so hard I'm sure he'll leave a bruise, and we run from communications back into the safety of the spiral staircase.

"What you just did was dangerous. You may not like it—I never have either—but there are rules to this game we play." He slides his finger across my cheek. "Shall we eat?"

"Are you honestly hungry?"

"No, but food always helps. And with my father and the rest of them in there"—Perth points behind us with his thumb—"we can eat without putting on a major show."

"No kissing?"

He cringes. "No kissing."

"Let's go then."

"Would you like to take a walk? Just you and me? We can try to find a place where no one else is," Perth whispers.

I glance at the growing crowd. I haven't seen Arland or Brit all day. No one else has heard from them either. Sitting around and hoping, waiting, is not what I want to do anymore. He's mad at me—she's probably mad at me—so *I* probably won't see them any time soon. "Sounds like a pl—"

Squeaking hinges echo around the cavernous great room, followed by a loud thud of the wooden door against the stone wall. The Leaders barge in with my mom trailing at the back.

Dufaigh spots Perth and me then smiles. "May I have everyone's attention, please?"

A hush settles over the mix of Ground Dwellers, Light Lovers, and Sea Dwellers all gathered around their tables.

"Leader Wilde has an announcement she would like to make before you all today. If you remember, she and her husband Leader Brian Wilde broke a High Leader's law over twenty years ago and abandoned their people."

Dufaigh pauses, raising his arms above his head and looking around the room with wide, expectant eyes, but no one moves or speaks. "We have decided not to execute her—against my better judgment—and today she would like to apologize. So without further chatter by me, I give you Leader Wilde."

Mom approaches Dufaigh then stands directly in front of me and Perth, head held high, body as still as stone. "Thank you, Leader Dufaigh, for reminding the people of the sacrifice I had to make for them. I do not wish it upon anyone *ever* to have to go against what a High Leader deems unlawful; however, if it were not for our abandonment and travel into another world, you would not all be blessed with the hope you are today—"

Cheers erupt from the crowd, and Dufaigh clamps his hand over Mom's mouth. "Have you any respect? You were supposed to denounce what you did, not goad these people." He removes his hand, leaving a red impression of his fingers across her cheeks.

"You want your son and my daughter to marry, to bring happiness to these people, to unite these people before they are all killed?"

"Of course. Of course."

"Well, I believe I just brought them happiness, and Katriona already brought them hope. You live inside your head making your power plays, and if you would ever just look at the world around you, you would see uniting our kinds would merely take a Leader like you to denounce what Foghlad did to your people all those years ago." Mom crosses her arms over her chest. "Arrest me if you must, but I will die proud while you die wrong."

I gasp, and both Leaders turn to face me. She's my mother and she'd rather die than stand for Dufaigh's behavior. Mom's always fighting, always giving her all to save this world. But after what he did to Rhoswen, I have no doubt he will kill Mom for her words. This game is too difficult. I want to grab her and run away, protect the woman who has protected me my entire life, but I can't. The only thing I can do is scowl at her, to keep up *my* act.

"Punish her, Father. I will escort Katriona to her quarters for the evening; she does not need to see this—she has done nothing but support you." Without waiting for his father to respond, Perth stands, pulls out my chair, then takes my hand and we flee the great room.

We run through the hall, passing no one, holding hands all the way to my quarters. Pushing through the door, we slam it closed then lock it.

"She was right, you know?" I whisper once we're sitting on the edge of my bed.

"Yes. That is why I feared for your safety. She has her own role in this, Katriona, and it should not bring you down."

He takes a deep breath. "So, what would you like to do?"

I raise a brow. "Do?"

He chuckles, trailing a finger from my shoulder down to my hand. "Yes, love, do. If I leave this room, they will expect us to be together. If we stay here, we can be alone, away from all their watchful eyes. So what would you like to do to occupy your time?"

Shivering, I grab his hand then drop it in his lap. "First, I'd like you to stop touching me when we're alone. I understand how difficult this is for you, but it's not exactly easy for anyone else either."

Perth sighs. "I am sorry. I feel like—"

"One of the youth smitten with lust?" I repeat the words Arland said to me once.

Perth meets my eyes and laughs. "How did you know?"

"You aren't the first person to feel that way." I offer him a smile, but pain radiates deep in my heart. I miss Arland. I miss the soldiers from Watchers Hall. I miss freedom, the sun, Brad, Mirain. There's no way I can deal with two weeks of this. I may not even make it through one. But something about Rhoswen's words—about how I need to learn all the magic—unsettles the pit of my stomach. I cannot possibly unite all these people and fulfill my duty here if I don't understand all the races. "Can you teach me Ground Dweller magic?"

"I can." He draws out 'can', reminding me of a teacher scolding children for asking questions incorrectly.

"*Will* you teach me?" I jab him in the shoulder.

"Ow!" Perth rubs his bicep. "I will teach you if you promise me something first."

"If it has anything to do with a kiss—"

"Katriona, I am serious. Just promise to bring me with you if you decide to run away. If it gets so bad you cannot handle it anymore and you and Arland and everyone else escape this place to live out your prophecy, please, take me with you. Do not leave me behind with these . . . these—"

I place my fist over my heart. "I promise."

"Thank you," he says, mirroring my action. "So what would you like to know?"

"Well, Rhoswen snapped her fingers and lit most of the candles in here. I'm sure I could do that if I wanted, but is there a word I need to say? She said she couldn't believe I didn't know Ground or Sea Dweller magic."

"She spoke with you again?" His loud gulp shakes me.

"Y-yes. Why?"

Perth paces across the room, running his fingers through his short, blond locks. "Were you planning to tell anyone?"

"I forgot. I sent her away, then you came in, and my mom, and . . . ."

"*Katriona.*" He growls. "How could you be so—?"

"If you say stupid, I will burn you."

He rolls his eyes. "Careless."

I get to my feet, march to the brooding Ground Dweller standing by my silly throne-like chair, then cross my arms over my chest. "I trust her. Don't ask me why; I just do. I know you will say I shouldn't, like so many said I shouldn't trust you. So if you plan on letting me down, tell me now, then I won't trust her either."

Perth strides up to me till our faces are mere inches apart. "Even if she has turned, the others will tell."

"You don't know that. Your father will kill her if he discovers she is on the path of Light. And who would want to die? Who would want to be beaten for your father's cause?"

He leans back, shaking his head as if he's just been slapped. "No, you are right. My kind is too selfish to sacrifice themselves, but if she tells anyone, anyone who might not be on the right path, we will all be doomed."

"Now will you teach me Ground Dweller magic?"

Perth pulls out a chair from the table. "Sit. This will take a while."

CHAPTER TWENTY-THREE

"You're telling me to think only of myself when I want to build a weapon? Weapons—"

"Protections, Katriona. The magic was manipulated because we thought of the *weapons* as protection. We lied to nature about our intentions, confusing the magic. And in the end, we confused ourselves." Perth stares at a floating piece of broken chair between us as it transforms into a dagger. The wood stretches out, snapping and blending into a handle all at once. The blade grows, splintering and dropping shards of oak onto the table.

"Go ahead, touch it."

I reach out my hand, and the newly created dagger darts across the room then lands on my pillow. "What . . . ?"

He flashes a boyish, lopsided grin. "When I requested help from the magic, I told it to keep you safe while you rest."

"*Why?*"

"If someone comes in here, anyone, I want you to protect yourself." Perth tips his head toward my poster bed.

"It will be invisible to all but you and me. Do you see how dangerous this is?"

"You mean your father could be heavily armed and no one would know the difference?"

He narrows his eyes ever so slightly. "*Is* heavily armed, and only those who he allows to see know the difference."

I close my eyes. "Perth?"

"Yes?"

"Does he plan on killing anyone we know?" I try to hide my caution, but it lines my tone, thick and dark.

"The thought has crossed his mind on more than one occasion."

Standing, I stare at him. "He's not only a pig, he's insane!"

Perth catches my hand before I storm away from the table. "Please, do not lose faith in him."

"Faith? I never had faith in him, Perth."

"No one has ever taught him the difference between right and wrong."

"No one ever taught you either and yet here you are. And I don't have much faith in anyone right now. High Leader Maher caves into everyone's demands, your father . . . I have no words for him, my mother is doing her own thing, Arland and Brit are God knows where—"

"And yet, here I am."

I laugh, high-pitched and shrill, and then the laughter sinks to my stomach, doubling me over until I can't breathe. "Perth"—I gasp for air—"you always have a way of making me laugh. You're right; you are here, and I have not lost faith in you."

Thump, thump, thump.

I freeze. "Who . . . ?"

"I cannot see through walls." He shrugs. "But grab the dagger, and find a place for it on you."

"You said I could only use it in bed."

"I lied. Just grab it and walk with me. If Rhoswen said anything, they will certainly be here to take you away."

Turning around, I head for the wooden bed adorned with red drapery, snatch the dagger then shove it down the front of my dress. "Are you positive no one can see this?"

"Only me." He clasps my hand then leads me toward the door. "Who is it?"

"Vanora." She clears her throat. "Your father requires you and Katriona be present for a dance in the great room."

"Why did he send her?" I whisper.

"I do not know. Maybe he wishes to have you view your mother's next punishment." Perth's shoulders slump and he sighs. "Tell him we will be there shortly. Katriona and I are just finishing up a few things."

"I bet you are finishing her up quite well." Cyric's muffled voice echoes through the door.

Vanora snorts. "So have they made a lot of noise then?"

"Oh you know, the occasional giggle, a few raised voices, but none of *those* noises Deverell and I have so hoped to hear."

The distinct sound of skin meeting skin rings out, and I know someone was slapped. "You disgust me, Cyric."

"I thought you liked us Ground Dwellers."

"There is only one . . . ."

"Oh, Vanora, wait!"

I imagine Cyric chasing after Vanora, and laugh at how funny that must look; she's at least a foot taller and as vibrant as life itself, and he's colorless.

I cross my arms over my chest. "What was that all about?"

Perth's chin quivers then he shakes his head. "Nothing."

"And you think I believe that?" I ask, raising my voice.

He puts his fingers to his lips, hushing me. "She and I met when we were little. Long before I ever knew of you or my father's plans for us, I promised I would be Bound to her. But . . . ."

"Then you learned of your father's plans, and he ripped you two apart."

"We were just children, Katriona, but she has never forgiven me. I had no clue about love or longevity, or my father's sanity," he says, running his fingers through his hair.

"Are you trying to tell me you no longer have any feelings for her?"

Perth focuses on me, intensity burning through me, hand squeezing hard around mine. "My heart is tormented, just like my past. Whether I had or have feelings for her is of little or no consequence." He reaches for the door handle then pauses. "Is this how your friend Brad felt all those years by your side?"

My breath escapes me. Tears build behind my eyes, bringing heat into my cheeks and shaking in my core. "How dare you! He may not have had the courage to say he had feelings for me, but at least *he* didn't make me feel like a jerk when I didn't reciprocate them. A god did. I'm sorry, Perth. I can't make everyone happy. I can't even make myself happy. Arland is gone, my sister, Mom, my best friend—their fates are mostly out of my control—and you're standing here before me, trying to make me . . . what? What is it you want from me? You want me to kiss you again? You want me to go out there and pretend to be your future wife a little longer so you can get your fill? Hell, Perth, my mom was right. If a Leader would just denounce what Foghlad did, maybe your people *would* be better off. You could be that Leader, but all you want is another kiss. I'll give it to you if you'll promise to grow up."

Moving into him, I grab his face with my hands then crash my lips onto his. I part his cold, thin mouth forcefully, greet his unmoving tongue with mine, then push him away. Tears stream down my face. "I love Arland, Perth. I can't help that. I love him, and he loves me. Together we are the key. Not Perth and Katriona. Remember what the Seer told you, or you will wind up very much alone."

I storm from the room. Deverell doesn't even look at me, but I spot a glimpse of blue in his eyes, and I know he's on the right path. Hopefully he stays that way and keeps this to himself. I'm sure he heard.

"Did you see which way she went?" Perth's voice is distant from where I hide on the stairwell outside the great room, but I know he'll find me.

Wiping the tears from my eyes, I stand, back braced against the crumbling stone wall for support. Waiting.

Footsteps clop up the stairs.

My heart sinks to my stomach.

"Katriona?" he calls.

"I am here," I say, stepping out of the shadows into the dim light cast by one of the burning sconces.

He turns and sighs. "I am so sorry. What I said, it was uncalled for. I did not want that kiss, not that way."

"Let's not talk about it." I glance at the wall where so many candles are missing from their holders. "Have you noticed an unusual amount of light missing? I mean, it is always dark, but now even more."

"I have. I worry we are running low on wax." Perth reaches out for me then quickly clasps his hands behind his back.

"Give me your hand. We would not want to disappoint. We have to play this game, remember?" I whisper. "I am sorry for accusing you otherwise. The line between you doing the right thing and you doing this for your own selfish reasons keeps getting skewed in my head."

"You are not the one who skewed it; that was all my doing. I do have feelings for you, how could I not? As a child I loved Vanora, but she wishes to be evil just for a chance of being with me, and I do not need any more darkness in my life. Please, forgive me for what I said and for the feelings I have no control over?"

"Of course."

Perth takes my hand, and we enter into the great room to play this game a little longer.

"May I walk the children to their rooms?" Mom asks Dufaigh.

He didn't bring us in here to watch her be punished again. In fact, he hasn't allowed her to move from his side or speak until now. The twisted Leader brought Perth and me in here to dance in front of everyone, to smile and laugh, to be in love.

Perth glances at his father. "I do not mind, sir."

"Very well. Do not keep them up long. Your daughter carries a lack of sleep under her eyes. Katriona needs to be well rested. We have many more events planned for the next two weeks."

"I understand." Mom offers me her arm, and I hook mine through. "Shall we go then?"

I smile. "Yes."

Perth walks next to us, keeping up the slow pace, hands behind his back, gaze on the floor. He steps aside, allowing us to exit first. The wooden doors rattle closed then we all walk a little faster.

"Mom, have you seen Brit?"

She shakes her head.

"Are you not worried?"

"Katriona," she chides. "Of course I worry for my child, but she is a grown woman. She chose to spend her time with Arland Maher, and there is nothing I can do to stop her."

Glancing around, I spot the small Ground Dwellers behind us, standing guard over the giant doors. I sigh. "It pains me to know she cares more for him than the rest of her family."

Mom pats my hand. "I know, dear."

We enter my room, slide the locks over my cell gate, then take seats around the table. Mom sits next to me while Perth sits across from us.

I rest my head on her shoulder, something I haven't done since I was little. "Where are they?"

"Honestly I don't know, Kate."

I bolt up. "What? How could you not know?"

Her face softens, and her green eyes turn down. "I am just as in the dark as everyone else, and not in a position to go asking questions."

"The night they left, when I kissed Perth, I had a vi—"

"Shh." She holds up a hand. "Don't speak of what you saw. Not to me. The less I know, the less you know, the better off we all are. You should push it from your mind, don't talk or think about it . . . just let it go, Kate. Arland would not endanger his people by leaving you alone. He cannot be far."

Perth meets my eyes then nods, as if he's agreeing. He cannot possibly agree with this. Or he can—of course he can. He wants me. I'm sure he's quite happy Arland and Brit are gone.

No.

I have to stop thinking about that. Perth wants to do the right thing.

"My personal feelings aside, Katriona, if you knew where they were . . . in fact if any one of us knew where they were, we would not appear as worried. The worry comes across for your sister even though your mother and I know it to be different. The emotion works well for us. People see you and me together; they see you looking around for Brit and feel sorry for us. These Draíochtans are blinded by my father's callous ways, by his bending of truth. And not just my people, Light Lovers and Sea Dwellers alike are confused by him."

"These people are under some sick impression my presence has saved them, yet your father doesn't want me to fight. He doesn't want *you* to fight. He just wants the power. He's led by pride."

"His father is under a spell just like the rest of them. Deep in his heart he wants our people to be united. Did you hear him in the great room? When he wanted to condemn me, I asked him if he wanted to unite our people . . . ."

I purse my lips. "I heard. But what I don't understand is why he isn't hurting you."

"Did you forget I am the only person alive who can perform your Binding?"

"I guess I did. So is everyone under Foghlad's spell?"

"Yes," they say in unison.

I look at Perth sitting with his arms crossed over his chest. "But your father is worse than the rest of them."

"If the spell is ever broken, he may still be a cruel, heartless man, but I do not know that for sure. And pray it is not his truth."

"I should go." Mom stands, smiling down on me and tucking a strand of hair behind my ear. "You have done well, Kate. Your father would be proud of your strength, of your courage, of your pureness."

"Do you really have to go so soon?" I stand then wrap my arms around her.

She holds me at arm's length. "This will be our routine. You and Perth will spend every day together. He will come for you in the morning, you will keep your head low, try not to say anything that will give you away to anyone, smile at one another, hold hands, kiss, whatever you must do while we figure out what it is that will bring us together."

"You mean whatever it is that will break the spell?"

"Yes." Mom crosses the room then presses her palm on the door handle. "Spend the evenings together as well. And Perth—"

He looks up, no emotion on his face, but his features are even more colored. His cheeks appear rosy, and his eyes are a deep shade of gorgeous green. "Yes, Leader Wilde?"

"I'm trusting you to keep her safe."

He smiles, eyes turning even darker green, and places his fist over his heart. "I promise not to let either of you down."

CHAPTER TWENTY-FOUR

Sleep is the furthest thing from my mind. It's been fourteen days since I've seen Arland. I don't blame him for not coming around, but I miss him. Miss his hands, warm and strong, wrapped around mine. Miss his lips, full and sweet, trailing along my skin. Miss the smell of the morning forest drifting off him. Miss his emerald eyes always radiating with love, locked with mine.

I cannot stand holding hands with Perth, cannot stand the quick kisses in front of our captive audience. He plays into it so well. All the smiling, waving, and telling everyone how excited he is about our Binding—sometimes I forget he's acting. Sometimes I think he doesn't want to be.

The lie is more difficult for me.

I've had to profess my love for Perth in front of my true love.

The torment on Arland's face when I ignited in flames during that kiss with Perth has not stopped haunting me. Every day I exit my room and expect to see Arland there, guarding me with his life the way he swore he always would, but the same two Ground Dwellers who've followed me everywhere for the last two weeks are the only ones who greet me.

Sitting next to High Leader Maher during meals hasn't helped any. Our conversations haven't gone beyond two words—good morning, good afternoon, or good evening—but everything about his appearance reminds me of Arland.

And that's as far as the similarities go.

The highest, most powerful Leader of Encardia is a fool. He's weak and scared. I'm not sure how my mom and dad could have ever been friends with him, and I'm not sure where Arland inherited his strength. He and his father are complete opposites. If Leader Maher was different in the past, his current self does little to prove it. Dufaigh walks all over him, all over everyone. He and his people—and some of my own—revel in the glory of having me, Katriona Wilde, deliverer of Light, attached to the Ground Dwellers' side.

Arland's soldiers—*my soldiers*—have been non-existent in my life since we arrived. The few times I've run into any of them, they barely looked in my direction. They know this is all smoke and mirrors, but the respect they have for Arland is far greater than what they have for anyone else.

I'm betraying their greatest Leader on a daily basis.

Someone taps on the heavy wooden door. The rolled-up wool sock I've been throwing at the ceiling hits my face. Tossing the makeshift ball aside, I prop myself on my elbows then create a flame in my hand. The light illuminates the door decorated with gold-lined carvings of ivy and jasmine—proving yet again how lost these people are.

"Katriona?" my mom whispers.

There is no Kate at Willow Falls—I'm so tired of the lies, but we haven't come up with a single idea for uniting our people. "What do you want, Mom?"

"May I come in?"

I don't know why she feels the need to ask . . . I haven't locked the door for days. "Sure."

The rusted hinges squeak like nails raking down a chalkboard. Mom pokes her head through, holding something behind her back and wearing an expression I haven't seen since the caves by the river. She's standing tall, shoulders squared, and she's smiling. "It is time."

I bolt upright; the crimson silken covers fall around my waist. My fingers tingle, and my legs fill with the urge to flee. "Time for *what*?"

She crosses the room, takes a seat on the edge of the bed, then places a hand on mine. "Arland is waiting. It is time for the Binding. Are you ready?"

"Where is he? Where has he been? Isn't he mad at me? Are you sure now is the right time? How are we supposed to get away with this?" Millions of questions swim inside my head, but those are the only ones I can put into words.

Mom squeezes my fingers—her way of reassuring me. "Now is the only time, and he has never been upset with you."

"Where has he been? Where has *everyone* been?"

"You are not even aware, are you?"

I scowl at her, heat flaring in my cheeks. "Aware of what? You wouldn't tell me anything. Brit wouldn't let me in her head. Perth didn't have a clue. So no, Mom, I'm not aware of anything."

"After your vision, on the evening you kissed Perth, you looked at Arland in a way so powerful no one could ever doubt you had feelings for him. The fact any of us remain alive is beyond me, but if Dufaigh had been in the room when that happened, I am afraid we would not be. We may have a few more people on our side than we think."

Rhoswen . . . she mentioned *we*, but I didn't realize there are so many.

"So he knows I didn't betray him . . . he knows about the vi . . .vision?" My heart pounds wildly in my chest, sending blood thrumming in my ears.

"Brit saw the vision when you did. We thought it would be safer for everyone you have formed a relationship with to stay away—allow you to truly feel alone, so if there was another vision, your eyes could not endanger our mission. It has worked well; to our knowledge, the Dufaighs suspect nothing."

"What would have happened if I had another visit from Darkness?" I ask, running my hands up and down my goose bump riddled arms.

"Arland has never been that far away, Kate. He has spent every moment with Brit in her quarters, or they waited in the halls while you ate dinner, drummed up conversations with people outside the washroom doors. His time with her has not only helped to build their lie, but has also given him direct access to you in case she sensed something was wrong."

Mom stares at the wall separating me from my sister. "We know her prophecy."

Taking in her blank stare, I gasp. "And?"

She keeps looking at the wall. "And your sister is happy with her news."

"You aren't going to tell me?" My sister lying on the ground in ruins . . . blood draining from her mouth, telling me to kill Dughbal . . .

"It is not for me to say, and now is not the time. You have a wedding to attend." Mom tilts her head to the side then locks eyes with me.

I put my hands over my cheeks to force the smile from my face.

"Now, we do not have much time. At this point, we all feel it will be better for you two to go on your own to seek out Darkness. I will perform the Binding spell, you will return inside while we will prepare those on the right path for departure, then you will leave tomorrow before Dufaigh has an opportunity to force you into a life without choice."

"But Griandor said I have to unite everyone. And what about my army?"

Mom cups my cheek with her hand. "Things will work out the way they are supposed to, and if they do not, you and Arland will at least have each other. He is outside the base. I'll ask again, are you ready?"

Arland waits for me . . . *to marry me.* I run my fingers through my hair, look down at my clothes, suddenly feel like I'm the ugliest, smelliest woman in the world. Of course with the velvet robes Dufaigh has dressed me in, I'm far from hideous, but wearing these things doesn't feel right.

Mom watches me appraise myself, giving one of those mother looks—the kind that says she's proud, she's sad, and happy all at the same time—then hands me a package wrapped in brown paper, tied with twine.

"What's this?"

She pushes the package at me. "Something Brit, Flanna, and Shay have worked tirelessly to create for you. Go ahead, open it."

I feel like a child on Christmas day, tearing at the package in a hurry to see the treasures locked inside. The last bit of brown paper falls to the floor, and what I'm left holding takes my breath away.

White silk.

"Other than Binding Spells, Encardia has no marriage traditions. Brit was desperate to dress you up. I imagine if we lived in Virginia, she would have planned a huge wedding for you, but I think we are all aware you would rather not have that. She was insistent you have something beautiful to wear. Brit described wedding gowns to Flanna and Shay, and the three of them sewed this for you."

Mom takes the silk from my hands then stands and allows the material to unfold, revealing the most stunning dress. Real white jasmine flowers line the scooped neck and thin shoulder straps—the fragrance so sweet I taste it. The bodice ties are also made of silk, and from the waist, the dress flows to the floor. "We had to sneak the flowers from the gardens. The children work very hard to use magic to grow them, but I do not believe any of them would mind if they knew their hard work was for you. So what do you think?"

There are so many things I think; I'm not sure which is the most appropriate to say first. Brit's a genius—the best sister in the world. Flanna and Shay are wonderful for risking their lives to make this for me. The gown is gorgeous. Let's go now. I can't wait. "Thank you, Mom. It's beautiful and . . . ."

My words stick in my throat. I'm about to get what I want: Arland. Our time together may not last forever. The visions, the warnings, the war, all of these things have shown me how easily life can be taken away, but for now, my little piece of heaven has arrived.

She hands me the dress. "You will have to wait until we are outside to put it on, but everything has been arranged."

More potential problems with their plan pop into my head. Every night we've been watched, Perth and me, watched by guards, watched by Leaders, soldiers, whoever's interested in our affairs. What would someone say if they caught me outside the base with my mom, wearing a white gown? Then I think of Perth as an issue, too. "What about Perth? He usually makes a nightly visit, to keep up the pretense of our love. It must be about time—"

"Everything has been arranged, Katri-Kate, *everything*. High Leader Maher is aware of our plan. He informed Dufaigh you and I will take a walk to discuss a Binding Spell with Perth—his father wants you and Perth Bound by tomorrow night, remember?"

"I know." Perth told me his father has pulled him aside every evening for the last week to discuss us finally taking that step, and every time Perth came up with another reason not to. He cannot continue to go against his father without suspicions growing.

"I stopped by his room on the way here and told him you would be out for a while and there would be no need to pop in here this evening. Now are you ready?"

"I am." I grab the dagger Perth made for me, shove it down the front of my dress, then stand, legs trembling below me.

"Ground Dweller magic?"

"Yes. Perth made it for me."

"He was wise to arm you, and with something no one else can see. Cheilt," Mom whispers, running her hand across the silk. The gown disappears. She takes it from me, slips it under her belt, then wraps her arm around my shoulders and ushers me toward the door.

"I have to apologize, Kate; Perth has surprised me. It appears trusting in him was the right thing to do. I am sorry for ever doubting you."

We walk into the hall at the same time.

Brit, Flanna, and Shay stand huddled with wide eyes looking everywhere but forward, hands clenched in fists at their sides.

"What are you guys doing here?" I ask. "Where are Deverell and Cyric?"

Brit responds with a squeal and a hug, knocking me into Mom with the force of it.

"Are you trying to kill me, Brit?"

She steps away, but rocks up and down on her toes. "Sorry," she whispers. "I'm just so excited for you. And your guards are off duty."

Shay places her hand on my shoulder and grins. She's never been a woman of many words.

Flanna hasn't moved or spoken; she waits behind Brit and Shay, glancing around our small group of women.

I take a few steps in Flanna's direction.

She offers me her best sarcastic smile—one that I've missed since Lann died. "It is about time you and my cousin have your alone time. Sorry for all the interruptions before. Part of my prophecy was to make you wait until the right time, which is now."

"Oh, Flanna, I always wondered if you interrupted us for a reason." I wrap my arms around her neck, soaking in her warmth and her heart-warming smell of potatoes and chicken worn into her from years of working in the kitchen.

We hold each other for longer than a quick hug, but Flanna has been so distant, so missing from my everyday life, I need to hold her.

"This is something I wished to share with Lann one day. Cherish it. Not everyone has these opportunities, but you and Arland deserve it more than most," she whispers next to my ear.

For a moment, I will every good feeling inside me to go into her and fill her with peace and love. "I love you, Flanna. You are the best Confidant a girl could have."

We break our embrace, tears streaking our cheeks, then I turn to Mom. "Ready?"

She takes my hand in hers. "Yes. We should go before time runs out."

I wave good-bye to the others. Brit blows me a kiss, then Mom leads me up the stairs toward the great hall. She holds her head high and walks without trepidation. Me on the other hand, my feet seem too large; I keep tripping over them. My knees are weak and buckle every few steps.

"Relax, Katriona," Mom says without looking at me.

Thankfully no one else is around to see my ridiculous display of nerves, and even if they were, they'd think my behavior was over Perth and not Arland. "Sorry. I'm nervous and scared."

"What are you afraid of, Katriona? Perth will make a wonderful husband. He loves you as much, if not more, than your father ever loved me."

Somehow I get the feeling we're being watched, and Mom is *not* talking about Perth. "Yes, I know he does, Mom. Our relationship has just moved all so fast, but he has shown me kindness unmatched by any other." Talking like this for these people makes me want to gag, and I'm also *not* talking about Perth.

She spares a glance at me then looks over my shoulder. I follow her gaze to Leader Dufaigh. He sits at a table in the far corner of the room, waving his hands in conversation with High Leader Maher.

They stop talking, tip their head, then return to whatever it is that's so important—which is probably something vain or self-serving for Dufaigh and something weak for Maher.

Mom wraps her arm around my shoulders, sweeping me through the rest of the great room. We enter the small foyer-like area then climb the last set of stairs leading to the exit; each step fills my chest with burning exhilaration.

I picture Arland waiting for me in his white tunic, brown leather pants and boots, green eyes blazing in the night. I cannot wait to kiss his soft lips, stare at his slightly crooked nose, hold his strong face in my hands.

Reaching the top step, Mom pulls the invisible gown from her belt, whispers *nochtann* then places the dress in my hands. "You will have to put this on outside the door."

I open my mouth to protest, but she holds up her hand before I even utter a word.

"Do not worry, Kate, no one will see you. Arland, Flanna, and many of the others have cast concealment spells over much of the base. These Draíochtans have forgotten how to use and notice even some of the most simplistic of magic." She shakes her head. "It saddens me to see my home this way, but their ignorance aids us now."

Leader Maher's lackadaisical ways infuriate me beyond belief. Dughbal was able to enter Encardia because Draíochtans stopped practicing old magic. What does Leader Maher think will happen if *all* magic disappears? "Why would Arland's father allow this to happen? Why isn't he stronger like his son?"

"Do you honestly believe High Leader Maher is so foolish?"

"I'm surprised he's allowed *this* to happen, Mom. He caves to everything Dufaigh wants."

"Kate, he plays the game the same way as everyone else. The people suffer from the game, but Kimball has no other choice than to allow them to forget. Before this is over, you will be teaching Draíochtans how to use magic. This place will be as it once was."

She prods my shoulder with her hand, pushing me toward the door. "We are wasting time. You're going to be late for your own wedding."

The door in the ground groans as I push it open. The air is heavy, but colder than most nights; fog blankets the forest floor.

Mom closes the door behind her then nudges me forward about ten feet through a concealment spell. The magic caresses my skin as I pass through, telling me I'm safe, reminding me I'm powerful. It's been so long since I've been near strong magic.

"You should change here," she says.

I untie the golden ropes securing me in my velvet prison, slip my arms out of the sleeves then allow the dress to fall to the ground. The dagger drops next to my feet, but I leave it there. I don't want to carry a weapon on my wedding night.

Mom helps me fit the silk gown over my head then laces the bodice in the back. The material slides over my skin, cool and soft. Chills run along my arms and legs.

"How's my hair?" I ask.

Mom runs her fingers through the back of my hair. "The braids all look good, and what is not braided is smooth. I am so happy you allowed Rhoswen to work on your hair again. Now turn around and let me see you."

Picking up the skirt of the dress, I twirl.

Tears roll down Mom's cheeks.

"What's wrong?"

She dabs at her red face with her sleeve. "Nothing is wrong. I cannot believe how grown up you are. You look beautiful, Kate. So beautiful. I just . . . I wish your father could see you."

Wrapping my arms around her waist, I rest my head on her shoulder, and for a moment, I cry too. I have a mom, someone who is proud of her little girl, someone who has emotions for her daughter, someone who maybe even sees a little bit of herself in me.

Sniffling, she holds me at arm's length. "We better stop or we are going to get tears all over your gorgeous dress."

Mom bends down to pick up my other clothes, folds them and makes them invisible. "You will have to put these back on when you are ready to return inside."

I laugh. "That may be never, Mom."

She gives me a knowing look, shaking her head. "I understand, but you must return. And you need to keep your dagger. Put it with these clothes, but do not leave it behind. Ever."

How did she know? Grabbing the dagger, I place it on top of the invisible clothes. "How much time will we have?"

"No more than two hours. I will be waiting here for you, so when you—"

"Got it. Let's go, then." I don't want to waste any more time talking to Mom. I want to see Arland, kiss Arland, *marry* Arland. And I want as much time to enjoy him as possible.

Kneeling, she squeezes her right hand into a fist, opens it then transfers a blue flame onto a torch.

"You guys have been planning a lot together, haven't you?" I wonder who all has been involved and what I should expect.

"We had to." Mom reaches the torch out to her right and touches it to some invisible barrier. Blue flames ignite in a straight line ahead of us. She does the same to another barrier on the left. A ten-foot tall wall on both sides of us, as well as our path and my white, silk dress now glow with a soft-blue hue.

My breath catches.

Mom looks over at me with a smile. "You did not think I would allow you to get married without something beautiful to remember it by, did you?"

I don't know what I thought, but it wasn't this.

She puts out her hand, indicating for me to walk ahead of her, but instead I link my arm through hers and we proceed together toward Arland and my new future.

I memorize every tree the flames illuminate. Soak in every smell of the forest—pine, dried leaves, dirt, dew, the light sulfuric smell of the fog. The fog itself is beautiful, clouds glowing gray and blue around us.

Mom glances at me from the corner of her eye. "It only gets better. Just you wait."

Better? "I cannot imagine anything being better than this."

"Your sister had almost every one of *your* soldiers out here trying to get this just right. What should I tell her when I return?"

"That I love her."

"I believe that is appropriate, and I will tell her you were speechless."

The path takes a sudden turn to the left and leads us down a short hill.

Mom and I fall quiet as we descend flat stone steps built into the side of the hill, placing each foot in front of the other with care. I lift the silk skirt in my hands.

Thank the gods Brit didn't design any special shoes for me.

The boots are an odd accompaniment with the white gown, but they are more appropriate than any stiletto money could buy.

Reaching the last step, I look up and have to fight against every urge inside me not to let tears fall. Arland stands under a healthy willow tree in front of the river, hands clasped in front of him, wearing his perfect-for-any-occasion regular clothes. Surrounding him are hundreds of white candles, lit with real flames, not blue. Warm yellow light fills the space around him. White jasmine flowers, matching the ones on my gown, sprinkle the ground with their pureness. The air smells sweet from the natural perfume.

We lock eyes, and Arland smiles.

I'm frozen in place.

The sight is more magical than any power I've been graced by the gods with, and I want to remember this—all of this—forever.

I inhale a deep breath, holding it in.

"Are you coming, Kate?"

"Yes. I'm just . . . just . . . I don't even know what to say, Mom. It's beautiful. I'm amazed." I gasp. "The tree . . . ."

"It is a tree of life." She takes my hand in hers. "You should not keep Arland waiting. He has suffered without you as much, if not more, than you have suffered without him."

I don't meet her eyes or ask about the implication of the tree; instead I stare ahead at Arland, watching for some indication of pain. He's had to witness me kiss Perth, hug him, hold his hand, sneak in and out of his room at night and vice-versa, but Arland reveals nothing more than joy. The yellow light glows on his skin, flickering in his eyes. The corners of his mouth twist up, melting my heart.

The distance between us is unbearable—my feet want to run to him, my body craves to be held in his arms, my lips tingle with excitement for an encounter with his. Every step I take sends another thrilling jolt of excitement through me. The protective barrier around us fades in the corner of my vision and all that's left is Arland, smiling at me, *for* me.

Arriving next to him, Mom bends and places my invisible clothes and weapon on the ground, then takes our hands and places them together. Arland's warmth shoots up my arms, makes my heart do summersaults in my chest. Mom places a palm on each of our shoulders.

Goose bumps line my skin from head to toe.

"You look beautiful," he says in a deep, sultry voice.

I glance down, cheeks warming. "Thank you."

Arland kisses my forehead. "You have no idea how much I have missed your hands in mine."

I squeeze his fingers. "I think I have a very good idea."

Mom lets go of us then picks up a candle from the ground. "We should get started."

Arland and I turn to face her. The crashing waterfalls in the distance behind Mom give me a strong sense of déjà vu, but I shake the thought.

She waves the candle above and below mine and Arland's connection, then sets it down. When Mom returns upright, she places one hand under mine and one on top of Arland's, then closes her eyes. "Cheangal orthu, banna iad, iad a choinneáil le chéile Arland agus Katriona. For you, Kate, it means Bind them, bond them, keep them together, Arland and Katriona."

My skin warms. I look from Mom to Arland to my hand. Golden lines twisted around each other in braids swirl from my fingertips, loop around my palm, and curve up my wrist like an intricate tattoo of light. Matching braided lines appear on Arland.

We meet eyes and hold each other's gaze. I feel his heart beating and the relief each breath of air brings his lungs—we are one.

"Le Chéile deo. Together forever." Mom releases us, kisses Arland on the cheek, then me. "Anois agus i gcónaí. Now and always."

The warmth in my hand races up my arm, across my shoulders, down my back and legs. My entire body is hot and swollen, ready to burst, ready to meet lips with Arland's . . . ready to love.

He's beautiful. Gone is the sadness he carried when we arrived at Willow Falls. Gone are the small dark circles under his eyes.

Every exposed part us radiates with light from the golden braids. The magic swirls around us, keeping us together, drawing us closer.

Mom sucks in a sharp breath. "I have never seen a Binding so strong . . . ."

"*There has never been a Binding reinforced by the gods.*" Arland's voice floats through my mind, seductive, hungry.

My head fills with memories—Arland's memories—full of love, sadness, joy, pain, desire. I see the girl I used to be, dropping a plate of food on the ground, feel his excitement when he saw my face. Even before he knew I was Katriona Wilde, he thought I was beautiful, captivating.

The next memory hits: our first kiss. He swore to never let anything happen to me, swore never to kiss another, swore to sacrifice his life to save me. The pain the first time I saved his life brought him is almost unbearable, buckling my knees. He felt like he'd betrayed me, like he'd failed me, like he should leave me.

I shake my head.

His thoughts change, and he shows me images of us in the stables, in the bath, all of our soldiers working to prepare for our marriage and then our marriage itself. Intense pleasure is what he feels; his entire body emanates with it. He sees no world beyond me, beyond my lips, beyond my eyes.

I don't know what memories he's received of mine, but he hasn't stopped smiling, hasn't loosened his grip on my hand, hasn't looked away from me once.

I thought I'd be nervous about what to do once we were Bound and had to follow through with things we'd been interrupted on so many times. Instead, I find myself wishing my mom would disappear, run as fast as possible, go anywhere but here so Arland and I can complete our marriage.

My breaths come out heavy, and my head almost refuses to turn, but I face Mom.

She's gone.

I look toward the hill, but she's not there either. "Where did—?"

Arland ignores my half-asked question and crashes his lips against mine. His hands make their way to my face, mouth trailing along my jaw, up to my ear, down my neck. I lean my head back, allow him to kiss a line straight to my chest where he stops at the row of flowers on my scooped-neck gown.

Electricity shoots out to every nerve ending in my body.

I run my fingers through Arland's hair, grab his brown locks then pull him up to my mouth again. He grips me with one rough, yet tender hand at the waist, while fumbling with the silky tie of my bodice with the other. Each lace removed sends relief through my chest, replaced by a breathless desire.

Abandoning my mouth, he kisses every inch of my neck, slides a strap of my dress off my right shoulder and kisses there, too. Lifting me from the ground, he takes a few steps forward then sets me on my feet on a blanket under the lush weeping willow—never once breaking the intimate connection we both so desperately crave.

Our eyes lock. We stare long and hard, exchanging unspoken emotions and memories, but longing wins out over all. Without looking, he slides off my other shoulder strap. The white gown flutters to the ground, landing in a pool of silk around my feet.

My body is his to do with as he wishes, and he just looks into my eyes. *"What's wrong?"*

"I am memorizing you. Parts of you which were not already memorized."

I sit on the blanket, unlace my boots then slide them from my feet. When I'm left with nothing on, I smile at Arland and lie back. *"Memorize away."*

He rids himself of his leather belt, flinging it aside, removes his boots then joins me. Our lips reunite, settling my craving for more, but giving way to a more powerful ache. Arland shifts so he's hovering over my body, arms on either side of my head.

I cannot wait any longer.

It's torment.

Grabbing a fistful of tunic, I lift it over his head. I trail my hands down his back, find the waist of his pants, then work to get them down. When he's freed of his barriers, our skin meets, and I'm filled with heat, with intensity, with love.

His sculpted chest presses against mine with each deepening kiss. Our breathing in sync. He pulls away, and our eyes lock once more. "I love you, Katriona Maher."

Hearing him utter my name, his name, *our* name sends me over the edge. My breathing speeds up. I fight the animalistic urge to force him into me. "I love you, too, Arland Maher."

He smiles, and our bodies truly become one. Flooded with warmth, with love, with Arland, I'm happier than I've ever been in my life.

CHAPTER TWENTY-FIVE

Our legs are tangled. Arland lies next to me, arm draped over my stomach, fingers tracing lines along my side. I stare at the stars through the green leaves on the Willow while running my hands through his knotted hair. The candles have very little wax remaining. Time is coming to an end. Soon I will have to stand, get dressed and part with my love. Return to living a lie. Be burned for each kiss I give to Perth.

Stars? I haven't seen stars since the cave, but here there are millions of them above us. Not a small patch of the heavens, a huge patch as far as I can see. Stars! The sun will shine over everything when it rises. Plants here will thrive, food will grow naturally—that is assuming, of course, these stars are not figments of my imagination and they do not fade like they have so many times before. "Arland?"

He lifts his head and smiles at me in a way suggesting he wants more time, more of me, of us.

I point to the sky and am surprised again. The golden bands still cover my hand. I sit upright, and Arland rolls over. "What are we going to do?"

Face turning white, he looks us over. "We need more time. Look"—he takes my hand and points at one of the bands which first appeared—"this one is lighter than the rest."

"We don't have more time. Mom said we had two hours, max. The candles have almost completely melted away; I'm sure we're already over our limit." I look around, afraid of being in the open, afraid the concealment spells might have broken.

Afraid.

Arland wraps his arms around me. "Do not fear, my love. Everything will be okay. We should get dressed and find your mother. She will know what to do."

"I am afraid her mother has already done enough." Leader Dufaigh's cold tone matches the sudden temperature shift in the air. "Stand up, offenders."

Turning his head in Dufaigh's direction, Arland's eyes widen.

I'm frozen. Afraid to see what's behind me. I don't want to think of the consequences we somehow knew we'd have to pay for our love, or care about the hideous nature of the man who wishes to steal my life from me.

"Do not stand up. Do not move. Cover yourself with the blanket. Remember, we knew this might happen, and everything will be okay." Arland kisses my forehead, gets to his feet, wraps the blanket around me then stands tall, proud, emotionless.

Naked.

"Arrest him!" Dufaigh shouts.

Arland doesn't flinch. *"I love you, Kate. Every fiber of your being is pure, beautiful and a part of me. Do not go lightly. Give them what they deserve."*

"I will fight, for you, I will fight." I think of the dagger, but am unable to move. Everyone might realize what I'm reaching for and kill one of us for it.

Cyric and Deverell march up to Arland, keeping their heads low. They cast me an apologetic glance, take Arland by the arms then lead him away. The two guards have sat by Dufaigh's side, followed his orders and watched me every evening when I'd grace the great hall outfitted in something new his dressers designed. Neither guard ever appeared happy about his job babysitting me, but I've broken laws. I have no idea how deep their loyalties run with Perth, Dufaigh, or High Leader Maher.

"Gather his clothing, Perth. We do not want to scare the women and children in the base with his appearance."

Perth? I turn my head but wish I didn't. Arland stands naked, hands tied behind his back, head still held high, face to face with

Dufaigh. Perth trots toward me, eyes revealing the man I thought was long gone—the icy nature of the Ground Dweller Perth swore he was not.

When he reaches me, I glare. "What did you do?"

"I am sorry." He kneels beside me. "I thought everyone was sneaking away without me. This place, these people, they have lost touch with reality of the world around them—I did not want to be left alone. I followed you and your mother outside. When I saw you disappear behind the concealment spell, I lost faith in our agreement. I broke the edge of the spell and followed you in." For a split second Perth's eyes flash a brilliant shade of green.

"How could you, Perth? I gave you my word. You said you trusted *me*. Why would you think we were leaving you?" The fury boiling inside makes it near impossible to keep my voice at a whisper. I want to wrap my hands around his neck and squeeze.

"Calm down." Shaking his head, Perth glances over his shoulder.

"I made a mistake. As soon as I realized what was happening, I left, but my father followed me. He watched your mother perform the Binding spell, watched as the magic enforced your bond, even commented on how he has never seen one so strong." Perth wipes his hand over his face like he's seen things he'd like to forget.

I swallow hard. "You *watched*?"

"No. When your mother came back, we dragged her inside, questioned her and got the guards. No one saw anything." He shakes his head again. "I am so sorry."

"Son, leave her to rot. I am sure daemons will find her unchaste body and deal with her. If you would like to punish her for her behavior, I understand, but aside from that she is of no concern to you," Dufaigh shouts.

Anger inundates Arland's mind.

We're still connected.

His thoughts turn murderous. Wiggling his hands, he tries to free himself.

"Arland, no! We knew this might happen, remember? I will be okay."

"*Somehow I knew Perth would be behind this.*"

"*It was a misunderstanding. Please, don't do anything to make this worse.*"

"I am coming, Father," Perth says like the perfect son.

"Wait." I grab Perth by the arm. "If your father was there, why didn't he try to stop us?"

Perth brushes my arm from his, always keeping up the façade. "My father is cruel, Katriona. He wanted you to suffer for your *transgressions.*"

The only way to make me suffer is . . . Arland. "What does he plan to do to Arland?"

Perth narrows his eyes then glances toward his father. "He will not do anything to Arland because we will not allow him. Get dressed. Meet me outside the door to the base in half an hour.

"My father was right about you. You are worthless like the rest of them." Perth clutches the clothes to his chest then runs toward his father, leaving me all alone and naked under the weeping willow.

I've been here before. In my visions. I knew this was coming—my mom pretty much told me this was coming—so why does it feel like I've just been punched in the gut?

"Put your clothes on, Arland Maher, fallen Leader of Encardia. You will never see her again, do you understand? How dare you go against the law of a High Leader, against your own father . . . ?"

I turn my head to see Arland one more time before he's taken away. I want to bask in his healthy glow because I fear the next time we see each other, he will have been punished, and I'm sure punishment will come in a physical form.

Cyric and Deverell free his hands for him to dress then tie the rope around his wrists again.

Dufaigh catches me looking at Arland. "On second thought, Perth, go get the girl and bring her to me."

The blanket seems very thin all of a sudden; I tighten it around my chest and do not make any effort to stand. Perth runs over, takes me by the arm, lifts me to my feet then leads me to his father.

The red and black plaid blanket trails at my feet.

"Do not be afraid. We will beat this. It is my fault, and I will somehow make it right," Perth whispers.

"I hope you're right," I say, staring straight ahead. I'm watching the back of Arland, afraid he might suddenly fall over dead, or disappear, or be punched—anything where I may need to step in.

Perth stops in front of Dufaigh and releases my elbow. I stand, not as proud and tall as Arland, but I meet Dufaigh's eyes with defiance in my heart.

"You may have disgraced yourself, but I will not allow you to live easily and disgrace my family. We will keep your crime between us and you will marry my son and be punished every day. An impressive amount of magic secured your Binding to Arland. I have a feeling it will bring you great pain to break that bond." Dufaigh smiles and bounces on his toes.

My skin crawls.

He's always wanted to hurt my family and Arland's. This situation must be like a bonus to what Dufaigh has already done.

Perth shakes his head. "No, Father, I will not marry Katriona."

Dufaigh places his pale, fat hands on Perth's shoulders. "Think of the pain it will bring the two of them, and with her in our family we will be safe."

"You are right, Father." Perth sighs. "I cannot imagine touching her, let alone marrying her, but she deserves to suffer for her actions."

No! This was Perth's chance to stand up to his father, to fight for his people, to help me and Arland, and he chose Darkness. He chose to stray from the path of Light. Fire burns in my heart, spreads like a flame in a dry forest—

"*Kate, calm down. Perth is playing the game. Look at his eyes, he is not genuine.*" The calm in Arland's thoughts mimics his exterior.

So many times I've seen Perth's eyes, so many times I wish I hadn't, but now I find myself captivated by the look of utter terror for all to see in his eyes. Wide and wild, glancing in all directions, as if mapping his escape. Maybe his father believes it to be because of my

319

transgressions, but I recognize it as fear of something Perth's about to do.

Dufaigh slaps Perth on the back, nearly knocking him over. "So it is settled. Take her to your quarters and do not allow anyone to see you. If they do, tell them you were out for a stroll and attacked by daemons. Make up a story about how you saved her life. She will be crying, no doubt, so anything she does will only corroborate your story. Make sure you kiss her if she does not shed tears, the pain will aid you."

The cruel Leader turns away from us then walks next to his guards. "Now, Deverell, take Arland to the High Leader's quarters with Leader Wilde."

Dufaigh turns to me and reveals his yellowed teeth. "We need to discuss how to deliver their death sentences."

Death sentences? I hold back a gasp. *Oh, Griandor, please help me. This can't be happening.*

Dufaigh and his guards leave with Arland in tow.

Perth grabs my hand, lacing his fingers with mine.

My life flashes before my eyes in fading clips. Riding horses on the farm. Hiking with my family. Holding hands with Brad when I was scared. Stepping into Encardia. Brad changing our relationship forever. Meeting Arland. Loving Arland. Discovering magic. Helping people. People dying. Marrying Arland.

No! He will not die for this. Brad suffered enough for loving me. No more madness. There are bigger things in life to worry about other than who has the most power, the most influential family, or the best wife. There is a god who seeks to destroy this world, and Arland and I together are the only ones who can fight him.

Dropping the blanket, I let it fall around my feet and concentrate on my power, my love, and what I need to do . . . *form an army.* No more wasting time. No more waiting for other people or some imaginary perfect moment. This is my life, and I will no longer listen to anyone else.

Fire unfolds from my heart and engulfs my skin, igniting the dead forest in brilliant blue light. My tattooed braids brighten and burn warm and golden. I conjure more strength than I ever have before. "Stop!"

My words spark something in Arland . . . *hope*. It builds in him. He's never had it before, not like this. He's always thought he was going to die, even when he told me he wasn't going to, and he was sure his death would occur here.

"*Show him how powerful you are, how powerful* we *are. Show him you are unafraid.*" Flames cover him as well, blue and gold, warm and beautiful.

The guards back away from Arland, smacking their hands against their clothes as if they've been set on fire.

Dufaigh turns. A look of shock turns to scorn when he sees me. "Perth, control your woman, she is—"

I turn my head towards the sky and raise my arms. "Gag him."

Sprites burst from the ground and swell around Dufaigh's feet, holding him in place. They climb out from the rocks then land on his shoulders, peel themselves from trunks of trees then cover his body, rush out of the river then pool in front of his mouth. The beings do not transform from their representations of nature; Leader Dufaigh looks like a barren tree, rooted to the ground, covered in rocks and water.

"No more, Father," Perth startles me with his words. He gives my hand a light squeeze and glows in the same magical colors as Arland and me. "Your time of rule has gone on long enough. There is a war much more worthy of our attention than the war you wage for power."

While Perth pauses, I take a moment to send another request to the magic. *Go inside the base. Gather the Draíochtans and bring them here. Let them bear witness to this. Suspend Perth, his father, Deverell and Cyric until everyone reaches us. Free Arland, and please, restore my clothes.* In a torrent of light, the sprites fill the air, swirl around everyone in different intense colors.

Crimson colored flames sever the ropes around Arland's wrists. He runs to my side when he's freed, takes my hand then places his lips on it. "I never would have allowed Dufaigh to follow through with his threat. No one could ever force you to be with Perth."

Glancing at him from the corner of my eye, I smile. "I know. I wasn't concerned."

We fall silent and watch as a fog swirls around Cyric and Deverell, holding them in place, removing the hard-pressed lines in their foreheads. The already blue flames on Perth's body grow larger and suspend him in his angry, I-will-speak-my-mind stance.

Arland steps away as a flood of light arrives from behind us. White silk flies above my head then descends my body, returning dignity to its proper place. Smooth and sleek, the gown flows to my feet, caresses my skin, reminds me of the happiness I still feel from the events of the evening—before the interruptions.

The magical beings float out and away from everyone, forming a circle of fire around the base, Dufaigh and his guards, Perth, Arland and me. Arland locks eyes with me, takes my hands in his again. We wait for the door in the ground to open so we can end this constant bickering between our own. We have to form an army. This has to be the time. Just like Mom said.

From the edge of my vision, I catch a glimpse of stars cascading through the horizon. Turning my face toward the sky, I suck in a sharp breath. Millions of white specks twinkle in the black night, more brilliant than the Milky Way, more breathtaking than what appears over the Rocky Mountains.

"Why do you think . . . ?" I trail off as I can find no words to describe the utter beauty of what I see.

Arland runs his thumb over my knuckles. "The sky is visible because we are on the correct path, Kate. Magic has awoken again, and the more we use it, the more we follow our path given to us by the gods, the more alive magic will become."

"But all we did was—"

"Get married," Arland finishes for me. "That has been what the gods have wanted all along, has it not? Gramhara would not allow you to return through the portal until we realized our love. Griandor specifically told you Brad was not meant for you and you knew it. Your mother—descendant of the gods—might have groveled on her hands and knees to Bind us—"

A small laugh escapes my mouth.

Arland grins. "But we are far from through this, Kate. If uniting our people is what we must do, it will not be easy. Dufaigh is cold and calculating. Even though you sent magic for the other Draíochtans, I do not doubt Dufaigh will attempt to have his own son executed for rebuking him in front of them."

I look at Perth: a good man, ready to come into his own, ready to lead, ready to live. I cannot imagine his own father putting him to death for it. "I called for them to be witness to Dufaigh's behavior, not to bring punishment to Perth."

Arland cups my cheek in his hand, turning my face to his, staring at me with complete adoration. "You did the right thing, but Draíochtans have witnessed his—and those of all the other Ground Dweller Leaders before him—heinous acts for years. The four of us: you, myself, Perth, and your mother—and to be honest, anyone who had a hand in helping arrange our Binding—will have to prove to everyone we are on the path of Light."

I press my forehead against his. "But your father, he should tell them. Stand up for what he believes. Help us. You are his son; I am his daughter through you."

He leans back, still cupping my cheek in his warm hand. "My father would appear guilty if he outright sided with us. This will not end here, not now. Time is needed to right the many years worth of wrongs which have happened in Encardia," Arland's voice is full of tension.

He pauses, allowing tears to fall down his strong face. His forehead creases together in a twisted, sad expression. "Kate, we will once again be separated. I do not know for how long, but I do know you have the power to stop this. All of this. Allow Perth to say what he must say. Allow Dufaigh to paint us as criminals . . . ."

Anger rumbles inside me. Arland is playing by the Draíochtan rules, but I was not raised as a Draíochtan, and I refuse to play games. I refuse to be separated from him. I will not allow him or anyone else I love to be punished. "No, Arland. This ends here, and it ends now. If they try to take you away from me, I will show them exactly what I'm capable of. I will release every magical spell cast over this place, then travel to Wickward and any other base to do the same. I will force these people to remember the dark reality of the world they live in. I will force them to fight."

The truth behind my words, the resolve, sends currents of fire from my body, stretching out in all directions.

Sprites fly around me, singing soothing angelic songs in my ears.

I know I'm receiving approval from the gods.

Arland lightly places his lips on mine; the fire grows stronger. "I hope you are correct, but say nothing of the gods and what you have been instructed to do until the time is right. Speak from your heart—"

Old, rusty hinges squeak and echo through the forest, preventing me from asking when that time may be. We both turn and look in the direction of the door.

High Leader Maher appears first, then Mom, Leader Murchadha and his wife Ula, Brit, Flanna, Anna, Marcus . . . the remaining soldiers from Watchers Hall, Ground and Sea Dwellers from around the world.

Quiet murmurs give way to riotous babble as the Draíochtans climb from the hole in the earth then spread out around us, everyone watching the Dufaighs and guards in their frozen states.

Arland and I face the gathered crowd with our matching golden braids, hands joined. We hold our heads high.

"Are you going to speak first, or are you going to release them?" he asks, pointing at Perth and his father.

"*Neither. I'm going to wait for your father to speak,*" I think, without taking my eyes off High Leader Maher. I'm watching him, looking for a glimpse of the man my mom swears him to be, for a hint of where Arland inherits his strength, love and passion from, for an indication the Leader is on our side.

High Leader Maher's eyes flash to Arland, giving him a once over that would make any son proud, then Maher straightens, steps forward, and lifts his hands. "What is the meaning of all this? Why is a Leader of Encardia encased in magic, and why are you and my son glowing with a Binding Spell?"

He turns to my mom, gives her a reproachful look, then does the same for me.

The façade I've played into for weeks while living here will be no more. "You know why; yet you lie."

Arland tightens his grip on my hand.

I do the same. "*Trust me.*"

"*I do. Just be careful.*"

Leader Maher laughs, a mocking laugh, low and throaty. "Why, Miss Wilde, whatever do you mean?"

"No, sir, I am no longer Miss Wilde." I look up at Arland. "*I'm going to tell him the truth . . . I'm going to tell them all the truth.*"

He nods an approval, and I return my sights to his father.

"Your son and I are now Bound, but you were aware we'd be together, from before I was born, is that correct?"

Leader Maher glances around the group of onlookers. Some of them wear expressions of shock and whisper to each other while others look proud, happy and ready to congratulate. I bet more than just Leader Murchadha knew of the prophecy surrounding Arland and me.

"Well? Am I correct? Should you have to think about your answer?"

"She is correct. I knew the two would find love in one another," he says, receiving a few gasps and angry shouts from the Ground Dwellers.

"But before you chastise me, you should know my son was not supposed to be Bound to her. I instructed he keep his distance from her, the same way I instructed her to keep her distance. Neither listened. Foolish children."

"Stop," I shout.

Leader Maher turns from his misinformed followers to set his narrowed eyes upon me, but even though I realize it to be an act, it is not good enough. He should be honest and forthright with his people. Ignorance is not bliss. If Dufaigh throws us all out of the bases then we will fight, and these stupid holes in the ground will be where he lives out the rest of his days.

"Enough with the lies. Isn't this world already abundant with Darkness? Do you need to make it worse? You should be ashamed of yourself. I don't care what your reasons for leading these innocent people into ignorance are, but it must stop. Tell them the truth. Tell them the only way for Encardia to have light is for me to have happiness with your son. Tell them!"

Leader Murchadha steps forward from the crowd, Ula at his side. The pair appear as twins with gray hair flowing down the middle of their backs, skin tan and leathered from age. He looks sympathetic, but I'm not sure who it's geared toward. "Kimball, what is the meaning of this? Is what the girl says true?"

Apparently he's lying too.

Does Dufaigh really have that much control? He's not able to speak or move and yet they still do not speak against him.

Leader Maher turns to his peer, hanging his head.

"*This moment could break us,*" Arland thinks, squeezing my hand.

Please, Griandor, help us.

"*Arland, let go of my hand then walk away from me. Away from everyone. Let them see how the magic fades when we aren't together.*"

"Yes, Afton, it is true. The only way for Encardia to survive is for my son and Katriona to be together." Leader Maher clasps his hands behind his back, pacing a line between me, Arland, and everyone else.

"*Step away now, Arland.*" I shake my hand free.

His absence leaves me cold. My resolve melts away with his fading presence. Fire still burns on me, but not as bright, not as strong. No one in the angry and confused crowd looks at me; their eyes remain focused on High Leader Maher and Leader Murchadha.

"Why would you not be truthful with us? Draíochtans deserve knowledge." Leader Murchadha does not yell, does not look angry, he's just the opposite . . . his face is red like he's going to cry.

I feel sorry for everyone. Most Draíochtans have lived their lives in the dark as I have, but these Leaders pretend to be in the dark out of fear.

Cold looks pass over the faces of most of the Ground Dwellers. People who have showered me with affections during the past couple weeks now have murder in their eyes, fists balled—they're ready to fight, and I have good suspicions they'd like to fight me.

"Arrest him!" Lorne calls from the crowd. "Arrest her—and Arland, too. They imprison Leader Dufaigh and his son!"

"We should punish High Leader Maher's son and his disgraceful wife! She makes us all look like fools," Maura says, pushing from behind Lorne and throwing her hands into the air.

Finally I understand why Arland's father has kept everyone ignorant. If anyone knew—Light Lover or Sea Dweller alike—and it somehow got back to the Ground Dwellers, they would have called for my blood long ago. I thought Maura was on our side. Maybe she wasn't ready. Griandor was right to tell me to take my time.

"It has pained him to act less of a man than he is, Kate. I am happy you see this." Arland's thoughts resonate with pride.

Turning, I see the pride painted on Arland's face, too. *"I'm sorry it took me so long to figure it out. I shouldn't have doubted you or my mom's faith in him, but he has played the game well."*

"Why is one of our Leaders imprisoned?" Vanora asks, drawing my attention to those gathered before me. I search for her in the crowd, racing past so many scowling faces, so many smiling ones too, and find her leaning forward with her fists balled.

Everyone turns their eyes toward me. I'm transported back in time to some school play where I had one line to recite—I spoke that line with confidence, with perfection. The courage oozed from me that day and fills me now. "Do—"

"Where has Arland gone?" Leader Maher interrupts.

I ignore him. "Do you not see? Look at the sky. Stars shine because of the connection Arland and I share. They shine because I'm happy, because we follow the path of Light. Look at them."

Gasps, as though they've never seen the sky before—and maybe some haven't—surge through the crowd.

"Now, look at me. Look at how pale my skin glows when he and I are not connected. I am tired of these games," I say, once I'm sure everyone has seen the sky.

Nodded agreements between many onlookers tell me this might work, but most of them return their gazes heavenward—a lot of them wear grins from ear to ear.

"Watch what happens when Arland returns to me."

I motion for Arland to come forward. He takes my hand and the flames re-ignite. Braids of our bond glow even brighter. Brit was right when she said everyone would know when I lost my virginity . . . because there would be no way to hide this—although I doubt she knew that.

Leader Murchadha whispers something in his wife's ear. She glances at me and Arland then whispers something back to her husband. He smiles. "We see the connection makes you stronger, but it does not explain why High Leader Maher kept the people in the dark. It also does not excuse you or your mother for parading around here like you had intentions of marrying Perth Dufaigh, and it also does not explain why Leader Dufaigh is imprisoned and looks like a tree."

A snort makes its way above the crowd. It doesn't take a genius to realize it belongs to Flanna; she's probably thrilled with Leader Dufaigh's current vegetative state, but Leader Murchadha goes on as though he never heard her.

Keeping a firm grip on Arland's hand, I take a few steps closer to the Leaders, closer to loss of my love, closer to imprisonment, but I want to be close, want them to see I am not afraid. "High Leader Maher kept things from you because he had to. Because he had to keep me and Arland safe from Dufaigh—who has sought to destroy my family for power for years—and safe from the evil possessing this land."

I should add just as you kept things from your people, but keep that to myself. Murchadha is trying to make this right . . . I hope.

The Leader of the Sea Dwellers looks to Maher. "Is this true?"

"It is."

"Go on," Murchadha says, tipping his head in my direction.

"You have to excuse me and my mother from parading around here as part of the lie, because if you choose not to, you will be forced to die with Darkness looming over you forever. And Leader Dufaigh looks like a tree because I asked the gods to gag him, and that is how they responded. Perth was in the middle of delivering a speech to his father, but I thought it best to have an audience for it. If you wish me to release him and the others, I want word from you and High Leader Maher on a number of things first."

No one yells for me to be arrested. There are no whispers drifting through the crowd. There is nothing but silence. Most still have their faces pointed toward the sky.

Leader Murchadha considers my words for a moment then raises a brow. "And what is it you wish us to promise you, Mrs. Maher?"

Hearing my new name makes me smile. "I want you to promise me no matter what Dufaigh says, no matter what anyone desires, Arland and I will be free. I want you to promise me our love will be allowed and there will *never* be another arranged marriage in Encardia again."

He rubs his chin between his thumb and index finger. "Is that all?"

I shake my head. "No, sir. I want Perth to replace his father as Leader of the Ground Dwellers, and I want councils to be elected by the people—"

Murchadha raises a bushy, white eyebrow. "You wish to have us force a resignation and redesign our political infrastructure?" he asks, disbelief flooding his voice.

"Yes, sir. When Perth is allowed to speak, you will see and understand why he must lead his people. And as far as the political structure, too much power rests in the hands of three Leaders. I know there are other Leaders across the world, but you three make the most important of decisions—and look at you. You have yourself buried underground, trying to punish a woman for being in love . . . a woman who wants to help. Your population is dwindling; your food sources are becoming difficult to procure because there are less and less children to grow produce. Face it; you are barely hanging on. You have two choices: stay here and die, or follow me for a chance to live."

A look passes over both Murchadha and Maher, telling me I've overstepped my boundaries. Maher grabs Murchadha by the elbow and directs him to the side of my circle protected by magic. The two men confer over something while everyone else is left with nothing else to do but stare.

"I do not know if talking through this will work. I believe my father will have very little influence now the truth is out about him keeping secrets. Murchadha is a friend, but we rely on the Ground Dwellers for our protections. Dufaigh will certainly call for my father's head when he is freed, and Leader Murchadha's if he agrees to your demands."

The two men return to the center of the circle. Leader Maher steps in front of Arland and me, placing a hand on my shoulder. "Do you have any other requests?"

"I need the army we spoke of."

Inching closer to Arland and me, Leader Maher nods. "You must find a way to convince Dufaigh and his people. Otherwise, if we send our soldiers with you, we will be outnumbered and vulnerable to an attack from within," he whispers.

"So you are willing to send your soldiers to follow Kate?" Arland asks.

Leader Maher clamps his hands on Arland's shoulders. "I always have been, son, but she still has quite a bit of convincing to do. Without Dufaigh's approval, I fear you two will be alone."

I draw in a ragged breath.

Arland and his father both glance at me.

Alone. The word unsettles me to my very core, raises the hair on my neck, makes my palms hot. *Alone.* Why does it bother me so much?

Leader Maher gives me a thorough once over then looks back to Arland. "Murchadha has agreed to allow you to be free, but you understand I cannot send soldiers unless—"

"What was her last request, Leader Maher?" Murchadha breaks in.

Arland's father turns to face Murchadha. "She desires an army."

He smiles and looks around the crowd, arms raised at his sides. "An army? What does *she* need an army for? *We* already have one."

Like I haven't heard *that* one before.

Leader Maher drops his hands from Arland's shoulders. "I am glad you two had your moment of happiness, and I pray for all our sakes it lasts into eternity." The High Leader turns to face Murchadha.

Arland takes my hand in his.

"She wishes to lead our people on the path of Light and seek out Darkness, Afton. The Seer who foretold of my son and his bhean chéile's prophecies saw they would accomplish that goal, but only together and only with an army following Katriona."

All pretense of anger drops from Murchadha's face, making him appear as a child eager for a treat. "Did the Seer receive the message in the utmost clarity?"

Now they are playing the angry crowd.

"Afton, you know as well as I do things can change at any time. If someone decides to stray from the path of Light, or—there could be any number of things which make them fail. But one thing I do know, we will all rot if we continue to sit here pretending like nothing is going on."

Leader Maher paces closer to Murchadha. "Look up. *Everyone*, look up. When was the last time you saw the night sky? Katriona already brings light to Encardia, and look what it took . . . their Binding. Do you deny the power between them?"

Murchadha shakes his head as he looks from me to Arland.

Walking before the onlookers, Leader Maher continues, "Will anyone else here deny the magic between them? See for yourself the glow"—he points at us—"Has anyone ever seen a Binding so strong? The bands have not faded, yet they are Bound."

Lorne and Maura step forward, joining Leader Maher and Murchadha.

"Dufaigh will not allow any Ground Dweller to fight for *her*—she has deceived us. Nor will I allow my sons to fight," Lorne says, jaw clenched. He flashes narrowed eyes in my direction.

"The girl imprisoned our Leader and has still not allowed him to speak for himself. I do not trust her. Our people will not fight for her. We would rather rot happily than die in a bloody war, serving a disgraced woman." Maura's words are lathered with animosity.

She's never truly shown me kindness, but to choose death over life. To choose Darkness. What kind of person wants that? Perth was right about the Ground Dweller's hatred being long ingrained, but I think the problem runs deeper than that. I think the spell they're under binds hatred to their core.

Murchadha straightens his back. "Katriona, would you mind allowing Leader Dufaigh and the other Ground Dwellers to be free?"

My heart flutters in my chest. "Do we have your word on my requests?"

"You have my word, but I will not send anyone to fight for you who are unwilling. If you want an army, the army will choose you," Murchadha says.

"I think that's fair."

"Now will you release them?" he asks, pointing to the tree which is Dufaigh.

"No matter what happens, Kate, know that I love you. Know I will never stop fighting for you." Arland's sadness weighs his soul down. Sweat slickens his palm. He's hiding something from me, something he knows but doesn't want me to.

Forgetting about everyone gathered around us, I turn to him, leaning against his tall, strong body. *"This feels like goodbye, Arland. What is it? What happens? Why won't you tell me?"*

He shakes his head. *"Not a goodbye, just caution, Kate. Dufaigh is not as sensible as my father or Murchadha."*

"Arland?"

Standing straight, I take in the twisted expression on his face begging me not to ask anything else. There is no hint of smile in his eyes, no spark of youth I saw under the willow, no Arland.

I remove my gaze from him then set my sights on Dufaigh. This is my fight, this is my problem yet everyone still knows things I don't. Everyone continues to withhold information from me when they know I'll do what I must no matter what.

Arland has never been one of them.

He has his reasons—they all do—but it does nothing to ease the hurt.

I focus on the burning in my heart and the confused thoughts in my head, let them build inside me until they boil over, then channel them into my intent gaze on Dufaigh's face. *He* is my problem. He is *everyone's* problem.

I know you're already with us tonight, but we need more. Release the Dufaighs and the guards. Bring peace to Perth for the decision he is making, bring peace upon everyone. Let them see through the anger of the man who would rather have power than life.

Protect Arland.

Protect all I love.

The longest request I've ever sent up sits in my chest like a boulder on paper. I'm flattened, hopeless, lost. I've gone from being the happiest I've ever been to being baffled.

When Dufaigh wanted to take Arland away, I thought I'd deliver my uniting speech Mom told me about then. When it wasn't, I thought for sure I'd deliver when everyone came out here.

I've failed already.

I cannot unite these people.

Murchadha and Maher have promised Arland to me . . . alone— and as much as being alone with him both thrills and terrifies me, I doubt when Dufaigh is freed he will allow it. No, I fear I have just started another war within the Draíochtans.

Or secured one of my visions.

I will be sent alone into Darkness.

The Willow, the water, the stars, the guards—why must I always realize what my warnings mean too late?

I don't want to be without Arland, without love. I want us in the Meadow with the children from my dreams. I want life. I don't care about this war, don't care about power . . . I care about my heart and freedom.

Why should I have to lie about who I love to earn an army to fight Darkness? Why should we hide in underground facilities, parading around in fancy dresses with braided hair, eating food we can barely maintain supplies for? Why should Perth have to live in fear of his father just to prove to his people they should do good?

Perth doesn't want to marry me; he wants real love, he wants freedom just like I do. Like everyone does. These people need to learn to use old magic and learn to trust in the gods again. They need to fight.

My breaths come at a rapid pace; air refuses to fill my lungs. I'm hyperventilating and can do nothing to stop it.

I've lost control.

My legs tremble beneath me as though my body is too heavy for them to hold. The grip I have on Arland's hand dissolves, and before I know it, I'm on my knees.

My will to get up . . . shattered.

Black fills my sight; there is no world in front of me. Blood boils in my veins and travels throughout my body, singeing every nerve ending. The magic in me rages.

I am Katriona Maher and I have fire—these people do not.

They need me yet are unwilling to follow me, unwilling to believe anything I say because of what? Desire for power? For wealth?

The nightmares I had for years, the visions I've experienced in Encardia and the visits from the gods play through my mind. I search my memories for clues, for a way to explain to these people they have to fight, and fight for me, but no clues present themselves.

Logh orthu! For they know not their ignorance, Griandor. Forgive them for their desire to punish for love. Forgive them for their weakness, for their unwillingness to fight.

Forgive them, because here they will die.

CHAPTER TWENTY-SIX

Slow breaths in and out through my nose revive my lungs and remove the painful constriction from the lack of air, but do little to calm my shaking body. I'm cocooned in flames, in mind-numbing rage. My temples throb with it. If I don't regain control, Dufaigh will remain trapped, and I will remain alone.

Stand up, Kate. You can do this. I ball my fists, nails digging into my palms. Fighting with every muscle, every ounce of magic erupting from my soul, I get up, open my eyes and face the cruel reality of my life.

What I see before me is nothing I could have expected. Dufaigh no longer looks like a tree—the sprites surrounding him have disappeared into the protective blue circle around us—and he stands by Murchadha and Maher. The guard's arms no longer hold an empty space where Arland stood before I took over. Perth is positioned on my left, wide eyes a deeper green than ever. He's smiling, mouth closed, but relaxed.

I get the feeling I've done something right; his face screams pride, but . . . .

Turning, I see Arland wears the same expression.

Everyone wears the same expression.

What did I do? An urge to run, to hide, to just be out of here, creeps into my thoughts and takes over my muscles. I'm on my toes, ready to grab Arland by the hand again and go—

He reaches for me first. *"There is no need to run. You have done what you needed to do, Kate. You have given a speech powerful enough to unite our people."*

The bravado in Arland's thoughts matches the look on his face, but I haven't given a speech. I haven't said a word since I agreed to the terms of an army with Murchadha. And since then, I've only spoken internally to the gods—to their magic—for help with Dufaigh.

I shake my head. "*What speech, Arland?*"

"Dearest Katriona, you must be confused," Leader Murchadha says, interrupting my silent conversation with Arland.

Arland's eyes break their lock with mine then he turns toward Murchadha.

I do the same.

The Leader of the Sea Dwellers steps toward us, arms outstretched before him like a welcoming embrace. "While you lost control of your emotions, your thoughts betrayed you. Magic carried out your thoughtful words. The images you have seen of death—of war—played around the circle you cast to protect us. To say your thoughts were horrifying would be a misstatement. However, what you said was what we needed to hear. What you have seen, we needed to see. We are a tired people, Katriona, and have lost sight of what remains important. Years of living in the Darkness—living as captives in our own world—have diminished our sanity, and for that we apologize."

My jaw falls slack. Tears well in my eyes, blurring my vision and turning everything blue. Arland wraps his arm around my shoulders, pulling me into an embrace he hasn't given me in public since . . . ever. I rest my head on his chest, inhale his scent, revel in his warmth and love.

"The two of you have broken the law, but Leader Dufaigh, High Leader Maher and I forgive you—everyone forgives you—and when the war is over, you will be returned to your Leader status. Encardia needs more High Leaders like the two of you, but since we agreed to adjust our political structure . . . ." he trails off, and everything falls silent.

Dufaigh forgives me? A minute ago he was ready to punish me for the rest of my life. Murder my mother and Arland.

"Whether his forgiveness is real or not does not matter, Kate."

Maybe Arland is right, but if Leader Murchadha's waiting for me to tell them how I plan to restructure, he'll be waiting awhile. There is no plan. I'd like to say be more like America, but they wouldn't understand that, and I'm not even sure if I do. *Revolutionize.* The word spoken in Griandor's voice floats through my head again, but what does it mean? Revolution. America. American Revolution. Patrick Henry. Brad's speech in fifth grade . . . .

Wiping my tears on Arland's soft tunic, I take a deep breath, let my arms fall from him, then once again face Murchadha. "The political structure needs to be adjusted, but you will still need High Leaders. There only needs to be a more equal division of power. And individuals need to be afforded rights, protecting them from ever being harmed by anyone in a leadership position. The government should be for the people, by the people."

If only I'd paid more attention in my history classes. I'd never found them interesting, but now I'd like to travel back in time and be the star student.

Murchadha holds up his hand. "We will discuss these things after the war is over. For now, I would like to ask of everyone gathered, who will fight for Katriona?"

Before anyone answers, a black spot appears in my peripheral vision. Standing in my protective barrier are Cadman, Saidear, and the other soldiers from Watchers Hall who ran the rescue mission to Wickward. They all glow with fire . . . with magic. They step through the barrier then join the crowd, bringing with them hundreds of faces I don't recognize.

"Cadman! You made it. We were beginning to worry when chatter box communications discontinued." High Leader Maher watches behind Cadman as more and more soldiers, women, and children come through the barrier. "I take it all has been lost at Wickward?"

Cadman shakes his head. "No, sir."

He looks at the gathered crowd then smiles when he sees me and Arland. "From the looks of things, I think it safe to say their truth has come out?"

Leader Maher laughs. "Yes, Cadman. If Wickward has not been lost, why have you brought everyone with you?"

"To fight for Katriona, sir."

Those who were staring at the sky now stare at Cadman in all his glory. His normally deep wrinkles appear smooth, his red hair has grown at least an inch, reaching down to his ears, and his body is covered in leather armor.

"So you knew she needed an army?" Leader Maher asks.

Cadman doesn't look away from his High Leader. "Yes, sir, and after what I witnessed during our travels between Watchers Hall and Willow Falls . . . I vowed to be a part of that army."

Dufaigh steps forward. "What is it you witnessed, soldier?"

"Katriona rescued every one of us. She was attacked by a shifter—the same creatures which infiltrated both Watchers Hall and Wickward—and nearly bled to death. She protected us through the forests, fought off daemons when we were attacked, but what made me vow to always fight for her . . . with her . . . was when she died." Cadman meets my eyes, crossing his fist over his chest like he did so long ago.

Murchadha and Maher exchange glances.

"She died?" Leader Maher asks.

"Yes, and was brought back to life moments later. Do you know what she did? She did not give up nor did she allow the rest of us to keep fighting without help . . . she fought harder until every daemon was dead. Right then I knew we were on the right path. Before I traveled to Wickward, she instructed me how to use old magic, and I was able to save our people from the same fate many of our fellow Draíochtans have already faced. They followed me here to fight. Without Katriona, they would all be dead."

Leader Dufaigh squints his beady, white eyes then comes closer to me.

Although his demeanor appears to be one of a more friendly nature, his presence disturbs me. I rub my hands together and shift from foot to foot.

Arland holds out his arm at his side, pushing me slightly behind him.

He doesn't believe in Dufaigh any more than I do, but the Leader makes his way around Arland then stands in front of me anyway.

"For years, I have been more concerned with control rather than life. Tonight, Katriona, you reminded us we were all going to perish. I will agree with your restructure, but more importantly, *I* will fight for you. Tell us what we must do and we will do it."

I'm not sure what to make of him, but I can't call him a liar either. "I—"

"I would also like to fight." Deverell steps forward, fist over his heart.

Lorne, Cyric, Flanna, Brit, Mom, hundreds of soldiers, children, and friends step forward and announce their willingness to fight for me. Some take a knee and mimic Cadman and Deverell's salutes—how Arland did when he swore his life for mine—others speak the oath with tears rolling down their cheeks, some with eyes flitting around.

Mom steps forward, out of the crowd, around the Leaders, *around everyone*, and takes my hands in hers. "I have always fought for you, and will continue to fight for as long as I live. There is no doubt in my mind your father is smiling down upon you from the heavens, Kate." She speaks slowly, resonate . . . proud.

High Leader Maher returns to his feet. "You have your army, Katriona, now what do you wish us to do?"

His words drive understanding into me, a deep-rooted understanding of everything I've accomplished since venturing off the horse farm in Virginia. No longer am I Kate Wilde, college student, horse lover, best friend to Brad. Now I am Katriona Maher. I have fire. I have united a people who have battled for centuries. And now, I have an army.

I must seek out Dughbal and destroy him with these things. The Draíochtans know not why they fight, but I do, and I think it's time I finally shared. "We have to find a fallen god and kill him. Dughbal is no longer an immortal, but the powers he has stolen from us will make the fight harder than it should be."

"*A god?* We cannot fight the gods, Katriona," Leader Maher says.

"Not gods, god. But you are right; you should not fight. You should remain here with the children and keep them safe. If we succeed, they will be our future, and if we do not, they may still be our future. Anna and Marcus, Kent and Keely—Encardia depends on them and all the other children like them."

Anna and Marcus bounce up and down when they hear their names and wave. I don't wave back, but I'd love to. I've missed my cheerleader and her enthusiasm, her wide smile and big brown eyes.

I look back to Leader Maher. "Griandor informed me I am the only one who can kill Dughbal, and I have many reasons why I want to."

Taking a deep breath, Arland tightens his hold on me. "She is correct, Father . . . to an extent. Although Kate's visions showed mostly death and failure—which I believe to be her own personal fears—those visions showed Perth, Flanna, Cadman, Brit, Kate and myself fighting. No one else. We only need a small army because we seek out one god, one god who has stolen the body of someone close to Kate. This will be a personal journey for her, for all of us. Aside from Cadman, we are all Leaders of Encardia. Does it not speak to you that the future Leaders must fight together?"

I already had an army and didn't realize it. The only other thing Griandor wanted me to do was unite our people, and it appears as though I've done that. Flanna smiles at me, fist over her heart. I glance around at the others: Cadman, Brit, Perth, they all wear the same proud look, mimicking Flanna's gesture. Arland is always able to figure these situations out so fast. I lean into him while the three Leaders gather in a small circle then confer with one another.

"*Are you sure we must go alone?*"

Arland kisses the top of my head. "*I—*"

"We have considered both of your opinions and approve your request for a small army. The soldiers from Wickward shall remain here; we will *all* remain here until this war is over. It is safer for us to be together," Arland's father says then directs his attention to me. "When would you like to leave?"

I don't want to waste time any more. The war needs to end, Brad needs to go home, and I want my life with Arland to start, but I know everyone needs rest. "In a few days."

Leader Maher nods. "We will prepare provisions for your departure. Shall we go inside and discuss?"

I stare at Arland. The gathered crowd forgotten, the war a small blip on my radar. Soon we will depart this place, we will be free, and we will be one step closer to a death I've seen Arland die too many times. Whether those visions were accurate or not, I don't know, but what I do know is I'll find out.

He looks down on me with what I interpret as both happiness and longing. Arland doesn't worry about his death anymore—I read that emotion straight from his brain; instead, he feels complete with the acceptance we've been offered. He traces my jaw with the tips of his fingers, then threads them through my hair.

He's forgotten the crowd as well.

"On second thought, we can discuss details with the two of you in the morning. Come along everyone, return to your quarters. There is much to be arranged inside. The soldiers need rest and Arland and Katriona need time."

Without waiting for everyone to return inside, Arland takes my hand in his. We turn and go the opposite direction, back toward the willow, the candles, the river, back toward where our life together truly began.

There will be time for war tomorrow.

Tonight is time for us.

THANK YOU FOR READING.

Curiosity Quills Press
http://curiosityquills.com

Please visit http://curiosityquills.com/reader-survey/ to share your reading experience with the author of this book!

ABOUT THE AUTHOR:

Krystal Wade can be found in the sluglines outside Washington D.C. every morning, Monday through Friday. With coffee in hand, iPod plugged in, and strangers – who sometimes snore, smell, or have incredibly bad gas – sitting next to her, she zones out and thinks of fantastical worlds for you and me to read.

How else can she cope with a fifty mile commute?

Good thing she has her husband and three kids to go home to. They keep her sane.

MORE FROM CURIOSITY QUILLS PRESS

Worlds Burn Through, by Vicki Keire

Chloe Burke has nightmares of a world burned to ash and the strange boy who saves them both. Underneath the dreams lurks a deeply buried reality; Chloe and a handful of others are survivors of a decade old apocalypse that burned their home world to the ground.

Now their ancient enemies hunt them again. To keep their adopted world safe, Chloe must undergo a ritual of blood sacrifice that will have life-long consequences if she survives. Her lethal protector, Eliot Gray, must keep her alive long enough to do it. Together they will uncover even more dangerous secrets buried in the past's deepest, darkest ashes.

Dinosaur Jazz, by Michael Panush

Acheron Island is a world lost to time, home to prehistoric creatures from earth's savage past – and Sir Edwin Crowe, son of one of the world's last Gentleman Adventurers. When ruthless American businessman, Selwyn Slade, brings an army of corporate cronies and modern industrial power to conquer this world from the past, it's up to Sir Edwin to protect these prehistoric lands.

Its Jazz Age meets the Mesozoic Age in a world where cave men, gangsters, hunters, zeppelins, pirates, warlords and dinosaurs clash for a chance of survival. All that and more is waiting for you in Dinosaur Jazz, a tale of high adventure in a prehistoric world.

Blood Redemption, by Vicki Keire

Trapped in the Dark Realms, Caspia finds herself the unwitting leader of a growing Nephilim rebellion. Plagued by strange dreams and intrigue, she learns to master her Azalene abilities when all she wants is to find her way back home. To Whitfield. To Ethan.

But a new enemy gathers, and it isn't just Belial. To avoid another Nephilim war, the Realms of Light decide to attack their ancient enemy first. Caspia, her hometown, and everyone she loves happens to be in the way. She and Ethan must fight their way back to each other and try to protect the life they've built.

Daughter of Glass, by Vicki Keire

Sasha Alexander has a powerful ability. Either that, or she's dangerously mad.

Her father shrouds her in isolation, convinced he's protecting her. But the seven guardians that only she can see insist she's gifted. Her companions since her mother's suicide, they protect her from hurt, pain, fear, love.

Sasha doesn't know how to react when Noah explodes through her defenses. This strange young man with the scarred hands suddenly makes her feel again. But unless she can learn to control her own emotions, the biggest danger to them all may be Sasha herself.

CPSIA information can be obtained at www.ICGtesting.com
Printed in the USA
BVOW010909030712

294188BV00005B/1/P